THE ACADEMIC BACK STREET

THE ACADEMIC BACK STREET

LAWRENCE A. CURTIS

Copyright © 2020 by Nova Science Publishers, Inc.

All rights reserved. No part of this book may be reproduced, stored in a retrieval system or transmitted in any form or by any means: electronic, electrostatic, magnetic, tape, mechanical photocopying, recording or otherwise without the written permission of the Publisher.

We have partnered with Copyright Clearance Center to make it easy for you to obtain permissions to reuse content from this publication. Simply navigate to this publication's page on Nova's website and locate the "Get Permission" button below the title description. This button is linked directly to the title's permission page on copyright.com. Alternatively, you can visit copyright.com and search by title, ISBN, or ISSN.

For further questions about using the service on copyright.com, please contact:
Copyright Clearance Center
Phone: +1-(978) 750-8400   Fax: +1-(978) 750-4470   E-mail: info@copyright.com

NOTICE TO THE READER

The Publisher has taken reasonable care in the preparation of this book, but makes no expressed or implied warranty of any kind and assumes no responsibility for any errors or omissions. No liability is assumed for incidental or consequential damages in connection with or arising out of information contained in this book. The Publisher shall not be liable for any special, consequential, or exemplary damages resulting, in whole or in part, from the readers' use of, or reliance upon, this material. Any parts of this book based on government reports are so indicated and copyright is claimed for those parts to the extent applicable to compilations of such works.

Independent verification should be sought for any data, advice or recommendations contained in this book. In addition, no responsibility is assumed by the Publisher for any injury and/or damage to persons or property arising from any methods, products, instructions, ideas or otherwise contained in this publication.

This publication is designed to provide accurate and authoritative information with regard to the subject matter covered herein. It is sold with the clear understanding that the Publisher is not engaged in rendering legal or any other professional services. If legal or any other expert assistance is required, the services of a competent person should be sought. FROM A DECLARATION OF PARTICIPANTS JOINTLY ADOPTED BY A COMMITTEE OF THE AMERICAN BAR ASSOCIATION AND A COMMITTEE OF PUBLISHERS.

Additional color graphics may be available in the e-book version of this book.

Library of Congress Cataloging-in-Publication Data

Names: Curtis, Lawrence A., author.
Title: The academic back street / Lawrence A. Curtis.
Description: New York : Nova Science Publishers, Inc., [2019] |
Identifiers: LCCN 2020001384 (print) | LCCN 2020001385 (ebook) | ISBN 9781536172799 (hardcover) | ISBN 9781536174014 (adobe pdf)
Subjects: LCSH: College teachers--Fiction. | Zoology--Research--Fiction.
Classification: LCC PS3603.U7784 A64 2019 (print) | LCC PS3603.U7784 (ebook) | DDC 813/.6--dc23
LC record available at https://lccn.loc.gov/2020001384
LC ebook record available at https://lccn.loc.gov/2020001385

Published by Nova Science Publishers, Inc. † New York

Contents

Introduction		vii
Disclaimer		ix
Acknowledgments		xi
Chapter 1	College Is First	1
Chapter 2	The College Environment	5
Chapter 3	A Master's Degree Is the Next Thing	15
Chapter 4	A PhD Degree Is Sought and Obtained	29
Chapter 5	Beginning Work at an Unenlightened University Branch	49
Chapter 6	Some Success with a Research Problem: Seeds of Problems to Come	67
Chapter 7	A Discovery of Interest to Mankind	93
Chapter 8	My World Gets Smeared	105
Chapter 9	Apocalypse, the Spring Semester of Year Five at Visitopolis	121
Chapter 10	The University's Local Branch Gets Under Way Anew	133
Chapter 11	Teaching, Research Proposals, and a New Abode Occupy My Time	159
Chapter 12	A Last Research Summer at Visitopolis Gets Underway	185
Chapter 13	An Undergraduate Investigation Takes Precedence	199

Chapter 14	Boeuf Bourguignonne and a Confession	**219**
Chapter 15	Snails, Fan Worms, and a Hint of Tangled Wire to Come	**227**
Chapter 16	The End of My Final Summer at Visitopolis Arrives	**245**
Chapter 17	The Wire Strangles Me: Goodbye to Visitopolis	**255**
Conclusion		**311**
About the Author		**317**

INTRODUCTION

This is a novel about the all too common practice in higher academia of hiring part time, non-tenure track faculty to teach students. The faculty hired in these situations often cannot pursue research even though they likely have a Ph.D. This fictional story is mostly set in the 1970s. It follows the tumultuous career of a professor interested in teaching and doing research in biological science. The people who administered the university at the place of his employment expressly do not want faculty to be involved with research. The professor in the story owns a Ph.D., which is a research degree. He holds that being involved in research adds a beneficial dimension to his teaching. Problems arise when he decides to undertake a research problem at his own expense and on his own time. A marine invertebrate zoologist, his search for knowledge centers on the marine organisms that have settled on a lengthy set of pier pilings. When this ultimately leads to publications by himself and with students, his bosses at the university find that seriously troublesome and they try to make him cease. Dire consequences result.

  The author is a marine biologist and has taught university students for years. So he has extensive experience with this subject area. Of course, what is supposedly found out in the research undertaken in the story is fiction. On the other hand, the marine organisms investigated are real enough species. While the research findings of his main character may be imagined, the approaches to formulating questions and ways to answer them are very much as they might have been in reality. What this author creates here is a telling of the troubles, trials, and tribulations that may come from pursuing new knowledge.

DISCLAIMER

The organisms mentioned in this fictional account are real enough; things supposedly found out about them in the story are not.

ACKNOWLEDGMENTS

Many thanks to Karen Hubbard for making extensive comments and suggestions on earlier versions of this work. My sister, Tina Sculerati, and Read McLean also kindly read and commented on earlier versions.

Chapter 1

COLLEGE IS FIRST

During college as a biology major I had almost nothing to do with research. In the early 1960's I was one Blake Turner among about 450 other students at a small four year liberal arts institution in New England. Masters or Ph.D. degree students and offerings were not to be found there. Maybe things would have turned out differently if I'd had some early experience with discovering knowledge, but that's not the way it went. Maybe it's just as well. What I needed was to get grounded in some area of knowledge. Maybe I unfairly denigrate my high school experience, but not much had been done in the realm of knowledge discovery during that time. What I needed was to confront some area of established knowledge, to see what I could handle and what, if anything, I would be good at. In a school dedicated to liberal arts there were many subject areas to pit myself against. Among them were Economics, French, English Composition and Literature, ancient Greek History, Psychology, Chemistry, and not least Biology.

By way of my first biology professor and a course in botany it was to biology that I became attracted. I entertained taking up majors in history and psychology, but decided on biology. When I took my first exam in botany I found myself befuddled and scored a wondrous 27% on it. Dr. Burke, rather than writing me off as a waste of time, as I probably deserved, asked me to come see him after class. I went, not knowing what to expect. A major component of that botany course was to understand plant life cycles. Dr. Burke observed, "I see from your test that plant life cycles are not coming through to you. We had better see if we can fix that. Let me revisit and explain one to you." He chose an example we had covered in class and did that, emphasizing the key points for attention. How and at what point did gametes form, where in the cycle did fertilization take place, and where did meiosis occur and what life cycle stage was produced? I should have picked up on those points at first, but now, at least that life cycle made more sense to me. Then he did something for which, even some 50 odd years later, I continue to be grateful. He chose a plant species we had not mentioned in class yet. It was *Ulva lactuca*, a marine green alga. What he wanted me to do was take a couple of days and figure out the life cycle of this alga then come back and (notes free) explain it to him. That was a challenge. I had no idea what *Ulva lactuca* was. I had to look it up and figure out the life cycle. Not only figure it out, but I had to grasp it well enough to be able to explain it all to someone else, not least to the intimidating Dr. Burke. That was the key thing. When you have to explain something to even one other person the prime goal is to be correct and not make a fool of yourself, issues about which I had never much concerned myself. It was a marvelous thing to have me do. I looked into the life cycle of *Ulva lactuca* and developed my explanation of it. When the time came I went in and presented it. It was not without flaw, but it taught me a lesson: when you need to learn something (as for a test), learn it so you can explain it to someone else and practice that explanation. It is not too much for me to say, that lesson in a very real sense ultimately got me through college and graduate school. For example, my new acumen in learning allowed me to earn a B in that botany course even with that 27% on the first test. I was very pleased with that.

Dr. Burke had a more complex motivation. After my explanation of the *Ulva lactuca* life cycle he determined that his little ploy had worked quite well. Taking his challenge seriously had made me thoroughly learn something, a new experience for me, and I had made a good explanation of that life cycle. There were other students in the class who had not done very well on that exam. He suggested that we set things up with another such student to come in and see if, in his presence, I could get a life cycle across to that student. Being somewhat enthused by all this, I readily agreed. We got together in two days and I commenced doing my new act. The bonus was that this other student was an attractive female named Linda Pomeroy. No harm there. My short lecture on a plant life cycle gave her a better understanding too. The fact that another student who had also failed the test had done the lecture was not lost on her. Dr. Burke presented her with a challenge like the one he had given me several days ago. She learned her new life cycle, developed her explanation, and presented it to the professor. I listened in. She had taken the challenge to heart and did a very good job. Now he had two students that he could call upon to make other students realize that learning something was well within their grasp. There were several in need.

This was an excellent approach to student learning that Dr. Burke had taken. We all strove to get our explanations correct. The help with instruction saved him some time and it enabled students to learn a method for handling the subject matter of his course. Speaking for myself, it gave me a method for learning all kinds of material. I got pretty good at doing that. During my undergraduate and graduate school careers I spent a lot of time talking to myself as I practiced lectures about some new piece of material. On more than one occasion people in the neighborhood of my studying threatened to have me committed, but it proved a method that led to a lot of success. Thank you Dr. Burke.

Before too long I became a lab assistant for that botany course. There was only a little pay involved, but it was a great experience. My duties included helping to get labs set up and ready for the two lab sections. Ultimately, I would do that for the next three years for that botany course and a zoology course, the second course for biology majors. These were four credit courses and they could be quite rigorous to assist in. Not only were there the set ups to do, but there were students to help out. Doing that for three years added in a major way to my foundation in biology. It gave me practical experience in lab preparation and I was able to materially help a number of students. I felt a little heroic and I learned a lot, great for myself image.

I won't go on much further about the academics of my time as an undergraduate. Suffice it to say that I, Blake Turner, stayed at college for four years and graduated with a B.A. in Biology. I truly enjoyed that time. My parents suffered some monetary stress financing their reprobate son's way through. I thank them and hope they felt rewarded. I did. Money was not something I ever had much of, but at the same time I and almost all other students lived on campus in a dormitory and got meals in the college dining room. So there was no rent for me to pay or food to buy. I had enough in the way of incidental spending funds to get by.

In the senior year to graduate it was necessary to take and pass something called the Graduate Record Examination (G.R.E.). So it had been ordained by the college. The examination I took was the one for biology majors. I had not had much experience with official exams like this one and I had no idea how I would do. The night before the exam I misbehaved. The shaky, somewhat delinquent circumstance under which I took the exam is a bit of a story, but that is not my point here. Apparently I had gotten my grounding in a field of knowledge during my time at this institution. I ended up with the second highest score in any subject in the history of the college. Nobody was more surprised than me, but the college expressed its surprise with administrative accolades (read as, self-congratulations) and there was laudatory mention in the college newspaper. Another benefit was that biology department faculty members took more than usual note of me. They began suggesting that I go to graduate school. I had developed a real love of biology and found it to be of sustained interest to me, but the idea of going on into graduate school had not entered my mind. What I was going to do after graduating had not occupied my mind much either. I just figured I would get a job somewhere, maybe selling biological supplies and equipment to educational customers. But, nothing like that was ever going to be. At the suggestion of one faculty member, who was himself taking graduate classes at a nearby university, I applied to a Master's Degree program in Zoology at that university. Three kindly biology faculty wrote letters to aid my application. An aid those letters must have been because in the end and all things considered I did get accepted to pursue a Master of Science Degree in Zoology. On graduation from college in the spring I did not have the money to begin graduate school. So that had to wait for a time while I worked (as a construction laborer) and saved. By the beginning of the next spring semester I had managed to obtain a tuition scholarship from the university to which I had been accepted and with some help from relatives I was sort of set up and funded to begin my graduate career. Off I went.

Chapter 2

THE COLLEGE ENVIRONMENT

Aside from becoming a pretty good biologist, my college years affected me in a number of other ways. One of the major factors was broadening by my fellow students. As with anyone, I had made friends and acquaintances during high school and they were pretty cool, but they all came from my local environment. The students attending this college and that I got to know were from all over New England and New York and they presented me with an impressive, and for me an unheard of, array of people with whom to deal. They were mostly around 20 years old. They had not had time to develop all their ultimate characters, but there were some among them who had already become very much characters.

The dormitory I lived in for three years was Gulliver Hall. Some 15 male students occupied a fairly small old house that the college owned on the main street of the small town in which the college was located. Surrounding the town was extremely rural, pastoral territory. Coeds were not allowed in the dorm except on the occasion of official parties or other special circumstances. In the dormitory there were no cooking facilities, except maybe a hotplate or two, and alcohol consumption or even possession was prohibited. We almost never violated that last ordinance. Penalties for breaking the rule were severe, but of course we found ways around those. I had a berth in two rooms and a bath on the first floor with two roommates. There were two bunk beds and a single bed at floor level, which I managed to occupy. Over the years and semesters roommates changed around some, but two of them, Henry and Tim, both math majors, were more or less constant. When we had to move out of Gulliver Hall into a newly built dormitory in our last college year Henry and Tim remained my roommates. We went on many adventures together and were fast friends well beyond our college years.

One student who lived in the Gulliver dorm had been at the college long enough to be an upperclassman during my freshman year. Jim Burnis was indeed a character. The first time I was aware of him was one night when a bunch of us were communing in the common room with the lights out. The object of the darkness was to see who could light the best fart. Before this get together I did not understand that could even be done. When Jim was ready he lit a dandy. There he sat on a cheap couch, the decorating mode of the room, with his knees drawn up near his chest and lit match in his hand. The flame that resulted was about a foot long and it snapped at the end. It was the best one that night and he was awarded the prize, a can of baked beans. I had to try this out. My attempt was far less spectacular, barely worthy of an honorable mention. There were only about three inches of flame and I was very happy to have kept my pants on. Otherwise I might have been singed. Anyway, the things I was learning! My parents would have been so proud.

Jim Burnis was an agile contortionist. He was a slim guy and could bend himself around in unbelievable ways. He had this sort of Quasimodo character that he would lapse into. On some nights he would bend himself up into his unearthly, hunched over, and frightening character and move around a room accosting people and at least making them nervous. A person not familiar with his act, like me the first time, might be literally scared. It really was an effective portrayal of a deranged monster. One Halloween we got some powerful sound equipment together and poised speakers in the dorm windows. The creepy music we had found wafted out onto the main street of the town and really set the stage. It was about 10 o'clock. The street was as usual pretty quiet by this time, not many pedestrians or cars moving about. Jim put on a costume and some makeup for his character and commenced to stalk around the main street in his scary way. On the sidewalk harassing pedestrians was bad enough, but it got worse when he would maraud out in the street and the few cars would have to slow down or stop. Twice he actually sprung up onto the engine cover of a vehicle in his stocking feet and did his deranged act through the windshield. We are lucky that some non-expecting motorist did not have a heart attack. In all Jim was out there in costume, make up, and character doing his bit for about a half hour. After that he came back into the dorm, ditched his costume, and we took down the window speaker set up for the music. As quick as we made it all happen, the town went deathly silent, no trace that anything had happened. I don't know how the people on the sidewalk and motorists felt about Jim's act. The people of the town were used to the antics of pesky college students and being

Halloween maybe they thought it was a good show. There was never any upshot, no cops, and no college administrator remonstrations. Probably we were fortunate not to have persisted longer, but while it was on it was indeed a good show. Not many people could have carried it off as well as Jim did. I thought it was immensely cool.

Another dorm compatriot was a guy named Stan Ford. I did not know him all that well and he only lasted in college for a couple of years. At our first convocation a speaker asked us to look at the people on either side of us. The prediction was that one of those people would not complete college. How true that prediction proved to be. Stan did not finish, but for me during the time he was there his legendary status was established. Had he lived in the south years ago he would no doubt have been running moonshine to customers along dark back roads and evading the law. He may not have been fitted for academics, but he sure could drive a car. I never directly knew, and have not known since, anybody with such skills as he had. It was early in the 1960s and he ran a Power Pack 1957 Chevrolet. It was carbureted and had a stick shift, a 283 cubic inch displacement engine, and dual exhausts. There seemed to be no limit as to what he could make that thing do. I never spent much time in his car with him driving, too much adventure, but a couple of times he gave me a demonstration. One time he navigated a curvy back road with me on board. Curves included a virtual right angle turn. This was by my lights a 30 mph road, maybe 35. Stan was handling it at 70 mph and more and loving it. I had a different idea about his performance, stark terror. When he took that very sharp corner he put the car into a four wheel slide, made the turn, and accelerated out of the corner. Wow, what a maneuver! Another time he demonstrated an 180° power turn. We were on a blacktop road heading east at about 50 mph. With screeching tires he brought the car around to face west. We were suddenly going in the opposite direction. The whole operation involved considerable manipulation on his part. I couldn't follow what he did to accomplish the feat and he wasn't much given to explaining things, but I was mightily impressed.

I was not directly involved in these two other events, but I have them on pretty good authority. One time my two roommates were with Stan in his car. They had a case of beer and none of them were of legal age. He was peeling out laying down strips of rubber and making quick braking stops. Apparently he had abused the tires on this and other occasions, leaving all that rubber on the pavement, to a point where they were ready to pop. He had attracted the attention of a policeman in a cruiser. When the cruiser started to approach him he decided to take off. It wouldn't do to get arrested with a case of beer in the car. He began leading the cop on a merry chase, moving fast and taking corners at high speed.

Soon the tires started to give out, one after the other, and before long they were riding on three rims and only one inflated tire, still managing to evade the cop. I can only imagine how tricky that driving was. He got enough of a lead to duck onto a side dirt road without being seen. Stan put his lights out and the chasing cop on the road went right on by. That was it for the chase. There, hidden on the side road, sat the car with shreds for tires and severely damaged rims. I remember being in on finding replacement wheels and tires to retrieve it and get it back on the road. Once that was done this event just went into the books.

As you might suspect Stan liked to gamble and this one all started with a bet. It was about 25 miles down to a particular beach town from campus. Somehow a bet was placed on the table that Stan could not get there and back in less than 45 minutes. The bet was for $50, a dollar a mile. A group of people put $50 together and with Stan's money $100 went into a holding pot. It was about midnight on a clear fall night. Another student, one with some money at stake, stupidly agreed to ride along to witness that he had actually gone the whole way. I suppose it is possible that the witness became so terrified that he agreed to say anything if Stan would just take him safely back. But let's assume that did not happen. Stan and the witness said it did not. Stan and his unwise passenger loaded into the car. As they peeled out and moved rapidly down the road toward the beach town, the exit time was noted and written down. The gathered audience, of course, could not watch much of what happened. It's not like they could keep up. They had to depend on the witness. The challenge was abundantly substantial: cover 50 miles in 45 minutes or less. It would be necessary to travel 1.11 miles per minute or average about 67 mph. This had to be done on public roads and at night. There were stops to be dealt with, police were a high probability, and there were untold dangers. I only heard about this deal later, but I figured if anyone could do it Stan could. And so it turned out. He rolled back in with just under 43 minutes on the clock and collected the money.

The witness had quite a tale to tell. Remarkably they did not see a cop and that was more than a little fortunate. Most of the road they had to cover was 40 or 50 mph two lane blacktop. In the early 1960s at that time of night there was only a little traffic. To compensate for stop signs, a few traffic lights, and other hazards, for which he had to slow down some, Stan had to run 80 or 90 mph most of the time. All corners were taken very fast. It's a good thing the car was equipped with almost new tires at the time. Stan no doubt figured that into his bet. The witness recounted that things, road signs, and telephone poles just zipped by and there were a number of hair raising corners. It took them about 23 minutes to get to the beach town and the agreed upon turn around point. Stan would have to go a little faster on the way back. He did and came in well under time. I know little of what Stan got into after he left college. I hear he raced professionally for a time. As far as I know, he never got himself killed. He certainly did enrich my college years just by being him.

I picked up a couple of "bad" habits once I got to college, smoking, beer drinking, and playing bridge. None of these were part of my life during high school. Smoking involved Lucky Strikes, Chesterfields, and Camels, which at the time were about 30 cents per pack and I remember getting a little high on them when I first started. I wasn't fussy about beer and would drink any available brand. Some ten years later I quit smoking for good, but even now I still like beer. Quite a number of students were into playing bridge. There was a social gathering place on campus where we could buy maybe a hamburger, french fries, and coffee. We called it *The Scrounge*. You could almost always find a bridge game going on there. I learned how to play the game pretty well and accomplished bridge players would not avoid me as a partner. I haven't played since leaving college. Most of the time points were just kept track of so some team would win bragging rights. However, sometimes marathon games would get going for a penny a point and lasting all day or night. At a penny a point you can lose or win a lot of money. In one such game I was in on I lost $36.54, which at the time hurt a lot. Gambling had not much been a part of my experience before this time. The lesson was that there are many people around much better than me at playing cards. Thanks to that lesson even now, if I bet any money on a game of chance, it's not much. At only $36.54, a good lesson like that was well worth it.

Because we could not consume or keep beer in the dorm and no women were allowed, we used to party in what we called "the pits." The pits were not a bar or club of any kind. They were about three or four acres of sand pits out in the boondocks about five miles from campus. Seldom did the cops bother us at the pits. Whoever owned it, they never complained about us. Probably we were out of the way out there, a danger to nobody but ourselves, and the cops basically left well enough alone. Anyway, there we often were, partying or doing a variety of other things. For example, there was an old wrecked car sitting on its roof in the pits. One day my roommate Tim and I decided we should turn that car over. It proved to be quite a challenge. We got out there one morning and spent all that day getting the wreck upright. It was only the two of us alone out there all day. We had some basic equipment, a couple of jacks, a crow bar and a shovel. The car had to be freed from the sand and levered over, engine block and all. It took about all our ingenuity and a supply of beer, but by late afternoon we had gotten the job done. We felt accomplished, damn clever, and very pleased with ourselves for the effort.

Another biology major and friend was Fred Campbell. Fred was a little bit of a guy just over five feet tall, but his fiery personality made him seem much bigger. We started out by studying together. We used to lecture each other about course materials we had to learn. I recall in particular studying organic chemistry with him. There was a lot of memorizing to do. We used to quiz each other repeatedly: how is an alcohol structured; how is that different from an alkane; tell me about the structure of proteins; what about the structure of nucleic acid molecules, DNA and RNA? We got pretty good at rattling such things off and we both ended up with an A in both semesters of the course, quite an accomplishment.

Fred and I did not only study. We spent time in the pits. At the time it was legal to walk around with an exposed gun on your hip. Nobody would get too excited. One time he showed up with a revolver, a Smith and Wesson .357 magnum. As a kid my Dad had guns around and I had experience with them, but the only large caliber pistol I had ever fired was a relatively tame six shooter, a Colt .38 Special Police Positive. This was my first experience with a magnum anything. The diameter of a bullet is about the same in the two pistols, but there was much more powder behind the round in the magnum. The pits were host to some target shooting. Compared to the .38 of my experience this pistol was simply amazing. We started out drilling a five gallon gas can, a relic of some sort we found resident in the pits. Such resources were aplenty there. The pistol was very powerful with a pretty good kick to it and seemed very accurate. Little did I know? We moved the can back, 20, 30, 40, and ultimately 50 yards, taking shots at the can at each distance. Eventually we had to find another can. Even at 50 yards the pistol was amazingly accurate. A couple of times I fired off hand at the can at that distance. It was propped up about shoulder high on a stake. Wham, the can was struck and disintegrated yet more. Such accuracy in a pistol, especially not leaning on anything, was as far as I was concerned not possible. Resting on something or not, with a .38 caliber revolver one wouldn't have a prayer of hitting a five gallon can 50 yards away. Fred opined, "That is one hell of a pistol." I could heartily agree.

We had just shot up all the ammunition we had and something else to do was necessary. There was a very small stream flowing through the pits. For the rest of the day we busied ourselves damming it up and creating a small pond. It took quite a bit of doing, but eventually we found enough debris to make a sizeable dam. The originally nonexistent pond ended up around 20 yards across and we proclaimed it quite beautiful and consumed a beer. Later we removed the dam and the pits were restored pretty much to their former self. When we left we were amused and satisfied. This was a great way to spend a day. Fred and I remained friends and continued to be study partners throughout our college years. I learned a lot from him and because of him. This is just a couple of examples of our times together.

Of course, not only guys were interested in partying and beer. I can remember many pit parties in which female students would just somehow be involved. In New England during the school year it was often damned cold outside. Typically we would get a fire going and there were blankets and sleeping bags around to keep warm. Music was blasting. Some of these pit parties got pretty wild others were quiet and more reserved. With a roaring fire and young people partying amidst blankets and sleeping bags on usually cold nights all sorts of naughty things went on. I had a little experience with the fairer sex during high school, but not all that much. Here I was near 20 years old and my virginal status had been pretty well maintained. Not by design, but that's the way it had gone. At one of these pit parties that status came to an end. An opportunity was made available to me by one Rachel. What can I say? Using a precaution I didn't let the chance slip by. That night was special for me and likely for her. But who knows? There is always some wondering about the opinions of our partners. Our relationship kept on for a while afterward, but a visit from a boyfriend from home brought an end to it. Oh well. Rachel was gorgeous, a psychology major, and an A student. I really did like her, but so things go. I guess the point here is that the pits were the site of yet another good experience in my broadening out at college.

Another occurrence, that had to do with the pits, happened quite a bit later in my time in college. It was early in fall of my junior year. My roommate Tim had an old station wagon on campus at that time. Five of us piled in and went to the pits (where else?) to drink some beer and have a fire. Tim was driving, I was there, as was my other roommate Henry, another friend of us all, Fez, was in attendance, as was another scoundrel named Peter. We hung around in the pits most of the early night, drinking beer, telling stories, laughing a lot, and frequently pissing in the sand. As midnight approached Henry made the pitch that we should stay up all night. The consequences of this idle pitch were unknown to us all at the time, but we all thought it was a great idea. Back into the car we all piled. Our first plan was to go down to the beach town (the Stan Ford destination) and watch the sun come up over the water. So there we went. It took us some 40 minutes just to get there. We went into the parking lot of an open drive-in and got some food. I was sitting in the car eating. All of a sudden I became aware of an altercation out in the parking lot and Tim was involved.

Tim is a feisty guy and some words were exchanged with a group of young local residents. Tim said they started it. There was some quick pushing and shoving and Tim ended up belted in the mouth. Very quickly it all stopped. We were all out there, two sides facing the possibility of a fight. But nothing came of it. Tim had to nurse a cut lip for days afterward, but that was all there was to it. On getting back in the car, Tim still driving, we decided we had better get out of that parking lot, which we did. Cruising around to various local places, we burned up most of the rest of the night. With dawn in the not too distant future Henry again made a suggestion, "Let's go back to campus and find some high ground to watch the sunrise." For some reason he really wanted to see the sun come up. "Great idea!" We all exclaimed. This plan would have dire consequences. Because it was Henry's suggestion, we had an excuse to blame all the consequences on him.

We traveled back and were cruising around in the dim pre-dawn light on narrow roads among farmer's cornfields looking for a propitious place to watch the sunrise. The corn was still erect, unharvested in the field. Tim's wild hair showed itself again. This time, with ample backing from his passengers, he plunged his car into a field of corn. Slipping and sliding around, he left wide paths behind him. Of course, we passengers were hooting and hollering as we all thought this was great fun. The owner of the cornfield did not think so. Somehow, we supposed with binoculars, he got Tim's license plate number before we vacated his field after sunrise. This was unknown to us and we went back to our dormitories, got some sleep, and for a short while marveled at what a night we had.

A day later the police came to the dorm and collected Tim. He spent some time behind bars. That unnerved us all, especially Tim. During his incarceration Tim did not reveal the names of any of his co-violators. The field owner called the college president and complained. After he was freed from jail, the president as a euphemism "invited" Tim into his office. We were all well aware of what was going to happen by this time and the other four miscreants were not about to let Tim take alone whatever additional heat was going to come down. At the appointed hour five of us trooped into the president's office. I suppose in his private moments he saw some humor in the whole affair, but in his office he certainly seemed pissed. It seems we had besmirched the wonderful reputation of the whole college in the town in which it resided. The field owner's name was Tom Calibri. It turns out that he had quite a sense of humor and was much more reasonable than we deserved. After all, he had planted that corn in the early summer, brought it along through the summer and into the fall, and then we had mowed down a large swatch of it with our inexcusable action.

Nevertheless, he was not going to press charges. We would not be punished by the college we took it on Mr. Calibri's recommendation. In our office confrontation there had been a number of threats by the president that we might all be kicked out of college. But no, none of that occurred. Rather, Mr. Calibri would put the five of us to work on his farm for a long day. The work he decided on was ignominious at best, which was only appropriate. Officially we never saw his humor at work, but this must have been part of it.

The work wasn't, as you might expect, shoveling shit. Another plan was devised. Mr. Calibri had another large field that was plowed, but full of stones, a problem in tilling and planting. It was early fall and, as luck would have it, it was hotter than the hinges of hell on the Saturday we were due to pay for our atrocity with labor. He had a hired hand. He was about 35 or 40 years old and at first he didn't know what the hell to make of us. His job that day was to drive an open tractor towing a flatbed trailer, about five feet on a side, enclosed with boards about 10 inches high. Early that morning we had close quarters as we were all hauled to the field on that trailer. The owner met us there and told us what was expected of us. Basically we were to remove the stones from that field. He left and we never saw Mr. Calibri again.

So there we were for about ten hours that hot day walking in a rank of five behind the tractor and trailer, in the dust, picking up the numerous stones from the plowed dirt and throwing them into the trailer. It was a big field and we just barely finished collecting stones from it all before it got dark. The tractor driver must have had to go empty the trailer 15-20 times that day. We did turns going with him to do that job and there was a huge pile of stones when the job was done. At first we were pretty quiet in our task line. We were being punished and it seemed appropriate. But after we had been at it for a while things began to change. Fez, among other things, had quite a sense of humor and could be a very funny guy. One time in a mixed crowd of people he got forcibly de-pants and just coolly walked off the "stage" lamenting aloud that he wished he could be more impressive. Peter was no slouch either. Eventually the humor of the situation was not to be bottled up inside Fez any longer. He started commenting facetiously on the intellectual challenge of the work that we, a bunch of smart-ass college kids, were doing. He kept at it. For example, he commented on the problems of dealing with recalcitrant stones when I missed the trailer with a stone I picked up. When I picked it up again and hit the trailer with it this time. He excessively marveled at how damned clever I was, "Did you learn that in college?" We all started to chime in, cracking wise about this that and the other thing. Some of the impromptu jokes were outright funny. We laughed as we worked. Even the tractor driver began to laugh at the situation. He had shown no emotion of any kind at first, but we found him to be a likeable guy and got along famously with him as the day went along. He told us his name, Zeke, and we all offered ours. The whole character of the day was now filled with humor and jocularity and so it remained for the rest of the day.

We had made arrangements with female friends to come out to our field of labor and bring along food and water (no beer here). Seven of them showed up and they added materially to the scene. With the heat, we all had built up running sweats, and in the dust the water in particular was very welcome. The girls could get right up close to our line of stone-picker-uppers as we were working and carrying on and they could add their own humor to the goings on. They stayed around most of the day and were a source of immense joy and interest to Zeke. I and the other laborers were also major beneficiaries. Thanks very much to you girls for helping to liven things up. There were some trials and tribulations in this whole happening, but in retrospect it was fun to have lived through it all. I found it superbly instructive.

Well, this deal with the farmer's field of stones was all said and done. Things slowly got back to normal as the memory of the whole affair began to fade in police, college administrators, and perhaps even the assaulted Mr. Calibri, but only somewhat in us the perpetrators. After all this time it is but one memory among many of our time in college. This and other events during this time had much to do with making me what I have become. The connection is sometimes obscure, but it is there and influences my actions and reactions to this day. There may not be much emphasis on research and the discovery of knowledge in what I have told so far. There had not been much dealing with that. Except for Dr. Burke, who had made it a point to tell me of the voluminous research he had done. Most of that will come later in graduate school and in my years as a university professor. For now just recognize my undergraduate college days as my foundation in biology. Also the environment, the place, time, and events of it all, became fodder for the development of what was to come in research and how I reacted to it. The connection between my college experiences and what ultimately happened will become obvious as the story unfolds.

Chapter 3

A MASTER'S DEGREE IS THE NEXT THING

As I indicated previously, when I started graduate school in a university of about 15,000 students I did not have much money. This place was much bigger than my college had been. It was the semester starting in January and ending in May. I had gotten a tuition scholarship, no small deal, and I had paid for dorm space. It was a big multi-story dormitory and I had three roommates. I hated it, but it was a roof over my head. Feeding properly was a constant problem. For one thing I did not have a car to get to a restaurant and even getting to one there was not much cash to pay for an order. There was a local eatery some miles from campus that I could afford and the food was good. One of my dorm mates went there regularly and I would hitch a ride. I made it a point to eat at least one good meal a day. Other meals were mostly crap. When you are young you can withstand such circumstances and I did not get sick. So, under these somewhat unfavorable conditions I commenced on my quest for a Master's degree.

The biology department at that university put an emphasis on marine and estuarine organisms. It was there I became involved with what became my chosen field of study, marine invertebrates. Marine of course means that the organisms in question live in a saltwater environment and invertebrate means that, as opposed to the vertebrates which possess one, they are animals lacking a backbone. There are at least one million animal species; invertebrates make up about 95% of them and vertebrates the rest. I had dealt with many invertebrate groups from marine, freshwater, and terrestrial environments in zoology courses as an undergraduate. But that was pretty much child's play by comparison. One of my first courses was on the natural history of marine invertebrates. A large part of the game in that course involved going to the ocean shore in the winter months and collecting and identifying as many species as possible. You would have to manipulate a specimen with bare hands. A gloved hand was prohibitive and most of the time your hands would be gloveless and wet. The wind and cold made it rough. Every time I would come back to the vehicle from a field trip my hands would be numbed and about useless. They would hurt like hell as they were warming up.

We would have to learn the mode of life of each species we collected: where it would be found; what it ate; how it ate it; and how it reproduced. That was infinitely reasonable, after all most of what an organism's biology involves has to do with either food or sex, or both. The final exam in the course involved collecting, correctly identifying, classifying, and knowing the mode of life of at least 100 different species. The weather had warmed some by the time of this final and that was good. This was very different from what I had experienced in college. There we mostly dealt with preserved specimens, or if alive, they were shipped in some unnatural container. These specimens were all initially alive and had come from their natural environment. Their names, how classified, and how they lived were the objects of study. Though there was discomfort in the specimen collection process in winter, I really got off on this area of study. Add to this the 30 hours of courses I got while pursuing my Masters, for example, in Invertebrate Zoology (two semesters), Marine Ecology, Algology (the study of algae, I got to collect live *Ulva lactuca*!), and Evolution this place equipped me pretty well for what I would eventually become. Initially my living situation may not have been ideal, but I rapidly became enamored with the idea of going to graduate school and the subject area I had more or less fallen into.

At the end of that semester my living situation improved. A friend by the name of Herb who had been living in the dorm with me came up with a rental and he needed a roommate to share expenses. I was more than happy to partake. Herb was enrolled in a program for a graduate degree in business. Our interests did not run along the same lines, but we respected each other's privacy, shared expenses honestly and amicably, and got along very well. He was a great housemate. The place was only a simple cottage, but it was fantastic. There were four main rooms, a kitchen, a living room, and a couple of bed rooms. No more space was needed and that kitchen was a godsend. I could now eat better, not perfectly, but better. The surroundings of the place were fantastic. It sat on a hillside overlooking a tidal river that after several miles ultimately led into a large estuarine embayment, about two or three miles across, called Big Neck Bay. The currents were very strong in that river and a boat had to constantly fight them, first one way and then the other. Big Neck Bay would become a major part of my existence very soon.

During that first semester an elderly professor involved in that natural history of marine invertebrates course and I had developed a relationship. Dr. Filbert knew an amazing amount about marine invertebrates and was quite a well-known expert. He offered me a summer job as a research associate (how I loved that title) working on a research project he had going in the Big Neck Bay vicinity and having to do with the natural culturing of oysters. I don't wish to clutter this up with species names any more than necessary, but the scientific name of the oyster being studied was *Crassostrea virginica*. As usual these jobs did not pay much, but it was an amount you could get along on. So, I had a paying summer job in research. I did not know what that was, but I would learn.

As it turned out I lived in that cottage for the next two summers and the intervening winter with Herb as a housemate. Great! To do the work associated with his project Dr. Filbert had acquired a 30 foot lobster boat with funds he had gotten for his research. It was named the Veliger (after the larval stage of the oyster). Two other graduate students had also been recruited. One of them, Joe, had been on the job for the two previous summers and was very experienced. Joe was a Ph.D. candidate in Zoology. The other one, Sebastian (Seb), a Master of Zoology degree seeker like me, was also new to the job. At first either Joe or Dr. Filbert handled the boat. We other two got to do the grunt work. Gradually we learned to pilot the boat and became more useful in other ways.

Most of the work involved maintaining several rafts that had oyster shells suspended from them like beads on strings. The object was to see how successful these rafts with their suspended oyster shell strings would be at collecting juvenile oysters. The idea was that oyster larvae (veligers) present in the water (a planktonic organism) when sufficiently developed would settle onto the shells and metamorphose into juvenile oysters. The idea of plankton is that the organisms that make it up cannot swim strongly enough to swim against currents. So, all plankters are drifters. There was a lot of work to be done. Ranks of oyster shell strings had to be assembled, they would have to be put out on the rafts, they would have to be checked to sure something hadn't fouled in them, eventually they would be retrieved, and the settled juvenile oysters had to be counted. Oyster shells were obviously needed and had to be collected. They were found on the bottom of the estuary, which meant they were retrieved with oyster tongs, something I had never done before. Hard work! All this provided me with a background in what it takes to run a research project. It takes quite a bit, lots of jobs had to be done, and many contingencies had to be overcome. Turning a wrecked car over in the pits or damming a small stream during my undergraduate days may have been less productive, but it was good practice.

Anyway, this summer marks my first involvement with doing any kind of research. It taught me a great deal.

I began to learn something that summer, which has, subject to further development, been with me ever since. That something is rope splicing and knotting. Splicing three-strand rope is not something a person needs to know how to do, but it is a handy skill on some occasions. Working around the Veliger and other boats all that summer, there were many examples of the product of that skill; all sorts of ropes were spliced. This was in the days before braided ropes were as common as now. One of the "old salts" that worked at the marina where we docked Dr. Filbert's lobster boat agreed, after a little begging and cajoling, to show me how it was done. First he said, "A boat only has one rope on it and that is the bell rope. The rest of them are lines." Having got that out of the way, Jobe demonstrated a back splice (he called it a dog cock). These are used to keep a cut rope end from unraveling and to give a user of a line a hand hold. He also showed me an eye splice, which is a loop joined back into the line with a splice, such as often used in mooring lines. I found the crowning of the three strands, which is the first operation of a back splice, to be the most difficult thing to master. Sometimes when I haven't done one in a while it still gives me pause. I spent days practicing and finally got it. In my other world, people kept asking, "What in the hell are you wasting your time with that for?" I would say, "It may be pretty useless, but it's really neat." That was a pretty good predictor of how I would choose things to do.

Once they let up a little on the hard crust they liked to present to people, Jobe and his boss Charlie, the person in charge of the marina, were great guys to be around. They had been in the boat game for a decade or more and knew a lot of stuff about fixing motors, hulls of boats, and in general boating. I learned much from them. After work we used to swim off the docks of the marina. There was one pier with a winch system that was about 12 feet off the water. It was used for raising and lowering boats from/to the water. In that place there was usually a four or five foot tidal range. Charlie was an athletic individual. He did some amazing dives and flips off that pier. Joe, Seb, and I contributed less wonderfully to the scene. Jobe wasn't much interested in nonsense such as that. It's likely he could not swim.

Shortly I became adequate at splicing ropes and tying a few knots. I did not know all that many knots, but there were a few essentials. I learned to tie a bowline. That was a handy knot, quickly tied and very efficient. I also learned the sheet bend, for bending two lines together, and the clove hitch for tying a boat to a post or cleat on a dock. All these knots were very useful. They were all secure and would not jam up no matter how much strain was put on the line. They could always be untied.

These newfound rope skills created the need for a better knife. They had one for sale in the marina store, a sheath knife with a five inch blade. It was replete with a marlinspike in the sheath, used for working splices and knots. Hans Anderson in the seafaring country of Denmark was the manufacturer. How cool is that! I hemmed and hawed for a bit. At the time it was quite a lot of money for me to part with, $13 as I recall, but I soon came up with the cash and bought it. The knife is still a used possession of this Blake Turner. It is all beat up now from worthy usage, but still very functional. It was a great purchase and I am still very pleased with it. It serves among other things to remind me of my time around that marina.

The Veliger was a wooden boat and not very fast. Maximum speed was maybe 12 knots. It had an inboard six cylinder engine, a single prop, and one lonely rudder. Onboard accommodations were pretty austere. There was no head. There was a small closed in area about 10 feet long and too low to stand up in under the bow deck. There were no bunks, but long pads were there and you could sleep in there, which I did once in a while. Mostly, gear was stored there out of the weather. Where you stood to steer the boat by a spoked wheel, there was a windshield in front of you and short roof over your head almost as wide as the boat, which gave you some protection from weather. You had to be careful of a misstep getting around that roof to get forward to deploy the anchor or tie the craft to a dock. In the center of the boat immediately on your left when you stood at the steering position was the engine compartment. It had a wooden cover that you could sit on. The rest of the spacious deck was open. This was a tough work boat you did not have to worry much about denting or hurting. It was well suited to the work we had to do. From the marina up into Big Neck Bay proper it was about four or five miles and this was more than enough boat to handle anything we might run into.

One constant problem was getting the boat into its slip at the marina. Virtually every work day this had to be performed. The problem was that strong tidal currents moved through the docking area. Joe was especially excellent at this maneuver, Dr. Filbert was adequate at it, and I eventually learned. Seb never felt like getting the method down and preferred not dealing with it. Depending on whether the tide was coming in or going out the current would be going one way or the other past our slip. At the brief slack water was the only current-free time. The challenge was to back the Veliger into its slip so gear could be loaded and unloaded over the stern. As a boat pilot you would nose into the row of slips, which was a box with boats docked at floating slips on three sides. Where you nosed in was of course open. There was about 50 feet between the boat slips on either side and the row of slips was about 150 feet long. Boats protruded out of their slips and there was not much room to maneuver a 30 foot boat.

Assume the tide is coming in. (If not, a reverse set of problems would set in.) This means that as you nosed into that three sided box of boat slips the current would be pushing you along into the box. A problem to be dealt with was that the Veliger would respond poorly to its single rudder in reverse. Ordinarily a boat could be steered in reverse by moving the rudder to the right (crank the wheel left) to go right and left (crank the wheel right) to go left. This boat would just plow essentially straight back in reverse regardless of what you did with the rudder. So, when you got to an appropriate distance from our slip, which was on the starboard (right) side, the maneuver was to point the bow to port (left) while you still had pretty good steerage in forward gear and line up the stern with the slips on the right. Now you are crossways with the current being pushed vigorously along into the box toward our slip. When you were still pretty well shy of our slip the idea was to pull the gear control out to put the boat in reverse and increase the throttle so the boat would begin to go straight backward. On coming abreast of our slip another gun of the engine would put the stern of the boat into the target slip. That is if you lined everything up and timed things correctly. If you went by the slip, you would have to avoid colliding with protruding boats and motor back to the entrance of the box and nose in again. Then you would try again. More than once it took me two sometimes three tries to get the job done. Of course, we had our slip well-padded with bumpers (tires) so when you got the stern into the slip and hit the sides, which normally happened, no damage would be done. Only once during my time there did anyone actually collide with another boat. Dr. Filbert was the unlucky one. Some damage was done, but his grant money had bought insurance to pay for such eventualities and things were put right. Every day we took the boat out, which was most days, we had to face this. Docking the Veliger was always an adventure, but add a wind, rain, or fog and things got even more complicated. Among other things this problem with docking the boat gave me a lifelong lesson: it is one thing to propose, for example, that you go out and test whether it is feasible to naturally culture oysters by putting strings of oyster shells in the water. It is quite another to actually do it and it will be expensive.

So you will not think graduate school was all about having fun, such things as dealing with the Veliger. Let me tell you about my own research project. At the time this university did not require you to write and defend a Master's Thesis to qualify for a Master's Degree in Zoology. Maybe it was a mistake, it would have been good practice, but I did not sign on for a thesis. Rather, one of the things I had to do was a piece of original research presumably less extensive than a thesis and submit a typewritten paper on it. This would be worth some course credits and it would be graded by faculty members. Dr. Filbert and two others on the faculty did this job.

One of the things I noted while working on those strings of oyster shells was that many species of invertebrates settled on the shells. It's not as if this was a clever observation on my part, it was immediately obvious. To do any piece research you need to specify a question and that basic observation would not serve that purpose. One of the species, besides the oyster, that settled on the shells was a tunicate by the name of *Molgula manhattensis*. If you don't already know, to give you a clue the tunicates are a kind of invertebrate, but in the Phylum Chordata. That phylum also contains the Subphylum Vertebrata, which have a backbone and are therefore not invertebrates. *Molgula manhattensis* belongs to a different subphylum, the Urochordata, within the phylum Chordata. The "Uro" in that name refers to a larval tail. This signals the possession of a chordate notochord only in the tail of the tadpole-like larva that members of the group have. A notochord is a stiffening rod, a sort of primitive skeleton, located just above the intestine. Muscles work against the notochord and give a larva better swimming ability. Most chordates, for example the tunicates and vertebrates, lose their basic chordate characters, including the notochord, when they grow up into adults. The tunicate name of the group to which *Molgula manhattensis* belongs refers to a tunic that envelopes the body and is characteristic of the group. In the organism we are talking about here, called a solitary (as opposed to colonial) tunicate, the tunic contains cellulose fibers, which is unusual because cellulose normally occurs only in plants. Adults of *Molgula manhattensis* are known commonly as sea squirts or sea grapes. Grape conveys well about what they looks like. Protruding from "the grape" are a water intake inhalant siphon (a fleshy tube) and a water output exhalant siphon. If you pick one of these critters up and handle it, the organism will likely squirt water on you, hence the common name. The purpose of the inhalant siphon is to haul water in, so it can be filtered through gill slits and a pharynx to remove food from the plankton. After filtering the water is pushed out via the exhalant siphon. In short, a sea squirt is a filter feeder, as is an oyster. *Molgula manhattensis* in the Big Neck Bay estuary occurs all over the place. You could find their squirting, grape-like selves on things in the water such as mooring lines, buoys, wooden posts, and on floating docks around marinas.

So, that is the invertebrate I decided to do my research project on, but what exactly is the question that I would address? The general question was: does the settlement of *Molgula manhattensis* on our deployed oyster shells inhibit the settlement of oyster larvae on those same shells. If the answer came up yes, the tunicate could be an obstacle to the success of Dr. Filbert's oyster culturing project. If the answer was no, then the tunicate would not be barrier to the project's success. How could I begin to answer the question posed? Well, for one thing the amount of room taken up by the tunicate on our oyster shells could be important. If space on oyster shells is taken up by *Molgula manhattensis*, then it can't be used by *Crassostrea virginica*. One thing I needed to do was count the numbers of this tunicate on deployed oyster shells. Because a large tunicate takes up more room than a small one, I also needed to measure the sizes of the tunicates present on deployed shells.

If the tunicate does not merely take up space, but actually consumes oyster veligers when filter feeding, this would also be important to know. (The reverse question is also of interest: do adult oysters, which are filter feeders, consume tunicate tadpole larvae? Well possibly so, but we can't do everything.) Observing whether microscopic oyster veligers can be consumed by a tunicate when it filter feeds, is not something you can do in the field. Maybe you could try to find oyster larvae inside the pharynx of tunicates from the field, but I didn't do that. Too bad, I wish I had thought of it. What I tried to do, without much success, was to expose oyster veligers to *Molgula manhattensis* in the laboratory. I was able to observe a few very young veligers that I cultured being taken in by large tunicates, but did the size of the veligers or the tunicates matter? I did not have sufficient luck with this to get enough observations to answer the question. It proved too difficult for me to get the cultured oyster larvae, tunicates, glassware, and other facilities together all at one time. All I can say about this is that oyster larvae can be consumed by tunicates, but how frequently this occurs in nature remains unknown. This aspect of my first research attempt was not a resounding success.

The counting and measuring of *Molgula manhattensis* on deployed oyster shells in the field was more of a success. This aspect of my research project, as was the other, was a lot of work. There is a previously unmentioned wrinkle in what I did in this regard. In addition to strings of oyster shells, shells were also deployed in something called vexar bagging. Vexar comes in large rolls of tubular material and the material is made with a large mesh. Mesh size is about two inches, plenty of room for an oyster or tunicate larva to pass through. All you had to do to create a bag was lace off one end of tubular vexar material, fill the bag with oyster shells, and lace up the other end. These bags were about two feet long by one foot wide and were loosely packed with oyster shells. These could be hung off rafts much like strings of shells to see how well oyster larvae settled in them. Because each shell did not have to be drilled to make a hole for stringing purposes it was much easier to make bags of oyster shells. Dr. Filbert wanted to know if as many oyster larvae settled on shells in bags as on strings. What I wanted to know was whether shells in bags accumulated *Molgula manhattensis* as well as shells on strings.

The arrangement of strings and bags of oyster shells on rafts is important. Rafts were constructed of wood and floatation material. They were 10 feet long and five feet wide and there were 10 of them anchored and deployed around Big Neck Bay. Strings of shells were three feet long and suspended off a raft on three foot pipes that went from one side of the raft interior to the other. There were five of these crossways pipes along a raft and eight strings of shells were arrayed on each pipe. Bags of shells could be hung in the water from rafts either in place of strings on pipes or around the outside edge of rafts.

To get a random sample of shell strings I used a table of random numbers. On a raft strings of shells were each given a number. There were five pipes with eight strings on each (40 strings) and numbers were assigned from one corner of the raft to the opposite corner. With closed eyes a position in the random numbers table was determined and, if the number there was between one and 40, that string was chosen. If some other number was there, I would try again. In all that amounts to 30 strings of shells, three randomly chosen from each of 10 rafts, on which the *Molgula manhattensis* would have to be counted and measured. Bags of shells were more haphazardly arranged than strings, there were fewer of them, and I used a smaller random sample of 10 bags. I simply counted the bags on a raft, assigned them all numbers, and selected one of them randomly with a random numbers table. This is the kind of stuff, as I learned, that you have to go through when you do a research project. It would not do to examine a biased set of shell strings or bags.

After my data were assembled the tunicate counts and measurements revealed some basic facts, but this is not without its complications. Oyster shells are not all the same. There are of course different sizes and they have various shapes and configurations. Figuring out just how much space is available on an oyster shell is not a simple matter. With regard to the tunicate, in the end all I could do is estimate the amount of space taken on oyster shells. This was less than perfect, but the estimate was at least pretty good. A given number of tunicates of given sizes take up a given amount of space and that was determined by data. Basically you just add the population up. The big problem arises when you try to understand how much space is available on a string, or in a bag, of oyster shells. That requires a more involved estimate. I took clean oyster shells of various sizes and estimated the amounts of obvious (measurable) space available. I did this by moving a square centimeter frame over the shells and keeping track of how many cm^2 I counted. This again was not perfect, but I got most of the area. In the end I figured that the tunicate occupied about 20 to 30% of space on shells. This is a reduction in space available to settling oysters on shells and that could be an important competition for space. Based on a simple statistical test, there was no difference in space taken up by tunicates on shells in bags and on strings. In his project Dr. Filbert had found that oysters settled in bags about as well as on strings. So, because it was simpler to construct bags, maybe it would be better for him to have bags of shells assembled rather than strings. That, as was the amount of space taken up by the tunicate on potential oyster settlement surface, was useful information. However, compared to what I learned from my project about doing research it was a minimal finding. The project was only a little less complicated than doing a Master's thesis. Even the simplest research project was difficult, complicated, could cost a lot of time, and would be an expensive proposition. This told me a lot, especially what fun it was to do such things.

Dr. Filbert seldom came out in the Veliger with Joe, Seb, and me particularly in the second summer. He really enjoyed working with that boat and being in the field with his marine invertebrates. It was inspiring how much, but teaching, writing papers and research grants, meetings, and other duties ganged up on him. He had too much else to do.

We were still working steadily, but every once in a while we would do things that, had Dr. Filbert known, would have gotten us in trouble or censured in some fashion. At that time there was very little populace out near the entrance into Big Neck Bay proper. This was a good distance from the marina and not many boats were around there either. Most of the time, we had the place to ourselves. The Veliger, as I have already indicated, was not very fast, but it had pretty good pulling power. Were you to pull a water skier with it you might have difficulty keeping the skier comfortably on the surface of the water. The engine was good. It ran well and powered the boat adequately, but we never felt like it could be run wide open for that long. Maybe it would take it, but we tried not to abuse the boat. It had much to do, what with hauling rafts around, putting out and taking in strings and bags of oyster shells, and many other jobs.

There were many occasions when we had to get over the side of the Veliger and into the water. There was no option if a line got tangled in the prop, or something had to be done below one of the rafts. Sometimes it was just for fun. One day we decided to see if someone could be pulled along behind the boat on the engine cover. Joe got in the water first and tried it out with me driving the boat. Just barely would the boat go fast enough to allow the engine cover to gain the surface of the water, but Joe did O.K. with it. It was difficult for him to stabilize the board as he got up, but once there he deftly got it under pretty good control. After some rough water dumped him Joe climbed back onboard. Next Seb tried it. He got up immediately and was an absolute star back there. He even took the engine cover over the wake. I don't know where he practiced such skills. It was my turn next and Joe took over at the helm. I dove off the stern and gathered up the towrope and positioned the engine cover in front of me. I had done some water skiing when younger and so had some idea what the job was. The engine cover was a clumsy piece of wood for this purpose. It was much harder to keep it aligned than it looked when the other guys were doing it. The boat started to pull. The cover plowed and started to rise up on the water, but wavered left and right as it did so. I had a hard time keeping my feet under me. I managed to overcome this after a ways and got up. So there I was skimming along the surface at about 10 knots, barely keeping my balance. When Joe had to turn the boat around and go the other way the increased speed at the end of the whip was too much for me and the cover went one way and I the other. When I and the engine cover regained the deck we thought just maybe water skiing on the engine cover was not a wise thing to spend our time doing. If Dr. Filbert found out, he would be justifiably angry. The boat might not handle it. It was fun to have done, but we did it no more.

But we did not stop challenging each other. It seems there was always a challenge of some sort at issue. For example, on another day the challenge went out that one of us could not swim across Fleming Strait. There was a fairly narrow passage before you got into Big Neck Bay. It was about 1500 feet across Fleming Strait and there was a strong tidal current running through there. The challenge was to get across before getting swept too far past the target point on the opposite shore. I was the one challenged. I jumped off the Veliger and started to swim. I didn't have to go far before I was made aware that the tidal current would be a major problem. It was an exhausting swim. I had a particular point on the opposite shore for which I was aiming. Before I was half way across, the current had carried me way past that point. I finally got all the way across, but missed my target by quite a bit. I had to swim back about 500 feet against the current, but along shore where the current was less strong. When I got to the point we had agreed on I was totally played out, but I had made it, was still able to swim, and not in any trouble. Joe and Seb brought the Veliger alongside where I was. As I was about to claim victory, which they just would not have, Seb mischievously jumped over the side with a couple of life preservers to fake saving me. Protest as I might they would not let go of the claim that I needed to be rescued. There was no money involved so it mattered in no way. All I can say is, "Guys, we all know the truth of the matter."

During the second summer my parents came to visit their graduate student son at his university. Their visit is still a source of pride to me. The idea of college, never mind graduate school, was totally foreign to my father. It was just never on his horizons, but he had my respect. My mother, at whose insistence we had all taken on the college challenge, also had that. They had treated this son very well. I knew they were coming and asked Dr. Filbert if it would be alright if I took them out in the Veliger to show them Big Neck Bay and tong up some oysters. He said, "You have been handling that boat very well for two summers now and that will be fine." I was happy he did not know about our abusive use of the engine cover. His response might have been different. Anyway, they showed up on a Saturday. We visited a bit and I showed them around campus then I told them what we could do and we went to the marina. My Dad had many boats during his life. I had gotten some experience with boats through him, but he never let me drive very much. On the other hand, I had learned to water ski. We got out of the car and brought stuff, some food and drink, down to the Veliger. When my father saw the 30 foot boat we were going to take out he was taken aback. He did not say anything, but I could tell he was a bit nervous.

I put some oyster tongs that were about 10 feet long on board and we helped my mother get on. It was a sparkling day with almost no wind. I fired up the boat, we took off the bow, stern, and springer lines (which by this time I had put splices in) and we pulled out of the slip. That was much easier than backing it in, which would come later. We all enjoyed the four or so miles we had to go to reach Big Neck Bay. It was a beautiful place with a number of things to point out as we went along at a moderate speed. When we got to where the oysters would be tonged we had to anchor the boat and this went without a hitch. Things had gone well so far and my father was loosening up. He wasn't used to his son being able to do all these things. Once the boat was anchored we sat in the sun on the boat gunnels and ate sandwiches and drank sodas. Now refreshed we decided to get the oysters we had come after. The boat I knew was in about six feet of water. I gathered up the oyster tongs and standing on the stern lowered them over the side. Neither of my parents had been around working oyster tongs before. The first haul raked up from the bottom had only two live oysters in it, but that was two. I dowsed off the rake and tried again. This time there were five oysters. Before too long we had 35 good sized oysters in a bucket.

It was the middle of the afternoon by now and it was time to head back to the marina. I fired up the boat and pulled up a bit to take the strain off the anchor line. My father pulled up the anchor, stowed it and the line, and we headed back. The trip back to the marina was uneventful, but pleasant. On the way I explained to my father the problem with backing the boat into its slip. I guess I did that to guard myself against any unfortunate eventualities. When we nosed into the box of slips the tide was going out. I tried to be confident, but I knew there was always a risk. When the time came I was able to point the bow to the left and line up the stern with slips on the right. As we drifted along crossways to the current I chose exactly the right time to throw the boat into reverse and begin backing up. It all worked perfectly. The Veliger entered the slip with hardly an impact. My dad said, "That was a tricky maneuver and was nicely done." That was all there was to it, but I was happy it had gone that way. My father was sort of mystified by this graduate school thing, but the fact that he had, even if briefly, verbally complimented me on something like that meant a lot to me. We buttoned up the boat, got in the car, and left the marina with our oysters.

The plan was to go back to my hillside cottage alongside the river and make dinner. Herb was away. We stopped at a store and got some steaks, a vegetable, and a dessert. I had some potatoes at home. My folks were really taken with my cottage and where it was situated on that hillside. The first order of business was making oyster stew. I had a couple of oyster knives and gave my dad a lesson in shucking oysters. Somewhere in his almost 60 years he probably already knew, but listened. We put the 35 shucked oysters in a pot to simmer for a few minutes then added some milk and seasoning and simmered gently for a bit longer. The stew was excellent and made for a great appetizer following the day we had. A few beers were consumed as we cooked the rest of the meal and ate it. It was a good time with them. After dinner they got into their car and went back to their motel. They were gone the next day.

This certainly does not cover all of my experiences while obtaining my Master's Degree, but it at least mentions the shaping ones. I have not emphasized much the academics of my time there, but of course they were absolutely key to what I gained there. As indicated earlier this was where I happened upon my field of study, marine invertebrate zoology. I would eventually go into doing research in that area and what I learned at this university was fundamental to that enterprise. Dr. Filbert of course had done his research in the same general field, but I would take a very different approach to it. The other thing I got there was the confidence to take on a research project. Knowing what to do is necessary and academics give you that. Equally important is the belief that you can actually do it. Handling my own research project and aiding Dr. Filbert with one of his had told me about all the uncertainties that can be involved in research. You have to be able to recognize and overcome these and press on to find the truth you seek. I did not know this when I came to this university, but I certainly left there with a good understanding of it, valuable, valuable, valuable.

Chapter 4

A PhD Degree Is Sought and Obtained

As I was about to graduate with my Master's degree I contacted Dr. Burke, of undergraduate days, to tell him that I had succeeded at getting my Master's Degree in Zoology. He was very pleased with that. I have since had the experience of former students going on and succeeding in graduate school and I understand why he was pleased. Late in my undergraduate days Dr. Burke had taken a teaching position out of New England and quite a few miles to the south. I wasn't contacting him to see if he could help me find a job, but that was the way it worked out. His department needed someone to handle botany and zoology laboratories for freshmen at the university where he was teaching. It was not a full-fledged faculty position, which I did not expect with my degree, but Dr. Burke knowing I could handle the job suggested I apply. Here was an available and paying academic position. Not a lot of money was to be paid (it was about $6,000 per year), but it was more than I had made so far.

I had a cheap wreck of a car that had come into my possession while getting my Master's Degree, it ran but not a whole lot better than the one Tim and I had turned over in the pits. It wasn't up to the five or six hour trip down to this new university so I gathered my resources and bought a used sports car for around $1500. It was a convertible and a Sunbeam Alpine. It had a four cylinder 1600 cc engine, not the V8 engine that they had in the Sunbeam Tiger of Get Smart fame. It was not all that fast, but with four on the floor it was fun to drive and would corner like the very dickens. It got me down and back for an interview, which was mainly what I wanted. The interview, my first ever, went pretty well. It was very good seeing Dr. Burke again and the other people I talked to seemed receptive to me as I made my case for the job. I suppose at the behest of my former professor they offered me the job and I accepted the offer.

In the very early fall that year, at the age of 24 years I got my few belongings packed easily into my two-seat sports car and moved myself away from my hillside cottage. I was glad to have a job to go to, but I really hated leaving that cottage and the situation there. The location of my new job was much more citified than I had been used to either in college or at the university where I got my Master's Degree. This was a smaller university with about 6,500 students. I searched for and found a place to live, an efficiency apartment, fairly close to where I would teach. It wasn't a walk to work distance, but it was only a 15 minute drive, even with the traffic around there.

The campus of this university was on a luxurious old estate and was very pleasant. Whoever had the original money to build the place surely had good taste. The laboratory I was going to teach in and my office were in a now defunct old brick carriage house that was modernized and well set up. It was a pretty cool environment to exist in while I was there. The laboratory was set up much like the one at college had been. That was undoubtedly because Dr. Burke had been running laboratories for his courses out of there. I collected the syllabus for the botany course that contained the schedule of labs I would have to run. I took an inventory, ordered some things, and generally got ready to present the labs to students. I had done all this before and it wasn't much of a problem to get it done again. There were the usual 24 student spaces in the laboratory and three sections. I would be responsible for giving up to 72 students their laboratory grade, which would be figured into their overall grade for the course. The students were students. I had changed, but they had not. Some were very capable and did fine all of the time all by themselves, some did not seem to need or want much assistance most of the time, and some were as befuddled as me in my first college biology course. I tried, with some success, to salvage as many of these as I could. The students were well worth dealing with. In fact they were outright inspiring, but the whole job did not meet up with or draw upon what I had come to be during my Masters experience. In short, there was no marine research going on here and I missed it.

Blake Turner was contracted for a year. I stayed there and taught my botany labs in the fall semester and zoology labs in the spring. I was responsible for 60-70 students each semester. It was far from a bad experience, but was not what I had come to want for myself. During that early spring I started looking in earnest for a place to go after a Ph.D. I really wanted to be involved with research. It would be necessary to obtain a Ph.D. and ultimately a faculty position to have my own research project, take it my own way and not be an underling working on somebody else's project, as much fun as that could be. So, even though I could have stayed, I decided I had to leave this particular situation.

Applications went out to several research universities. Pardon that redundancy. I didn't know what a university not involved with research would be. I was accepted to pursue a Ph.D. in Biology at one of these universities and there was a Research Fellowship available that I could have. This university's Department of Biology had a good emphasis on Marine Biology. There was even a field station at the shore some distance from the main campus. The fellowship as usual did not pay much money, but it meant I would not have to pay tuition. It was a sort of bare subsistence wage (about $2,000 per semester), but until just recently I had been used to that kind of situation. When you are interested in doing something, money is not too important. With that in mind I went to the university that had accepted me and started on a Ph.D. program.

I made a trip to my prospective university during the summer prior to the fall I was scheduled to begin classes. It was necessary to talk with the faculty member who controlled the fellowship that would employ me. He, one Dr. Dexter P. Franklin, was the leader of the Marine Biology section of the Department of Biology and an accomplished man somewhere in his fifties. Fish physiology was his area of expertise. A grant for a good sum of money had been gotten by Dr. Franklin to collect three species of mollusks to see what levels of pesticides were present in their tissues. The species were *Mercenaria mercenaria* (the hard shell clam), *Geukensia demissa* (the ribbed mussel, in the late 1960s it was *Modiolus demissa*), and an old friend of mine *Crassostrea virginica* (the eastern oyster). I had previous experience with all of these species and that was a meaningful thing to be able to tell Dr. Franklin. He would be my initial, but temporary, faculty advisor to help me take a first step and get me on my way.

Dr. Franklin had identified nine sites around the state where one or the other of these three species could be collected. My job would be to go to these sites, collect 12 specimens of whatever species was at the site, bring them back, grind them up, dry them out into a powder, and mail their dried carcasses off to another lab to be analyzed for pesticide content. This would have to be done once per month. I did not know it at this telling by Dr. Franklin, but this would be quite a bit to get done.

To get my Ph.D., I would have to select a permanent faculty advisor and arrange to develop a problem for my dissertation research. Oh yes, I also would have to take 60 course credit hours. At this meeting I didn't grasp the immensity of what was before me, but it would take four years to get it all done. I believe it was Confucius that said, "The longest of journeys begin with a single step." It was nice to have that first step somewhat organized.

Later that summer before classes were to begin I found a room near campus that I could call home. It was a private residence. The owner rented out four rooms to university students. There were no kitchen facilities and we were not meant to cook in there, back to a hotplate again. My fellow renters were for the most part pretty quiet. One guy kept playing a record player too loud. He was flatly obnoxious. Eventually the owner got so angry at this guy that in a large scale confrontation he summarily kicked the guy out and put his stuff out on the street. Most of the time, the owner was much more laid back. Anyway, I started my classes. That first semester it was oceanography, ichthyology (the study of fishes), and a geology course. I had a little more money now than I had when I started my Masters classes and found restaurants where I could eat. Eating well was again a problem, but at least I had a little more money than before. I wasn't set up very well as far as living arrangements went, but it was at least O.K. I lived in that room for that first whole school year.

Things went along and pretty soon it was time to go and make my first collections. Some of the sites I had to collect from were under docks or in other places you could walk to. For several a boat was required. The graduate student, Bruce, who had done this work before went with me the first time to show me where and how collections were to be made. It was fortunate that he was available for that. I never would have found my way around without him. We started at 0500 hours. The first thing we did was drive a university car south to the field station. That took about two hours. There we picked up an open 15 foot long outboard motor boat with a 25 hp engine, which was on a trailer. There was no steering wheel on this boat. The operator had to sit in the rear and operate the engine hands on. There was no electric starter either. It was a manual mechanism, a pull-rope, to fire up the engine. After we got the boat hooked up to a truck we were off to the first collection site. I was glad I had all that experience with field work when I did my Master's work. There were new things to do at every turn, figuring out and abiding by the rules of the field station, learning to back the boat trailer and launch and reload the boat (only a minimal amount of that had been required of me previously), and not least to remember where the usually remote collection sites were located. Had I not worked around boats so much I would have been hopelessly swamped. Likely Dr. Franklin had chosen me for this particular job because I had advertised that in my application. The boat was necessary for the first three collection sites. First we had to put the boat in the water, travel several miles down a long canal, and enter into a large bay. It was late September and still warm out. The trip so far was pleasant and the scenery was outstanding, though very different from New England, no hills. The first site was off a beach in that bay. At this site hard shell clams were to be collected with clam rakes. We got over the side of the boat in waist deep water and raked for clams while stepping backward. Only twice had I ever done this before, but picked it up again pretty quickly. After about 20-30 minutes my partner and I had gotten our 12 hard clams.

Back in the boat now we had to go south across the bay we were in. It was something like four miles to the next pair of sites. After going south across the bay we had to find a short canal-like passageway. I hoped I could find it next time. After going through that passageway we entered yet another bay, the site of the next two collection stations. At one site oysters were to be collected from under a dock. We pulled the boat in next to the dock and got out. You had to go under the dock and chisel 12 of them off rocks. The rocks were put there by someone years ago to stabilize the dock. All rocks in this geographical area were at some point put there by man. I believe the southernmost natural (glacially delivered) rock is on Cape Ann Massachusetts. The other site in this bay was along a shore populated with marsh grass (*Spartina alterniflora*, as I learned) and ribbed mussels were to be collected there. They occur in bunches and it was relatively easy to gather 12 of them. Our prize so far then was three plastic bags with live shellfish in them. Now this bay's open water and the short passageway were to be traveled again. The bay of the first sample was to be crossed again and that long canal re-navigated to get back to where we could take the boat out of the water. That would take most of an hour. I noted out loud that, "In the winter these sites will be a bitch to get collections from." Bruce responded, "Let me tell you, in my experience yes indeed they can!"

For the next site, number four, it was necessary to put the boat back in the water and motor up a tidal creek into a salt marsh to get more mussels. At collection site number five the boat was left on the trailer and we walked out on a sandflat and raked for hard clams. Then we traveled north for the remaining four sites. At two, oysters were taken from rocks under docks in waterside towns. That was quickly done. At the other two mussels had to be collected from salt marsh sites and those sites required the boat to be put in and taken out twice more. At the last site we were about 50 miles north of the field station. We had to haul the boat back, clean it up, be sure the boat and truck were gassed up, and everything was in order. With all that done and with our 12 bags of catch we headed north back up the road to campus. We got everything put away in the lab on campus by about 2300 hours and thankfully quit. It had been a very long day. Processing the shellfish and shipping them, a boring endeavor, could wait until the next day.

If I was to collect these samples every month, this whirlwind tour of sampling sites had told me a couple of things. For one, it would be wise to recruit another graduate student to come along and help whenever possible. Things would get done more easily. Most of the time a helper was realized, but not always. I remember one winter trip in particular, in which alone I went down that canal and across those bays. There was a wind generating lots of spray. It was above freezing, but in the thirties. I was bundled up and in chest high waders and it wasn't that much of a boat. Getting dumped in the water would have made for a bad situation. I still had my Han Andersen knife and had it handy. Maybe, just maybe, I could have cut my way out of those waders. But even if I managed that, in that cold water it would still have been a very dire situation. It was a miserable job collecting those samples that day.

A second realization was that I would be lucky to get all 12 samples in a single day. Bruce had attained Ph.D. candidacy and had a year's worth of previous experience with this. He knew exactly what had to be done, where, and when. If everything went perfectly, e.g., weather, mechanical things, and sufficient number of daylight hours, it was possible to do the job in a single day, but if anything went even slightly out of skew it would be two or more days to get it all done.

The experience also told me once more that this, or any, bit of research was very expensive to run. In this case there was my own measly salary, the support for Bruce, the university car, the boat, the truck to haul it, various equipment and supplies, and a food allowance. Working that long and hard, one had to be nourished. Many services within the university enterprise, and outside, accrued some of the money. And, that leaves unmentioned the cost of preparing and analyzing shellfish bodies for pesticide content. This little piece of research has had and will continue to have significant challenges for many university people. The reason it was being done at all was because Dr. Franklin had the idea, written the proposal, and gotten the money appropriated. For me it meant getting monthly samples regardless of what that took. For many other university people it also meant just doing their jobs. The garage mechanics, secretaries, and boat maintenance people all deserved to be thanked and of course paid.

So, in outline that was what I was paid for about two years running. In addition to keeping up with my collection of samples I had to take two or three courses a semester and I had to come up with a dissertation advisor, not to mention a dissertation project. One faculty member that I got to know well was a recently graduated Ph.D. from another university and was just hired the year I got there. His name was Stephen Victor and he was not that much older than I was at the time. He was an ecologist, the first one I ever met that wasn't something else first such as an invertebrate zoologist, or a physiologist. He was teaching an ecology course down at the field station in summer. I too was down there then and that's where I first got to know him. He read and collected lots of books (got me interested in doing that) and knew lots of stuff about a wide variety of things. He worked on fish populations, but as I said first and foremost he thought of himself as an ecologist. Dr. Victor, I eventually took on using his first name, was the first professor with whom I came to feel an approximate equality of status. I wasn't equal in actuality, but he made me feel that way. In our conversations he not only brought up interesting topics, of which he seemed to have an inexhaustible supply, he was genuinely interested in what I had to contribute. During my four years at this university he expanded me a lot. I took two of his courses, population ecology and community ecology. These courses introduced me to subject areas about which I previously knew almost nothing. I value having the chance to listen to and come to know him, but I wanted to work on a marine invertebrate and being mostly interested in vertebrates he would not be a suitable advisor.

It turned out that another faculty member, Dr. Veblen Postelwaite, agreed to take me on as an advisee. That is one distinctive name. I could get next to being advised by a professor with a name like that. He was a sort of frail little man about 50 years old and had been studying marine invertebrates for years. Notable discoveries and his work in general had made him quite famous among invertebrate zoologists. During my Masters work he had been brought up more than once in classes. At the time he did not have much grant money, but because I had a research fellowship that wasn't an immediate problem.

Dr. Postelwaite had been thinking about an organism on shores local to the area. In fact there was more of this species in a local estuary than anywhere else he had looked, which generated his interest. I knew about the group that it belonged to, but had not yet heard of this species. It was a polychaete. A polychaete is in the same group as the earthworms and leeches (the Phylum Annelida). Members of the Class Polychaeta, like the earthworms, are obviously segmented with essentially identical repeating segments making up the body. There are many uniquely defining characters to the Polychaeta. Main ones are that these segmented worms are marine and have many (poly) fairly long bristles (chaetae) on each segment, earthworms in comparison, have only four short ones per segment. This particular polychaete species is named *Sabellaria vulgaris*. The adult is a worm about an inch long. It lives in tubes constructed of mineral sand grains (of quartz and feldspar) that it cements together. Normally it lives always submerged with only a few in one place. For example it is common to see a few tubes with live worms inside them on live horseshoe crab shells. However, on some estuarine beaches in this area it lived in large aggregations in the intertidal zone. The worms do not form these aggregations on open ocean beaches because wave action is too intense. These guys need an intermediate level of wave action. Aggregations were so large in this estuary, that the sand grain tubes all cemented together formed intertidal reefs up to as much as a foot high off the sand.

I still had my Sunbeam Alpine and I made a trip down to a beach where it occurred. There were the reefs standing "tall" in the intertidal zone. They were a major feature of that beach. I had never seen anything like that before and took an immediate interest. It seems that almost nothing was known about this species other than where it could be found. Dr. Postelwaite had written one brief paper on the species. He and I started to figure out what aspects of that ignorance might be addressed.

With Dr. Postelwaite's help I began to look into the literature on the species. The species had been noted and described back in the 1800s. It had a larval stage that, like the oyster's, lived in the plankton, but very little was known about that important stage in the life cycle: what stages did the larva go through in its development; how long did its development take before it could change into a juvenile worm and start tube building; at what time or times of year did the larvae settle out of the plankton; how widespread and how abundant were these larvae in the plankton; and could they be identified with any surety? There were lots of questions to answer.

It took a couple of months, but Dr. Postelwaite and I developed a plan to investigate this species. In quick outline its three basic parts looked like this. One was that I should attempt to take some sperm from male worms and eggs from females, use the sperm to fertilize the eggs, and see if raising the larvae in the laboratory was possible. If it was, I could learn the developmental stages of larvae. By raising them at different temperatures I could get an idea of how long development would take in the plankton in various seasons of the year. Another part was that with knowledge of larval stages, I could look for the larvae of *Sabellaria vulgaris* in field plankton samples from various places and times. A third part was that I would put out a series of clean settling plates to observe when the larvae settled out of the plankton and became adult worms. This was a plausible plan of action and with success would tell us a great deal about this species that was not presently known. But would it all work, could I do it?

By this time I had arranged a faculty committee to oversee my work. There were five people on it, Dr. Postelwaite, Dr. Franklin, Dr. Victor, and two others that I shall leave nameless. The challenge before me was first to write a research proposal and get an O.K. on the plan from my committee. The people on my committee had all done a lot of research and knew where the pitfalls were likely to emerge. It was difficult constructing a detailed proposal that I could be hopeful would get their approval. When I had done that and submitted it to them, there were a lot of questions and many suggestions from the committee. They all felt that I had proposed a very ambitious research plan, too much work. There was indeed a void in the knowledge that needed to be addressed, but so much work was proposed it was unlikely that I would finish. It would be better to set my sights at a lower level. It was difficult defending my proposal, but the whole committee agreed that if I thought I could do it I should have the chance. So my first interaction with my committee, even if difficult, was a success. Now all I had to do was make it work and that would take about three years.

The small research problem I had done for a Masters was a start, but this Ph.D. research, by comparison, would be a Herculean effort. As my Ph.D. dissertation work has much to do with my future attitude toward research and the way I go about it, let me summarize how it went and fundamentally what was found out. The first part to get underway, and the thing on which most of the rest of it depended, was the culturing, raising, and description of *Sabellaria vulgaris* larvae. I did not know what they looked like and if I was going to look for them in plankton samples, I had to know. This was mostly laboratory work and was far from cut and dried. By about this time I had moved off campus and was living down near the field station. I had an office/lab down there. The living situation near the shore was better, much more to my liking. Also it was much closer to the work I had to do for my research fellowship and for my dissertation. The first thing I did was look into the culturing of larvae. I collected some ripe worms (with egg and sperm present) from the intertidal zone and brought them back to the lab. I had acquired some petri dishes and other glassware from the biology stockroom. It turned out that females would shed eggs and males would shed sperm into dishes of seawater without much problem. I put the eggs on a slide and observed them with a microscope and took some photographs. Sperm were treated similarly. When I introduced sperm into a dish with unfertilized eggs in it the sperm fertilized the eggs and after about 24 hours there were young larvae swimming about in the dish. How about that!

The Polychaeta have a larva called a trochophore. They look like a microscopic globe with a mouth, a simple intestinal track, and an anus. There is a single band of cilia (whip-like short extensions from the cells) around the middle of the globe (called the prototroch). Anyway, there they were and on the first try. It took about a year and a half, but with this start what remained was to rear larvae all the way through to the stage where they could settle to the bottom and become juvenile worms. It took about three weeks for this to happen depending on the temperature at which larvae were raised. When this was done I knew what *Sabellaria vulgaris* larvae looked like at all stages of development and I could identify them in plankton samples from the field. They developed long bristles only a few days after the eggs were fertilized and those bristles were the first clue when I ran into them in a plankton sample.

Sampling the plankton to find out when, where, and what larval stages were present was a major undertaking. Monthly samples were collected at three places along about 12 miles of estuarine coastline. In the winter this could be particularly rough. In the warmer part of the year it could be pleasant, but even that could present its challenges. The university made an open 17 foot Boston Whaler with a 55 hp engine available to me for this purpose. That was a well set up boat. It could handle rough water, but it would not keep you dry as it did so. I had some wild times in that boat just getting the samples taken. It wasn't merely playing around, just wild. There was a console in the center of the boat that had a steering wheel, gear shift, and throttle control. One time in cold weather and rough water the steering wheel just broke off in my hands. A tricky time was had steering with just a wheel stub to get back to shore. Another time in summer the engine conked out on me about an hour and a half before dusk when I was five or six miles away from home port. It is not like there was a radio onboard. I had to anchor the boat, swim about three quarters of a mile to shore with sneakers around my neck, hitchhike a couple of miles to a phone in the near dark, and put in a call to a maintenance guy I was friendly with to come pick me up. He had quit for the day and wasn't happy with that call, but he did come to get me. The next day we used another boat to go get the crippled Whaler. I was hoping as we went on this mission that the stranded boat was O.K. Somebody could have easily towed it away. Well, fortunately that didn't happen and it was a gorgeous day for the trip. You have to take the good times when you can get them. Collecting those plankton samples every month was sometimes difficult to do, but it was a time of adventure that I won't forget.

The idea behind taking these plankton samples was to figure out what stages of development and at what times of year *Sabellaria vulgaris* larvae were present in the plankton. A secondary purpose was to find out how widespread they were in the plankton. That was why I sampled over 12 miles of estuarine shoreline. Sampling the plankton is normally done with a plankton net with a mesh size appropriate to the size of planktonic organism being sought. The net is usually towed horizontally though the water behind a boat. A plankton net is conical in shape. On the net I used, the mouth, where the water enters the net, was about a foot in diameter and it narrowed down to some three inches in diameter where there was a removable, blind end cup that captured the plankton. The problem with towing a net horizontally behind a boat is that the plankton of interest, *Sabellaria vulgaris* larvae in this case, may be at a different depth than the net. Because this was intended as a survey I did not want to miss larvae at different depths. So I employed vertical rather than horizontal tows. The net was rigged with six three ounce weights suspended around the brass ring that held the mouth of the net open. Knots and splices again, it could have been done less professionally than it was, but we are what we are and the weights remained fast and worked without a hitch.

Sampling at a location was done by lowering the net to the bottom, somewhere from 10 to 30 feet down, and when the bottom impact was felt the net would be pulled vertically to the surface. Three vertical tows gave three samples, which were put in separate jars and preserved with formalin. Because the current was moving by the anchored boat, these represented samples from different water masses. Based on the net mouth diameter and depth the volume of water filtered by the net could be figured. With three stations sampled each month that gave nine samples per month and I did this for 15 months, giving 135 total plankton samples to examine.

Examining those samples took much longer than collecting them and was much more tedious. Using a dissecting microscope, the sample was shaken up and then one third was checked through for *Sabellaria vulgaris* larvae. They had to be counted and identified as to stage of development. There were sometimes hundreds of larvae, a tedious process indeed. A single sample would take at least an hour, often two or three. But all research at some point comes down to some such tedium.

The information gained was pretty substantial and it told me a lot about the species that was not previously known. First let me address the question of how widespread larvae were in the plankton. If larvae were present at one station on a day, they were likely present at all. This speaks for larvae being widespread. After all, they do drift around at the mercy of currents. I also did some 24-hour plankton studies, two in winter and two in summer, wherein I would take a vertical tow every hour off the end of a long pier. The two winter studies, which revealed zero larvae, were ordeals. I used a bicycle for trips to and from the end of the pier. Trips to the end of the pier each hour and the taking of samples were indeed trials. In summer 24-hour studies the larvae were present, but very patchy in abundance from hour to hour. In some hours larvae would be very abundant, in others very rare.

With regard to the monthly time scale, in the spring young stage larvae appeared in the plankton during April and they were quite abundant until June, then there seemed to be a decrease, and in September and October there was another increase. Larvae were absent during the winter in the monthly samples. I assumed the April-June increase in larval prevalence was because of spawning by adults that survived the winter. The September-October increase in larvae probably came from new worms that had settled out of the plankton earlier in the year. What I had learned from culturing and studying larvae in the lab came into play here. I was able to observe in plankton samples the progressive development of larvae from very young stages earlier in the year (April) to later stages later in the year. The presence of those later larval stages correlated well with the occurrence of *Sabellaria vulgaris* settlement that was observed in the third part of my research.

The third part of my project was keeping track of larval settlement in the intertidal zone and that required quite a bit of effort. It was important to know when larvae settled out of the plankton and metamorphosed into juvenile worms. After several tries I came up with a rack for my settlement plates that would withstand the rigors of the intertidal zone. A rack was made from two by six inch lumber and was about a foot high. A flange was attached to the bottom of a rack so it could be screwed onto a pipe well buried in the sand. That way a rack would stand solidly against wave action and other hazards such as ice. Only on two occasions did racks fail. Each rack would hold three plates on which *Sabellaria vulgaris* was known to be able to settle. The positions of settling plate racks in the intertidal zone would be in the middle of a sabellariid reef where larvae would be most likely to settle. Plates were maintained at several places along the estuarine coastline. They were changed out monthly and replaced with clean plates. By observing the tubes that showed up on plates I could keep track of when *Sabellaria vulgaris* larval settlement had occurred, where it occurred, and how much had occurred.

As I indicated above, only if late stage larvae showed up in the plankton did settlement occur in the intertidal zone. There was indication that adult worms did not simply spawn all the time during from about April onward during summer. If worms spawned continuously, one would expect there to be continuous settlement on settlement plates once early batches of larvae became old enough to settle. My examination of settlement plates demonstrated that was not the case. Settlement was not continuous. Also, if continuous spawning were the case, you would expect early stage larvae to always be the most abundant in the plankton. Plankton samples demonstrated they were not. Many times, including in one of the summer 24-hour plankton studies, later stage larvae were most abundant all day. This suggests that spawning had occurred a while ago, I figured two weeks, and then abated. If worms do spawn according to some schedule, it would be nice to know, but my study did not address that. *Sabellaria vulgaris* appears to spawn in episodes, but what controls those episodes remains a mystery. What is that cue? Maybe I will have a chance to get back to that.

As I have just outlined, my study and the results from it added a lot to the knowledge about this worm. That's the kind of thing invertebrate zoologists do. Of course, in the general public this worm was not a high profile item. Almost nobody knew or cared the first thing about it. There were a few other scholars in the world who had studied various aspects of sabellariid worms. I had read their works and was very interested. Even if all of them read about my work, they would make for a small audience. When it was finished and written up, I had about a 200 page dissertation. I had previously been though my written and oral qualifying exams and had taken all my required course work. I had been admitted to official Ph.D. candidacy. The final thing that had to be accomplished was to defend my dissertation work. So I got my 200 page work typed up in accordance with university regulations, replicated it, and presented a copy to each of my committee members. They would have about three weeks to read and consider.

It was a harder defense than I expected. Two committee members felt I had spent too much time (space) covering what I considered to be the connection between spawning and settlement of larvae. I had what I thought was a clever explanation of how *Sabellaria vulgaris* larvae were retained in the estuary where I had done the study. That was part of the reason, so Blake Turner claimed, why so many local intertidal reefs existed there. I freely admit that this was not the original purpose of my study. Further, I had not proven the explanation beyond all doubt. But most of the original proposal had been accomplished. The critics did not specify and I am not sure what kind of data would answer their criticism, but the estuarine system was too big and the required data too extensive to tackle with a lonely Ph.D. project.

People have been interested in larval retention in estuaries for a long time. The basic problem is that river flow constantly enters at the head of an estuary. This means that the estuary would fill up and overflow if more water did not flow out than comes in with the tides. Put another way, because estuaries do not fill up and overflow there must be a net outflow of water to match river inflow. How could planktonic larvae that drift around at the mercy of currents manage to resist this net outflow and be retained in the estuary? That was what I tried to explain.

Here is an outline of my explanation. It basically involved vertical migrations of larvae so they would be in the surface waters during the day, attracted to the light, and down deeper at night. If larvae enter the tidal system (by being spawned) at certain times, they can experience more net tidal flood time than net tidal ebb time and thus be retained in an estuary. Consider a conveyor belt that runs to the right more of the time (symbolizing estuarine tidal outflow) than to the left (estuarine tidal inflow). Even though the belt moves to the right more than to the left, by choosing when you get on the belt (by spawning) and when you get off (by settlement) you can move leftward, into the estuary. Anyway, two committee members did not like the explanation because I had no data to prove it was going on. Well, definitive data maybe not, but I did have data in the form of a connection between spawning, settlement, and my proposed mechanism of retention. I have to agree that my explanation was not proven, but it was pretty clever and added an idea to the business of larval retention in estuaries. Things do not always go smoothly and there sat our conflict, three committee members would sign, two would not. There were some changes they wanted me to make in my dissertation before they would sign off. I had some four years at stake and I took this very seriously. I did want my Doctor of Philosophy Degree. They wanted me to back off on the certitude of some of the things I had said and remove some sections altogether. I went as far as I could with the changes they wanted without compromising myself too much. It was a rough two weeks for everybody, but in the end they all signed and I ultimately got my Ph.D. To put it mildly, that was a relief.

Another event that happened when I was going for my Ph.D. was my first attempt at presenting a talk at a scientific meeting. I went to a few small meetings first to get an idea of what went on. As I was getting close to defending my dissertation I ventured to submit a paper to be given at a meeting. I was put on the schedule and went to the meeting. It was only some 80 miles away. The talk was to be on my proposed mechanism of larval retention in estuaries that would be in such contention at my dissertation defense. The lead up to giving a talk at a meeting is a great deal of preparation and practicing and as it gets closer to the day for it the pressure increases. It's not as if the atmosphere at these assemblages of people with scientific mind sets is unfriendly or threatening. However, there is a chance that you will forget something or somehow make a fool of yourself. For an academic that would be a serious faux pas. They only schedule you for usually 10, 15, or on the outside 20 minutes and time for questions must be allowed within your time. You want to sound confident, but not arrogant. The usual advice you get from old hands at this goes something like this with respect to the structure of your talk: "Tell them what you are going to tell them, tell them, and then tell them what you told them." It is probably true that the best made point is the point made most often, but you have to have a worthy point and deliver it competently. That's the challenge and it is felt most acutely the first time out. Well, I presented my idea and at the time it seemed to go over well. There were a number of questions and people seemed to think the idea was at least interesting. One person in the audience, a biology professor at another university, was quite taken with my little talk. He came up, introduced himself as John Phillips, and indicated interest in what I had to say. He said, if I didn't mind, he would really like to model my proposed mechanism of larval retention on a computer. No, I did not mind. This was in the days before desktop computers were all over the place. Thus far I had done all my model construction (calculations) on a hand held calculator. Those calculations took a lot of time and the idea of a computer program to handle most of the tedium was very attractive to me.

We, Dr. Phillips and I, parted ways after the meeting and he went back to his home campus and went to work. He contacted me later and his computer model of my mechanism worked very well. If larvae were spawned at the right time and behaved the way I specified (in surface water during daylight and deeper down at night), they were indeed retained in the estuary. In fact, larvae were sometimes run up into the freshwater river at the estuary's head. That would not do. The freshwater would kill them. There are two possibilities: 1) larvae are actually lost in river water; or 2) there is some important factor absent from my model. The second possibility is most likely, which would mean there is more thinking to do. When he got back to me with all this I had already defended and gone through that episode. In any case it was rewarding to have a faculty member from another university sufficiently interested in my idea to develop it further.

Of course in four years at a university a lot of things happened to me. A few of them really affected my long term self. One of them was accidental, as I guess most things are, but it nevertheless made a lasting point for me. It was while I was living in a trailer down near the field station. I met a neighbor while playing darts in a local bar. He was a guy maybe 15 or 20 years older than me. I didn't know he was a neighbor at the time, but so it turned out and it led to an informative exchange of ideas. As usual I lost at darts. It was just for drinks and I paid up. In the conversation that followed I learned that he had been to a university as a philosophy major and was currently into being a real estate agent. Mike had been a successful real estate agent and unlike me had established himself financially. He lived alone in a house. He made it a point to tell me that he owned it outright. It was near my trailer park and he invited me over for some drinks the next night. I was still a pretty confirmed beer drinker. He said he wasn't, but that was no problem. I agreed to come over.

When I arrived he gave me an expensive beer and he drank some scotch and water on ice. He had various nibbles around, nuts, dip, crackers, cheese, and the like. We began to talk and pretty quickly I thought I was seeing a suspicious side to Mike that I had not picked up on in our brief meeting at the bar. He asked a few questions and made a few comments that made me feel like he was more interested in me and what I did than what I thought about things. For example, he asked: whether I had a girlfriend, what I did in my spare time, and did I have any friends in the area? I did not know this guy very well and I saw all this as too personal and strangely pushy. I guess my suspicions made my mannerisms change suddenly. I persistently avoided his questions and in general backed up on him. At the time I was a young, fairly large individual in very good physical shape, and I really didn't feel threatened by him in any way. Mike must have gotten the idea that I wasn't going to have any of whatever he was vaguely driving at and the side of him that irked me quickly disappeared. Once we had put to the side whatever he formerly he had in mind, probably some desire to get in my pants, the guy that I had liked at the bar reappeared. He had some incisive and different perspectives on many things and adopted a different tack altogether.

Mike already knew that I was working on my Ph.D. at the university and asked me what I did for my research. I gave him an explanation suitable for a person not versed in biology. He understood well and asked a few good questions about the research problem. He indicated that this was more interesting than selling real estate. Then he asked me an interesting general question. I don't know if it was a practiced question, sort of his stock and trade, but he wanted to know: what was it like to work so hard and long for so little money and way out on the edge of humankind's perceived need? When you are intimately involved with something you are interested in you don't think of things that way. I never had, it was just important to do.

I tried to answer the question. I thought for a minute and then took on the question. My answer consisted of three parts. First, humankind's need goes beyond what you might call everyman's recognized need. It may be that the average person will never need to care that much, or even be aware of, something like *Sabellaria vulgaris*, but humankind as a whole has a duty to know about the world of which it is a part. You never know what knowledge will be needed for. Second, one might conclude there is no classic need for, e.g., philosophy, sports, music, painting, sculpting, poetry, or prose. These pursuits do not house or feed the masses, but they certainly enliven and enrich our lives. Third, for my own selfish motivation I find scientific research to be a challenge, fun to do, and superbly interesting. In short, it amuses me. I find that satisfying and reason enough to busy myself with it regardless of low pay and lack of a general feeling by everyone that what I do is important and much needed. I said to Mike, "That is a question about which I had not thought before and it seems fundamental, one that I should ponder. Anyway, that's what I can come up with on the spot so to speak." We dickered some on other possible values to doing scientific research, but he basically accepted my answer. I drank another couple of beers, he had more scotch and water, and the remainder of the evening passed with good conversation. For example, I had not published anything yet, but he was interested to know why it was that scientists were so avid to publish papers in journals that almost nobody reads. It takes so much effort, even with effort it is difficult to do, and seldom do authors get any recognition for their work. I recognized this issue as being a more specific version of the overall question he had asked before, but it too was a good question. I answered, "It may be that most papers in journals go unrecognized and they do require a lot of effort, but through the pages of those journals and their authors and readers, pass one of the flowers of mankind. If you want to have a good idea, you need to have a lot of them." He said, "Well maybe, but they are still pretty much unrecognized and there is little gain." And there we were. As far as I was concerned, once he put aside his other agenda, Mike was good company. I saw him a few other times after that, but did not have another exchange like that evening. His question, on the other hand, has stayed with me. It made me have a more pointed understanding of my life's work and how I got to be me.

Another thing that sort of got cemented into my being during this time was a dearth of interest in taking on a wife, home, and family. I had been tacitly working on that attitude for a while. By this time, getting a B.A., an M.S., and now a Ph.D., it had been about 10 years with only shoestring resources. There had of course been girlfriends and girls who were friends. In some cases I tried to convert the latter. Maybe by this time I should think of them as women. I suppose I was a reasonably attractive male. In any event I liked females. Not only for the obvious reason, but because they otherwise had a lot to offer. I liked a party and the socializing that went with it. But, living off research grants and the like doesn't leave much financial room for entertaining ideas of permanent relationships. Even now, about to get my Ph.D., my prospects were pretty dismal for good paying employment. That will have to be dealt with, but whatever was to happen I had no regrets about how I had spent my time.

In my later years at this university the research fellowship that had at first supported me dried up. The project was done and the fellowship went with it. I switched to being funded as a teaching assistant. In that role you would normally be required to spend about 20 hours a week running laboratories of one kind or another. I had a lot of practice doing that and it was fun getting a chance to get back into it. I was recognized by associates and students as a good teacher. At the very end of my time at the university where I got my Ph.D., I took on being in total charge of a course. It was an invertebrate zoology course and it was quite an experience. It honed my skills in that discipline and made me think that a job that mostly required me to teach would not be a bad choice. Maybe I could put my desire to discover knowledge aside for a time.

In point of fact a teaching job was the only sort of paying work that I was likely to come by. After all, I had gotten my Ph.D. from a fairly low level university and further my chosen area of study was invertebrate zoology. Those are pretty good credentials for obscurity. On top of that I had studied an obscure beast, of which even most academics were unaware. I knew quite a lot about biology and could teach a variety of courses, but almost no one in a hiring position (e.g., a dean) would be excited about the subject of my dissertation. There were a number of ads from universities and colleges with open teaching positions. I applied mostly to universities because at those there would be at least some fealty to the discovery of knowledge and I would not have to abandon that altogether.

I made an application to Visitopolis University. They had advertised for someone to fill the position of Assistant Professor of Biology at an away from the main campus branch of the University. That branch was near the coast and was in a region that was populated by marine invertebrate species about which I already had some knowledge. That boded well. Now all I had to do was get them interested in my application. My pitch basically was: 1) my experience with teaching dates back to undergraduate days and runs through to just recently so I can contribute substantially in that area; and 2) I do understand that what would be required of me is mostly teaching, but it would not be honest to hide my interest in being involved in research and I plan to develop something in that venue. I guess my application portrayed a smart, capable guy and they invited me for an interview. That's always a good sign.

Most of the day of that interview was spent interviewing with faculty, various administrators, and the guy in charge of that branch of the University. His name was Jacob Flannery. He was titled the Provost for this branch of the University. I only spent about five or ten minutes with him. He was a youngish man, younger than I expected in that position. Before assuming his present position, the Provost's academic discipline had been in political science and I guessed he was about 40 years old. He was good looking, about six feet tall, and looked very fit. Jacob Flannery was very cordial and encouraging in that short meeting, which I felt good about. Biology faculty were very few. Only a few biology courses were taught at this campus and only three faculty were needed to teach them. Were I successful, I would be the third. The former third had recently quit, hence the open position. Usually at these interviews some kind of presentation by the applier (a seminar) is required, but faculty did not have time, or were not interested in a seminar given by me. The two biology faculty I talked to did ask about my research and I explained in very basic terms because time was short. They were politely interested. I asked, but neither indicated any current investigations that they had going on. That seemed strange for faculty at a large university. When I asked about the normal teaching load for biology faculty they said it was normally two courses, with labs, per semester, but sometimes three. I should have been forewarned by the heavy teaching load, but the biology laboratories seemed well set up, the buildings were quite impressive for an off the main campus site, and most everybody I talked to said acceptable things about the mission of the university and this branch's role in it. Let me impart to you my favorite one liner for the mission of a university. It is to foster the discovery and dissemination of knowledge. I deployed this several times during my interview and no one had disagreed.

About three weeks later Visitopolis University contacted me and offered me the job. It's not as if I had several offers to choose among. Here was an available university position as an Assistant Professor and with, by comparison with my history, really good pay. The first year's pay would be about $20,000. I knew that was not very much money in the grand scheme of things, but I had never made anywhere near that much. With a couple of reservations Blake Turner decided to accept the offer. It was 1973 and in the fall semester I would begin teaching.

Chapter 5

BEGINNING WORK AT AN UNENLIGHTENED UNIVERSITY BRANCH

I arrived in the locale of "my" branch of Visitopolis University in late July. Arrangements for a place to live were the first order of business. As I have said, this branch of the University was located near the coast. It was north of Cape Hatteras in the mid-Atlantic region. Naturally the first place I went to look for a dwelling was near the ocean. I found a furnished house to rent. It was about 25 miles from that house to the site where I would teach. So it would be a reasonably short commute. I had finally sold my Sunbeam Alpine and bought a two year old Datsun 2000. This was another two seat sports car and it too was a convertible. With its two liter engine and five speed standard transmission, it was much faster than the Sunbeam had been, but it would not corner as well. The speedometer went up to 140 miles per hour. That was cool. Whether it would do all of that I leave up to Datsun (now Nissan) engineers, but it would do at least about 80% of that. I drove that car for several years and while it lasted it was a lot of fun to drive and for me good transportation. I had a few more books now, but I could still fit all my stuff into a car of that style and I did not have much to do to move into my new abode. The new place to live was quite inspiring. It was only about half a kilometer walk to an open estuarine beach. The ocean was very nearby and you could sense that. This area was pretty flat and looking down on the water from a hillside, as in my Masters days, was not in the cards, but you could smell and taste the salt in the air and see its sculpting effects on vegetation in the area. That was certainly a plus. There was only a low dune between me and the water. Getting flooded out was a definite possibility. A storm tide with an onshore wind could do that and I would have to be on my guard for that eventuality.

The nearness of an estuary and the ocean meant there were many marine invertebrate species in the immediate area. This place was within about 200 miles of the university where I had gotten my Ph.D. So I was familiar with the species around here. Unlike on the New England coast, rocks were in absence in this coastal area. This meant that most of the local invertebrates would be organisms that live in as opposed to on the bottom. Put another way most species I might work with would be infauna, living in sand or mud bottoms. There were of course manmade structures along the coast, such things as breakwaters, groins, and piers. On those invertebrates might live on a hard substratum. I did not know at this point what local organisms might interest me. Maybe *Sabellaria vulgaris* would be a possibility as it did occur around here, but only more or less isolated individuals here and there were to be found. Intertidal reefs built by that species were absent. It would be a different situation from my previous one, but would have to be looked into. This whole area would require some exploration.

With my living arrangements reasonably settled I had to start getting ready to teach this fall. It was about a month away and there was much to do. The University had decided to "ease" me into teaching with only two courses. Each one had a lab with it, which increased dramatically the amount of time a professor must devote to a course. One course was intended as part of an introductory sequence for biology majors. It was called Introductory Biology I. In the spring semester the companion course Introductory Biology II would be offered. Students other than biology majors often took these courses. There were about 1,000 students taking classes at this branch of Visitopolis University. Anyone majoring in biology would usually only spend a year or at most two at this branch campus because few advanced courses were offered. They would quickly run out of courses to take and they had to get to the main campus to finish their degree requirements in a reasonable time. There were several courses for non-biology majors offered on this campus. One that was on the books was a baby ecology course. The former third biology faculty member was a terrestrial type ecologist and he had been teaching the course along those lines. I wanted to emphasize marine ecology in such a course. Because there was no template for it the course would have to be developed from scratch. Between my Masters and Ph.D. work I had quite a bit of experience with ecology. It would be a lot of work, but as a second course I agreed to develop and teach a course in ecology. So, in this fall semester I was to teach Introductory Biology I and Introductory Ecology.

With who had I agreed on this course load? On this campus there was a dean in charge of making such assignments. It was a powerful position because as I came to learn most of what was done by faculty on this campus was teaching. The woman in charge of teaching assignments was Dean Abigail Terkel. Her academic credentials were in education and she had a doctorate, an Ed.D. She was about 45 years old, a little stout, professedly knew very little about biology, and had an officious, almost imperious, manner about her. She had been doing this job for several years and was accustomed to wielding her power. I had spoken with her for about 15 minutes during my interview process and had communicated with her previously by mail and by phone concerning what I would teach. My teaching responsibility had been pretty well settled as they had to get whatever we decided upon on the schedule. When we spoke in a brief meeting in that July, Dean Terkel was momentarily interested in my thoughts on teaching, as was I in her academic background and philosophy. She quickly went past all that as she wanted to finalize what I was going to teach this coming fall. Students were beginning to register as we spoke. Scheduling what I would teach did not take long. Introductory Biology I was already on the books, needed an instructor, and I readily agreed to do it. The ecology course took a little more haggling, but she was in favor of it being taught and I thought it was the best option. I accepted doing it as a challenge. That business being done, she claimed to have another appointment and said a quick goodbye. I felt a little anxious about being sort of officially dismissed, but maybe she had good cause. There were a couple of very competent assistants in her office. I got together with them and we agreed on what days of the week and at what time my courses would be offered. I was out of Dean Terkel's office in pretty rapid order. I next had to get into the lab I would use primarily for introductory biology to see how it was set up. Ecology labs would be taught in there too, but would be mostly outdoors and were a different sort of problem.

When I got into room 108 Hartley Hall where labs would be taught I was pleased with the setup. There were slots for 24 students, each equipped with compound and dissecting microscopes that were of acceptable quality. Good, that meant that I could not have more than 24 students in my Introductory Biology I class or in ecology. A spacious prep room was off to the side of the teaching lab in 108a. There was quite a bit of vacant space as only a portion of it was used. Existing glassware, basic supplies, and the like seemed to be in good supply. A semester lasted for 12 weeks and labs met once per week for two or three hours. The Introductory Biology course had been offered for some time at this location and there was a schedule of laboratories that were usually offered. Most supplies and equipment were on hand to teach those labs. I could change what labs were offered if I wished, but the basic setup was there. Still, I would have to make a list of chemicals and other supplies necessary for labs, compare that with what was already available in the lab, and order the rest. Dr.

Eric Mortimer would be teaching a section of this course to another 24 students. They would do basically the same labs in the same room. The subject matter of Biology I was concerned with introductory matters of cell biology (biochemistry, parts and pieces of cells, photosynthesis, respiration), molecular genetics (DNA, RNA, protein synthesis), and classical transmission genetics (passage of genes from parents to offspring). Dr. Mortimer's specific area of expertise was genetics. This far from the start of classes other faculty members were not much around on this campus. I would have to get together with Dr. Mortimer when I had the chance and collaborate on lab supplies. I had not personally done research in the subject area of this course, but had taken many courses covering those aspects of biology and I was not worried about being able to teach it to students. It would take some preparation, but that was O.K. as that was largely what they were paying me for. Anyway, here it was about a month before classes would start and I now had at least a basic handle on one major question: what had to be done with laboratories for biology.

The ecology labs would be done mostly in the field, but not entirely. They would have to be designed. It was a low level ecology course and I would have to get a feel for what I might expect my students to be able to do. I had not yet even met a student, but they probably had not even previously thought about ecology, except maybe in a newspaper save-the-world context. I would have to look around the local area to see what sorts of habitats and organisms were available to study. That would take some time, but there was another month of summer to get it done. In any case, in search of a possible avenue for research I wanted to get a look at the marine habitats and the invertebrates in the area.

It may be that you already know most of the material you want to teach, but you have to prepare and get lectures organized so they can be presented with as few hitches as possible and in a logical sequence. I had done this as far back as undergraduate school, thanks once more to Dr. Burke, so I knew what had to be done. It would just take time and I would spend a lot of the next month constructing lectures so I would not be utterly swamped when classes began. Lecture notes had to be designed and organized. You can do it, but in science it is best not to walk in to give a lecture you have just barely finished preparing. You need time to go over and over your plans to get it all straight in your mind. Only then will it seem to be all coming freely from an organized mind. No student wants to sit in class while a professor fumbles around for some fact or the next point. I probably would not get all lectures together before classes started, but I should be able to get a month or so covered. That's six hours of lectures per week for the two courses times four weeks, or 24 lectures to prepare. It would have to be a busy and productive August.

Beginning Work at an Unenlightened University Branch 53

At most universities when a faculty member is hired it is common to include with the hiring what are called setup funds. These are funds awarded to new hires to enable them to set up their labs, buy microscopes, a gas chromatograph, or whatever other equipment they might need for their research. They are not unlimited these funds, but setup funds give a faculty member a head start, money with which to get his or her research underway. On the main campus of Visitopolis University, about 200 miles away and north from my branch, a setup fund was the practice in the biology department. The idea is that these funds will eventually result in more funds and more equipment when a new hire has time to apply for and get research funds from an agency outside the university. When I was hired nobody had mentioned setup funds. I must admit that it was not my major concern. Visitopolis University's only recommendation to me was that it was an academic job. This branch of the University was near the coast, but there was not much interest in marine science either by faculty at this branch or indeed by faculty on the main campus. Main campus faculty were involved with research in other areas, such a genetics, embryology, physiology, anatomy, and terrestrial and river ecology. What all this meant for me, and my desire to develop a research program of some sort on marine invertebrates, was that whatever I did would have to be done on a shoestring. Some basic equipment was around, e.g., microscopes, glassware, but not much else. The services of a field station with its boats and equipment were not to be had. If I was going to amuse myself with research, it would be like finding things to do and managing to do them in the sand pits during my undergraduate days. There wouldn't be much more in the way of equipment and resources.

In terms of my research I had two items presently on my agenda. One was to get aspects of my dissertation published. That would be a major undertaking and would have to wait a bit. The other was to get out and explore for research topics. When I made my first trip out to survey available habitats and organisms in the local marine area near my acquired abode I checked out a number of places. There were salt marshes, marine beaches, estuarine beaches, and a sandflat. The invertebrate species I encountered were essentially the same ones I would have expected around the field station at my former university.

The habitat that peaked my interest was a long pier that extended out into the water a little more than a quarter of a mile. Information on a sign near the pier said that it had been built by the U.S. Army some 35 years ago during World War II. It was not located on the open ocean coast. It was close to the ocean, but inside an estuary and therefore somewhat protected. It was a very sturdy structure. Originally its purpose was as a place to load and unload ships. Trucks were used to transport goods along the pier between ship and shore. The seaward end of the pier was in, depending on tidal state, about 20 feet of water. Back toward shore where the tides played back and forth and exposed the bottom there was a vast sandflat on either side of the pier. Tides in this area usually went up and down about three feet. The upper surface of the pier was about 15 feet off the intertidal ground. Not even the highest of high tides would cover the pier with water. The pier was supported by ranks of six pier pilings along its whole length except for the offshore end, which capped the pier so it looked like a giant T. Each of the pilings was about a foot in diameter. Within the range of the tides, which was all that was visible to me, pilings were festooned with a variety of invertebrate species. In a quick examination I found snails, blue mussels, a few oysters, barnacles, polychaetes, sea anemones, hydrozoans, tunicates (recall *Molgula manhattensis*), echinoderms (sea stars), and several species of algae attached to pilings. Hard substrata such as these pilings were in short supply around here and this collection of species was taking advantage of what little was available. There were lots of natural replicates (the pilings) for assemblages of species in this community of organisms, which statistically made the system attractive from a survey or even a manipulative experiment point of view. I didn't have time right now to look further into this assemblage of species, too many lectures to prepare and teaching to get going, but I wanted to get back to this promising system.

I did manage to get back to my discovered pier on a couple of occasions, but worked steadily on lectures during August and made a lot of progress getting that job under control. I did not want to be in the position of putting lectures together only a day or two ahead of giving them.

Toward the end of the month, just before classes were to start, Dean Terkel called a faculty meeting. I was happy to attend as I wanted to meet my fellow faculty members and I supposed them me. On the day and time we were all to meet her, Dean Terkel was in her very-much-in-charge persona. After welcoming everybody back for a new school year she took a moment to introduce me and another new faculty member that had been hired to teach history. I got up at my introduction and politely and I thought somewhat humorously bowed to the assembled group of 22. In retrospect, that fell pretty flat. As I would find, humor was in short supply among faculty. The Dean went on for about 20 minutes extolling the virtues of this campus and the job we were doing in its area of operation. We were performing a service for the local population that would be in absence was this campus not here. The faculty were all absolutely wonderful and we could be proud of what we were doing. She went on a little about the perceived mission of the University on this campus. I hadn't heard this expressed as such before. Our role was solely to teach. As she put it, "This distant from the main campus site, is mainly to get students interested in pursuing a university education essentially by offering the first two years of courses that would allow them to continue on in a major on the main campus." I already pretty well understood that, but then she went on and it wasn't good for my plans to get busy with a research project. She continued, "Faculty on this campus are not historically afforded sufficient time to be involved in the research aspect of what the overall University does. There has been some agitation to change that principle of late, but most faculty here are more interested in teaching than in doing any kind of research and I am in favor of leaving it that way." She went on for a while about some other things such as the number of registered students this fall, 957, and the number of classes being offered, 45, and then stopped. I had a lot to say about the attitude she expressed about research in the context of a university, but kept my mouth shut for the time being. There was no reason to belabor folks with my apparently radical viewpoint without first talking with some other faculty and assessing the lay of the land. Most pointedly, I would have to discover who the source of that "agitation" Dean Terkel spoke of was and what the motivation was.

After the meeting, we spent some time over refreshments. It was good to have a chance to meet other faculty members and introduce myself personally to them. Most faculty were men. Many disciplines were represented. Included were business, accounting, economics, history, English, physical education and of course two more in biology besides myself. There were three women. One taught American History, another taught English, and another taught Social Studies. I was most impressed with a history teacher. She had a Ph.D. from The University of Notre Dame, was about my age, smart as a whip, and at five feet ten inches tall just plain beautiful. The main feature she possessed was an incredible symmetry of face and body. I found myself surreptitiously starring at her when I could get away with it. I thought I was not too obvious about it, but I am not totally sure. Her name was Sylvia Armbruster. Her marital status was not revealed that day, but I must admit I was interested. She did not sport a wedding ring.

It turned out that Sylvia was the agitation source, which made me even more impressed. We spoke for about 20 or 25 minutes and she was the author of a couple of published books dealing with the history of the American Revolution and had another in the works. I told her about my pier pilings and indicated that it was a site that was promising for research. She said, "That's good to hear. It will be useful to have somebody else around here with the idea that research is something that all of a university's faculty should be pursuing." She indicated further that on this campus a research program would be very difficult to get going. People would not actually stand in your way. On the other hand nobody would help, or be supportive of whatever effort you put in.

Sylvia had been on the faculty for two years and I asked what sort of relationship faculty here had with faculty on the main campus. She said, "They are pretty far removed from concern with us." Main campus faculty and administrators had apparently gotten used to not seeing research done by faculty at our branch. We were colleagues in name only. I asked how she had published two books. She informed me that she published one before coming here and the other one she had put on the finishing touches and sent it off to a publisher just after she got here. It was tough finding time to work on the book she had in progress, but she was committed to finishing it. For me research had always been a selfish endeavor, but Sylvia made the point that university students have the right to experience professors with a keen interest in the discovery of knowledge. As she phrased it, "It adds another dimension to a faculty member's teaching, one that university students must have available to them as they move on through their courses." I had never thought of it that way. It was a good point that I stored away for later use.

It wasn't as much fun as my talk with Sylvia, but I spent some time talking to three other faculty. I found another biology faculty member, Eric Mortimer. I had prepared a list of things I planned to order for my Introductory Biology I laboratory. Because he was teaching the same course with basically the same labs to another set of students I thought it would be good to give him my list so we would not unnecessarily duplicate things. After greetings were gotten out of the way, Eric took the list and said he would compare it with what he intended to order. We exchanged a few pleasantries and that was about all there was to it.

The other biology teacher that I had spoken with very briefly during my interview was a part-timer consistently referred to as Mr., meaning most likely that he did not have a Ph.D. Toby MacMurtry was in his thirties, an affable, pleasant sort of guy, and wasn't present for this faculty meeting. He was a cellular anatomist. A guy who was schooled in the techniques of microscopy and other means to get at the microscopic structure of cells. I had not done much of that and he might be a useful colleague to have.

A second faculty I spoke with was an English teacher named Dexter Mublai. I only spoke with him momentarily, but he was quite an experience. A black man, equipped with a Ph.D. from Michigan he was a most interesting guy. He was over six feet tall. His voice was mellifluous and that must have been pure dynamite for teaching. Dexter was very bright and knowledgeable, given to dropping clever quotes and ideas from various authors. Just listening to him do his thing was hellishly entertaining as well as informative. Aside from just listening to him I did mention my fledgling interest in used books and my former professor, Stephen Victor. Dexter offered, "That'is something I do too. I've got a pretty good collection. Do let me know if you find anything interesting in your travels." I agreed to do that and then we both went on to other people.

The third faculty member was a talkative guy by the name of John Landsby. He was an Economics professor. Having previously achieved the rank of Full Professor he was hired at that rank. Dr. Landsby was a real honest to goodness, official professor. I had read a bit about him before talking with him. In an earlier life at another institution he had done some incisive analysis of what and why people do what they do when confronted with unforeseen and poorly understood economic challenges. His discoveries were written up in economics textbooks and he was therefore somewhat famous. He had come here to avoid the publishing rat race and now spent his time on teaching alone. He asked me about my Ph.D. dissertation work and was genuinely interested by the tale. Anyone following your tale with interest always makes you favorably disposed toward them and I immediately was. He said, "Minus the field work you describe, I can well remember being involved in analysis and discovery such as that. There is much to recommend it, but I have given it up. Now I teach and that's all I want to do for employment. I find that to be fulfilling enough. I put a lot of time these days into my paintings." I thought to myself, well at least he did it once, was successful, and currently is well aware of what motivates him. I guessed he was a fine professor and well suited to this place.

All of a sudden the meeting was over and people rapidly began to melt away. I can't say I noted much comradery among the faculty, but maybe this wasn't the venue for it. With regard to how this place was run, certain things were made crystal clear to me. The Dean's little speech had made it plain that at least she was not in favor of faculty involving themselves in research. As a powerful person on this campus her attitude was something to be taken into account. Sylvia's "agitation" and comments suggested that Dean Terkel's attitude was at least not universal.

This year's overall University catalog stated that faculty responsibility revolved around three areas teaching, research, and service. These three areas sometimes overlap. Service involves serving on committees within the institution and service to local, state, and national communities. Teaching and research are traditionally clear. Members of university faculty generally have a Ph.D. The abbreviation means a Doctor of Philosophy, a lover of wisdom. To get the degree you have to discover something new and convey it to others in writing. It is above all a research degree. After graduation it does not seem reasonable or desirable to want an earner of a Ph.D. to stop using research skills that were years in development. Why do universities highly prize research and faculty equipped to do it? Well, the discovery of knowledge is one of the businesses of a university, as indicated by the inclusion of research among the three areas of faculty responsibility. If faculty are busy pursuing new knowledge the odds are that at least one of them will make a discovery of great importance. Most will make discoveries of value only in their particular discipline, but occasionally one will discover some knowledge of wider importance, perhaps of general importance to mankind. Also, there is an associated issue, overhead funds. When faculty make discoveries they almost invariably wish to look further into what they have discovered. They apply for grants to support further study. For a large faculty total faculty grants can mean a big sum of money. Universities get a percentage of that sum to support their facilities. For most universities the overhead percentage of a total grant is about 30%. These overhead funds can mean a lot of support money for a university. So a university gets to increase the total knowledge available to mankind, which is ostensibly one of the reasons for its existence, but it also rakes in substantial monetary support for itself as a result.

After the faculty meeting a few days passed and before I knew it classes of the fall semester were scheduled to begin. I spent those days working on lectures and finalizing laboratory content and materials. Labs would begin in the second week. Biology labs were pretty standard. The first one dealt with learning to use and understand compound and dissecting microscopes, the second with learning to distinguish procaryotic (e.g., bacteria) from eukaryotic (e.g., plant and animal) cells. On the other hand, ecology labs were still something of a problem. Most ecology labs are not easily canned into a two hour, indoor exercise. They require getting out in the field. Further, I needed to assess what my students were capable of doing. I had figured out a couple of lab sessions dealing with sampling techniques that could be done in the lab to get started. With a little luck students would later be able to apply some of these techniques in the field to see how much more difficult sampling in the field could be from sampling in the lab. In short, I had to wing it for a while.

My classes were set up for Tuesday and Thursday at 8 and 10 A.M. Labs were on Tuesday afternoon for Introductory Biology and Thursday afternoon for Introductory Ecology. Especially Tuesdays and Thursdays would be quite full. Lectures would be an hour and a half. The Biology lab was three hours while the Ecology lab was two. When the first Tuesday rolled around I was all revved up to meet my students. I had already met a few, but most were unknown to me. The first class was Biology and there were the full 24 students in attendance. There was no more room in the lab and I could not add any of the students that tried to sign up late unless somebody dropped the course. Anyway, there they all were assembled in a room that would accommodate about 35 people. One very good thing that the University did on this campus at this time was keep classes small. No huge classes of perhaps a hundred or more students, was the policy.

You don't learn much about students on the first day. There are those given to selling themselves to the professor, but you can't know whether this is just bullshit, a scam to get a good grade, or if they are serious students and just outgoing. The majority of them just keep quiet, not a word is spoken to the professor. These too are a mystery. Students are generally at least a little apprehensive about any new course. I know I was and my way of handling that was to be quiet and see what happened. So, the quiet students could be competent or completely overwhelmed. In time I would see how this shook out.

In that first class one of the students, a recent high school graduate and a girl named Linda Pomeroy, came up to the podium before I started my lecture. Her name brought back memories of a girl in my first biology course. Her purpose was to tell me that she just loved biology and she was thrilled to be taking her first college course in it. She related that she had taken every advanced biology course her high school offered. Of course, that could mean anything. She seemed to be an intelligent girl, but was she just making a sale of some kind, or was she going to be a good student? Only time would tell, but right now I had to get started with class. I began by introducing myself as Dr. Blake Turner and gave them a quick rundown of my historical background, where I was from, where I had gone to school, and what my specific area of biological expertise was, which they likely did not understand. I introduced the course. My intent was to make it rigorous, but fair. As a rule of thumb a student should figure to put in three hours outside of class for every hour in class. If you figure that out for a full 15 hour course load, you will find that a student is expected to spend about 60 hours per week dealing with school. Taking a full college load is more than a full time job and will require some effort no matter how smart you are. I then made the point that this course is intended as a foundation for biology majors and those needing such a foundation for other majors. I then launched ahead into a sketchy outline of what we were going cover in the course.

The first topic on the syllabus I had prepared was a little of the history of biology, the human origin of some of the major ideas and concepts we were about lay out in the course. This would take up the rest of the first lecture and most or all of the second. Students should be aware of the contributions of, for example, Hook, Leewenhoek, Harvey, Mendel, Darwin, Morgan, and Watson and Crick. They would not yet really understand the advances made by such people. That would maybe come, but going through all that would definitely begin introducing them to the language of biology. Two students, having signed up for the wrong course, came up to drop after class. They were made up by two of the attempted late registrants that came to the first class just in case somebody dropped. Anyway, the lecture in that course went well that day. I think I made a good first impression on them.

The Ecology class was made up of students that were a little more hapless. They were in some major other than biology and had simply signed up for the course to satisfy a science requirement. There were undoubtedly some great students in there, but one could sense the uncomprehending and mystified nature of the group whenever the subject matter of ecology was broached. These guys would have to be brought along slowly and carefully. All this was not too surprising. It was the early 1970s and Earth Day had just recently happened. Ecology had gotten a lot of note and many people were aware of "the ecology," but few were at all aware of its basic tenets, as confusing as they could sometimes be. The science of ecology was relatively new. The word itself had only been coined in the early years of the 1900s. The content of the science that made it potentially useful for "saving the planet" was unappreciated by almost everyone. While recognizing my audience's uninformed state, my intention was to get them a little beyond that condition. As far as the lecture itself was concerned the first lecture went pretty well. I went through some of the terms that ecology uses in specific ways to refer to and describe the household [ecology comes from *oikos* (pronounced eekos), or the household, plus *logos*, or to know]. However, it was clear to me that there was little comprehension afoot among students as I went over the topics I planned to cover. This was not the ecology most expected, with big-eyed, fuzzy creatures to fawn over. Despite that they received me well and here too I seemed to have made a good impression. None of the 22 students came up to drop after class.

Because labs did not start till next week I had a chance on Wednesday to go and explore further the pier I had designs on for research. I did so even though I might incur the displeasure of Dean Terkel. Well, so it might go, even though at this stage that was unlikely. Mainly, how would she know what I did? If I just met and taught my classes, she would likely be most pleased. On that Wednesday there was a good low tide in the middle of the day. I brought two manuals along that would aid in the identification of intertidal invertebrates and algae that had settled on the pilings. It would require some lab space and the use of microscopes to make more careful identifications. I'd have to see what could be done about that, but not today.

When I got to the pier the tide was falling and already quite a way out. It was a beautiful September day. As I walked and waded along, heading offshore among the pilings, I could see an interesting polychaete on most of them. I had seen this species before. There is no common name except a fan worm, but the scientific name is *Eupomatus dianthus*. The worms built and lived in calcareous tubes, unlike the sand grain tubes of *Sabellaria vulgaris*. There were a very few of my old friend around down low on pilings near the sandy bottom. Apparently wave action was either too rough here to allow much tube building by *Sabellaria vulgaris*, or possibly there was not enough sand kicked up for tube building. Both worms are filter feeders. They feed by expanding their tentacles outside of their tubes and filtering microscopic food out of the plankton. The calcium of the fan worm's tube is produced, secreted, and laid down by the worm itself. A polychaete with calcareous tubes is not dependent on suspended sand grains for tube building and calcareous tubes may be able to better withstand heavier wave action. I didn't know what the correct answer was, but questions began to formulate. *Eupomatus* occurred in the lower intertidal zone, well above where the few *Sabellaria* were, and usually formed a skirt all the way around a piling. The tubes that made up the skirt stood out from most pilings, as much as five inches, and formed a sort of catch pan. Several other species could be found amongst this polychaete's tubes.

I found a snail species among the fan worm's tubes and in other places peripheral to the skirt. There were quite a few around. It was *Urosalpinx cinerea*, the oyster drill. This snail made its living by drilling with its radula (sort of like a rasping tongue) through an oyster's (or other bivalve's) shell and feeding on the meat inside. Could it also drill the calcareous tubes of *Eupomatus*? There was another oyster drill species there on the pilings, one called *Eupleura caudatum*. It was larger and much less abundant than *Urosalpinx cinerea*.

On the sand at the base of pilings was an abundant intertidal snail, something called the mud snail *Nassarius obsoletus* (as it was called then, its name is now *Ilyanassa obsoleta*). On pilings in about a three foot high zone above the *Eupomatus* skirt there occurred a band of the blue mussel, *Mytilus edulis*. There were a few horse mussels, *Modiolus modiolus*, also in this zone, but the blue mussel was definitely the predominant species. When I got well offshore, in about chest deep water, I found another snail species, the periwinkle *Littorina littorea*. This, unlike the oyster drills, is an herbivorous snail that is very abundant on New England rocky shores. I didn't expect it here, but here they were no matter what I expected. I was getting quite an array of species on my pilings and I haven't even thought about the algae and hydroid species that occurred there. I could not be sure what these species were until I could get back to the microscopes in the lab. This, however, was enough for today and I made my way back toward shore. I collected a few hydroids and algae on my way and put them in a bucket with a little seawater until I could get to them back to the lab where I could look at them more carefully.

The very next day after classes I went to see Dr. Terkel. Under the guise of setting up Ecology labs, which was partly true, I asked if she would write a memo giving me permission to use the open space in the large set up room adjacent to the Biology lab. Unsuspectingly she said, "Sure, go ahead. I'll have the memo typed up immediately." When the memo was typed, dated, and signed by Dean Abigail Terkel it said simply that Dr. Blake Turner has permission to utilize the currently unused space in Room 108a of Hartley Hall. It was only two lab benches about six or eight feet long, but it meant a place to work. I had keys to get in the lab and I could work in there any time I wished. That was a good start. Now I needed to organize microscopes. There was a quite good compound scope dedicated to that room that nobody used very much. That would work well. I would have to borrow a dissecting scope from the Biology lab when needed. They were of pretty good quality and would work well too. So, in fairly short order I had a place to work and basic equipment. What could I develop in the way of research?

Within the next couple of days with the aid of manuals and a microscope, I had a chance to confirm my invertebrate identifications so far. Also, I was able to identify the hydrozoans and algae I had collected. I had collected only two hydrozoan species, *Tubularia crocea* and *Bougainvillia carolensis.* These species are primitive colonial organisms that live attached to a substratum (in this case piling surfaces). There are many individuals in a colony with various functions (feeding, reproduction, and defense) joined together by a common digestive space. They are in the same group as the jellyfish, the Phylum Cnidaria. With regard to algae I happened to collect three species, my now ancient old friend the green alga *Ulva lactuca*, another green alga *Enteromorpha linza*, and the brown alga *Fucus vesiculosus*. The last species is a kelp and in its vertical zone takes up a lot of room on the pilings. There were undoubtedly more species on those pilings. Only further exploration would reveal them, but now at 12, the species list was rapidly growing. What sorts of interactions were there among the species that inhabited those pilings? This was not like a rocky New England shore where hard substratum organisms have abundant places to settle. Most of the shorelines in this area were beaches, salt marshes, or other soft substrata. Organisms that required a hard substratum for attachment had only a few jetties, docks, and the pilings available to them. Even the numerous pilings on this pier were an isolated, minor habitat in the middle of an expansive sandflat. Organisms requiring a hard substratum would not have much in the way of substrata to colonize. Because that resource was present in a short supply, species interactions were very likely. I did not yet know what might emerge from a study of those pilings, but the odds were that something would.

With that little delving into a potential research problem I had to devote myself to getting my lectures and labs going. I had the lectures under good control for a while, but in the second week labs would begin and they would require an input of attention. The first lab had to do with the parts, pieces, and functions of compound and dissection microscopes and a number of exercises to get students familiar with using them. It was the first time I actually ran a lab in that room and it took some time and a few missteps to get used to it. My introduction to lab rules and regulations, general mode of behavior expected, and how this section of the course would be graded went well enough. There would be two labs (on enzymes and genetics) for which a report would be required, two different lab practical exams, and some number of brief surprise quizzes. The exercises for this lab were a success overall. You learn a lot about students in their first lab. Things like names of students, personalities, who wants to learn, and who curious all come to the fore. Other than this you don't really get to know students until the first exam. That's when they begin to emerge as individuals. But, that would be down the road.

The first lab in Ecology was necessary, but they would not find it too exciting. All 22 students showed up. I wanted them to get an introduction to sampling. I had prepared some jars with four differently colored beans in them. You can think of the different colored beans as representing different species, perhaps scattered in a field or on a sandflat. Some bean colors were rare, others more common. The total number of each color bean in each jar was known. I had counted them and gave that information to students. Each jar held one liter (1000 ml) of beans. One jar went to each pair of students. The idea was to try different sampling techniques to see which led to the best estimate of the number of beans of each color (species) in the jar. We looked into dealing with sample size. The jar was shaken to mix the beans up, a hand was put in deep among the beans, and initially a single 50 ml beaker of beans was extracted. Now, 50 ml is 5% of a liter so you would multiply, in this example, the number of each color bean in the sample by 20 to get an estimate of the total of each color bean in the jar. The smallest sample size (50 ml) was expected to be the least accurate. Bigger sample sizes (multiple 50 ml beakers) should improve the estimate. The most difficult to estimate accurately was the total number of the rarest colored beans in the liter jar. Most often with smaller samples the number of that colored bean in a sample was zero, giving the erroneous estimate for the number in the whole jar of zero. In actuality there was some number of that color bean in the jar. Particularly the rarest bean, sample size had to be adequate to estimate how many of each colored bean accurately.

We also tried random sampling *versus* uniform sampling *versus* haphazard sampling in determining the total population size of a single species. For random sampling we spread a goodly number of one color bean (several hundred) out onto a piece of brown paper divided into a grid of 100 squares. There were various numbers of beans (individuals of the species) per grid location. We used a table of random numbers to pick out which 10 grids would have the resident beans counted. This would allow the students to calculate an estimated average number of beans per sampled grid. Multiplying the total number grids on the paper (=100) times the average number per sampled grid gave an estimate of the total bean population being tested. For uniform sampling we spread the beans out on the paper again and counted the beans in every tenth square. Again, multiplying the average obtained by the total number of squares gave an estimate of total population size by the uniform sampling method. The haphazard sample was gathered in the same way except that no pattern was followed. Students just decided at whim which 10 squares would have the beans counted. These two exercises well filled up the two-hour lab and I thought it went pretty well. They got to see some of the methods and problems in obtaining estimates of a whole population from samples. How large a sample is necessary and what will be the pattern of sampling? They would see how some of this might be applied in the field later on.

Now we got into the long haul of the semester. Lectures and labs were on Tuesday and Thursday. The other days of the week did not have official duties, but they were pretty full for me nevertheless. Both courses were brand new to me. The first time through a course lectures had to be prepared essentially from scratch and labs required an extraordinary amount of thought and set up. Two new courses are a lot to organize and keep going. A professor has to stay on top of things. If you lose the respect of your students, a course can utterly devolve into crap. We can't have that.

I am committed to essay exams. When the time came for the first exam in both courses I announced that would be the test type. I said in class, "There will be five or six questions, of which you will have to answer your choice of four or five in an hour and 15 minutes. Make your choices, think, divide up your time, and then write. What I am interested in is whether in the time allotted you can create a logical, correct, and complete answer to the questions asked."

When the tests were taken and I had put in hours getting them graded the results were not too bad, quite good in fact. Students did about equally well in both classes. Using the Ecology class as an example, there were two A, four B, eight C, three D, and five F grades. The Fs were people who were just lost and could not handle the questions. Maybe I could get them on the right track. I invited all students to come see me if there were issues they wished to discuss. A more pointed invitation was extended to the eight with D and F grades. Five came. Following Dr. Burke from years ago I selected topics that should have been in their answers and spent time trying to make them understand those topics. With that under their respective belts I challenged them to go and figure out an answer to one of the questions on the exam that would work. "Come in and verbally with only a few notes give your answer to me in a couple of days." Three of them, Matty, Joe, and Gus, took the challenge seriously and came in to present their answers. Matty did a wonderful job, Joe and Gus did quite well. I pointed out that, as a means of studying, they could devise questions and answers on their own, or with other students. I related the story of getting a 27% on my first botany test and told them that this approach had led to success for me. If it worked, I hoped they would adopt the method. I presented similar challenges to Biology students that had done poorly, three of them accepted, and did well in presenting their answers. I could only hope that the considerable amount of my time, and that of the students, had been profitable and that word about the method would spread among students. If it worked as well as it did for me, it would indeed be well spent time.

I intend my courses to be difficult and rigorous, but not impossible. Students should not get good grades without having worked hard for them. As might be expected, some students fell down on the next exam. Some did about as well. Others did better. Most did not seek any sort of help from me and this didn't happen because of anything in particular I did. Students often don't want or require help. I was very pleased by the fact that Ecology and Biology students that had accepted my assistance on the first exam did indeed do better. They all managed a C or better on their next exam. Most, including Matty, Joe, and Gus, did markedly better than on the first exam. As it turned out, Dr. Burke had a long reach.

So, the semester proceeded along. I kept control of the lectures and labs and indeed both courses went quite well. There were many details and specific interactions with students, but what I have mentioned covers the semester adequately. I found it necessary to fail some students. That is always a downer.

It was usually because students were absent too much, or were incapable of understanding the material, or refused to work hard enough. Because I have mentioned them previously let me report on Matty, Joe, and Gus. They all passed Ecology, with an A, a C, and a B, respectively. That was certainly rewarding to me and to them. Course/Professor evaluation forms were filled out anonymously by students still in class near the end of the semester. I have my reservations about such evaluations, but for me they came out quite well. I had not done anything to piss her off yet and Dean Abigail Terkel even took time to express to me her congratulations on the job I had done in my first semester. That was nice of her, but I was happier with the accomplishments and good feelings of my students.

Chapter 6

SOME SUCCESS WITH A RESEARCH PROBLEM: SEEDS OF PROBLEMS TO COME

A moment to moment history of my teaching at Visitopolis University is unnecessary. My interest in teaching remained high and I always put much effort into it. Suffice it to say that each semester there were two, sometimes three, courses to teach. Teaching Introductory Biology I and II continued and they became a steady part of my teaching duties. I had done what was considered a very good job with those courses in my first year and Dean Terkel was happy to have me continue to teach them. The Introductory Ecology course was offered once every year and I also eventually developed courses for non-majors in Human Physiology, Invertebrate Zoology, and General Biology. Most the time one or the other of these three would be offered in the semester when Ecology was not. I especially liked the years when Ecology and Invertebrate Zoology were offered. Summer and winter session courses were offered at our branch, but I consistently declined to teach during those times. My motivation for doing this was straight forward, but kept close to the vest. I needed the winter and summer sessions to conduct the various activities associated with my research. Among other things it meant that no extra money would be coming in, but that was a price I would have to pay for my research. My salary was pretty small. It was however enough to comfortably support me and my modest research needs. I designed both to not require much.

A sort of wet lab had been set up at my abode. It wasn't much, but there was a refrigerator and a saltwater aquarium and I could store organisms there for a while until I could get to campus where I had microscopes available. At my home lab I did have some good magnifying lenses, which were an important aid, and some other simple equipment. Working at home was a major convenience. It was closer to the coast and my pier pilings.

At the end of that first semester in my first year at Visitopolis I had about a month of time away from teaching. There were courses to get ready for the spring semester, but I had time to do some further exploration of the pier pilings. It was winter and the weather could be rough. On the other hand it was nicer at this location than it had been in New England during winter when collecting and identifying invertebrates could be difficult. Conditions there could be out and out brutal. At the end of that month I had quite a list of species I had found on the pilings. I kept track of when each species was found, as some species might disappear and others appear with the changing seasons and I needed to know about this if it occurred.

My first piece of research work at the branch of Visitopolis University was perhaps not too exciting to a person not steeped in invertebrate zoology and ecology. When it was finished and published the work was of interest only to maybe a few experts around the world. Such is often the way of science. Nevertheless, I need to go over this piece of work in a little detail because it was my first research project at my new university. It tells a lot about the way I had to go about things and something of the amount of effort that any piece of research entails. Above all a scientist in any field must be curious, busy, and keep good records. It is meaningful to include a firm notion of my motivations and methods. It is possible to skim over, even skip, the species names and some of the details without losing the thread of my here told tale, but it would not do to leave out all that was involved.

By that first winter session I had amassed a pretty complete list of invertebrate species that I was able to collect and identify either from or near those pilings. It would probably change as rarer species that I had missed collecting were found, but the list was pretty complete. It consisted of 39 species. The amassing of this list required a lot of my time and effort. All I will say about that is, here you have it. The list of species found at that time, organized by taxonomic kingdom and phylum, is given below:

Kingdom Protista (I mention here the algae, formerly considered in the Kingdom Plantae)

I am not going to look much into species capable of photosynthesis, but I have identified with reasonable surety some the algae that I found on the pilings. I will mention three algal Divisions.

Some Success with a Research Problem: Seeds of Problems to Come

Chlorophyta (green algae)
Ulva lactuca (grows all year in moderately wave exposed locations)
Enteromorpha linza (exposed locations, upper intertidal)
Phaeophyta (brown algae)
Ectocarpus conferoides
Fucus vesiculosus (low to mid tidal range)
Rhodophyta (red algae)
Ceramium rubrum
Polysiphonia nigrescens
Kingdom Animalia
Phylum Porifera (sponges)
Cliona lobata
Cliona vastifica
Mycale fibrexilis
Phylum Cnidaria (hydrozoans, jellyfish, sea anemones)
Hydrozoans
Bougainvillea carolensis
Campanularia amphora
Obelia bicuspidata
Obelia commissuralis
Obelia geniculata
Tubularia crocea
Sea anemone
Metridium senile
Phylum Platyhelminthes [this one is a free-living (nonparasitic) flatworm]
Euplana gracilis
Phylum Annelida (polychaetes, earthworms, leeches)
Polychaetes
Eupomatus (formerly *Hydroides*) *dianthus*
Sabellaria vulgaris
Phylum Mollusca
Gastropods (snails)
Littorina littorea (the periwinkle, rare on shoreward pilings)
Nassarius obsoletus (now called *Ilyanassa obsoleta*, mostly on sand at base of pilings)
Urosalpinx cinerea (the oyster drill)
Eupleura caudatum (a much less numerous and larger oyster drill)
Pelecypods (bivalves)
Crassostrea virginica (Eastern oyster)
Mytilus edulis (the blue mussel)
Modiolus demissus (ribbed mussel, now *Geukensia demissa*)
Modiolus modiolus (the horse mussel, rare on pilings)
Phylum Arthropoda (crustaceans)
Barnacles
Balanus balanoides
Balanus eburneus (low intertidal zone)
Balanus improvisus (low intertidal)
Chthamalus fragilis (upper intertidal)
Decapods (crabs, not attached, but found occasionally on pilings)
Callinectes sapidus (the blue crab)

Cancer irroratus
Carcinus maenus
Phylum Ectoprocta (moss animals, individuals small, colonies can be large)
Amathia vidovici
Aeverrillia armata
Phylum Echinodermata (spiny skinned animals, sea stars)
Asterias forbesi (found occasionally on pilings)
Phylum Chordata (at some stage of life cycle have a notochord, gill slits, a dorsal hollow nerve tube, includes fish, amphibians, reptiles, birds, mammals)
Urochordates
Molgula manhattensis (the common sea squirt)
Botryllus schlosseri

In this list of species the one that grabbed my interest the most was the snail *Urosalpinx cinerea*, the oyster drill. What were they doing there? How were they distributed on those pilings? Were they more abundant at other times of the year? The number of oysters on those pilings, I found only five, would not support the number of oyster drills I observed. They must be feeding mainly on some other species, maybe the blue mussel (*Mytilus edulis*), or possibly the fan worm *Eupomatus dianthus*. It was probably the blue mussel.

When an oyster drill drills through even a young oyster shell it takes a day or two or more to do it. Once the shell is drilled through it is a pretty sure thing that oyster meat will be inside to feed on. A fan worm tube is calcareous like an oyster shell. The worm can move along inside the length of its tube. A drill might invest considerable drilling time only to find no meat reward at the end. The *Eupomatus* tube may be thinner which could make it attractive to an oyster drill, but the blue mussel exists in a wider band and is abundant on those pilings. So I favored the hypothesis that drills feed mostly on the blue mussel.

I probably couldn't do much about this until the next summer after the spring semester was over, but what might I do then? Three questions about drills occurred to me: 1) how many drills did those pilings harbor; 2) how are drills distributed in space among pilings; and 3) does the number of drills and/or their spatial distribution change with the seasons? These seemed possible to answer on a limited budget and might reveal something interesting. I began to think about these questions. How could I go about answering them?

Here's what I decided upon. In my trips to this pier I found that on an average low tide I could get out to row of pilings number 50. At that distance from shore the water was usually a little more than knee deep when the tide was low. When the water was cold I could use waders to get there and work. In summer the waders wouldn't be necessary, except maybe as a guard against jelly fish. Shorts would do. With six pilings in a row, between piling rows one

Some Success with a Research Problem: Seeds of Problems to Come 71

and fifty that made 300 total pilings. Pilings close to shore tended not to have so many invertebrates on them. I guess they were left high and dry for too long by too many low tides and they were killed off. So I cut down on the number of pilings I would have to examine by choosing rows 10, 15, 20, 25, and 30. That was 30 poles to examine close to shore rather than all 180 in that range of pilings. This would give me a pretty good sample of any *Urosalpinx cinerea* (and other species) that occurred in toward the beach. All pilings in rows 31 to 50 would be examined for drills. The oyster drill (*Urosalpinx*) was the only snail inhabiting those pilings, other than the much rarer other oyster drill (*Eupleura caudatum*), and farther out the periwinkle (*Littorina littorea*). In total that amounted to 30 + 114 = 144 pilings to examine. Examinations were a fairly simple matter because intertidal drills were easily seen on pilings and were usually not all that numerous. In summer I had seen quite a few, but this winter I had noted only between 1 and 4 per pole and you could see them by walking around a piling.

Another piece of information I would get would be the size of each drill observed. This could be gotten without disturbing a snail from its position on a piling by putting a ruler alongside and measuring shell height. Shell height is the length of the shell from the siphonal notch in the shell aperture to the tip of the shell spire, which is considered ventral to dorsal. In snail anatomy it amounts to how tall the snail is rather than how long. Measuring this way was not as accurate as if I had removed snails and measured them with vernier calipers, but it was more important to not disturb snails any more than necessary. I did not want drills to fall off of pilings by my disturbing them. The largest drills were just over an inch (~30 mm) in shell height.

At the end of a run through the pilings the information I would have would be the number of drills on each examined pole and the approximate size of each. I could be relatively sure that few people, perhaps a few snail experts, would care much about this information. That was right up my alley, but you never know what you might uncover when you start to investigate. It was the dead of winter when I came up with this plan of action. Sometime in early spring I would have to see if I could accomplish my first run through the pilings. To get a feel for the correlation of seasons with *Urosalpinx* abundance and size on those pilings I would have to do this several times in at least one year.

I checked into the literature on *Urosalpinx cinerea*. There was, thank goodness, a pretty good library at this branch of Visitopolis University and I could borrow from the main campus library when needed. The snail is native to the east coast of North America from Canada to Florida. It lives in protected estuaries on rocks and other hard substrata, such as pilings, and in adjacent sand.

The species prefers higher salinity, saltier, waters. Some snail species, for example the periwinkle *Littorina littorea* and the mud snail *Nassarius obsoletus*, also occurring on or near the pilings, have a free- swimming larval stage that drifts around in the plankton at the mercy of currents, but *Urosalpinx* larvae develop in an egg case from which fully formed juvenile snails hatch and crawl away. Species with planktonic larvae drift about and can spread rapidly to new areas. Because it has crawl away juveniles *Urosalpinx* disperses slowly to new geographical areas. This snail is a major predator on oysters, but also eats other mollusks. It can decimate crops of young oysters, just settled from the plankton, and is a major problem in that regard. This oyster drill also occurs in Europe and on the west coast of North America where it has been spread by association with live shipments of the Eastern oyster (*Crassostrea virginica*).

When the end of March (1974) rolled around it was time to get out among the pilings and put the plan into action for the first time. The pier's direction shore to offshore was almost due north at 355°. Of the six pilings in a row the piling on the west side of the pier I called number one and pilings were numbered consecutively upward to number six on the east side of the pier. So with a row number and a pole number I knew exactly where a particular piling was located and therefore where and how many drills were found. The water was still quite cold and I used waders and a mini tape recorder to make my counts and measurements of oyster drills (*Urosalpinx* only, ignoring the much rarer *Eupleura*) in the intertidal zone on 144 pilings. On 30 March I counted only 5 drills on 135 pilings, with never more than two on a piling. I went out again on 23 April and this time I counted 25 drills. Of 144 pilings this time, 123 had no drills on them, 17 had one, and four had two. The smallest snail was 12 mm, the largest 26 mm, and the mean (average) size of the 25 drills was 20.9 mm. This represented a lot of work, but all by itself did not mean much. It might mean something more when compared with similar data from other times of the year. All I could say at this time was that in April there were only a few fairly large oyster drills on pilings.

How were they distributed among pilings? Were drills distributed randomly, uniformly, or did they have an aggregated (or clumped) distribution? Well, if the number of drills found on poles varied randomly, then there would be no pattern to where and how many you found at a time on a pole. You might run into zero, or one, or three, or seven, or maybe 10 drills on various pilings. If distributed uniformly, you might find the same number of drills on every pole, or maybe on every second or third pole. In a clumped distribution one would find drills gathered on a few poles with many poles bearing few or none. There is an index called Green's Index. This index isn't affected by the abundance of the organism in the habitat. Its calculation gives you a good idea of how organisms are distributed in space. Space in this case is among pilings. If Green's Index (GI) comes out close to zero, that indicates a random spatial distribution. If it comes out close to one that indicates a very clumped or aggregated spatial distribution. If it comes out close to minus one that means the organism is uniformly distributed. To calculate a GI you need to know the average number of drills per pole (in the 23 April sample the mean = 0.17 drills per piling), the statistical variance in the number per pole (that was = 0.20), and the total number of drills observed (25). Green's Index for the distribution of drills on pilings on 23 April 1974 was 0.0074, pretty close to zero and indicating that drills were distributed on pilings randomly. [The formula for Green's Index is (variance / average) -1 / the total number of drills observed - 1, or in this case (0.2/0.17) -1 / 25 -1) = 0.0074.]

As I have said above, all by themselves these spring observations on oyster drills on my pier pilings did not mean very much. There would have to be comparisons made with numbers present, sizes, and distribution pattern in different seasons. Over the span of the year I collected data 13 times. Rather than describe each occasion, let me present a table telling what happened. From an invertebrate zoologist's point of view the results are pretty interesting. They help in understanding the drill population on those pilings.

Data on *Urosalpinx cinerea* counted (#) and measured for shell height (SH) on pilings of an old military pier near Visitopolis University branch campus in 1974.

Date	# Poles	Total # Drills	Variance (#/pole)	Avg. (#/pole)	Range (#/pole)	Observed GI	Range of SHmm	Avg. SHmm
03/30	135	5	0.07	0.04	0 - 2	0.188	-	-
04/23	144	25	0.20	0.17	0 - 2	0.007	12 - 26	20.9
05/15	144	476	70.63	3.31	0 - 57	0.043	12 - 30	22.4
06/11	144	343	28.01	2.38	0 - 56	0.031	8 - 30	22.2
06/18	144	443	20.99	3.08	0 - 23	0.013	4 - 32	18.5
06/30	144	298	20.72	2.07	0 - 32	0.030	10 -33	23.1
07/09	144	172	20.98	1.19	0 - 39	0.097	2 - 31	20.6
07/20	144	177	3.16	1.23	0 - 9	0.009	10 - 31	18.9
07/21	144	288	8.38	2.00	0 - 16	0.011	9 - 31	19.2
08/25	144	167	16.59	1.16	0 - 42	0.080	3 - 28	13.5
09/25	144	46	1.16	0.38	0 - 6	0.046	4 - 30	15.5
10/06	141	136	3.52	0.97	0 - 13	0.019	4 - 30	14.1
11/22	138	102	2.19	0.74	0 - 9	0.019	4 - 29	11.1

From left to right the table gives the date of the observation (month/day), the number of pilings on which drills were counted and measured, the total number of drills observed, the statistical variance in number per pole, the mean (Avg.) number per pole, the range in number observed per pole, the Green's Index (GI) assessing drill distribution in space among pilings on that date, the range of shell heights (SH) observed, and the mean observed drill shell height.

Let me put into words some of what this table tells us. Observations were taken from late March through November. I did look for drills a little in winter months and found a single one in December. In January and February they were absent from pilings. It appears then that drills were present on pilings from about March to November and basically absent for the other three months of the year. I took a census of drills on about the same number of poles on each date listed. The total number of drills was very low in March, increased in April, was highest in May and June, somewhat reduced in July and August, and reduced in September through November. So the best time to observe drills on pilings appears to be May and June. Not surprisingly the variance in number per pole was greatest at times when more drills were present on pilings, as reflected by the average and range in number per pole. Note that over 50 drills were observed on a single pole in May and June. It's not evident in the table, but in most months snails were most concentrated on the lower numbered (westernmost) poles. However, numbers of drills were in all months pretty randomly distributed among poles as indicated by Green's Index, which was always very close to zero. Only in March, when two of only five total snails existed on the same pole, were drills somewhat more aggregated in their distribution. That surprised me. Organisms commonly have clumped spatial distributions because they cluster together for breeding or protective purposes (hiding together in protected places). Random spatial distributions are usually quite rare. In terms of drill size, smaller snails were not the ones to show up first on pilings in the spring. They showed up later.

How can these data be interpreted? Because *Urosalpinx cinerea* does not have a planktonic larval stage for dispersal and even adults move around only a little, we can assume that snails were resident in the sand at the base of pilings during winter. Where else could the first snails on the pilings have come from? They were already quite large? They must have become active in the spring and among other actions crawled up onto pilings. The fact that somewhat larger snails (see table) were the first to show up certainly indicates that the population on pilings did not arise from newly reproduced juveniles. Why do drills exhibit a random distribution among pilings when it would be more common for an organism to have an aggregated distribution? You would expect them to be aggregated on certain pilings because for one thing these snails need a partner of the opposite sex with which to breed. There is a distance of 10 feet between rows of pilings and the pier is 30 feet wide. To get out to row 50, the last row I made counts on, that's an area of sandy bottom of at least 30 feet X 500 feet = 15,000 square feet from which drills might be drawn to pilings. In early spring most pilings had zero drills on them. Even at times when the piling population was high not all that many drills show up on pilings. This indicates that there are not all that many available in the sand. If they were randomly distributed in the sand, it follows that they would climb the nearest available piling and be randomly distributed on them. In any case, that was my working hypothesis. Perhaps I will get to test it. Why did the mean size of drills go down toward the end of the year? That is probably because juvenile snails came out of egg cases produced by adult females and became part of the piling population, thus reducing the average size.

I have gotten somewhat ahead of myself with all these data and interpretations thereof, but that was my original piece of research at Visitopolis University. Getting these data had taken me into the fall semester of my second year (1974-75) as an Assistant Professor. Eventually I would write the data up and offer them for publication as a brief paper, but for now these data had to sit quiescent, unpublished for a time. First I had to get busy with publishing some of the content of my dissertation. That would be a major project. I began this undertaking during the winter session of my first year (1973-74) of employment at Visitopolis University. What I decided to emphasize in my wished for paper to be was the laboratory development of *Sabellaria vulgaris* larvae from the fertilized egg through mature stages, that were able to settle out of the plankton, and observations of larvae present in the natural plankton over the course of the year. This involved all sections of my long dissertation that had to do with culturing the larvae and the analysis of plankton samples. These had to be condensed down into a manuscript that would take up only a few journal pages. There was a lot of condensing to do and having never published anything before there were lots of challenges to overcome. The preparation of photographs, tables, and figures (graphs) for inclusion in a journal article requires the following of many rules and that does not even include coming up with the crisp and concise language that outside reviewers and a journal expect.

I had to enlist the services of a graphic artist at the University to help me produce the illustrations. Alice Manning was willing to do this and was a very big help. Around this University branch she had not had much practice getting illustrations ready for journal publication. Most of her work was in setting up visual aids for the classroom. Nevertheless, she knew her way around the technical details of her craft. Alice made it possible for me to overcome my illustration challenges and deserves abundant thanks for doing that. The writing was something with which nobody could help me, but eventually I got that done, at least to my satisfaction. In all it took nearly six months fussing around with various details to come up with the manuscript. In the summer between my first and second year, as far as I was concerned the paper was ready to go. I, with great hopes for its acceptance, submitted it to a journal.

Some six months after that (still in 1975) the reviews came back. It was accepted pending revision. The editor was I guess aware of the problems I had dealing with my first publication. In any case he was very helpful. Two anonymous reviewers were not overly negative, as I would find out they could sometimes be, and offered some good suggestions and asked some good questions. I was very pleased by the acceptance. That's true of any accepted manuscript, but especially your first. I worked for about a month on getting the revisions accommodated and sent it back in. After another month the editor replied and said he had sent the manuscript off to the printer. Close to four months later the galley proofs came back from the printer. These give you a final chance to correct any errors made in printing. I went over them with care in the allotted 24 hours as requested and sent them back. There were a few corrections, but nothing major. The paper would be published in the next issue of the journal to come out in 1975. So at this point I had one publication to my credit. That indeed was very satisfying.

Faculty members and administrators around school were verbally congratulatory. It was fun to include a reprint of the paper with my annual evaluation. How Dean Terkel really felt about a faculty member accomplishing something in research I can't know, but on the surface she seemed to recognize and appreciate it. (I and almost nobody else ever adopted calling her Abigail.) It was, after all, research done in the past and elsewhere that had just now seen print, only a small affront to her view of faculty duties. That aside, she was not above extolling the academic merits of her local faculty. A scholarly paper published by one of her biology faculty was worth a mention or two in her administrative and public circles. When the time came to determine raises in pay for the next year I got increased by $3,000, which put me up to a massive $23,000, a 15% increase. The Dean and the powers that be must have liked something I was doing. Would that continue?

I had gotten to know the history professor Sylvia Armbruster quite well by this time. She was single and we had been out a few times to talk, eat, drink a few beers, go to the movies, and the like. She was not only beautiful, her eyes could transfix me, she was also full of incites and a great conversationalist, which made her multiply fun to be around. Sylvia was dedicated to her subject area, the history of the Revolution. She had been around here a little longer than I had and moreover had been rebellious about faculty members being limited to only teaching. We had talked some about what had happened to her when she had published something. She summed it up as follows: as long as it was something based on past research from her dissertation, or at least done elsewhere, administrators were pretty positive about it with rewards and accolades. The project she was presently working on, however, was new research on the American Revolution and it was making demands on her time. She had gone so far as to ask Dean Terkel for a some time off and support to make trips to libraries that had the resources she needed. The Dean took umbrage at that request and verbally expressed that it was not the policy on this campus to support faculty time being devoted to such activity. Local administrators held: faculty are hired to teach and not to do research.

At about the time when I had finished my 13 trips to the pier pilings, Sylvia offered some advice. She of course had known about my piling project, had even been out to help a couple of times. Sylvia opined that it would be best to leave my research activities pretty well hidden as long as possible. She suggested that the old saw -- it is easier to obtain forgiveness than permission -- might be well applied here. She was now handling her work that way. I had mentioned my research to students, but not to any administrators. Aside from using some space in the room adjacent to the lab, I had not asked for anything to help me get the work done. As long as they did not spend time investigating, my research was basically an unknown endeavor as far as administrators were concerned. At the time I did not fully understand just why she thought I should keep quiet about my ongoing research, but I took her advice and continued to maintain a low profile for my research project. If I ever managed to publish anything on it, which I intended to try to do, that would come to an end.

While my first paper was in the process of being reviewed and published I started work on another manuscript based on my dissertation. This one had to do with the settling plate data and told of the times when *Sabellaria vulgaris* larvae had settled out of the plankton and became juvenile, tube-building worms. This was somewhat shorter than my first paper. In it the point was made about the connection between the times that mature larvae were present in the plankton and times when settlement occurred, but I confined myself to only hinting about the retention mechanism I had hypothesized. I sent it in to a different journal than the first and it was accepted. Good luck was mine, or so it seemed. You never know what will come as a consequence of a publication. Anyway, I made the revisions asked for, sent it back to the editor, and she quickly sent it off to the printer. About six months after my first paper had come out the second paper saw print. So I now had two published papers to my credit, not bad for a recently graduated Ph.D. Both were based on research in my dissertation and the response from Dean Terkel and other administrators was again pretty positive, about what it was for the first paper. I had about used up my dissertation data and if I was to continue being successful as a publishing researcher, I would have to make use of new data that had been collected while here at the branch campus of Visitopolis University. That would be an end to flying under the radar.

In the winter session of my second year (1975) I began writing a new manuscript concerning what I had learned about the oyster drill population on the pilings of that pier. People had studied that snail in oyster beds, on rocks, and other sorts of habitats, but so far as I could find out by searching the literature, a population on pilings had never been studied. I had been around sets of pilings before in various places where oyster drills could have been present and never observed any drills. This was usually in places where intertidal rocks and other hard substrata were more abundant than around here. I was not looking as carefully on those former pilings as I as I had on these, but certainly drills were not a prominent element of the invertebrate faunas on those other sets of pilings. It appeared that I was studying a somewhat unique situation and that alone made it potentially worthy of a publication.

One necessity reared its head immediately. To make the connection between drills in the sand in winter and recruitment of drills to pilings in spring, I had to look into the abundance and distribution of oyster drills in the sand around the bases of pilings. It was important that I could at least demonstrate their presence in the sand in winter. I rigged up a clam rake with a basket that would drain water and most sand, but retain drills. Five random piling rows were selected using a random numbers table. Row numbers 12, 33, 40, 41, and 48 were the rows selected. The plan was to systematically rake through the sand between the chosen rows and the next row landward and look for drills. Each plot of sand to be raked was 30 by 10 feet and in winter it was a hard bit of exhausting work getting it done. I was able to find a total of 24 drills in the five raked plots. It was January (1975) and water was cold. All the snails I found were adults and alive, but inactive and distributed according to no recognizable pattern. I took this to mean that drills were sparse in the sand in winter and randomly distributed. That was about what I expected, but it was good to have confirmatory data.

Over the next days I got busy composing my manuscript. I worked on it mostly at home and very little in my office at school. The paper to be would include an explanation of the season when drills showed up on pilings, their fluctuating abundance during summer, and when they disappeared for winter. Other workers had noted that abundant drills were a phenomenon of summer, but it was worthwhile to establish that it happened that way in a piling population as well as elsewhere. Other topics in the manuscript included: (1) the absence of very small drills among those that appeared first in spring; (2) the probable connection between the few drills found in winter sand and recruitment to pilings in the spring; (3) the unlikely random distribution of drills among pilings and its probable dependence on drill distribution in the sand; and (4), as evinced by the occurrence of the smallest snails later in summer, a discussion of the apparent breeding schedule of the *Urosalpinx cinerea* population on those pilings also seemed appropriate. I felt that I did not over analyze the data and told what they meant in an efficient manner. The spring semester of my second year was over before the manuscript was finished. This was still in the days before computers and word processors were everywhere. There certainly was not one on my desktop. The typewriter clacked clumsily away, I never managed to get very good at that, and it was submitted to a journal during that summer (1975). If it got accepted, Blake Turner's heretofore quiet local research cat would be out of the bag and loudly snarling. Well, the published product of research is worth whatever consequence flows from it.

In the spring semester of 1975 I had to teach three courses, Introductory Biology II, Ecology, and Invertebrate Zoology, and what with writing that manuscript there was not much time to do any research in the field. I did spend time in the library looking further into the biology of some of the species that occurred on the pilings. One of the bits of information I discovered was that two of the common species were parasitized, each by its own species of trematode parasite. The trematodes are parasitic flatworms. Parasitic of course means they depend on a host for their nutrition. The Platyhelminthes, the phylum which contains the class Trematoda, has about 15,000 species. Tapeworms are in a different class, but also belong to that phylum. Trematode flatworms are primitively structured invertebrates. The body is not divided up into segments and they lack a space between the outside of the intestinal wall and the inside of the outer body wall. In a more evolved animal, such as an earthworm, that space is called the coelom. Flatworms are described as acoelomates (without a coelom) due to lacking such a space. They also lack a lot of other things such as a blood system, respiratory system, and appendages.

Despite their relative simplicity trematodes often have very complicated life cycles, usually involving three different hosts. The adult worm typically lives in a vertebrate animal, which it uses as what is called a definitive host. In most trematode species the sexes are not in separate male and female bodies. Adult worms are sexually both male and female and produce both sperm and eggs (that is, they are hermaphrodites), but most often they copulate with and reciprocally trade sperm with another individual trematode. Usually in the definitive host's fecal material, fertilized eggs of the trematode exit the host and develop into larvae (called miracidia). These larvae infect what is called a first host, which is typically a mollusk of some kind and most often a snail. In that first host the first larval form of the parasite (the miracidium) develops into other larval forms, the sporocysts and/or rediae, (redia is singular, rediae is plural). Within the sporocysts or rediae yet another larval form, the cercaria (cercaria is singular, cercariae is plural), is produced. Cercariae typically exit the first host and swim to and infect a second host, which depending on the particular trematode is some invertebrate, or possibly a vertebrate species such as a fish. When the infected second host is eaten by the vertebrate that serves as the definitive host, the parasite develops into an adult worm, which makes more fertilized eggs and the cycle continues. That is an outline of a trematode's life cycle. This information, while perhaps a bit troublesome, is necessary to follow the direction my research would take on.

One of the common species on the pilings was the fan worm, *Eupomatus dianthus* and from the literature I learned that the trematode that infected this polychaete as a first host is called *Cercaria loossi*. Because the first host of trematode parasites is typically a snail it is unusual that this one uses a polychaete worm in that role. This is the only trematode infecting the fan worm and I will refer to it as the fan worm parasite. The sporocysts of the fan worm parasite have orange pigments associated with them and when they mass in the belly of a parasitized fan worm they impart an orangish color to it. The cercariae produced by those sporocysts have a long tail, forked at the end. This makes them quite distinctive when looked at with a microscope. It is not known for sure, but it is thought that a marine fish serves as the definitive host for the fan worm parasite and would be the source of fan worm infections.

The other common species on those pilings that had a trematode parasite was the blue mussel, *Mytilus edulis*. The mussel is, of course, a bivalve mollusk. So it is not so unusual for it to be used as a first host by a trematode, even though snails are more often used in that role. As an example of a snail first host, the oyster drill can be infected by a trematode. It can harbor the larvae of *Parorchis avitus*. The only trematode infecting the blue mussel is called *Protoeces maculatus*. When not using its scientific name, I will call it the mussel parasite. The definitive hosts for this species are known to be mollusk-eating fish and they would be the main source of mussel infections. The life cycle of this

Some Success with a Research Problem: Seeds of Problems to Come 81

parasite is not usual. This trematode has an abbreviated life cycle. The term for this is that it is a progenetic trematode. The unusual situation is that not only larval *Protoeces maculatus* (sporocysts and cercariae) occur in the mussel but adult, reproducing worms too. Apparently the whole life cycle can be completed in *Mytilus edulis* alone. Mollusk-eating fish (definitive hosts) have strong teeth and jaws that can crush a mussel shell and they can be infected with this parasite when they eat mussels. Either the fish ingest the adult worms from the mussel and take on an infection that way, or they ingest larvae and they develop into adult worms in the fish. Either way the fish becomes infected. In a mussel this parasite, like the one in the fan worm, has orange pigments associated with its sporocysts and it imparts an orange color to an infected mussel's gills. The cercariae produced by these sporocysts are very different from those produced by the trematode in the fan worm. Rather than a long and forked tail these cercariae have a short stub of a tail, almost no tail at all. Through a microscope it should be no trouble to distinguish the two kinds of cercariae. When I got back out in the field again it should not be too difficult to examine some fan worms and blue mussels and see how common these parasites were on those pilings.

One of the first things I did that next summer (1976) was to take a look at some blue mussels and fan worms. About a week was taken up doing it. It was a lot of fun. I had studied parasites quite extensively, mostly with preserved specimens, but had not previously spent much time looking for live parasites. It took a while to develop methods for dissecting and examining mussels and fan worms. In fairly short order I was able to convince myself that these parasites were quite common on those pilings.

On a piling the fan worm usually existed in a vertically narrow skirt around the pole located below the band of mussels. Mussels occupied a wider band that covered most of the pole's mid to high intertidal zone. On a piling that band of mussels could cover two or three feet of vertical extent. I examined 40 mussels and found nine (22.5%) infected with the mussel parasite. I didn't see any adult trematodes, only sporocysts and cercariae in any of the nine infected mussels. Of 40 fan worms, 17 (42.5%) were infected with their parasite. I knew that trematodes might be pretty common around that pier. For example, the mud snail (*Ilyanassa obsoleta*) from the adjacent sand flat was pretty famous among aficionados for being a first host for a number of species of trematodes, but it was damned interesting that so many of the mussels and fan worms on those pilings were infected by their trematodes. I would have to look into this.

During the summer of 1976 there were a number of questions concerning the oyster drill that might have been addressed: for some examples, what did the drills feed on, mussels, fan worms, or something else; what explains the apparent favoritism of drills for the pilings toward the west side of the pier; how much do individual drills move around on a piling; do they ever change pilings; and how fast do they grow; how old are drills of various sizes; and how old the largest of drills on those pilings? Many questions about drills should be answered and might have occupied my time, but the parasites I had found so common were more intriguing to me because they were a new arena for research. Anyway, to parasites went my 1976 summer at Visitopolis University. I was initially interested in whether the parasites of one or both species were more common in their respective hosts on more offshore pilings. Marine fish were likely the definitive hosts of both parasites and the sources of fan worm and mussel infections. A fish host would obviously spend more time in the environment away from shore and be more likely to transmit an infection to an offshore mussel or fan worm. Consequently, farther offshore is where infected mussels and fan worms were most likely to be found. Is that actually the case?

However, I could not wade offshore much farther than piling row 50. I needed some kind of boat. I thought about that for a while and decided that a canoe would be the best sort of boat for getting in amongst and around those pilings. The wind blew pretty hard sometimes and I would have to be mindful of that danger. A canoe could be carried on a car and one person could load, unload and launch it, but my Datsun 2000 was not suitable for that job. It was getting older anyway and had to go. I really liked tooling around in that car, but needs are needs. I did the best I could trading it in and buying a used Ford pickup truck. That was much better as a research vehicle. I soon had a sturdy canoe. The $900 I had to put out for it hurt quite a bit, but it was all pretty much fun. I rigged the truck up to carry it. I bought a wrack for the truck that carried the canoe up over the pickup's bed and out over the roof. There were many knots and splices to devise and it was most interesting getting lines together to tie it securely down on my new vehicle.

The first time I tried to get offshore in the canoe to take samples, a strong wind was blowing out of the northwest. That put the west side of the pier off limits so I paddled out on the east side. It was somewhat more protected on that side of the pier, but in amongst the pilings, with the waves filtering through from the west, it was bumpy as hell and it was next to impossible to keep from getting upset. Taking a spill would be a real mishap. I had only done a little previous canoeing and I couldn't get safely close to pilings to take samples of mussels and fan worms. The bouncing canoe gunnels would have scraped too many fan worms and mussels and other things off the pilings. It was too rough to work and I quit. That day was a bust. I would have to find days with less wind to work offshore in deeper water effectively.

Some Success with a Research Problem: Seeds of Problems to Come 83

When I was able to choose better days and get samples I showed that mussel and fan worm parasites were indeed more frequent offshore. Before long I had examined 50 mussels and 50 fan worms from the offshore area beyond piling row 50. Of the mussels, 60% were infected with the mussel parasite. Of the fan worms, 71% were infected with that parasite. I checked with a statistical test and that represented a statistically significant increase for both parasites in offshore as opposed to nearer shore hosts. Besides that, it was obvious just by taking a quick look at the data. In parasite ecology, prevalence is the term used for the % of examined hosts bearing a parasite. Inshore to offshore, the prevalence of the parasite in fan worms had increased by 28.5%. The corresponding increase for the mussel parasite was 37.5%.

I was working at school in the section of the prep room adjacent to the lab I had taken over. There I had microscopes available to me. I was examining offshore mussels to see if they were parasitized. It was there I made a superbly interesting discovery, one that shook the world of this lonesome invertebrate zoologist. It turned out to be that key moment of discovery of which scientists sometimes speak. In one of the mussels I found a fan worm trematode infection. There could be no mistake about it. The sporocysts in this mussel were in the gills and had an orange color, which made me think at first that I was looking at a typical mussel parasite infection, but when I looked at some of the cercariae in the infection they had long, forked tails and there could be no doubt that they belonged to the fan worm trematode, *Cercaria loossi*. I looked very carefully to see if maybe both species, the mussel and the fan worm parasite, were present in that mussel, but no it was just the fan worm parasite. The fan worm parasite was infecting that mussel alone. After I regained my composure I went on to examine other mussels. Two days later I found another blue mussel in my offshore sample that was infected with the fan worm parasite. I made the same observations and got the same result. That mussel too was infected only by the fan worm parasite. In the literature *Cercaria loossi* had never been observed in a blue mussel. All by itself this was an important discovery, worthy of a publication, but in that moment how little I knew. It had been my practice to discard mussels and fan worms after examining them. Those two mussel bodies with their infections were separately committed to 70% ethyl alcohol with a label saying when and where I had found them. I had taken to looking at parasite stages alive. They move and are more expressive that way. The alcohol would kill and alter them some, but at least they would available for future observations.

I continued investigating those two parasite species for the rest of that summer. More inshore and offshore mussels and fan worms were collected. I wanted to see if the fan worm parasite could be found in other mussels and if the mussel parasite ever occurred in fan worms. Examination of an additional 200 mussels revealed that about 4% of mussels were parasitized by the fan worm trematode and always alone. So far the fan worm parasite had never co-occurred with the mussel parasite in a mussel. A look at 200 fan worms indicated that never does the mussel parasite parasitize fan worms. The greater chance of running into both of these parasites in offshore hosts was confirmed. The rest of the summer was pretty well used up checking 400 hosts for parasites by dissection. I had to teach Introductory Biology I and General Biology in the fall and I had to devote time to getting them ready to go. For general biology it would be the first time through and getting lectures ready would be very time consuming. That fall and winter I hoped I would have time to take some samples of mussels and fan worms to see if there was any pronounced seasonality to their infections. They were definitely there in the summer, but what about other times of the year?

Another thing I set up in the summer of 1976 was the better equipment necessary to eventually write the manuscript about the discovery of the fan worm parasite in the mussel. Of course, I had no money to buy what I needed, but the equipment was already present on campus. A fellow faculty member, Toby MacMurtry, was a microscopist and cellular anatomist. He had some very fine microscopes equipped with cameras and extensive photographic paraphernalia. I could draw the stages of the fan worm parasite when it occurred in the mussel, but photographic depictions would be a better way to go. The cercariae of *Cercaria loossi* are very different from the cercariae of *Protoeces maculatus* and good photographs would make the case beyond any doubt. Maybe drawings would be needed too. Whatever way that went, I needed access to better equipped microscopes than were available in my lab space and Toby said he was willing to help out in that department. He had the equipment and the knowledge of how to use it to get the results I desired. I recruited him by telling him of the data I had indicating a host-switch by the fan worm parasite. He was immediately interested and eager to help however he could. My manuscript on oyster drills was still in review and unaccepted so my research efforts were still quiet on that front. However, taking another faculty member into my confidence had inherent dangers with it. Obviously, my friend Sylvia already knew about my research efforts, but I could count on her not saying anything. If there was talk about my discovery among other faculty, it wouldn't be long before it got to administrators and my heretofore quiet research activities would be revealed. Well, I was not about to be quiet about my neat finding. They would find out soon enough anyway and the fun would begin. The one thing I had going for me was that this was Visitopolis University and administrators couldn't be too directly damning of research without sullying the reputation of the whole institution. However, they have ways to get what they want. I would have to be on my guard.

Well, the beginning of my third year at Visitopolis University was a full semester indeed. Keeping ahead of General Biology lectures took a lot of time and was a serious challenge because of the other things I had in progress. Prime among those things was mastering and using Toby's rather complicated microscopes and cameras. He was a great help in this process and I owe him. One piece of equipment he had was a camera lucida setup that could be used to essentially trace images seen through a microscope onto paper. I had used one of those only once before, in my undergraduate days. Now, it resulted in some pretty good drawings of the sporocysts and cercariae of the two species of parasites. You can get some features better depicted in a drawing than you can in any photograph. By the end of the semester I had gotten the needed photographs and drawings together and I could get started on my manuscript during winter session.

One other thing of note that happened during the fall semester in 1976 was a student that showed up in the Introductory Biology I course. Her name was Annie Hall. She had heard about the research I had underway from another student and approached me to express her interest in getting involved in some way in my research. Annie was a year or two older than most other students. She did very well on tests and was capable in the lab. Above all she demonstrated a real curiosity about things. She was a tall, slender girl, handsome rather than pretty, and looked fit. I told her that during the coming winter session I was planning to go out to my pier pilings to collect some mussels and fan worms to see what the state of their infections were in the winter months. She didn't know what might be in front of her, but readily agreed to help. I told her that I was not sure how my administrator bosses felt about my carrying on research and we would have to be circumspect about broadcasting to others what we were doing. We did not need to keep it a deep dark secret, only be somewhat circumspect about what we told others. She said that she understood and agreed to keep things quiet.

When that semester was over the winter session saw a start on my manuscript about those two parasites and the host-switch I had found. It wasn't that difficult to write or very long. I had only last summer's sampling to describe, the features of the two parasites, and above all the fact that I had found the fan worm trematode in the mussel for the first time. The photographs and drawings developed in the past semester made things straight forward. I thought an acknowledgment of Toby's help in doing that would be appropriate. I asked him if he wanted me to do that and he said yes. May he not attract any grief for his involvement.

As for me, that snarling cat would be out of the bag pretty soon anyway. Recently the reviews on the manuscript about oyster drills had come back. The journal accepted the manuscript, but pending many revisions. Reviewers were mostly griping about how I had chosen to present data. That was perhaps reasonable, but in any case would mean a lot of work. Nevertheless, it was a success and meant my third published paper would eventually come out because very rarely do journals ultimately turn down a manuscript once they have accepted it pending revision. I would have to get to work making the revisions soon just as soon as I finished my manuscript on parasites.

When the first day came for Annie and I to go and make a collection it was for December a beautiful day. There was little wind, the sun was out, and it was over 50 degrees. We took the canoe out to pilings well offshore and made a collection of mussels and fan worms. Annie was a good helper. She was cheerful, handled her end of the canoe well, and took pains to not damage any invertebrates living on the pilings with the gunnels of the boat. The conditions were very benign, but she handled herself well. The help was welcome.

We met in the lab the next day and began dissecting 20 mussels and 20 fan worms. I had a lot of practice at this, but it was all new to Annie. We first examined the mussels. They had to be measured and one of the shells removed. The next job was to search the exposed gill for the mussel parasite, or if we were lucky, maybe the fan worm parasite. This was done first with a dissecting microscope and then if any orange sporocysts were found, a section of gill was cut away and viewed through a compound microscope to look for cercariae. The fan worms were a little trickier. These are small worms inside a calcareous tube. A hole had to be broken in a tube quite a ways back of the worm. Then using a probe the worm could be gently forced back into the tube and out the hole. If the worm was infected, the parasite's sporocysts would be concentrated along the worm's ventral surface (which might be called the belly of the worm). It would be possible to examine a worm's belly with both sorts of microscopes. It took us a couple of days, but we got our 20 mussels and 20 fan worms examined. Results were that 50% of mussels were infected with something. We could not always be sure with what, undoubtedly most had the mussel parasite, but nine of them did not have any cercariae present in the infection to aid in the identification. We found one that had an active infection with the fan worm parasite. In that one there were fully formed and active fan worm parasite cercariae present. Among 20 fan worms we found 40% infected with the fan worm parasite and they all had cercariae present. Apparently in winter, the mussel parasite is present, but there are no active cercariae, while the fan worm parasite has active cercariae at all times of the year. If I wanted active mussel parasite cercariae, I would have to collect mussels in the spring, summer, and fall. I wanted to get at least one other winter sample. This, however, probably told me what I needed to know and was a good start.

Annie and I went out sampling one more time that winter session. It was only about half as bad as that first time I took the canoe out alone, but that was bad enough. We were able to get enough samples offshore for five specimens of each host. After that we quit the canoe and switched to taking samples from the inshore pilings where we could wade. Annie had purchased a pair of waders, but not being as tall as me she had to stay closer to shore. Anyway, we got enough for a total of 20 mussels and 20 fan worms and Annie got a little taste of how difficult sampling can sometimes be. She handled the bouncy offshore water in her usual cheerful way. I was thoroughly impressed with the way she went about things. When we examined our catch the results were about the same except that fewer of both mussels and fan worms were parasitized. When we were finished I thanked Annie for all her good help. After she got introduced to the methods she really made things go faster. She said, "I too enjoyed what we did and I thank you for giving me a chance to be involved first hand in research." I replied that maybe we could do more along these lines and mentioned that the oyster drill also had a trematode parasite. Maybe that was an avenue for further investigation, but right now both she and I had to get back to handling classes.

During that second semester of my third year at Visitopolis University I had to teach Introductory Biology II and Ecology. I had taught both before and had lectures mostly in hand. The labs, tests, and reports to read took a lot of time, but I was able to finish my parasite host-switching manuscript. It came out well and I sent it off to a parasitology journal. After sending it away, I worked on revisions for my accepted drill paper and fairly quickly got that sent back to the editor of that journal. Maybe I would not see that one again until the galley proofs showed up in the mail. I fervently hoped so.

When the summer of 1977 came along I had a question and a plan for answering it. The fan worm parasite sometimes switched to mussel hosts, but never had I found the very common mussel parasite in the same mussel with the fan worm parasite. Why was that? There must be some explanation. It could be that if the mussel parasite was already there in a mussel, it was impossible for some reason for the fan worm parasite to get an infection going. Alternatively, it could be that if a mussel was already parasitized by the mussel parasite, when a fan worm parasite came along and started an infection in that mussel it killed off the mussel parasite. How might I begin to find out what was involved? Well, as a start I could attempt to separate the infections from fan worms. To repeat myself a little, when a fan worm is infected by its parasite the infection is localized in the worm's belly. You can see a pretty definite orange strip along the worm's belly. If I could get enough infected worms, I could with some deft scalpel work separate that orange strip from enough worm hosts to get enough of the parasite into a blender. Upon blending, with any luck I would have a pretty concentrated fluid of parasite material and some associated host worm chemicals. I could then see what happens to an existing infection of the mussel parasite in a mussel when some of the blended fan worm parasite mixture is put on the mussel gill.

When I took this on I spent five days cutting that orange strip away from the bellies of fan worms from the offshore pilings. I put the infections from 30 worms in a container with some filtered sea water from the area of the pier. I refrigerated the collection while I worked on additional worms. When I had them all in there I blended the contents. So I had a fluid in the blender made up almost entirely of fan worm sporocysts and cercariae. Whatever chemicals the parasite had produced and whatever host chemicals were contributed by the infected worms were also included. I could add that fluid to an infected mussel's gill and see what happened.

The experiment, however, had to be a little more complicated than just that. If there was an effect on the mussel parasite when the blender fluid was added to it, it might have been caused by the fan worm parasite in the fluid, or by worm fragments that happened to be included in that fluid, or by something in the sea water used to dilute the fluid. I would have to put three types of fluid on three different infected mussels to be sure which fluid caused whatever effect was observed if any. I already had the concentrated fan worm parasite fluid from the blender. That would be one fluid to test. I would have to make up fluids that contained fragments of uninfected worms and a fluid of only sea water. These fluids would be incorporated in my experiment.

The experiment I initially set up involved six infected mussels. One of the valves was taken off these bivalves. With the gills exposed I then added fan worm parasite fluid to two of them, worm fragment fluid to another two, and filtered sea water to the remaining two. I observed through a dissecting microscope for any effect of the three fluids on the mussel parasite infections. The results were surprisingly clear cut. Almost immediately both infected mussels to which the blended fan worm parasite fluid had been added showed signs of a breakdown of the mussel parasite. Sporocysts and most clearly cercariae were rendered inactive. Within three hours the mussel parasite stages in those two mussels appeared broken down and dead. With both of the other fluids there was no visible effect on the mussel parasite. Clearly, the blended fan worm parasite fluid had a pronounced negative effect on the mussel parasite, but uninfected worm fragments or plain sea water did not. It would be unlikely that plain sea water would have a negative effect, but I had to be sure it didn't. There was, however, a chance that uninfected worm fragments might have an effect, but no. Only the fan worm parasite fluid had a negative effect on the mussel parasite.

Needless to say I was excited by this outcome. On the face of it this result explained why the mussel parasite never co-occurred in a mussel with the fan worm parasite. The strong suggestion was that if a fan worm parasite came along and got a fan worm infection started in an infected mussel, the mussel parasite was rapidly killed off. It could also be that the fan worm parasite sometimes infects an uninfected mussel and subsequently prevents the mussel parasite from infecting that mussel. Deciding which was the correct idea, or maybe both occur, would be the subject of future experiments. In any case, the fan worm parasite had a clear negative effect on the mussel parasite in a mussel. Right away I contacted Sylvia and Annie to tell them what happened. Sylvia was suitably impressed with the clear cut result, but she was busy working on her new book and couldn't come to fawn over me and celebrate right then. O.K., I can certainly understand that. I didn't want or need to take her away from her book. Annie, on the other hand, acted more like a scientist. She wanted to see it work and readily agreed to help out with a repeat experiment.

Being a local resident she was there at the pilings next day to get started. We had to collect mussels and worms to work with. We went out to offshore pilings because the odds were better there that any specimens collected there would be parasitized. We went back to the lab and set to work locating parasitized fan worms. With Annie's help we fairly quickly found enough to make up a new batch of fan worm parasite fluid. We then made up the uninfected fan worm fragment and sea water fluids. We then doubled the number of parasitized mussels to be observed to 12, four exposed to each fluid. With two of us working it was easier to get all this done. Annie to say the least was a very capable aid. We started the experiment and followed the fate of the mussel parasite under the influence of the three fluids. Results were identical to the first experiment, but this time four mussels rather than two were exposed to each of the three fluids. Annie, the first time she had seen anything like this, was alive with wonder. Poor girl, she was probably now hooked on science for life. My thought was that science was very lucky. As for me, I was very pleased to see it work again. This was confirmation and science is supposed to be repeatable.

When I talked to Sylvia in person and revisited the first experiment and told her what had happened with the second she congratulated me. From past conversations and a little fieldwork with me she knew the blue mussel in particular was a very widespread intertidal animal. It was eaten by humans and had some economic importance. Parasite infections were pretty common in this mussel and it probably would not be a good idea to eat raw mussels. She could see that this was a result that would clearly be of interest to people with an interest in the mussel, the fan worm, or the fan worm or mussel parasite. She thought this was definitely publishable.

Then by her demeanor Sylvia betrayed a bit of reservation. I asked her what the problem was. She said, "I have known you long enough to know that you, like me, have the drive and dedication to pursue actively your chosen field of study. Now you have a string of successes while here at this University. When the paper on this discovery comes out it will be number four, the second one done here. I have never mentioned this because I am not very proud of the way I handled it, but now I think I should."

Sylvia then went on to recap with me some of her dealings with Dean Terkel concerning her request for research support. After that she said, "Here's the thing I feel some urgency to tell you about. The reticence to encourage faculty involvement in research activities does not begin and end with Dean Terkel. Its root is higher up in the administration. Provost Jacob Flannery is absolutely committed to that policy." I asked her what had happened to her to make her not mention this before. She said, "My little campaign for support did not stop with Dean Terkel."

She had made an appointment to see the Provost in his office to make her pitch for support. When she went to the meeting and made her pitch, surprisingly he immediately responded that he had been advised that she was a troublemaker. He went on to tell her in no uncertain terms that he was not going to have faculty on this campus using up their academic energies on anything but teaching. That would be counter to his idea of the mission of this branch of the University and he would not have it. She should just back off. He could not do anything about what she did on her own time, but his campus would not encourage or support such faculty research efforts in any way. If she persisted in her requests, he would review very carefully her contract the next time it came up. Sylvia said that as he said this he made a quick move around his desk and got disturbingly close, faces only inches apart. Sylvia emotionally said to me, "I felt a physical threat. It was not explicit, but it was pretty plain and I wish I had been stronger. As it was, it was just the two of us in that room and I could not wait to get out of there. I maintained my composure well enough to say something feeble like

Some Success with a Research Problem: Seeds of Problems to Come 91

I'm sorry you feel that way and quickly made for the door out." When she finished I said, "Holy shit, he went that far! Not only had he threatened the job of an excellent teacher over this, he added a physical threat to it." For whatever reason, Flannery must indeed be committed to that policy. Either that or he is manifestly unstable and given to treating people like that. I let Sylvia know that I was troubled and sorry that had happened to her. There's no need for that kind of crap in an institution of higher learning.

She wished she had been better able to handle Provost Flannery's not so veiled threat, but at that moment she admitted to being intimidated. "That's why I don't talk at all about the incident." Sylvia is not a woman who is shy and retiring. She has probably more guts than I do about most things. The Provost's way of expressing his point was way out of line and he undoubtedly took her by surprise. I thanked her for telling me about her incident with the Provost. I wondered how many other faculty had occasion to be subjected to his intimidation. Sylvia was likely not the first. If she was right about what my discovery meant, and I thought she was, I had a confrontation coming with Jacob Flannery in the not too distant future and it was good to be forewarned about what might happen. She did not want talk about Flannery anymore and we quickly dismissed the matter, had a couple of beers to celebrate the experiments, and enjoyed each other's company for a while.

When that night was over Sylvia's experience gave me a lot to think about. The next morning over coffee I thought: what on earth could explain the Provost's attitude about research by the faculty here? It could derive from a higher up on the main campus whose bidding he was doing, but that would not explain his intimidating tactics. He seemed to be driven by something more personal. Maybe it was just that he had run this branch campus for a number of years with success by keeping faculty from pursuing research objectives. But, what if a faculty chose to do both and did not let their teaching duties slide. It's not as if the dissemination of knowledge and the discovery of knowledge are independent and opposing endeavors. A teacher who is careful about research, which you must be, is likely to be just as attentive to teaching. Discovering knowledge and it effect on students must not be underestimated. What is happening with Annie Hall is a good case in point. Why should he feel so strongly that he must put an utter stop to that intertwined benefit on "his" campus? It seems a very unlikely anti-research attitude for a university administrator to have. I couldn't answer the question, but concluded that he must be very angry about something.

That summer I made use of Annie's help to run another experiment like the one we had run before. It came out with exactly the same results. That's three times now that something in the fan worm parasite fluid had caused the demise of mussel parasite infections in mussels. I was busy writing the manuscript and added that third experiment to it. Before the end of the summer I had the manuscript finished and sent in to a parasitology journal. I had little doubt that this one would be accepted. In the last month of that summer word had come back that the oyster drill paper had gone to press. It would be out this coming fall (1977). That cat would be out of the bag and making itself known. Also, in the fall semester word was back from the parasitology journal where I had submitted the host-switching manuscript. They had accepted the manuscript. There were a few minor things to change in it, but not many. Could I be getting better at this? In any case, it wouldn't take much to get it fixed and back to the editor.

Classes were about to start. I quickly had to do what I had to do to get ready to teach Introductory Biology I and Invertebrate Zoology. The invertebrate course was fully enrolled and I was happy about that. I really hoped that it would go over well with students. It was 1977 and this fall semester would be the beginning of my fifth year at Visitopolis University. Sylvia and I both had the premonition that it would be a portentous year for me. I hoped it would not be disastrous.

Chapter 7

A DISCOVERY OF INTEREST TO MANKIND

The fall semester in 1977 was a strange one. Both courses I had to teach I had already taught several times. That meant I had past lectures from which to work and did not have to make them up from scratch. On top of that I had nothing pressing in the research area and no plans afoot. Annie Hall had finished up Biology I and II with an A in both courses. She had decided to stay on this campus for another semester to take Invertebrate Zoology. I was happy to have her take the course, but it was a non-major's course and she really should have gone on to the main campus and gotten on with her biology major. When I pleaded that case with her she said, "No, I want to do this. Before going, I want to take this course from you and further look into the trematode that infects *Urosalpinx cinerea*. Who knows what I might find." Well, that does say about all of it, the girl is irrevocably hooked on science. If she is going to love something, she could do worse. I told her that I would certainly help in any way I could. As for me, my devotion just now would be mostly to teaching.

My lectures for Biology had been in play for four years now and were due for updating. Biology does not stand still and neither can lectures on the subject. I took the opportunity to update and improve lectures as the course went along. This was the second time through for Invertebrate Zoology and I decided to update some of the labs to take a more experimental approach and do a little more with parasites. Both these options alone kept me busy during the semester. Early in the semester I managed to make the few needed repairs to the host-switching manuscript and sent it back to the editor. In due time the oyster drill paper came out. If the shit was going to hit the fan, that would be the start of it. I was not planning to hide its existence, but it would take a little time before administrators became aware of it. They were not that on top of things.

However, I did plan to submit a copy of the paper with my annual evaluation. A brief check by anyone would make it plain that the considerable amount of work involved had been done while here. This was not a paper based on work done elsewhere and would definitely signal that I had involved myself in ongoing research while I was employed at this branch of the University. Well, if it took that long, that would put any reaction off until winter session, or maybe even the spring semester. Anyway, nothing happened when the paper first appeared.

As she had foretold, during that fall semester (1977) when the weather was still warm Annie started looking into that parasite in the oyster drill. In my work with drills I had been careful to not disturb them from pilings, but to do what she wanted she had to collect oyster drills and dissect them. At first she just independently collected a few snails from pilings near shore. We got them in the lab and tried to figure out how to go about dissecting them. With a little deftness the shell could be cracked with a hammer and the pieces of shell removed from the snail's body. The naked body of the snail could then be observed for a trematode parasite. There was only one trematode known to infect the drill. It was *Parorchis avitus* and I will mostly refer to it as the drill parasite. The snail, the first host, was infected by a larval stage called a miracidium derived by fertilization from adult worms living in shorebird final hosts. The larval stages of the parasite we could expect to see in the drill were rediae and cercariae. Cercariae are produced inside the rediae and eventually escape from the snail to infect second hosts. Actually in this case there is no second host. Cercariae will encyst, as metacercariae, on any available hard substratum; shells of blue mussels are an example.

There were not that many drills on pilings so Annie collected only a few. We at first only dissected 10. We found none of them parasitized, but at least we had developed a method of dissection. Annie suggested we collect some drills from pilings farther offshore because they were more likely to be parasitized. I had no idea whether that was true, but it was as good a plan as any. The next weekend we planned to go out in the canoe and do just that. On the day we chose the wind was blowing out of the northwest and it was pretty wavy, but we were both experienced at this and decided to give it a try. Curiosity is the root of many mishaps. We really wanted to see if more drills were parasitized offshore and so began this adventure. We put the canoe in on the east side of the pier and made our way out. It was stable enough on that protected side of the pier. However, at the site where collections were to be made it was bouncy, dangerous work in amongst the pilings. Drills were pretty scarce where we were trying to collect them, but we were able to collect 22 drills and put them in a plastic bag. The intention was to get 25, but before we could do that a larger than usual wave came through and upset the canoe.

Annie was in the front and just got dumped into the water with no damage to her person. The water was not over her head, only about up to her neck, so she could touch bottom. On the other hand, I was right next to a piling at the time of upset. I had shorts on and the barnacles, mussels, and fan worm tubes on the piling scraped my thigh pretty severely as I went into the water. We were both sort of O.K., but I could see down in the water that my leg was bleeding. There was nothing for it except to right the canoe, gather what stuff we could, put it aboard in the deepish water still on the floor, and walk the canoe back to shore. Both of us were a bit used up when we got there. Annie had a great attitude about all this. I was glad she wasn't hurt. We had gotten the 22 collected snails into a plastic bag before the spill and the bag was retrieved. We got the snails on board and they made it back to shore. So the day wasn't a total loss. As I emerged from the water I could see that the side of my thigh was deeply and extensively scraped. The first thing I had to do was find a wrap to stop the flow of blood. I found an elastic bandage in the truck. After taking care of that we could then get the canoe emptied out and tied down on the truck. We then headed back to campus.

When we got there we put our 22 drills in a little seawater in a bucket to keep overnight. I needed to get off my leg and have time to get the wound cleaned up and we quit for the day. We agreed to meet at 10 A.M. the next day to see what we had collected. Late that afternoon when I got a chance to examine the scrape on my thigh, it was worse than I thought when I had just come out of the water. The scraped area was about eight inches running along the outside of my thigh and five inches wide. Further, there were a couple of places within it where a barnacle or something had cut in deep. It's not like the cuts were in close to the bone, but nevertheless it was a pretty serious wound. I avoided putting warm shower water on the wound. That would likely make it bleed, but I managed to get myself and the wound cleaned up. I put some antibiotic on the scraped area and wrapped it all up with some tightness. It felt pretty good at that point. When I got up the next morning the whole wound was stiff, sore, and throbbing. I put myself together and made it into campus to meet Annie. She was waiting outside Hartley Hall when I arrived.

I hobbled myself into the lab and we got busy doing dissections. Over about four hours we had dissected all 22 of the drills we had collected and only one of them was infected with the larval stages of the trematode we expected to find in that snail. We opined for a while on what this effort meant. My thought was that it is just possible that not many drills on those pilings are infected because shorebirds (e.g., gulls and terns) infected with that trematode don't spend much time around those pilings and the water is deep most of the time. Birds too would have to guard against injury from those pilings. Perhaps there is too much chance of injury if birds spend too much time bouncing around in amongst and around those pilings. The microscopic parasite larval stages that infect snails (once again called miracidia) had to exit from the bird host in the bird's feces and swim to a suitable snail host to infect it. That might be difficult with snails living on vertical poles in fairly deep water. Annie liked that hypothesis. She said, "If that is the case, then drills in a population living on intertidal rocks where gulls and terns can hang out for longer should be more often infected." The girl was really getting it. Her plan was to look around for a rock inlet or beach groin where she might find a population of drills to study. I had a couple of suggestions where she might look and she did in fact continue to look into parasitism of oyster drills during that fall semester. Interestingly, she recruited another student to help her out, one Timothy Holt, who was also in the ongoing Invertebrate Zoology course. Maybe something of broader significance is getting started here.

Anyway, work was done for the day. Annie had watched me moving around badly on my leg all day and admonished me to get that taken care of. My claim was that as soon as I got home I planned to do that. When I got home I took the wrap and bandage off. The wound did not look good and it appeared that some kind of infection was taking hold. I cleaned it, put more of the antibiotic on it, and more loosely wrapped it up again. The next morning the wound was still throbbing and it was difficult to get myself going. I had some laboratory setup to get done for this week's labs and made it into school. So there I was working on my lab setups and dealing with a very troublesome leg. It was definitely developing an infection. I was wearing shorts and in the lab and I took the bandage off. All the cuts and scrapes were inflamed and oozing pus. I washed the area and found something to cover it. This was going to be a problem.

I was finishing up and putting some things away in the refrigerator when I noticed a bottle about half full of the concentrated fan worm parasite fluid left over from the last experiment Annie and I had run this summer. I thought to myself, you don't suppose? Three times now that fluid had eliminated a parasite infection from an infected blue mussel. Could it possibly help my wound? The nature of the infection in my leg would of course be very different, that one being most likely caused by bacteria and the one in the mussel by a larval trematode. Could the fluid be harmful to me? I thought, well maybe, but things seem to be pretty bad anyway. The fluid had been blended, homogenized and sitting for three weeks in the refrigerator. There wouldn't be any living trematodes in the fluid, just chemicals from them. I figured it would not do any harm if I put some of the fluid on my wound, probably it would have no effect at all. I fussed around for a while and then made my decision. I would give it a try. I took the covering off the wound. I took a clean cloth and doused it in fluid from the bottle and swabbed the wounded area with it. At least the wound did not feel horribly worse. I put the fluid back in the refrigerator, covered the affected area again, and went on home. By the time I got there the throbbing of the wound was noticeably less. When I took the covering off the wound to officially wrap and bandage it the wound looked a lot better. It was only about two hours later, the wound was not so inflamed, and there was less pus than earlier that day. I bandaged it up again not doing anything to the wound except covering it. I had an early class the next day and would have no time to change the bandage in the morning.

That next morning I got up, put on long pants, ate breakfast out, and went to teach my classes. My leg felt good. The Biology I lecture went well and the Invertebrate Zoology one too. I saw Annie after that class and told her what I had done. She let loose a small epithet on me, but was glad I was feeling O.K. For the Biology lab that afternoon I had to run around a lot. It gave me almost no trouble, unlike what I expected. When I went home that night and removed the bandage I was amazed how good the wound looked. It didn't hurt at all, there was no pus, and the redness had all but disappeared. I replaced the bandage and very pleased with myself slept well that night. Next morning I felt very good and the wound had all but completely healed up, just a little evidence of a scraped area left.

I had not yet told Sylvia what had happened with Annie and me that weekend or what I had done to treat my wound the day before yesterday. So I called her to tell the tale and pass along the good news. She informed me that I was one crazy dude, but was very happy all had turned out well. She probably thought the outcome was some kind of accident.

I had a different idea. There was something in that parasite fluid that had healed my wound much faster and more completely than otherwise would have happened! If I accept that last statement as a hypothesis, I would need to somehow test it. With my resources the only way I could think of was to do an experiment on myself. I came up with something that would tell me if the fluid worked again to heal a wound, but it would involve some pain. Suppose I had a similar wound on both arms. I could treat the wound on the left arm with the fan worm parasite fluid and the wound on the right arm with the same antibiotic I had used at first on my thigh wound. Both wounds would ultimately heal, but I could make observations to see if the parasite fluid-treated wound healed faster and how much faster. Neither wound would be infested with bacteria from the pier pilings. They would nevertheless be wounds and I should be able to discern whether the one treated with the parasite fluid healed up faster. Within the next couple of days I had the materials and my courage together for the experiment. It was an evening at home. What I did was get two sterile scalpels ready. I picked up one with my left hand and put a two inch slice in the outside bicep area of my right arm. It wasn't horribly deep, but the blood flowed pretty freely. Maybe this wasn't such a good idea. The next cut would be even more difficult with the experience from the first. In spite of this, I managed to make a nearly identical cut in the left arm with the second scalpel. Blood flowed freely from that one too. I put a compress on both wounds to stop the bleeding and sop up the blood. With that done I swabbed the wound on my left arm with a cloth soaked in parasite fluid and the wound on my right arm with antibiotic. I had kept the parasite fluid cold as I brought it home and in the refrigerator once I got there because I did not know if warming it up might deactivate the fluid. I then put a bandage over both wounds. The weekend was in front of me with not much strenuous to do, I only had to work on some lectures and I could observe how these wounds healed.

The next day when I took the bandage off, the right arm wound was about the same as it was last night when I covered it. It was not bleeding and looked clean, but it was not healed. The left arm wound was virtually closed up and was definitely better healed. I applied the respective treatments to both wounds and bandaged them up again. I wrote down in a notebook what I had done and observed last night and this morning. I plied my craft with the lectures and left the bandages on all that day. The next day the wound of the left arm was closed and all but completely healed; the wound on the right was still clean, but not healed over. Clearly, the fan worm parasite fluid led to a faster healing of the wound on the left arm. I wrote these observations in my notebook. I wished I had a camera so I could take pictures, but I didn't have one. I treated and bandaged both wounds and went back to the lectures I was working on. The third day, which was a Monday, showed a continuation. The parasite fluid-treated wound was well healed now and the antibiotic-treated wound was O.K., clean and partly healed, but not completely closed. After writing these observations down, I thought, well, there it is again. That parasite fluid surely does speed wound healing in a human. I had no illusions that this was a definitive experiment, but it was pretty strong nevertheless. I at least was convinced.

What could be in the parasite fluid that would cause wounds to heal more quickly? It wasn't my area and I could not push the inquiry too far. It would require an analytical chemist to figure what was in the fluid. For starters, it could have been something inorganic or something organic. If it was inorganic, the causative atom, ion, or molecule would not contain carbon. The only carbon containing inorganic molecule is carbon dioxide (CO_2). If it was organic, the molecule would contain carbon and it might be some kind of amino acid, or maybe a small protein, or possibly a nucleic acid, fat, or carbohydrate. With some simple experiments I should be able to figure out what broad class of chemical compounds was involved in the action of the fluid on wounds. The fluid contained many things all blended together, bits of fan worm, parasite sporocysts and cercariae, plus any chemicals associated with any of those. When I tested it previously there was no effect of the fan worm only fluid on the mussel parasite so it is not likely from the fan worm. Rather, it likely came from the sporocysts and/or cercariae of the fan worm parasite. To really go after this and figure out what it was and why it worked would require a person with a laboratory and much more versed than I in biochemistry.

I had to think carefully about how I would handle this discovery. A major problem was it certainly went outside my usual realm of invertebrate zoology. My training and predilections did not equip me to follow this to its logical conclusion, whatever that was. To prove its worth would certainly involve testing on human subjects or at least rats, neither of which was I equipped to do. This sort of research I did not know how to do and quite frankly no desire to do. It would likely require the corroboration of a hospital. I would maybe have to collaborate somehow with someone who was into research on human medical problems and had the contacts to arrange such a series of tests. None of my biology colleagues on this campus would be of any aid in this way. I had not gotten to know any of the faculty in the Biology Department on the main campus, but I knew that several were involved in medical research. This would be a better bet and I would have to look further into that possibility.

First I wanted to let my two local confidants in on what had happened subsequent to the wound I had gotten in that unfortunate spill out among the pilings. Neither of them would be too pleased with what I had done, but since I had brought them along on everything so far they should know. When I told Annie she was sort of put off by my experiment. I showed her the two wound sites and she expressed amazement at how much better the parasite fluid-treated wound looked. Always the biology professor, I said, "Unexpected findings are the way research goes some of the time and this discovery will mean that things will change a lot. In your case, who knows what may come from your looking into that parasite of the oyster drill? I must admit that I am uncomfortably outside my area of expertise with this and into something potentially of importance to humankind." I didn't know how I felt about that. A discovery of great medical importance was never seen by me as being on my horizon. Being an invertebrate zoologist lays out a career of finding things out that are interesting, but usually to mankind only marginally important. Annie said, "I am honored to have been involved in this and I would like to know how you are going to handle it." I told her what I was now thinking, which was very preliminary. She said, "If you bring someone else in, it will indeed change your circumstances and I wish you well with that prospect." Here she was a sophomore in college and already she was getting a lesson in how a discovery could mean so much to your way of doing things. If my history had gotten me started on research at a comparable stage to Annie, it might have better prepared me for this. Well, we are where we are. After this little exchange Annie and I parted ways for the day.

I had a dinner date with Sylvia that night. It was a chance to tell her what had happened. She too was appalled at my experiment. I showed her the two wounds and the noticeably better condition of the one treated with parasite fluid. She said, "That sure is well healed compared to the other one. That's pretty striking!" I indicated to her that I would appreciate her thoughts on what I should do about recruiting a collaborator. She agreed that nothing in my history had prepared me for an eventuality such as this and a trustworthy, expert collaborator was probably a good idea. But, there would be dangers in that. She said, "If you were in a different position in terms of expertise and resources in medical research, I would suggest you to look into patenting your discovery. There could be a lot of money involved and it would be good if you got a big piece of it. However, you probably would prefer to make this free and open to everyone, as you have done with all your discoveries so far. In any case you would need a lot of help in developing this as a medical product."

She had been to the main campus some to use the library and had been to a couple of gatherings where some biology faculty were present. She had met one biologist there who, if he could not help me out himself, would maybe lead me to someone who could. His name was Frank Scarpitti. She talked with him for a while and he came off as an honorable guy involved in medical research. Sylvia could not claim to know him all that well, but that's how he came off. I thought that was a good lead and I thanked her very much for it and her thoughts on this whole deal. Sylvia had an organized mind of great quality. On pretty much the spur of the moment she had come up with a cogent assessment of the situation and a good suggestion. Aside from her other womanly qualities this was a valuable woman to know and I was thankful for her advice.

I checked up on Frank Scarpitti and some other faculty in the Biology Department on the main campus by looking at the short bios in the University catalog. At the time there was not a medical school as part of the University, but a number of faculty were involved in research along those lines. Scarpitti had discovered a drug a few years ago that he was currently still writing papers on. His drug had promise in the treatment of severe pain. He must have contacts with at least one or two hospitals to test and improve his drug. If true, that meant he would indeed be a good person to ask about who, where, and how to release the information about my parasite fluid wound healing potion. As hard as it would be on populations of *Eupomatus dianthus* and *Cercaria loossi* were it successful, I felt that the word should be gotten out and that if there was money to be made I should get some of it. But, above all I wanted credit for the discovery. This was a real rat's nest because I had no idea how to proceed and guarantee those things.

For the next few days I mulled over this tangle, trying to decide what to do. I needed a plan, but what I had been thinking of so far did not set all that well with me. The idea of finding someone to help me navigate the ins and outs of medical research and hospitals seemed to me like a road I did not want to travel. It sounded like I was trying to go into business and I had decided long ago I was not suited to that. Something Sylvia had said kept coming back to my mind: "However, you probably would prefer to make this free and open to everyone, as you have done with all your discoveries so far." Whatever money might be made I would probably end up getting screwed out of it and anyway that was not the main point for me, never had been. Credit for the discovery was. These thoughts led me to what to do. I decided to try and publish a short note laying out what I had found about the wound healing properties of the fan worm parasite fluid. I would stay away from medical journals for this purpose and go with a parasitology journal. It would be an unusual note in such a journal, but as far as I could go (no pictures) the evidence is strong and it is clearly a property of a parasite. At the least it should interest parasitologists and should be publishable in a parasitology journal. Upon successful publication I would be guaranteed credit for the discovery, which was mainly what I wanted. Of course, it would also mean that anyone who read my note could take my finding and develop it further in any way they want. That would certainly be a problem in terms of getting any money from the medical development and sale of the fan worm parasite's properties by a pharmaceutical company. Oh well, that wasn't my desire anyway and probably would be more troublesome to me than it was worth. Comparatively speaking, I did not have a lot on my plate this fall. I should be able to write up the note and get it sent to a journal in pretty short order. So, whatever the consequences that was the road I decided to travel.

As is true in general of notes in journals, this note wouldn't be very long. I had two procedures to describe. One was what I did with my leg wound. The other, more of an experiment, concerned my bit of self-mutilation and the healing of those wounds. It would be helpful if my host-switching manuscript were published before this note was subjected to judgment, but that paper was still in the hands of referees and an editor. I should be hearing pretty soon, but I didn't know just when. Maybe that would work out in time. In the note I could at least legitimately cite it as accepted. Without waiting on that unknown I launched into writing the manuscript. Working around my teaching duties and Annie's pursuit of the oyster drill parasite, it took about a month to get it finished.

The guts of the manuscript were simple enough. For the scrape on my leg there was not any comparison. It had just healed very fast. It took only about two days after treatment, much faster than any wound of that general sort I had previously experienced. My self-mutilation experiment at least had something to compare against, healing of the antibiotic- treated wound could be compared with healing of the parasite fluid-treated wound on the other arm. The fan worm parasite treated wound was healed within about one day while the one treated with antibiotic was clean, but still not completely healed after about four days. The overall conclusion was that the parasite fluid made the wound heal at least twice as fast. The data I had cost me considerably and I hoped I had enough to securely make that point. With my resources I could only wound myself so much and volunteers were unlikely. I was hoping readers would recognize that and the need for more experiments and data. Other experiments of various sorts would definitely be required to find out exactly what in the parasite fluid was causing the effect and its mechanism of action. That would undoubtedly be in someone else's hands. A note may be short, but this one took longer than I expected to get written because the sort of data and the nature of the experiment were so strange to me. It took a while to get it written down effectively without making me the center of it all.

In fiction, Jekyll experimented on himself and created the sinister Mr. Hyde, but in fact many physiologists have done that sort of thing. As an example in biology, there is the true story of a physiologist that wanted to see how effectively the human body could cool itself when subjected to very high temperature conditions. He went into a sauna along with his dog, a piece of steak, and a small container of water and allowed the temperature to rise to about 240° F. The water boiled, the steak started to cook, but he and the dog were

O.K., if kind of uncomfortable. As long as the humidity was kept low they were able to evaporate enough water in sweat and from their respiratory systems to remain relatively cool. Evaporating water, changing it from a liquid to a gas, carries away heat. So experimenting on yourself is not unheard of and I'm not the first.

In about a week's time I had typed the manuscript in final form, written my cover letter to the editor, and committed them to the mail. Sylvia and Annie both read the note beforehand. In effect, they each told me that it read very well so far as they were able to judge. They thought it told the story with precision and accuracy. Again, I needed their thoughts and was happy and thankful to have them. So with heart in mouth that manuscript was gone. May it be accepted. We would see what would be its fate.

Chapter 8

MY WORLD GETS SMEARED

Annie continued to work on the oyster drill parasite during the fall semester. She had looked around and found an intertidal rocky habitat where drills were fairly numerous. It was a jetty that stabilized an inlet in an estuary. Salinity was only a little lower than open sea water. She and her compatriot Timothy Holt had done three things. They collected 200 drills from the inlet habitat and 100 more drills from moderately offshore pilings. Then they dissected them to examine for trematode infections. I loaned them the canoe and my truck to collect from the pilings, admonishing them to be sure and choose good weather days. Timothy was a sensible, strapping sort of guy and I thought they would be O.K. They were. I did enough of the dissections with them to be convinced that they were both recognizing the parasite in drills correctly. Also, they had made observations in both habitats. They kept watch over two days (about 12 hours at each site) wherein they had kept track of how many times gulls and terns visited in the immediate vicinity (defined as within 3 m) of the pilings or rocks where drills were collected. Gulls and terns are the likely definitive hosts of *Parorchis avitus* and those birds would be the source of infections in drills. Furthermore, they had tabulated and analyzed their data in quite an expert way. Basically what they had discovered was that drills in the intertidal zone of the jetty were more often parasitized than drills from pilings. Prevalence figures were 31% from the jetty and 3% from the pilings. Observations of gulls and terns at the habitats indicated that in over the 24 daylight hours of observation there were 78 visitations around the jetty and only 5 in the vicinity of the pilings. The message was that more drills were parasitized around the jetty and this correlated with the greater visitation of gulls and terns around that jetty. Pretty damn cool! I was very impressed with the way they had both handled this investigation.

In the 1970s marine parasitology was still pretty much in its infancy. Not that many researching zoologists were doing it. I told Annie and Timothy that it was likely that this little study was publishable. Documenting a difference in parasite prevalence in two habitats and offering evidence of why it was that way were not all that common. Annie came back that she would like to try. She said with poise and certitude, "I would like to see a three author paper with me as first author, Timothy as second, and you as third." She obviously had been thinking about this. I said, "Sounds good to me, how about you Timothy?" He readily agreed and we all committed to make the attempt. Annie had to go to the main campus for the spring semester, but she and Timothy could make a good start writing this thing up in the first part of this winter session. Those two should have first crack at the writing. I would see if I could improve on it after that. I would hate to see Annie go, but she had to get up to the main campus to get on with her biology degree. Annie was clearly the one mostly responsible, but she would be one hell of a student on campus to recommend what this campus could produce. If the paper we intended to write got published, that would be doubly true.

The winter session began. As usual I did not agree to teach a course, but among the other things on my plate I had to assemble materials for my annual evaluation. There was a self-evaluation, analyzed student evaluations, and my recently published paper on oyster drills and pilings to submit. My self-evaluation was as usual excellent and I only mentioned the research I had been doing in a general sort of way. Administrators for some reason put a lot of weight on self-evaluations. My student evaluations continued to be laudatory. Several questions were asked, but the key ones had to do with how did the student like the professor and the course. With exception of a few disgruntled students, student answers on those questions ranged between the choices of good and excellent, mostly very good and excellent. So there wasn't any problem there. If there was going to be a problem, it would be caused by the copy of my drill paper. So far as I could tell no notice of that paper had yet been made by administrators. At least nothing had been said. Word had recently come back that the paper on utilization of both fan worms and blue mussels as hosts (the switching of hosts) by the fan worm parasite had gone to press. That was very good news because the killing off of the mussel parasite in a mussel, when the fan worm parasite invaded that mussel, was a necessary piece of information for the wound-healing note. When the host-switching paper came out it would only add to any problem administrators had with faculty engaging in research, but for now it was only the drill paper.

With regard to this evaluation my only contact with an administrator was with Dean Terkel. When I had my annual evaluation meeting with her early that winter session, she opened with, "I see that you have published a paper based on work you have done here at this branch of Visitopolis University." Well, that was getting right to the point. She went on, "We don't make a point in written policy of this, but you must be aware that we do not encourage that type of activity by faculty on this campus." I replied, "Yes, I am aware of that, but this is a university the purpose of which is the discovery and dissemination of knowledge." Without noting the point about universities she said, "But you nevertheless went ahead and chose to do a research project, now you have published a paper, and that could develop into a problem. I and other administrators are concerned that other faculty will begin doing the same thing and we don't want that. It would disrupt the workings of the place." I made my point again, "But it seemed appropriate in the context of a university. I was trained to do research and indicated an interest in that when I was hired, which I gather everyone ignored." "But, you were secretive about doing your research," she said. To which I replied, "Well, maybe a little. I did not make it a point to advertise, but it was far from being kept a dark secret. It was more that no administrator took the trouble to notice. Only a little inquiry amongst students would have revealed my research activities." Her repetitious reply sort of shut off our exchange, "Well maybe so, but we don't want faculty on this campus to be involved in research. Do you have other research under way?" Leaving the details out I said, "Yes, there is another paper accepted and another in review." She sort of grunted and said, "Well, this definitely could be a problem even though the rest of your evaluation is very good. Maybe you should change your attitude about doing research or think about getting a job elsewhere." I was afraid that threat would come up, but was surprised that Dean Terkel offered it.

After that, our meeting was over. It was plain that Dean Terkel did not want to discuss anything further. She had not brought Provost Flannery into her assault on research activities, but I knew he must have been a prime mover in the attitude she expressed. Maybe not right away, but soon enough I guessed he would be heard from. When I told Sylvia about my meeting with Dean Terkel and what had been said by her and by me, she agreed saying "While she is probably not the originator of the attitude, Dean Terkel should be a concern. She certainly backs the policy, but based on my history Provost Flannery is the real threat. He should be your main worry."

Sylvia had gotten her Revolutionary War book finished and sent it for review to the outfit that had agreed to publish it. How to go Sylvia! The way my situation came out could easily affect her job status as well, but she also took a principled stand on that. We were in solid, fast agreement that university faculty should be involved with some kind of research. The discovery of knowledge is key to what a university is for. A policy barring university faculty from doing research, for whatever reason, is simply out of place. One would think that administrators on this campus must be aware of that. Most of them were probably just backing their boss' attitude and not avidly in favor of it, but still they do find themselves having to promote an ill-founded policy concept, a house built on mushy sand. They were in an untenable position. That is what made them dangerous. If Provost Flannery was indeed the originator and main proponent of the no-faculty-involvement-in-research idea, what in hell was he thinking? What drove him to this? I was back to thinking that he must be very angry about something, but what? I decided I had better look into this man's history as best I could. Up to now there had been no reason to do that. Maybe I could get a clue to what angered him, even if not I would make myself better prepared in my dealings with him.

Only about a week after I last saw them, Annie and Timothy got back to me with a write up of their work on the oyster drill parasite. For them that must have been an intense week. They had now completed the invertebrate zoology course, each with a grade of A. I took their rendition of the work in hand and told them I would read it over right away. I wanted to have time to suggest changes and work on the manuscript particularly with Annie before she had to leave. Very soon she would have to set off to take up main campus life. Timothy was a freshman. He was going to switch his major from chemistry to biology and was going to take Introductory Biology II this spring semester. So he was a convert and would be around, at least for a while. Annie's recruit was a little crude in terms of language skills, but demonstrated a capability and a true interest in biology and research. I would be happy and rewarded to have him in Biology II. I was eager to see how my two collaborators, a college sophomore and a college freshman, did with this write up. I was predicting pretty well.

I read the manuscript that night. They had it typed and it wasn't very long, only nine pages double spaced. Its title was "Difference in prevalence of the trematode parasite *Parorchis avitus* in the oyster drill (Gastropoda) in two habitats." I thought that was a good title, pretty short and nicely descriptive. The Abstract was too long and detailed. Those are always tough to write, especially on your first attempt. They had some trouble with the Introduction because they weren't aware of all the pertinent literature concerning the discoverer of the parasite, the original describer of the snail, and recent papers on the ecology of the snail. I could fix those problems. Except for using some complicated verb tenses here and there, the Materials and Methods and Results sections were professionally done. They did need a statistical test to make the point that prevalence was not only different in the two habitats, but it was statistically significantly different. I could supply that. For authors at their stage of education they did remarkably well and I was very pleased. The Discussion again required familiarity with the literature. I would have to bring that to the writing. There were correctly no Acknowledgments, no one other than the authors to thank. Their handling of the References, both in the text and in the bibliography was rough, but that was to be expected.

After reading it, I began the revision that night. I added the pertinent references and the necessary content to the Introduction. That alone would make the manuscript read better in the eyes of editors and reviewers. The idea is to keep verb tenses in the simple present or past as much as possible and I went through and made those changes. It was late at night when I finished those projects and then I stopped. I didn't have any classes to teach just now and the next day would be time enough to work further on it.

Next day I applied a statistical test to the data, beefed up the Discussion, and fixed the problems with referencing. When the day ended the manuscript was in pretty good shape. I got a chance to spend a couple of hours typing up the revised version. I still wasn't very good at that. I called Annie and told her about the revision. She said she would contact Timothy and I said I would be on campus tomorrow and could give my revision to her then. She would look for me in the lab. Before hanging up I made it a point to compliment her and Timothy on a great job of writing the first draft. I said in closing, "You two made it easy to make changes. Nobody knows for sure, but I think this thing will end up published."

When I got to campus that next day there was a message waiting for me. One of Jacob Flannery's secretaries had called. I immediately phoned her back. It seemed he would like to see me in his office at 9:00 A.M. two days hence. Well, that didn't take long. It was only about half way through winter session. I quickly agreed to be there. If I was going to look into this man's history, I would not have much time to do it. I was envisioning how I would do that when Annie and Timothy showed up to pick up my revision of their first draft. I gave them my typed revision as well as their typed first draft version that had my own notes on it. Between the two versions they could figure out what I was suggesting and why. Both were oozing excitement, eager to see what changes I had suggested and made. I told them that they had done a very good job on the first draft. At that a sort of calm wafted over both their countenances. I explained that I had a meeting with Provost Flannery in a couple of days and it probably had to do with my published paper on oyster drills and my yearly evaluation. A few things had to be done before that meeting and I would be busy until after it. Timothy was not aware of the meaning of this meeting. Unless Annie had filled him in on some of the situation, to Timothy nothing would be portended. I guessed she hadn't. Annie, on the other hand, would realize that this could be a meeting with very serious consequences. I had not told her about Sylvia's experience with Flannery in his office, but she had a good sense of the administration's attitude toward faculty on this campus being involved in research. All she said before they left to begin work on the manuscript was, "What could he, the head administrator on this campus, want to talk with you about concerning the oyster drill paper? Maybe he just wants to compliment you on the effort it took. Maybe, but I somehow doubt it. Good luck."

I visited the library to see what I could learn about our fearless leader Jacob Flannery. There was a brochure with a quick rundown of the main administrators for this campus. That was a good place to start. I had dealt with a number of people in administrative positions, but the main two I was interested in were of course Jacob Flannery and Abigail Terkel. Flannery had been at the University for about 15 years. As a man in his late twenties he was hired as an assistant to the original provost on this branch. At that time it was only a few years after the formation of this campus. His discipline was in Political Science. He had his Ph.D. from a prestigious California university, but no mention was made of his having published anything. That was strange because other administrators had their publications listed. What was going on there? Shortly after being hired the original provost retired and Flannery was chosen to lead this branch as Provost. After ascending to that position he hired virtually all of the current administrators under him, including Abigail Terkel.

Except for that short meeting associated with my hiring three or four years ago I had only seen him at various official gatherings and never in a one on one situation. The rundown listed all he had accomplished in his time here and that was considerable. The branch had come a long way under his leadership and apparently he was to be complimented. A hobby was noted. It was in the Korean taekwando martial arts. I commented previously that he looked very fit. In his twenties, some 17 years ago, he had achieved a second degree black belt. He continued to maintain interest in the martial arts, which I found most illuminating given his look and demeanor. When I contacted Sylvia to ask if she knew about his interest and abilities in martial arts the answer was no. The lack of publications had struck her as strange too and quite naturally she had already looked into the reason for it.

Sylvia got this history from a friend of hers in the political science department at the university where Jacob Flannery obtained his Ph.D. Her friend was a graduate student there just after Flannery left and this was the story told about him. Apparently it all started with a rift between Flannery and his Ph.D. advisor. It was traditional in the department that the advisor would be given second author status on publications resulting from Ph.D. research. That is often the way the system works and for good reason. Certainly not always, but often enough a newly minted Ph.D. does not have enough personal guile to navigate the difficulties of getting his or her work published. I know about my own struggles in that regard. This would be particularly true in the case of the rarified, highest quality book and journal publishers that handled works from a place such as the one from which Flannery came. The guidance and influence of a mentor is usually needed to see it through. Well, Jacob decided to publish on his own. He wanted to publish a sole-authored book and decided his advisor was not needed. So he adapted his dissertation into book form and submitted it for publication. It was rejected and devastatingly hammered by editors and reviewers. One of their choice conclusions was reputed to be that it was "infantile." That is pretty harsh as criticisms go. Flannery was totally put off by the process of trying to get something published. He thought his treatment was too harsh and he gave it all up. It was terminal. He apparently never entered the publication arena again.

Of course, he never accepted the blame for his failure. He simply took the position, without any evidence and untrue, that his advisor was angry about not getting authorship and used her influence with the publisher to cause the book's rejection. In fact the advisor had published several books as a sole author and sometimes with other students. There was no need to do anything of the sort. She did not need authorship on Jacob's book to enhance her reputation and she simply stayed away from any aspect of the book's preparation, as was Flannery' desire. His advisor even said once that she had done nothing of which Jacob accused her. She was considered by students above such nonsense.

Once again I was indebted to Sylvia. This was real intelligence and I don't know how else I might have gotten it. It gave me a pretty good idea of why Provost Flannery might have been so down on scholarly activity and publishing. In fact, as far as I could determine not only had he never published a refereed article, he had not taught even one course in political science at Visitopolis University during his whole time here. His energies had been confined to administrative duties, including the suppression of research involvement by faculty members.

I looked around some more, but did not find anything else that might be pertinent to my coming interaction with the Provost. I was under the impression that I knew enough. He had a bad experience with trying to publish a book. He wrongly and mischievously blamed that on his advisor and was turned off by the whole business of scholarly activity and publication.

There was a day to kill before my meeting with Provost Flannery. There is no denying that I was a little anxious about it. I had Sylvia's experience in a similar situation in mind, but I wasn't concerned if he tried to intimidate me. He might try a modicum of that, but even if we were alone in there it probably would not get to anything actually physical in his office. True, he was a black belt in taekwando, but that would not likely come into play. How could he justify a physical fight with a faculty member in his office? I was without martial arts training, but I was more than 10 years younger than he, about equal in size, and pretty fit myself. Anyway, I wouldn't precipitate such a thing. I was more concerned with how I would defend myself verbally. I did have my point that a university has as its business the discovery *and* dissemination of knowledge. However, if he took the position that this was his campus and he didn't want faculty spending their time on anything but teaching, what could one say to that? Arguments about the mission of a university, the fact that my teaching record was good, and that I had not asked for anything to support my research, save using Hartley Hall Room 108a, would likely descend into ignominy because he would see them as beside the point. We would be arguing at cross purposes, *i.e.*, on different grounds. Dean Terkel had undoubtedly informed Provost Flannery that I had one more paper accepted (the one about host-switching by the fan worm parasite) and another in review (the one about the wound-healing properties of the fan worm parasite). He would just recognize those items as details presaging that there was coming trouble.

Of course, this all presumed that I understood why he wanted to have that meeting. Maybe I didn't. In the final analysis my thought on the coming meeting was that Provost Flannery had not specified an agenda and I couldn't predict how it would go. There were too many unknowns. I would just have to wait and see what developed and depend on my not inconsiderable intelligence to be able to handle whatever came along. I had a contract through the spring semester and at least he couldn't fire me on the spot. He probably wouldn't do that anyway, too much inconvenience for next semester's teaching schedule.

The day before the meeting I spent the whole day working on lectures at home. I did think about the next day some, but for the most part I kept that off my mind and stuck to building lectures. I decided I was prepared. I knew quite a bit about the situation and would just have to wait and see how it played out.

In the morning I rose at 6:00 A.M. and went to eat a breakfast of pancakes, bacon, coffee, and orange juice. I then drove to campus in my pickup truck. By 8:00 I was at my office desk. Because there was no stated agenda for the meeting there was nothing to bring with me. I spent a little time putting some things in order in my office. It was a 15 minute walk to Fleming Hall where the Provost had his office and I arrived there at about 8:55. As might have been expected I was kept waiting for about 10 minutes before the Provost made himself available. The secretary ushered me into the Provost's inner sanctum. He was sitting behind his huge desk apparently busy with some papers. When I came in he stood and thanked me for coming. The man did look fit. His secretary quickly left. Still standing he said, "This is your fourth year here and I haven't had any contact with you during that time. Perhaps I should have. By Dean Terkel I am informed that unknown to her you have been engaged in a research project. I understand that you have published three papers, the work for one of them done here, and two other papers are either accepted or in review." I acknowledged that was the case. He went on, "You probably know that on this campus we don't encourage such activity. Teachers are hired to teach and it has been profitably run that way for the 14 years I have been Provost." His silence called for a response and just to get it on the table I said, "Yes, I am aware that most faculty do confine themselves to teaching, but I am not aware of any written rules that prohibit a faculty member from involving himself in research matters. In fact, one would think a faculty member at a university might be expected to engage in the discovery of knowledge." His rejoinder was emphatic, but was a repetition of his initial point, "On this campus that is not the way we do things. Our primary mission is to teach and we want our faculty to stick to that."

I figured I would open things up and asked, "At most universities, including this University according to the course catalog, there is recognition of a synergistic, re-enforcing relationship between the dissemination of knowledge and its discovery. Why does this campus not agree with that?" I used the term "this campus" in that because he had not yet made it clear where the idea came from that faculty here only involve themselves with teaching. He could have shifted the responsibility away from himself, but he didn't do that and instead made his previous point once again, "Our campus has been a success because faculty emphasize teaching and we want to keep it that way." I silently thought to myself that if he couldn't do any better than to keep repeating himself, then maybe the negative responses editors and reviewers had given to his proposed book were entirely appropriate. I gave him an out from his loop, "What would you have me do? Am I supposed to pull my pending papers from any chance of being published?"

The Provost was still standing. He said, "No, I wouldn't go that far." I wasn't sure why he didn't say I should do that. Maybe he just didn't want me to be able to say that he wanted me to withdraw papers from publication. Then he did something that, because of Sylvia's experience, I half expected. His quick move around the desk was menacingly done. Had I not been forewarned, I would have been utterly surprised and probably unnerved, but I managed to meet his steely look with one of my own. I did not allow myself to back up even a little. There he was threateningly only inches from my face when he delivered his take home point for this meeting, "I want you to stop doing research and quit publishing papers. It is disruptive of the functioning of this campus. If you do not, we will have to review your contract to see if it should be renewed when it comes up next time, which is this summer." I was still meeting his glare, faces very close, when I said, "Well, I am surprised to hear a Provost of this University take that attitude. But, I will take it all under advisement and get back to you at some point with what I decide to do. I gather that what you will do is already decided. Now, are we done here?" To a degree I had managed to take control of the situation. When he nodded I took that to mean yes and I simply turned away, opened the office door, walked out, and quietly closed the door behind me. The secretary had a sign on her desk saying Gail Pratt. With a little smile I said goodbye to Gail using her first name and exited. It was 9:25.

Sylvia was obviously interested in what had happened and had ordered that I come see her immediately when my meeting was over. I went straight to the history department and into her office where she was seated behind her desk. It was about a 15 minute walk. After closing the door I related that the Provost had done about the same thing he did when you made your visit to his office. She was listening intently. He was prepared with information from Dean Terkel. The meeting only lasted for 10 or 15 minutes and he kept making but one point: he was in charge on this campus and he didn't want faculty to use their time for anything but teaching. At least he tacitly owned up to the idea being his. The last thing he did was to try to intimidate me, as he had you, by coming quickly around his desk and getting face to face with a threat to my job. The move was in my case, thanks to you, not totally unexpected. It was, however, effectively done. I wonder how many faculty he has used that move on. In any case, I managed to meet his probably practiced, cold, intense look without backing up. I saw a chance to take some control and said, "Are we done here?" His nod allowed me to end the meeting on my terms and I left. Sylvia said, "You will have to give me the moment to moment details, but it is interesting that he used the same ploy." With that I invited her out to get some coffee and maybe some lunch. She readily agreed to that and we left for a local eatery.

On the way I filled her in as best I could on the moment to moment. When we had settled into a booth and got some coffee she was very apparently thinking about something. She put it this way, "You know, when the Provost threatened my job, I quit pressing for any support for my research. I just stopped asking for it and went on with my scholarship as best I could. My book is near to seeing print, but even when it does it should not be much of an effrontery to Provost Flannery. There should not be much if any retribution. You, on the other hand, have this remarkable wound-healing paper in the offing. The chances of that becoming a noteworthy discovery are good. Also likely is you achieving a little fame as a result. This will mean real problems for Provost Flannery and his agenda." Her point that Flannery's 14 year push of no research by faculty was about to be upset was well stated and perceptive. I thought there would probably be severe actions taken by the Provost to preserve the status quo and they would be directed at me. Sylvia then said, "I like having you around this place and I would not like to see that end." I was very pleased with her having that sentiment, but I guessed that I better pay attention to the other thing she had said. I had not previously put the discovery of the human wound-healing properties of the fan worm parasite in that context and she was probably right about the consequences. The Provost would be challenged. As demonstrated in our meeting he may not be too clever, but in his 14 years as Provost of this campus he must have learned some nefarious administrative moves. I thought that Blake Turner would have to be very clever to keep his job, if that was even possible. At least I had gotten some experience and maybe it would not be so difficult to obtain another, maybe.

As was her way, once her point was made Sylvia went on to other things. She asked if I had heard anything about my wound-healing manuscript. "Not yet," I said. She also asked if I knew when the host-switching paper would be out. "That would probably be next month." There wasn't much more to be said about the big meeting and we ate some lunch and discussed other things. A notable topic had to do with something she had said earlier. I asked what the exact stage of her book was. She said she had just sent it to her publisher two days ago. They were going to look it over as a final check and, assuming everything was in order, get the type set and the book would be out in about six months. I knew how hard she had worked to accomplish this. It had been more than two years of work. This was the first I had heard that the book was all but finalized and I heartily congratulated her on that milestone. I wondered out loud why I wasn't more up to date on this topic. She said, "With all you have going on I didn't want to bother you." I rejoined, "It is not a bother and I am very interested to know what's going on with your research. So, please don't do that again." This would be her third book, quite an accomplishment especially considering the virtual secrecy under which she felt she had to work. You go special girl!

Neither of us got back to work that day. It was winter session and neither of us was teaching so we had time on our hands. We spent it as inspiringly as we knew how.

The next day I didn't go to campus, but I got in touch with Annie to find out if she and Timothy had gone over my revision. Boy had they and they were waiting for me to get in touch. They wanted to come to my place to have a discussion about what they had done. I knew that Annie had to soon depart for the main campus. She and a roommate had found an apartment to rent and needed to get settled in before spring classes began. I readily agreed to meet with them. They said it would take about 45 minutes or an hour for the two of them to get here. While waiting I looked over the original draft and my revision one more time. I wanted the details to be fresh in my mind for our discussion.

They arrived and I invited them in. I asked them if they wanted anything like coffee, tea, or a soft drink. Sort of in unison they indicated that coffee would be good so I got busy and made a pot. While it was perking they began to spread materials on the kitchen table. I got out three of my cups, which were all different, and some milk and sugar. I poured the coffees and they adulterated their cups the way they wanted. It was good to have this little introductory respite, but now I and they were ready to get going. All of us seated around the table, Timothy was first to speak.

> I ain't tryin' to take over our time in this meet with you Dr. Turner, but I've got somethin' I want to say. The two of you have stirred somethin' up in me. When I came to school this fall I wondered what I was doin' here. I'm only a freshman and have just recently finished an invertebrate zoology course for non-majors. I'm happy and amazed about the A I managed to get. Your class Dr. Turner for some reason I found it interestin' as all git out. I never knew there was so many kinds of organisms that even existed, never mind know anythin' about 'em. When Annie told me about what you were doin' outside class, that impressed me. Annie said she also was investigatin' somethin' and I asked if I could help her out on her project. Her yes got me really interested. I just wanted to start this session off by sayin' that both your roles in wakin' somethin' up in me have been very important to me. Havin' an interest in knowin' somethin' has never been somethin' I cared about. I can't tell you how good this all makes me feel.

He acknowledged that he had to practice that little speech to make sure he got it all out. I said, "Well, thank you. It does me a lot of good to hear it."

Annie then said, "I probably cannot top that, but I definitely feel the same way. Regardless of whether our little paper gets published, my dealings with you Dr. Turner, and you Timothy, have given me the chance to find something I really love. Biological science is just wonderful." To which I said, "Annie, you have done extremely well ever since you approached me wishing to get involved in some way with research. You have become more like a colleague than merely a student and I thank you for that. Now let's talk about what you guys think of my suggested revisions."

They had spent a lot of time over the past three days talking about this and were pretty much in agreement. They were appreciative of what I had done with the Abstract and the Introduction. They weren't aware that you should stick to simple present and past tenses and avoid gumming things up with such things as the pluperfect tenses. I congratulated them on knowing about those. The extra references in the Introduction made it more complete and read better. They didn't know about all those. The addition of the statistical test was particularly good. Neither one had taken a course in statistics yet and didn't really understand the test. I spent some time explaining how it worked to bring them up to speed as best I could. Anyway, the difference in parasite prevalence was statistically significant and they followed it was important to cleanly make that point in the Results. Both of them were happy about the changes I made to the referencing system. It wasn't at all clear to them how all that worked. The Discussion is always a tough section to write. They had hit the main points, but in a less than professional form. The two of them were pleased with the way I had changed it. Both had read a couple of scientific papers to get a better feel for how they were presented and both thought that this manuscript now read like a scientific paper. It was in good shape. I didn't expect them to offer much in the way of arguments about my revisions and they did not, but it was good to have it all pretty much settled. It was a short manuscript, just under 11 pages typed double spaced, but I thought it made a valuable point and stood a good chance of being published as a note by Hall, Holt, and Turner. We would see. I told them I too was happy with it, would type it up in clean form, and suggested an appropriate journal to try for. I should have it together over this weekend and they could read the final version on Monday, which shouldn't change much. On their approval we should be able to send it off early next week. It was about 2 hours after arrival that they left to go home in the pre-darkness. Both of them were obviously enthused.

I was done for a while, but later that night I started getting the final manuscript together. There I was with a typing job once again. I checked the instructions to authors for the journal I had chosen to see what format a note had to take. I followed those instructions carefully and began with the Title Page, then did the Abstract, and then quit. Tomorrow and Sunday would be time enough to get the Introduction, Materials and Methods, Results, Discussion, References, and the data Table done before Monday. It was a pretty full January weekend, but I did all that and wrote a cover letter. On Monday I could make copies for Annie and Timothy to read. I dearly hoped they would find no corrections necessary. If they didn't, we could get it in the mail right away. I better bring my typewriter along so we could fix things.

The lab saw me pretty early and Timothy was already there looking for me. I got him to make two copies for him and Annie. She showed up shortly thereafter and they both sat down in 108a Hartley Hall to read over the latest version. They found a couple of typos, which required retyping a couple of pages. That done, we could make additional copies plus three copies of the cover letter after we had all signed it. We would all need a copy of the manuscript and cover letter. The original typescript plus two copies would be sent to the journal along with the original of the cover letter. There was some fanfare getting all this done and my two coauthors then happily took it to the post office to mail it.

We were all pleased to see it go. On my treat we all met for lunch afterward to celebrate. Annie asked what had happened at my meeting with Provost Flannery. I decided to just tell them the truth, absent the implied physical threat, and indicated that the Provost wanted me to cease doing research and publishing papers. He said it disrupted the functioning of this campus and, if I didn't my job was in jeopardy. Both were appalled! I said we would see what happens, but obviously I wasn't going to do that. The discovery of knowledge was just too important to me and the University. Annie chimed in, "The Provost's attitude is pretty sick. Why would he have it?" I evaded an answer, but said that it was a good question to which I needed an answer. Sometimes administrators have strange ideas and motivations. Timothy was appropriately puzzled. Anyway, we went on to discuss how cool it was that we had just put a manuscript in the mail. I contributed, "The manuscript is very pleasing to me and whatever consequences flow from it good or bad, our proposed paper is worth them. My job seems secure at least through the spring. So we shall see what will happen."

Annie was due to leave in two days to head for the main campus. She said she would be back next summer and wanted to continue working on the trematode that infects the oyster drill. On the main campus they had an option for undergraduates to do a senior thesis and she was interested in taking that on.

At this time she didn't know precisely what the topic might be, but if we could come up with something having to do with the oyster drill and its trematode that would be wonderful. I told her that I would be thrilled to work something out with her. I would have to study up on what was involved in a senior thesis at Visitopolis University. That was never mentioned around this branch, but I'd advise her on one if I still had a job at this University come next fall. If not, she would have to find another faculty member to serve in that role. Whatever happened, it was a worthwhile goal for her. The three of us finished lunch and two days later she was gone.

Chapter 9

APOCALYPSE, THE SPRING SEMESTER OF YEAR FIVE AT VISITOPOLIS

In the spring of my fifth year as an Assistant Professor at Visitopolis University (1978) I was scheduled to teach Ecology and Biology II. I had taught both courses several times and they were pretty well in hand by now. New things always cropped up, but lectures and labs were sort of established and should not present insurmountable problems. Making up tests, grading them, and reports would as usual take a lot of time. It's not like the semester would be easy, they never are, but as far as teaching goes it should not be too difficult.

In terms of research I learned something from the literature that there was something I could do to clean up my experiment with the fan worm parasite as a cause of the demise of mussel parasite infections in infected mussels. What I had done so far in making up the fan worm parasite fluid was simply to excise the orange bands along the bellies of host worms where the infection in the worms was pretty well localized. Upon blending in filtered seawater I had a quite concentrated parasite fluid that killed off mussel parasite infections when placed on an infected mussel's gills. The problem was that this fluid did not only contain the fan worm parasite; it had bits of host worm in it as well. My scalpel work was not (could not be) that precise. A way to avoid this contamination with worm parts in my parasite fluid presented itself. In each segment of a fan worm there is a pair of genital ducts located in the belly of the worm by which sperm or eggs normally exit the worm. Fertilization occurred external to the worm in the surrounding seawater. If you get an infected fan worm out of its tube and put it in a dish of seawater, within moments sporocysts and cercariae of the parasite are extruded through the worm's genital ducts. The host worm is not damaged as this happens. Hundreds of sporocysts show up on the bottom of the dish. Before long cercariae begin to emerge from them.

If you think of an infected worm in its tube in nature, there is a tract of cilia along the outside of a worm's belly that are originally meant to propel eggs or sperm, but when sporocysts and cercariae are released from genital ducts they too are propelled by these cilia toward the mouth of the tube and to the outside. The freed cercariae can then encyst on any available hard substratum. In an uninfected worm these cilia are used to propel sperm or eggs out of the tube where fertilization takes place. Now there's an open question that might be answered: on what hard surfaces do cercariae usually settle? Presumably the fish definitive host becomes infected when they eat something (e.g., a mussel) with encysted cercariae (metacercariae) onboard.

Regardless of what hard surfaces are involved in nature, this gives me a means to make a "cleaner" parasite fluid. All I have to do is let infected worms release sporocysts (and cercariae) into a dish of seawater, gather masses of them up with a pipette, and then blend them all together to make an essentially pure parasite fluid. If when placed on an infected mussel gill, that fluid causes demise of the mussel infection, this would be a demonstration that it is indeed the fan worm parasite that caused the demise. I could exclude infected host worm fragments as causing the effect, or aiding it in some way. It would be a cleaner result. I would have to do this in the spring or maybe Annie could help next summer when she came back. I had some new ideas on what she might do for her thesis too. It is also possible that I could get Timothy to help. Who knows? Maybe another student would like to get involved. All this depends of course on whether or not I am terminated from my job.

I had not been thinking much about new approaches to research of late and it was good to get back to it. There's nothing like perusing the literature to get new questions and ideas. We can always improve on our experiments. My proposed experiment would mean, if it worked out as I expected, that even if it was still unknown what exactly it was in the fluid that caused the demise of the mussel parasite, and probably the wound healing effect, something specifically associated with the fan worm parasite caused it. That would be a step forward.

Well, the winter session was over now and spring classes were about to begin. This would be a semester that would perhaps change everything. It was possible, even probable, that it would be my last associated with this University. I wasn't about to quit doing research and if Provost Flannery's threat about my job was to be taken seriously, which it probably was, he would likely seek to not renew my contract. He clearly had the power to do that. I should start now looking for another position. I wasn't looking forward to that prospect. Pursuing a new job is always a real pain in the ass. The application process, the travel, and the interviews all take a lot of time, time that I couldn't devote to teaching and research. But, I had better swallow hard and get on with it. At least I had four publications to my credit now to give me some weight in the application process. The last manuscript, about wound healing was still being reviewed, if accepted it stood to make me much more marketable as a potential hire. This branch of our University actively discouraged research and publication and would rather not deal with them at all. Most colleges and universities felt otherwise. I started reading about open positions that seemed to fit my qualifications.

I found three possibilities. Involved in applying to these three institutions were the applications themselves, individual cover letters advertising my potential worth, copies of the three papers I had published to date, and arranging for three letters of recommendation. The amount of time spent doing this was far from incidental, but I got it done. I felt I was in better shape applying for jobs this time. I now had considerable teaching experience, three published papers, and one more in review. We would see what would happen.

If you are in all likelihood going to be terminated, a case could be made that you might let your teaching slide. I decided not to do that. Students deserve to be taught by someone who cares about his or her discipline and about their intellectual development. Not all of them return that caring by working hard and trying to learn, but they deserve it nevertheless. When classes started some inspiring students showed up in my classes. Apparently word had spread about my research activities. Several expressed an interest in getting involved with research. It was too early to tell how serious or good they were, but I was happy to see it. Most of the students in Biology II had been in Biology I. Timothy was an exception, but there he was. If he wound up being an author on a published paper, he would perhaps assume something of a heroic status among the other students. This would in all likelihood be an interesting semester.

The semester had only gone for a week when I got a very surprising phone call. It was an in personal call from Provost Flannery, in person mind you. I thought it strange that he didn't delegate to a secretary the making of any call to me. He was only briefly on the line that Thursday afternoon. The gist of it was that he thought maybe we had gotten off on the wrong foot in our recent meeting in his office and he would like to have another meeting in less formal circumstances. Would I be able to come to his residence tomorrow evening at 8:00 so we could talk? I answered, "Yes, I don't see why we couldn't do that." He said something like that's good, I will expect you at that time, and then hung up. I was surprised by his invitation. What further did he want to discuss?

Normally I would have contacted Sylvia to see what she thought about this development, but there was no opportunity to do that. She was away traveling to a weekend historical society meeting and would not be back until very late Sunday. In the end maybe that was fortunate, but right at the moment it meant that there was no one to talk with about this most unusual situation. Well, once again Flannery had not specified an agenda and there was no way to prepare. I would just have to go and see what he had in mind.

That Thursday night I had nothing in particular to do. There was a local bar that I frequented sometimes and I went there and had a few brews. They had a really good dark beer on tap that I liked a lot. I just sat there alone at the bar with my thoughts. I must admit that they weren't very exciting. I couldn't come up with anything new about the position I had sort of tacitly taken at the last meeting with the Provost. If he wanted to know what I planned to do about his ultimatum, that was simple and straightforward. I wasn't going to give up research and publishing, even if it cost me my job. Beyond that there wasn't much to consider. So fairly early that night, I left the bar. I had only the hint of a buzz on as I went home. I watched some television and then to bed. I slept very soundly.

The next day was that Friday and I was on campus in the afternoon polishing up the next week's lectures. I brought a sports coat, but didn't think I would need it. For an informal one-on-one session I figured that informal attire would do fine. I wore a sweater. He hadn't indicated that he was going to feed me so I went out and got something to eat before I went out to his place. It had been a warm day for the middle of February. Even when I went out to dinner it was still well over 50° out. At that time of year, it was getting dark as I drove out to the Provost's house. The only thing I knew about his abode was that he lived there alone. Previous to my employment there it was my understanding that he had a wife, but she had moved away years ago. I had no idea of what had transpired to bring that about.

The Provost's house was quite a few miles away from campus in the middle of quite a large tract of pine forest. As I approached the address I could see that Provost Flannery had done very well for himself while in his position at this Visitopolis University branch. There stood the house in a cleared patch in the forest. There were no neighbors apparent anywhere around. It was pretty dark when I pulled into the driveway. Had it been lighter I imagined that the surroundings of the house would have been very beautiful. The house itself was nestled into the encircling landscape. It looked as though it were placed there by nature rather than some architectural force. The drive went in from the road, wound around the house, and ended in back of the house away from the road in

Apocalypse, the Spring Semester of Year Five at Visitopolis

a large paved area where quite a number of cars could be parked. When I added my pickup truck, there were just two vehicles there. The Provost drove a Lincoln and I parked beside it on its right hand side. There were garage doors in front of me and what appeared to be a large deck delimited by railing about 15 feet above the pavement. It looked like a great place for a party.

As I was getting out of my truck the Provost appeared on the deck above me. He said, "There is a door immediately to your left. Come up the stairs and please come in." A lighted stairway was easy to navigate and the door at the end of it opened as I got to it. Standing at the door was the Provost. There was a kitchen off to my right. He invited me in and asked if I wanted something to drink. I said, "Just a beer if you have one." To which he said, "Yes, I've got one. As for me I don't drink much beer, I'll have a bourbon." He fished a beer out of the refrigerator, opened it, and asked if I wanted a glass. I told him no the bottle was fine and took the beer from him. He then poured himself one hell of a big bourbon. So there we were, drinks in hand when he said, "It's such a nice night out that I thought we might spend some time out on the deck." I responded, "Sounds good to me." He flipped some lights on out on the deck. A door from the kitchen led to it and out we went. It was a little chilly out on the deck, but we were both adequately dressed for that. When I entered the deck I could see lights of two neighboring houses on a hillside way off in the distance. They must have been in their own cleared patches of forest. I guessed that it was the plan of the neighborhood that residents would not be routinely bothered by neighbors. It was an attractive place. I liked the atmosphere. He told me a little about his home such as how many acres he owned and how long he had lived there. Interesting I thought, but I was impatient to know why he had asked me over here.

I asked him, "What did you have in mind for this occasion?" He said, "You are a good teacher and I wouldn't like to lose you as a faculty member on this campus. We arrived at an unnecessarily contentious point in our meeting in my office the other day. I thought it might be good to have another occasion to talk. Maybe we could end in a better agreement." I did not argue and simply replied, "I hope that is the case." I thought that he had so far been very gracious and maybe there is a cause for some hope. I went on to ask, "What sort of accommodation did you have in mind?" He came back, "Well, I won't back off the idea that faculty on this campus should be mostly concerned with teaching, but we might make an agreement that you could pursue some research and perhaps publish one paper per year." I replied, "For my own purposes the publication of a single paper per year might do, but there are other things in the works that involve other people. That might put a wrinkle in such a plan." I then described the wound-healing paper that was in review at present. If that got published, there stood to be a number of folks wanting to learn about that polychaete host and how to get at its parasite. Likely some research money would be coming my way that would open up other research avenues and possibly a little fame. It might be difficult to keep me limited to one paper per year. I also told of my two students, without mentioning their names, who had been first and second authors with me on a short paper that we had just submitted for review at a journal during the recent winter session. Those students were very enthused about research and were likely to go on with it. One had just gone up to the main campus as a sophomore and was considering taking on a senior thesis, with which I would help her if I still were employed here. These students had told other students what they were doing and there had been something of an upsurge this semester in student interest in involvement in research. Who knows what that could portend?

When I finished explaining those things he said, "Goodness, this has gotten much further than I suspected. I must tell you that I am not pleased. This campus has been run successfully for too many years on the basis of faculty confining themselves to teaching. To allow it to change now would be counterproductive." My rejoinder was, "Well, perhaps it is time to open things up for faculty and students."

With that little exchange the whole character of the evening became different. He was no longer so gracious and friendly. He took a more aggressive stance on everything. He did, however, offer me another beer, which I took. He had another bourbon. I then ventured, "One thing that has bothered me some is why you decided to essentially bar faculty, and therefore students, from research activities. It seems a waste of a lot of talent and training. Most faculty here have a Ph.D. and that is mainly a research degree." He then offered the excuse of having started that way and it being successful for these past 14 years. I then said, "But, you have a Ph.D. and must have been trained in the research tradition. Why would you turn your back on it now?" In retrospect I should probably not have brought that up. He answered shortly, "That's none of your business." I said, "I think it is because it is likely going to cost me my job." I, of course, thought I knew what the issue with him was, his failure to get his dissertation published and his harsh handling by reviewers and editors of his purported book to be.

I should have left it alone, but my job was at stake and there was a fire in me to find out for sure what was driving him. So I unwisely said, "I have noticed that you have never published anything, not even your dissertation, and moreover have not taught even one course in your subject area while at this

University. That certainly seems like someone who has purposely abandoned his academic discipline. You seem to derive comfort from being surrounded by faculty on this campus that don't publish much either." Apparently there I struck a nerve because he noticeably tensed up. He had probably not been challenged by a faculty member in that fashion ever. He had that cold look in his eye that I had seen before. It was obvious from his demeanor that he had been stung and was really pissed. I began to be wary of him.

It didn't take but a few moments for him to make a move on me. He didn't say anything. I was standing there on the deck about two or three feet in from the railing with my back to it. He was in sort of the middle of the deck. He let the glass fall from his hand, it broke on the deck, and he closed the distance between us with two steps. I dropped the almost empty beer bottle I was holding. As he stepped forward his right arm was being cocked for a punch. I didn't know exactly what he was doing, but I assumed it was some kind of taekwando move of which I knew he was capable. The punch came with its own momentum plus that of his forward movement. To get out of its way on my left leg I stepped forward toward him and a bit to my left. I ducked away from him some too. From boxing, with which I had a little experience, I managed to slip his punch and considering his training I was damn lucky to do it. Maybe his being pissed, or the big bourbons he drank, or maybe some lack of current practice had screwed up his movement. Anyway I managed to slip the punch. I further deflected his punch by pushing on his outstretched arm with my left hand and I grabbed his wrist with my right. I didn't so much block the punch as just helped it go on by. The railing had a two by six inch inward slanted top face to it. His forward momentum was not impeded at all by the railing. His upper body just kept going. The railing kicked his legs up to the rear and over he went. I regained my composure a little and stepped nearer the railing to look over. There he was to the left of my truck crumpled on the pavement, not moving in the dim light down there.

My first thought was to get down there to see what happened to him. So I moved quickly back into the kitchen and down the stairs I had come up. When I opened the door he was still lying in the same place. I went over and spoke to him. There was no response. I knelt next to him and felt for a pulse on a wrist. There was none detectable. I checked again. This time I felt directly for a heartbeat. He had none and had not moved even a little. It looked like he was dead. From the relative angle of his head and neck as he lay there, it looked like he had broken his neck in the fall. I left him right there as he lay. I was pretty shook up, but I decided I'd better call the police and went back upstairs to do that. I had picked up a phone that was on the kitchen wall when I had some reservation. What was I going to tell them? Why was I here? What had happened that caused this? I hung up the phone.

I gathered myself and thought about the situation. Obviously the right, correct, and supposedly safest thing to do was call the cops. My reservation about doing this was that it could be construed that I had a reason to kill him. After all, he had threatened to not renew my contract when it came up this summer. Who knows where it would take them, if the cops got on to that piece of information. And, they eventually would get on to it because I had told Sylvia, Annie, and Timothy about that threat. I had told nobody else and the threat itself had been made in the privacy of his office. Maybe he had recorded the conversation, but that seemed very unlikely. He didn't seem to operate that way and further a high administrator of the University would not want a threat of like that for that reason on the record. The University is supposed to support research. At least so it says in its catalog. He may have wanted me out for taking on a research project and publishing, but it wouldn't do for him to fire me for that reason. He would have to come up with some other sort of justification. Perhaps his secretary and Dean Terkel knew about his threat, but even if they knew, it was very probable that no one else was privy to what exactly he had in mind. He more likely needed to be secretive about such thoughts. It was only about three weeks since our office meeting and the process of not renewing my contract probably had not gone that far yet, if it had gone forward at all.

The other thing to think about was that as far as I knew nobody, except Jacob Flannery and me, knew I was here. He certainly wasn't talking. If I just left, then no one could make a connection between me and what happened here this night. Flannery strangely had made a personal invitation rather than delegating the task to a secretary. I had not had occasion to tell anybody that I was invited or planning to come. The Provost apparently wanted to have the two of us here alone. He probably did not have anything violent in mind for me. I mean if he was planning to kill me, he would not do it in his own house. I could not be absolutely sure, but most likely nobody other than the two of us knew we were going to meet here tonight. It's not as if I had a known, running relationship with the Provost except as a faculty member on this campus. Until recently he had ignored me and there would be no connection between me and him, other than that I was in fact here on this night, if I stayed and reported this. There would be no connection to be made if I just left. Not even a neighbor or passerby could have seen my truck. That's all true, assuming Flannery had not mentioned our planned meeting to someone. He likely did not, but that would be a major gamble.

Then I had reservations on my reservations. Maybe I'm treating this too much like a science problem. What if one of my assumptions is wrong? If I just left and the police found out I was here, how would I explain myself then? I didn't murder him. He was trying to punch me, I managed to slip it, and his own momentum carried him over the railing. Nevertheless, I sure would look guilty if I left. Only about fifteen minutes had passed since Flannery went over the railing. I would have to make up my mind just what I was going to do, and soon. It would have to be one way or the other. I was thinking reasonably clearly now. After a little further hemming and hawing I decided that the best thing to do was to just leave. Assuming I wasn't eventually arrested, I hoped I could live with what had happened. Once I had made up my mind I thought hard and carefully about everything I had touched since coming to the house. My fingerprints were not on file anywhere. I used a rag so I wouldn't leave any more fingerprints anywhere. I went out on the deck to retrieve the two unbroken beer bottles I had used. I left his broken glass where it lay. I wiped the bottles off and threw them in the trash. Somebody might wonder why they were clean, but maybe whoever put them there was fastidious. Anyway, the absence of fingerprints is not evidence. I wiped off the phone and the upper door knob I had used to go downstairs. The only other door handle I had touched, was downstairs in the driveway. I stood and pondered the room for a moment and decided no one would know I had been there.

I went downstairs and lightly wiped the inside and outside door handle to smear any prints there. Maybe someone had a glove on when the door handle was last used. I got in my truck and drove out of the driveway with my lights out. About 500 feet down the road I turned on my headlights. There was no traffic on that back country road. I drove back to campus and on down the road to my place. And so the die was cast.

It was on the radio and came out in the paper on Sunday that someone had discovered the body Saturday afternoon. There was no real reason to, but for a time I expected a visit from the police and I was apprehensive about that possibility. It never happened, but it gave me some anxious moments for a while. The person who found the body, a housekeeper/maid, called the police and they investigated. In the article in the paper they said that Provost Jacob Flannery of Visitopolis University was found dead in his driveway. He had been a leader at the University for 15 years. He had somehow fallen off his deck and broken his neck in the fall. The police had said it was apparently an accident though it was a mystery how it had happened. There was no indication of foul play. They concluded that he was home alone and late in the day Friday he had somehow fallen off his deck. That was true enough and if the police left their thinking that way, I should be O.K.

The second in command in the administration, Associate Provost Joseph Bigelow, had risen to the occasion and expressed his sorrow at the death of Provost Flannery. The essence of his comments in the paper were that we are now bereft of a fine leader of this branch of the University and it would be difficult to get along without him, but we would strive to have things go on pretty much as usual. Next week there would be a memorial service at such and such a church in town. If everything stayed that way, and I could keep my cool and strike the appropriate pose, things should work out well. That pose should be that I was sorry, had never dealt with him much, and wondered what could have happened.

How would I handle the three or four people who knew that the dead Provost had threatened to fire me? Dean Terkel probably knew and certainly Sylvia, Annie, and Timothy knew. As long as they didn't know that I had a meeting with him on the night he died, even these people would not associate me with his death. Still, they did know that I had a major confrontation underway with the Provost. I didn't care about Dean Terkel, but I really hated to be less than honest with any of the others. It was necessary not to let on about that meeting, as that would be bad for me and further would embroil them in the whole mess. I decided that the best way to handle this would be to be puzzled about what had gone on at the Provost's house when he died. I could only hope that Joseph Bigelow was not kept informed of Flannery's problem with me. He would probably at least temporarily take over the deceased Provost's duties.

I thought it might be good to be on campus that Monday. No classes were on my schedule, but I wouldn't want anyone to think that I was for some reason avoiding the place. Besides, I wanted to see Sylvia. She should be back by now. That morning I traveled to campus and spent some time organizing the next day's lectures. I ran into Toby MacMurtry in a hallway and we exchanged a few words about the Provost and how strange that was, but that was it. Then I went over to Sylvia's office. She was there busily working on something. This would be the first occasion when I had to maybe talk in depth about the events of this weekend. I was worried about whether I would betray anything about my personal involvement. Especially with Sylvia there was reason to worry. She was very perceptive and would pick up on any unease on my part. Besides, I had always been utterly honest with her. But, I had to just leave out anything about my visit to the Provost's house. This would be a test. I comforted myself by thinking that if I ever became engaged to her I would tell her what happened.

She looked up and started right in by noting, "The Provost's untimely demise might lead to a change for the better around here. Maybe the new leadership that comes in will begin to recognize the value of scholarship activities on the part faculty." To which I said, "Hi, nice to see you again. How was your trip? And, I agree. That might be one benefit of this development." Sylvia went on to say, "Not only that, but it might be good for you keeping your job here. If Flannery didn't put into official motion not renewing your contract, which in all likelihood he did not do yet, it is not likely that there would be anyone to take up that cudgel. Maybe Abigail Terkel, but I doubt it. You might be free and clear of the threat. I hope so." Clearly, she did not mourn the Provost's passing. Why should she?

Sylvia was newly alive with strategy items. What they all boiled down to was that we should not lose this opportunity to open up possibilities for faculty to take on research/scholarship projects. Most of them have not recently been so engaged and there would be considerable momentum to overcome, but some would take up the challenge if they were encouraged to do so. She particularly liked the model I had going with Annie and Timothy. The idea of undergraduate students being involved in the publication of books and articles was indeed very promising. She really hoped that manuscript we had submitted would be a success. If they are willing to work, she could not imagine a more maturing thing for students to do. It could change the whole atmosphere around here. Published students would gain a respect for how difficult it is to discover new knowledge and the amount of work it takes. They would also come to understand the risk you take when you go public with a piece of work. Sylvia was absolutely renewed by this new opportunity and I was happy to see it. The idea of faculty being encouraged to do research on this campus was grist for her mill. Not small of importance, her reaction to the Provosts death made it unnecessary for me to hide anything from her. There was no reason she would suspect my involvement, but I did not want to be explaining what I was doing last Friday night.

Still, maybe her idea that this was an opportunity for the whole campus was the right one. Maybe the events of last Friday night were not so apocalyptic after all and her way was the right way to look at it. I had reasons for being otherwise concerned, but the Provost's attitude, which he had twice expressed to me, must have been the main driving force behind the exclusion of research by faculty. That had made the environment on this campus what it is. His absence stood to allow things to be different. When a new Ph.D. is hired that person is trained to do research of some type and usually there is an interest in a developed area to pursue. All that is required is an atmosphere in which that knowledge can be gained. It would be nice if the pursuit could be given monetary support, but that is not essential.

The discovery of knowledge is akin to pine tree reproduction. A male pine cone casts pollen about on the wind and with luck female pine cones will be pollinated and ultimately its eggs will be fertilized. With time, two or three years, that female cone will open up and spread seeds to generate a rebirth. It tends to be a leisurely process and must be given time, but it works. Especially if there is a population of Ph.D. equipped people around, that rebirth of new knowledge will naturally happen. It would not be a good idea for me to lead such a campaign, but this would be a worthy cause to take up. If she will have me, perhaps I could join in Sylvia's plans. She would be a great leader to follow in such an endeavor.

Chapter 10

THE UNIVERSITY'S LOCAL BRANCH GETS UNDER WAY ANEW

Well, here it was only about three weeks into the spring semester and the place was rife with new options. Admittedly they were mostly in Sylvia's head, but this was her new cause. She couldn't stop talking about it. Every time I saw her new plans, new strategies were what she was thinking about and the topics of our conversations. Even before I got my job here, four or five years ago now, Sylvia had been agitating for faculty not being barred from pursuing their research interests. So this was not a new cause with her, but now she could see a path to follow. And follow it she would. She had shown, as had I, that a faculty member could pursue scholarship with very few resources. My experience with Annie and Timothy had demonstrated that even freshman and sophomore undergraduate students can be profitably and meaningfully involved in the search for new knowledge. Not only faculty members benefit, but the students as well. Students are smarter than even they think they are. Seeking the answer to a question, whether in science or some other area, wakes up a student's intellect. They may need guidance, but all you have to do is let it loose and they mature quickly.

Sylvia was thinking way ahead. Way ahead of me for a distance I had not even considered. As I have already pointed out this branch of the University operated about 200 miles distant from the main campus. The students here were mostly freshmen and sophomores. They could not afford to stay much longer because very few upper level courses were offered here and they would get way behind in completing requirements for their major. Anyway, only about this far had I thought: if we could let loose the discovery-of-knowledge genii and begin to develop some of that on this campus, we could begin to offer more advanced courses and this would become a University branch that would serve students and the community hereabouts much better than it currently does.

Sylvia started there and went on. For this campus to grow, she thought the faculty are the best place to start. Administrators had been steeped in the tradition of Provost Flannery too long to work from that quarter. No, the place to start was with the faculty. They all had a research background, if not at the Ph.D. level, then at the Masters level. They either currently have an interest in research and discovering knowledge, or had it once. Either way most of them would be at least open to the idea. Many had not actively pursued new knowledge for a long time and it would be important not to threaten them in any way. No one would be forced into research if they wanted nothing to do with it, but anyone who was interested would be encouraged and to the degree possible helped in their efforts. This would take time to get off the ground and you would have to allow for that. Sylvia said, "As a first move we should try to get most of the faculty to vote in favor of allowing faculty members to undertake research if they so choose." I said in response, "You know, biology faculty will be a cases in point. I of course would be all for your proposition, one enthusiastic yes vote. I suspect that Toby, based on his interest and involvement in my host-switching paper, would be a yes vote. Eric on the other hand might not vote yes. As far as I know he has not even thought about doing research for many years. But, maybe he will surprise us." I told Sylvia that I agreed with her that the faculty were the place to start and that I would assist her in getting this vote taken. If we can go to the administration with a nearly unanimous faculty vote they will be hard pressed to just dismiss it.

Votes would have to be as lined up beforehand as much as possible so we have a pretty good idea of how it will come out. If it looked like most everyone would vote to keep things as they are, we would have to rethink our efforts. I volunteered to approach biology faculty as well as Dexter Mublai (English) and John Landsby (Economics). I had maintained a friendly relationship with both these guys since coming here. Sylvia thought we had better develop a list of all faculty and which of us was going to approach whom. We would not like to leave anybody out. She was better than yours truly at that kind of organizational thing.

Pretty quickly we had the faculty divided up between us. In all there were about 15 each. The pitch to them would be that: we are University faculty members and there is currently an unwritten policy on this campus that discourages faculty research and prevents any support for it. Would you contribute to a faculty vote on that issue? We, Sylvia and I, believe that such a ban on faculty is inappropriate in a university setting. Removal of that discouragement would open up new possibilities for this campus. Once the vote is taken we plan to submit the vote results to the administration. And lastly, would you as a faculty member likely vote to remove the ban on faculty research or would you vote to keep it in effect? We could embellish as called for and needed, but that would be the basic question. Sylvia and I thought it best to wait three weeks or a month before calling for a vote. There was no escaping that this would not have been an issue to promote were the former Provost still alive, but we didn't want it to seem too much as if we were taking advantage of his death, which of course we were.

The semester went on ahead. Joseph Bigelow was in fact installed as the temporary new Provost. He kept things running pretty much without a hitch. There would be an official search for a new Provost within the next year. I for one had few doubts that Bigelow would be a candidate for the permanent position. That might be good or bad. I didn't know much about him and we would have to see if he was a better leader than Flannery had been. Anyway, for the next year or so he would be the person in charge.

About a month later Sylvia and I began talking to individual faculty members about removing the ban on faculty research. I talked to 14 and only three indicated that they would probably vote to keep things as they are now. Sylvia conferred with 15 and only two of them indicated the same thing about their votes. The sort of common feeling about the issue was that it would be difficult to start thinking about research again and beginning to execute those thoughts would be particularly difficult, but certainly faculty should be allowed to do it and some support would be helpful. So, our preliminary results were 24 to remove the administrative ban on faculty research and five to keep it. That was pretty good so far. Interestingly, Eric Mortimer and John Landsby were both yes votes. When I talked to him Eric even mentioned that when he got here about eight years ago he attempted to begin a research project in genetics, but Provost Flannery had said he might lose his job if he persisted. The biology faculty member that I replaced apparently was put in the same circumstance and that was why he left. Eric said this wasn't a bad job, but he had been a little dispirited since Flannery had told him what the situation was. It was decidedly interesting to me that Flannery had been actively persecuting faculty research for a long time. Those make four faculty, Eric, another biology person, now me, and let's not forget Sylvia, that had their research efforts suppressed by the former Provost. I wondered if there were others. It seemed probable. In any case we now had the likelihood of a strong faculty vote to set up a different environment around here.

Of the three job applications I had sent out one had produced a response. A university on the east coast, but south of here, wanted to interview me. Usually that means that you are one of three applicants they chose to interview. It is far from a guarantee of a job, but it means your odds are quite good. At the present University, and by the standards of university professors, I was by now making a good salary. All this semester not a word had been said by anyone about the possibility of my contract not being renewed, even Dean Terkel was silent. Maybe that cudgel was indeed now gone. And, I was getting more comfortable with what had happened. It appeared that my just leaving Flannery's house without reporting the events there was not going to be found out. Was I to have to, that would be difficult to explain, but apparently I wouldn't have to. It was now into April and about a month and a half had gone by with no questions being asked of me about that night. I just wasn't associated with the Provost's death. I did not accept the interview that I had been offered. I felt that seeking a new job was a drag and if everything stayed the same I would stay in my present position for at least a couple more years.

In my fifth academic year here it was about time when I should think about going up for promotion from Assistant to Associate Professor. At universities promotion to Associate Professor usually carries tenure with it, but on this campus tenure was not made available to faculty. Faculty did get promoted to Associate Professorships on this campus, but without tenure and not too often. The promotion procedure at this University meant that your credentials had to be judged by committees on the main campus. Even if a candidate for promotion wasn't going to be awarded tenure, on campus people expected to see in your dossier evidence of teaching, *research* and service done while hired here. Obviously, candidates for promotion from this campus couldn't often provide evidence of research and it was difficult, but not impossible, to get promoted beyond Assistant Professor. Sylvia Armbruster was an untenured Associate Professor. She had managed to get the promotion two years ago based on her excellent teaching, the two books she had out at that time, and some committee work she had done. Both Sylvia and I thought it would be beneficial to have another person from this campus go up for promotion and actually have extensive evidence of local research activity. Maybe down the road we could get tenure available to our faculty, but for that faculty would need to be doing research.

About a month and a half into the semester Sylvia made up a ballot and we sent it out to all local faculty. The vote question was: do you want the administration to encourage and as possible support faculty research, or do you want it continued to be disallowed? Faculty members voted anonymously, but we kept track of what faculty had voted. The ballot was out for a week and after prompting a few faculty to return it we got the results back in. There were 29 ballots returned and the vote was 26 to allow faculty research and three to keep the ban in place. That was even two better than our preliminary counting. Apparently on consideration two people had seen the light. We now had the ballots as evidence that the majority of faculty no longer wanted the administration to discourage faculty research. Undoubtedly, through the grapevine the administration would have heard about the vote being taken. How would it be received?

Sylvia and I produced a letter to Joseph Bigelow stating the results of the vote. We secreted away the originals and enclosed copies of the ballots. We both signed the letter and sent it. Now, all we could do was wait for a reply.

At about this time the host-switching paper came out in print. As these things go there was a lot of response. I had purchased, with my own money, 250 reprints of the article. Some 200 post cards and letters came in requesting copies of it and I sent those out. My mailbox was very active for a while. I was happy to let the University pay for most of the postage. This was the greatest response to any of my papers so far. I found that rewarding. About two weeks after that word came back from the parasitology journal to which I had submitted the wound-healing manuscript. The referees and editor had some reservations, as they should, but they decided to accept it. Their general statement was that this needs further work, with which I wholeheartedly agreed, but if this parasite can somehow actually aid in the healing of wounds, this would be a very important discovery. There is ample evidence presented to strongly suggest that is the case. They accepted the manuscript without change, which was by my lights nothing short of amazing. The note would be published in the next issue of the journal this summer. I wondered if the publication of the host-switching paper had anything to do with this positive decision. Well, whatever. Anyway, I thought this was definitely good. When I assembled my promotion dossier this summer to hand in during the fall semester, the beginning of my sixth year, I would have five published papers with which to credit myself, the two based on my dissertation, the drill paper, the host-switching paper, and the wound-healing note. If the manuscript written by Annie, Timothy, and myself came through by then, that would be more frosting on an already tasty cake.

The semester was about over and the weather was getting nicer. I wanted to follow up on the piece of information I had discovered in the library at the very beginning of this semester. This involved a cleaner way to run the experiments on the demise of mussel parasites when a fan worm parasite fluid was added to an infected mussel's gill. Recall that sporocysts and cercariae of the fan worm parasite are naturally extruded though the genital ducts of the host worm when the infected worm is removed from its tube and placed in a dish of seawater. These parasite stages can then be gathered with a pipette without contaminating them with fragments of the host worm. If when blended this pure parasite material caused the demise of mussel parasite infections, as had the cruder blended parasite fluid used previously, which contained host worm fragments, we would know for sure that bits of host worm in the original parasite fluid were not the cause. But, something else could be shown. What if I never blended the fluid containing the isolated and purer sporocysts and cercariae? Would the live, intact fan worm parasite stages bring about the demise of mussel parasite infections, or did the fluid have to be blended? If blending was not necessary, then whatever chemicals were involved in the demise of mussel parasite infections were released naturally from live, intact fan worm parasite sporocysts and/or cercariae. It would be important to know if blending were necessary. To do the required experiments, fan worms infected with *Cercaria loossi* would have to be collected, as would blue mussels infected with *Protoeces maculatus*.

I contacted Timothy and explained to him what I needed and wanted to do for this project. He understood quickly. Would he like to help with the collections and running the experiments? He enthusiastically answered he would be more than happy to do that. In fact, he had been hoping there was some research project that he could take part in this summer. He missed it. Also, he mentioned a friend of his, Toby Gillus. He had been talking to Toby about the manuscript he had submitted with Annie and me. Toby was actively interested in becoming involved in research. Could he help us as well? I knew his friend. He was one of the black kids in class, a good student who had been in Biology I and now II. He had earned a B and an A in those courses. Timothy had also gotten an A in Biology II. I thought we could use Toby's help and agreed to bring him in. I warned Timothy that the both of them would have to expect to go slowly until I could be sure that they were both up to speed on the necessary procedures. He readily agreed. Annie was due home for the summer pretty soon. If she got back in time, having done the experiments with the cruder parasite fluid with me, she could help out with this. She would, to say the least, be a very big help.

The mussel parasite was active, produced fully developed cercariae, in the spring and early summer and the fan worm parasite seemed to be active at all times of the year. At the end of May classes were over and we made plans to go out and make our collections from the pier. Offshore pilings had more infected fan worms and mussels on them, probably because that is where the fish definitive hosts infected with the two parasites mostly occurred, and that is where we planned to collect. The day we selected was absolutely idyllic. Sunny, almost no wind, and about 80° were the stats for the day. The day being so cooperative we went farther out than usual. We counted our way out and got to piling row 80. Previously, I had not had occasion to collect this far out. The three of us got along famously in the canoe, me at the stern, Timothy in front, and Toby riding in the middle. I showed my two assistants how to collect fan worms and mussels and avoid damaging the assemblage of living things on pilings any more than could be helped.

We got our collections of fan worms and mussels from those offshore pilings. It turned out that quite a few were infected. After collecting we paddled around for a while among the offshore pilings taking advantage of the great conditions. We noted that there were quite a few periwinkle snails, *Littorina littorea*, out there on those pilings. They are a rarity in closer to shore. This was as far south as that snail had been observed. We collected eight of them to see if they were trematode infected. When they were checked they were not, which was something Annie and Timothy might have predicted considering our findings about the drill trematode, which was not very common on pier pilings either. The snail up north on the east coast, where it is much more abundant, carried two or three species of trematodes. Maybe the parasites in snails did not make it as far south as the snail did, or maybe definitive hosts (in this case shorebirds) didn't hang around in amongst those offshore pilings often enough? Or maybe miracidia coming from parasite eggs in a bird's feces were not able to swim to snails living on pilings out there, questions, questions, questions?

When we got back to the lab and started examining the fan worm collection for parasites we had a lot of work to do. Annie, who had by now returned from the main campus, Timothy, Toby, and I did the work. Thank goodness Annie was back. She had done this sort of work before, got right back into it, and helped a lot getting Timothy and Toby up to speed. Individual worms had to be removed from their tubes by making a hole in the posterior end of the tube and gently pushing the worm back with a blunt probe and out the hole. If the worm was infected and not damaged it could be put in filtered seawater to emit sporocysts and cercariae by way of the worm's genital ducts. In all we found 93 infected worms. Of those one third had the orangish strip of parasites on their bellies excised with clean scalpels and those strips were blended in filtered seawater to make the original, crude parasite fluid. One third had their naturally emitted sporocysts and cercariae blended and made into a pure parasite fluid by that method. Finally, another one third had their emitted parasite stages remain unblended. So in the end we had three different fan worm parasite fluids in the refrigerator, 1) there was the old style blended fluid with host worm fragments in it and sporocysts and cercariae, 2) the new style fluid with just blended parasite sporocysts and cercariae, and 3) another fluid with unblended, sporocysts and cercariae. We would have to use fluid 3) first, as I wanted to have surely alive sporocysts and cercariae in that fluid when we ran the test.

I decided that we would test each of the three fluids on six infected mussels. In the following three days we ran the three tests. Each time we found six infected mussels by removing one of the valves to expose an infected and therefore orangish gill. We added the fluid to be tested to all six mussel gills and observed over a matter of hours to see what the effect of the tested fluid was on the mussel parasite infections. Results were straightforward, easy to analyze, and gave a strong message. To sum up, all three fluids had the same effect on all six mussel infections. The sporocysts and cercariae of the mussel infections were rendered dead or inactive. After eight hours none of the infections had come back to life. So, as before, fluid (1), the "dirty" old style, blended parasite fluid, caused the demise of mussel parasite infections, but so did fluid (2), the blended parasite fluid with no host fragments, just sporocysts and cercariae in it, and so did fluid (3), the unblended parasite fluid with live, intact sporocysts and cercariae still in it. Based on this experiment we could now definitively say that the host worm fragments did not cause the demise of mussel parasites. It happened whether the fluid had host worm fragments in it or not. Further, blending of the fluid was not necessary to release the active chemical or chemicals that caused the demise of the mussel parasite in infected mussels. Alive, intact larval stages of the fan worm parasite released whatever chemicals were involved naturally.

It was inspiring to see Annie back in action. Her semester on the main campus had made her more experienced. She had taken an advanced course in ecology as well as the course in parasitology they ran on that campus. She also had learned what she had to do to undertake and execute a senior thesis. The pamphlet in her possession laid out all the particulars. Because I now expected to be here, I could advise her and we would have to conjure up the question we would ask and how to answer it. I could tell from her avidness that would not be long in coming.

I can't express how pleased I was with this experiment and its results. For one thing it confirmed yet again that the fan worm parasite caused the demise of mussel parasite infections. That the experiment came out so cleanly was a surprise to Timothy and Toby. Both had performed very well during its execution. It was a look at science in action and both exhibited a deep appreciation of the view. These two students were now, like Annie, irreversibly hooked on the enterprise of science.

As an added bonus Timothy was attempting to improve his spoken word. He had asked me to correct him when he made a mistake. Already he had stopped using "ain't" and dropping the "g" off "in" every time. I was happy to oblige. From a more selfish vantage point I was happy to be back into research. This was what I loved doing and I had not had a chance to do for almost a year. It was good to get my mind off the recent turmoil, the Provosts unfortunate death, and get back into doing science. Besides, the clean result likely meant that another paper could be written. I thought we would make a four author paper, with me, Annie, Timothy, and Toby as authors in that order. My coauthors had all worked very hard and well in bringing the experiment off. They certainly deserved at least an acknowledgment, but I decided to include them as authors. I would let them bask for a while in what they had already accomplished. When I got closer to writing it, I would spring that decision on them.

Shortly after running that experiment a letter came in the mail from Provost Bigelow addressed to both Sylvia and me. My copy of the letter was a xerox copy. Sylvia got the original. Brief and to the point, it said that he had been thinking about the unwritten policy banning faculty research for some time. As we probably knew, when he practiced his academic discipline it was in biochemistry and the barring of faculty, and therefore students, from research had in his opinion limited the growth of this campus. While the previous Provost was in charge there wasn't much impetus to change the policy. Now, especially since most of the faculty agrees that it should be changed, we can work on changing that policy. He invited the two of us to come to his office and talk about what changes should be made. He asked us to contact his secretary if June 10 at 9:00 A.M. would be alright with us. When I read the letter I immediately thought: Wow! That certainly didn't sound as if I was going to be fired, quite the opposite. When I talked to Sylvia she was utterly amazed that the new Provost had apparently been an unknown ally to our cause. I too was pretty amazed. It's not often you get a communication from an administrator that is substantive and in all appearances sympathetic to what you want to do. We both looked forward to our meeting with the new Provost. The both of us hoped we weren't going to be disappointed.

Sylvia got right into getting us organized. I was glad she was so good at that. We had about a week to get ready. The first thing she did was call the Provost's secretary and let her know that June 10 at 9:00 would be fine with both of us. Then she suggested that as a start we each write a three or so page summary of our beliefs concerning the role of faculty research in the character of a university. We had talked extensively about this and there would probably be much duplication in what we wrote, but we could make one document out of the two. She said, "We should have as unified a view on this as we can come up with."

Sylvia and I thought that as far as work goes this day should end there. We adjourned to a local establishment to have a couple of beers to celebrate our apparent good luck. Temporary Provost Joseph Bigelow was indeed a surprise. We spent a couple of hours discussing just what we were going to propose. It was pretty simple, the administration should no longer stand in the way of faculty research, but there were many details to consider. How much support and what kind would be available: would there be any money made available to faculty for research; could we ask for secretarial assistance, for example, could we reasonably ask that manuscripts be typed; and for assistance with graphics? Would whatever policy we came up with be written or unwritten? Especially if it were unwritten, what would Bigelow communicate to the administrators with various jobs around this University branch about the new policy? During our conversation Sylvia was busy jotting down these and other questions. We had another beer and adjourned our meeting. It had been productive. We agreed to get together in two days and parted to produce our three page summaries.

That night I managed to put together my summary. I had been thinking about this topic for a long while and it wasn't too hard. The next day I was commandeered by Annie. She was eager to talk about her proposed thesis. I had read the pamphlet she had on the topic. It was a pretty big deal, essentially like a master's thesis for an undergraduate. A student, with an advisor's help, had to formulate a question or questions to be answered, figure out how to answer whatever questions were asked, write a proposal about those things, get that accepted by a faculty committee of at least three members, do the necessary work, write the thesis according to rules set out by the University, and finally do an oral defense of the work before the faculty committee and an audience of students and other faculty. On the main campus it was even possible for the student to get some support funds. If this was all to be done, Annie and I had a lot of work to do. We had better get started.

We had sort of agreed that the topic of her thesis would be the trematode, *Parorchis avitus* that infected the oyster drill. If the manuscript by Annie, Timothy, and me got published, she would have one paper out on one aspect of this parasite. In a single sentence we had found that: definitive hosts (gulls and terns) visited an intertidal rock jetty drill population much more often than they did a piling drill population and that is likely why the drills on the jetty had a greater prevalence of infections with this parasite than the drills on the pilings.

A summary of the life cycle of this parasite is as follows. Definitive hosts (birds) have the adults of the parasite inside them in the intestine. The cloaca of a bird is a sort of "common sewer" where urine, feces, and genital products are briefly stored before being emitted from the bird. The adult parasite in a bird host has a uterus with active, free, living miracidia in it. Live miracidia exit the bird host via the cloaca with fecal material. Once again, a miracidium is the larval stage of the parasite that infects the snail. This larva is equipped with hair-like cilia and it uses these to swim to and burrow into a snail. Once burrowed into a snail the miracidium initiates the snail infection. Sporocysts are not involved in this life cycle, there is a single redia inside each miracidium and that initiates the infection. More rediae are formed and inside them are ultimately formed cercariae. When cercariae are released from the rediae and from the snail they swim away, settle, and encyst on any hard substratum as a metacercariae. There is no necessary second host in this life cycle. Mussel shells, oyster drill shells, fan worm tubes, pier pilings, and rocks can all be festooned with metacercariae of *Parorchis avitus*. Apparently gulls and terns become infected when they happen to ingest metacercariae when feeding. If that happens, the life cycle is completed.

The step in the life cycle that we decided to investigate is from the bird definitive host to the drill first host. In our talk that day Annie and I agreed on that. The question I had was did she think she could master investigating it in the time she had available?

She would have to collect bird shit from the jetty, ideally identify live *Parorchis avitus* miracidia within it, get some uninfected snails from somewhere, and see if she could infect them with miracidia gotten from the bird feces. That was a tall order, but nobody had ever tried to experimentally infect oyster drills with *Parorchis avitus*. It seemed like a good, if difficult, project for Annie's thesis. She might even be able to observe the snail infection process. We agreed that the first thing to do was see if the live miracidia could be found in gull droppings.

Not one to wait to get going, the next day found Annie at the jetty site with a spatula. The most common natural definitive host for the drill parasite was the herring gull, *Larus argentatus*. She watched until herring gulls left droppings on the sand. She would then quickly run out to the spot and use the spatula to scoop up the dropping and put it in a plastic bag or jar for transport back to the lab. She collected 10 herring gull droppings. I had requested a key so she could get into the lab on her own. I met her there that day and we began checking what was in the bags. We used a little seawater to dilute the feces and looked for miracidia, first with a dissecting and then with a compound microscope. Some droppings were just teeming with very tiny ciliated miracidia. They could best be seen with a compound microscope. Because alive and active miracidia of *Parorchis avitus* are born from adult worms in bird hosts they appear alive in the feces. Adults of a congeneric species of trematode, *Parorchis acanthus* (which also occurs in herring gulls), puts out inactive eggs in the fecal material that later develop into miracidia. So there was little chance of confusing them. Of the ten bird droppings two had oyster drill parasite miracidia in them. Does that mean that about 20% of gulls are infected?

Well, only the first day out and that was a big step forward. We had developed a method that actually found the parasite stage we needed to try and infect oyster drills. I had to go and meet Sylvia to compare our summaries, but Annie, who was now all enthused and fired up, wanted to stay in the lab and get things set up for her work. I indicated an eight foot section of bench that she could have as her domain. She was thrilled.

When I got to Sylvia's office she was out for a moment, but she soon came back. She handed me her summary and I handed her mine. When I read hers I noted there was a lot of overlap, but she had done a classier of writing. One thing, in mine I had made a big point about the purpose of a university being the *discovery and dissemination of knowledge*. I didn't personally come up with it, but I did like that phrase. If we just incorporated that, we could basically use her summary. That done, she went on to say that we ought to, in addition to handing Bigelow a copy of our summary, prepare a 10 or 15 minute oral presentation about what we thought we should do to effectively change the policy of banning research by faculty. We could present it or bag it as the meeting seemed to call for, but better to be prepared. I said, "That is a good idea. It will help us formulate and organize our thoughts better." Sylvia volunteered to make up this little talk and present it. I acceded to her volunteering. For reasons I could not say to Sylvia, I still felt a little anxious about taking too strong a lead on this campaign. Probably there was no reason for that. I wanted to be involved, help, and play a role without actually being the prime motive force. So this was good. After she had put it together I would give a listen to give her some practice and make comments. I had no doubt that she would do it marvelously. She too had been thinking about this for a long time. We closed up shop and went our separate ways on this night.

I went back to the lab to pick some things up. Annie was still there. She had been working and thinking. The section of bench that was to be hers was all cleaned off and readied for work. There was a pair of aquaria set up that only wanted seawater. She had been considering how she could come up with very likely uninfected oyster drills to try infecting them with *Parorchis avitus* miracidia from gull feces. That parasitology course she had taken had equipped her to understand what had to be done and how to do it. I was tired and wanted to go home, but she wasn't going to let me depart, not right now. She had data that showed that drills infected with the drill parasite were pretty rare on the pilings. The prevalence figure was 3% in our manuscript. Her proposal was that especially offshore, where drills were scarce, we could nevertheless collect drills. They would most likely be uninfected. The collected drills would have to be kept alive. They couldn't be dissected to check for infections. She had learned in her parasitology course that infected marine snails may emit cercariae when placed in seawater. Any snail that emitted cercariae was clearly already infected. We could eliminate such infected snails from our experiment and would therefore avoid trying to infect already infected snails. She laid this all out on the blackboard with considerable aplomb. I said, "That's pretty good. You would have a double check on the snails that you try to infect. If they come from the pier pilings, right there they are likely to be uninfected. If they also do not release cercariae, that makes them even more likely to be uninfected. You might have a few snails sneak through your screen in the infected state, but not many. You could dissect some of the snails that did not release cercariae to check on how probable it is that an infected snail would get through your test as uninfected. I like that a lot. Good plan!" Annie then said, "O.K. you can go home now." I replied, "I guess we need to go out in my canoe and get some offshore piling snails that can be checked for release of cercariae and how about tomorrow?" She answered, "That will be fine. I checked and the tide is at 11:30 A.M." At that we parted company for the night.

The next day the weather was suitable and we paddled out and collected 25 oyster drills. Out there we had to look hard to find them. We also collected a quantity of seawater to be filtered for experiments and Annie's aquaria. After a nice day in the field we returned to the lab, filled the aquaria and got them running, and put each of the 25 drills in its own beaker of filtered seawater. The drills would sit in their water for 24 hours under natural lighting near a window, *i.e.*, as natural as obtainable in the lab. At that time we would come back and observe each beaker with a dissecting microscope to see if there were cercariae in evidence. They might be swimming around in the beaker or encysted (as metacercariae) on the glass. In either case, the waiting was next.

I called Sylvia to see how the talk was developing. She was not teaching in summer school and of course had already finished it. Would I like to come over to her office and give a listen? Yes, I would. When I got there she was looking even more gorgeous than usual. I should ever look so good. She was ready to go and got right to the task at hand. The lead sentences in her talk were, "The purpose of a university is the discovery and dissemination of knowledge. By keeping faculty from searching out new knowledge, by doing research, we are denying that this branch performs one of the basic functions of a university." I thought that was a great lead in. Her talk went on, "We should change that policy because it robs students of the opportunity to engage faculty that are themselves actively seeking new knowledge. Being so involved provides an additional dimension to a faculty's teaching. Not only that, but it provides a chance for students to be involved in trying to answer real questions, which fires up their intellect." Another good point to include, I thought. Sylvia's talk kept going for a while. I timed it as nine minutes. Her last point was that if we were to change that policy and promote faculty research (not just allow it) this branch stood to serve the local community better and grow as an educational enterprise. My comment was, "Sylvia, I have been thinking about this for years and that is just perfect. Great job! It quickly makes the points that need to be made and Bigelow should be impressed."

I didn't say why and she didn't ask, but I then told Sylvia that I did not want to be the leader of our, and maybe Bigelow's too, campaign. I said, "Based on what you have done so far you would be the best leader that could be hoped for. I will help and support in any way I can, but you would be better as the main leader." She didn't argue. I think she wanted to lead this fight. She just replied, "O.K. we need an identifiable face, but what you have underway with Annie, and now Timothy and Toby, will do more to make the point of our message than anything I can presently do." She hoped to involve some history students in a similar way. We had about finished our business on the campaign for the day and I asked her out for some coffee. A local eatery, Flannigan's, got our patronage. There were three days to go until our meeting with Bigelow and because of the way Sylvia had nicely organized things, there was nothing left to do.

At the coffee shop she asked me for more detail on what was going on with Annie and the other research students. I had told her some of it, but not in great detail. As was generally the case among faculty here she had not yet even considered a student taking on an undergraduate thesis. When I related what Annie was doing and what was involved she was keenly interested. Then I described the most recent experiment that Annie, Timothy, and Toby had been involved in. I told her what the results were, what they meant, and that it was likely publishable. I mentioned that they all had worked so hard in the execution and, though I hadn't told them yet, I was planning to make it a Turner, Hall, Holt, and Gillus manuscript when it got written. She thought that was a great idea. We talked a little more and then I invited her out to dinner at Flannigan's, which also included a fairly upscale restaurant. She allowed as how she was getting hungry and that would be fun. We did that and talked about work things no more.

When I got to campus the next day Annie was already in the lab checking the beakers with drills in them for cercariae. She had found one in which she thought cercariae had been released. I looked and sure enough there were indeed metacercariae encysted on the beaker. So the snail in that beaker was clearly already infected and we would not experimentally expose it to infection by miracidia. There would be no point. It would just screw up results. If a snail was already infected we would eventually re-release it at the pilings. We checked all the rest of the beakers and found no more snails to be already infected. So, based on this sample of 25 oyster drills, one (or 4%) had revealed its infection by releasing cercariae. The next question was: how many of the snails that failed to release cercariae were nevertheless infected? The only way to find out was to dissect them. We were not ready to try infecting any drills yet so we put them all under the hammer to break the shells and observe. It took us the rest of that day and part of the next to do that. In the end one of the 24 snails we thought to be uninfected actually bore a "silent" infection. It had rediae and cercariae, but did not release the latter. So, one (4.17%) of 24 snails that tested as uninfected actually had an infection. It got through our infection screen undetected. More snails would have to be processed in the same way by testing them for release of cercariae and dissection of those passing as supposedly uninfected. We had to know how reliable that testing procedure was. We would eventually find out. I continued to be very happy with the way Annie was comporting herself. She was aggressively pursuing her objectives and not taking up my time with less than essential issues. If she could just have some success infecting oyster drills, her thesis would be most of the way home.

As far as it goes that was very comforting to me, but tomorrow morning would be that meeting with Provost Bigelow. That was a big deal and none too comforting. I warned Annie that I had that meeting and might not be around for the rest of the day. I went back to my office and gave Sylvia a call. As usual she was remarkably composed. I told her I would meet her in her office at 8:45 tomorrow morning and we could go over to the Provost's office together. She agreed to that plan and we signed off.

The next morning I arose early to a pretty day. I ate breakfast out, and made a leisurely drive to campus. I was in my office by about 8:00. After a little fussing around I went over to Sylvia's office for an 8:45 arrival. I was a little bit anxious about what was about what was coming up, but Sylvia's continued composure pretty much wiped away any worries I had. She said, "Let's go so we won't be late getting there." I followed her out the door and closed it behind me. We walked into the Provost's outer office a few minutes before 9:00. Gail Pratt was there with a smiling face. Bigelow had Flannery's former secretary and the same office. "Good morning Drs. Armbruster and Turner," she said. Both of us had been here before to receive Flannery's job threats, but Gail probably didn't know about that and she was just being friendly. She got on the phone and announced that we had arrived. We could hear a voice on her intercom saying, "Please show them right in." At that Gail rose and ushered us in. I let Sylvia negotiate the door first and followed right on her heels.

I had seen Joseph Bigelow before, but hadn't yet had any face to face dealings with him. He was a distinguished looking man in his early 60's. He came right around his desk to greet us saying, "I am so pleased that you both could come and talk with me today." Sylvia was silent, but I acknowledged his greeting. The secretary left the room and the Provost asked us to take a seat and then took a chair next to us. He opened, "Let me put some of my cards on the table. As I said in my letter, I have been thinking about this idea of keeping faculty from engaging in research for some time now and I am eager to hear some of your thoughts on the situation. Even though it is an unofficial, unwritten policy, it has nevertheless been effective and it is a ridiculous policy for any university to have. Now, what are some of your thoughts?" At which time I motioned to Sylvia that this would be a good time to present her prepared talk. She then said, "We have prepared a short summary of some of our thoughts." After she had handed the summary to him she said, "Dr. Turner and I have discussed this issue extensively and by way of starting this I will say a few things for both of us about what is in our summary as well as a few other things." She then eased into her prepared talk, but did it in a way that hid any preparation. Masterful, I thought. When she finished her nine minutes or so the Provost said, "Based on what you have said, I can see that we are pretty much of a mind on this topic. When I was active in biochemistry it was at a university that held faculty research in high esteem. It was a very important criterion for faculty promotion and student participation in research was particularly valued." To which Sylvia said, "We have someone right here that has done that with some of our students. Blake, please tell him some of what you have going on." I took the cue and briefly told about Annie's undergraduate thesis, the student manuscript currently in review, and something about the one planned. He said, "Goodness, I had no idea that such things were going on at this branch of the University and it is very good to hear. Thank you." To which I said, "If we have any luck (or not) with publishing either of these papers, I will make it a point to keep you informed."

The Provost then changed the focus of our meeting. He said, "We are in more or less the same mind about what needs to be done here, but now how should it be done?" I chimed in, "Most of the faculty here have for good reason not been seeking to develop new knowledge for a long time. The one thing we should not do is threaten them in any way. The will to get into research has to develop slowly and naturally. Most of them have a Ph.D. and they have been trained in a research tradition. I have faith that faculty doing research will happen, but it will take time." The Provost said, "I agree with that sentiment. The last thing we should do is demand that they start research, but what can we do to start the ball rolling? I have a proposal. Let's see if you like it." He was the only one in the room who had real power to do things and both Sylvia and I listened intently. What he said was reasonable and not too pushy. "Let's just make an announcement from me in writing that no longer would faculty be hampered in any plans for research they might have. Support would be limited at first, but the administration would attempt to facilitate such activities as they could. Proposals for aid would be vetted through me." Both Sylvia and I thought that as worded the statement would be quite a shock to faculty and not much else needed to be done right away.

I then told the Provost about my wound-healing paper that was due out this summer. The Provost said, "That's incredibly interesting. You were able to do that here?" I said, "Yes, and with publication of that it is likely some research funding will be coming my way. Is there some administrative branch that could officially handle managing those funds, and others that might come along? For example, suppose Sylvia were to get a grant to investigate some aspect of history." He said, "We ought to be able to figure something out. Give me a little time."

We had been in the meeting for nearly an hour and the Provost had other engagements to attend to. He requested that we bring this meeting to an end. He wanted to get his announcement out to administrators and faculty as soon as possible and he would think about how to manage any research funds that might be coming in. He closed by saying, "I have really enjoyed talking with the two of you here today. You have given me much food for thought regarding the future of this branch of the University. Thank you both for taking the initiative." We all got up. Sylvia and I said our thanks for an inspiring meeting and we headed for the door out. The Provost went back around his desk and sat down. After saying good bye to Gail in the outer office we left. It was 10:10 A.M. on the 10th of June in 1978.

Outside I said, "I had a favorable impression of Provost Bigelow before this meeting, but never thought he would turn out to be a real champion of what a university is supposed to be. I have a real faith that he will make great strides forward for this University's branch. Things are looking up. What was your take on our meeting?" Sylvia returned, "That meeting was very encouraging. I too believe that Provost Bigelow's is, surprisingly, very much in accord with what we both think should the purpose of a university and I am very much heartened by this meeting. Let's see how it goes from here." My only rejoinder was, "Let's go get a classy cup of coffee at the local gourmet coffee shop by way of celebrating a real victory." We did that.

When I got back to the lab Annie was there. She wanted to hear how the meeting with the Provost had gone. I told her that because of the meeting I had real hope for the faculty here having the way open for research, real hope. She then said, "I am very happy that things came out that way. It would be nice to have this branch begin acting like a real university." She went right on to ask whether she and Timothy could use my canoe and truck tomorrow, to go and get more drills from the pilings, and more gull feces from the inlet. I indicated my truck and canoe would be at my place and they would be welcome to use them. She allowed as how she planned to collect 50 more drills. Did I think that would be too many? She also wanted to collect as many more droppings as they could manage. I said, "This is the time of year when drills are most abundant on the pilings and I didn't think that would be too many. I'll come back to the lab when you return to help with processing the drills and fecal samples." She said, "It was not really necessary for me to come back to the lab. She would only stay long enough to put the drills in beakers of seawater and isolate any droppings with live miracidia in them. That shouldn't take too long." I thought to myself now that is something. I had become unnecessary. Well, that's the way it goes. I said wryly, "Could I come in the next day to go through checking for presumptively uninfected snails and maybe trying to infect some of them with miracidia?" Mercifully she returned, "Yes, you should be here for that." We then sat down and planned out just how we were going to try to infect snails.

Our plan was to put a likely uninfected oyster drill in a finger bowl with 50 live miracidia and leave it there for 24 hours. There would be 100 ml of filtered seawater in the dish with the snail and miracidia. At the end of 24 hours a supposedly now infected drill would be transferred to an aerated aquarium to be maintained until it began to release cercariae or it had to be dissected to see if an infection with rediae had begun. That might be a while, weeks or even months. We would provide food on which to maintain drills. With that plan made we called it quits.

I went home to my bar with that great dark beer on tap. I ordered a hamburger with lettuce, tomato, and onion and some french fries. I sat there and ate and drank and thought about that meeting with the Provost today. Both Sylvia and I were very pleased and surprised about that meeting. It really looked like Bigelow had his heart in the right place. The Acting Provost is only human and an administrator, but nevertheless that's a superb start. And so I thought, over my third beer, as I sat there self-satisfied.

Next day, to catch the morning low tide, Annie and Timothy appeared at my place at 6:00 A.M. We loaded the canoe on my truck and with a small, probably unnecessary, lesson on how to tie it down so it wouldn't fly off on the road and they left pretty quickly. They returned in a few hours with 50 drills from offshore pilings and 15 bags with herring gull droppings in them. I guessed I really had made myself unnecessary. Too bad, I really enjoyed getting out in the field. My two students unloaded the canoe, hosed it off, put it back on its rack, and almost immediately left to get back to campus. They did have quite a bit of work to do before quitting for the day. Me, I had put the day so far into reading a novel written in 1915. It was a Grosset and Dunlap edition of *A Princess of Mars* by Edgar Rice Burroughs. I had found this book in a used bookstore. They had a first edition too, but at $80 it was too expensive for my taste. This one sold for $10 and I enjoyed reading it. It was fun following the heroic adventures on Mars of the Virginian John Carter, billed by Burroughs as the best fighting man on two planets, and the red woman he loved Dejah Thoris, Princess of Helium. Burroughs does not produce the heaviest of literature, but it does make for imaginative and fun reading. I managed to finish the book. It was a relaxing day.

Annie called that night and told me that she had gotten the snails into their water by 1:30 P.M. About the same time tomorrow we could begin checking the containers for cercariae. So I made it to campus the next day about 1:00 O'clock. We spent a couple of hours and went through the 50 dishes housing a single snail. We eliminated one snail we found to be already infected. An attempt would be made to infect 10 of the presumably uninfected snails. When we looked through the 15 gull droppings for live miracidia we got stopped. These droppings were collected early yesterday morning and alive, active miracidia were not present in any of them. We could see miracidia in some, but they were mostly dead. Apparently they don't last too long in a collected host dropping. We had to get more, fresher herring gull droppings. There was a late day low tide coming on, but maybe those wouldn't be fresh enough in the morning. Annie said, "I will go down there tomorrow morning and try to collect more droppings. I will bring them right back and with any luck there will be live miracidia in some of them." I said, "I will meet you at the jetty. I want to see the process of collecting bird droppings." We put the snails that had passed the test as uninfected in an aerated aquarium and left for the day.

On the morning low tide we were able to collect seven herring gull droppings. It was a simple procedure and I was happy with her method of collecting them. We rushed them back to the lab and began examining them. Three droppings had hundreds of alive and active miracidia in them. We were ready to go. We set out 10 finger bowls. With a pipette each got 50 miracidia in 100 ml of filtered seawater. That took some time. Once we had those organized, the next thing was to select 10 snails that failed to release cercariae from the aquarium. We selected the ones to use at random by getting all 49 out and using a random numbers table to choose 10. A single snail of the chosen 10 was placed in each finger bowl. We didn't know how long to leave the snails in there, but had agreed on 24 hours as being reasonable. Probably the miracidia wouldn't live much longer than that anyway. It was late afternoon now and Annie agreed to come back tomorrow afternoon, remove the snails from their finger bowls, and put them together in one aquarium. I told her that when I come in the day after tomorrow and we will have two jobs. The remaining 39 drills that were thought to be uninfected would have to be dissected to determine what proportion was "silently" infected. A second job would be coming up with young oysters (spat) to feed the 10 snails we were trying to infect in the aquarium. The snails had to be fed. Even if we were lucky and actually managed to infect some snails, it might take a long time for the infections to develop.

When we dissected those 39 oyster drills none of them bore an infection. Using all available data so far, that meant that 1 out of 63 drills (or 1.6%) was actually infected, but did not release cercariae when tested. Put another way, this means if we tried to experimentally infect 100 uninfected drills by our procedures, then one or two of them would have had an infection initially and were not newly infected by us. This would serve as a proper correction on any success we had trying to infect oyster drills.

With regard to that other job, finding food for the snails that had to be maintained in an aquarium, there was a local enterprise that harvested oysters and brought them into a processing plant. We went to that plant and asked if we could look over some of the oysters they brought in to search for young oysters. If we found them, they would be way too small to be of market value. Oyster larvae settle on older, larger oyster shells, as I knew from my Master's Degree days, and this might be a good source of young oysters. It was. We would have to return many times, but that is where we got food for our experimental snails and, with any luck, for the infections they carried. We could witness the drills in the aquarium drilling away on oyster spat. So things were pretty well in order.

Now all we needed was for some of those experimental snails to bloom with infections.

When I next saw Annie I asked her whether she had thought about forming a committee to oversee her thesis. She said, "I have developed a good relationship with my parasitology professor, from whom I earned an A. The only other thought I had was my ecology professor. I got an A in that course as well. Maybe I could ask him too." It turns out that Annie's mode of operation was to always get an A in all her courses. It was almost dumbfounding. I said in response, "They sound like reasonable choices. Ask them if they would be willing to serve. The reason I ask about this is you will soon have to come up with a research proposal and your committee will have to judge it. We have made good progress in a short time this summer, but who knows where it will go from here. If some infections develop in those 10 snails, that would be impressive preliminary success to add to your proposal. Anyway, the proposal is your next job." She then said, "I will call up Drs. Lang and Berkowitz and ask. And, it would indeed be wonderful if some of those snails began to show infections. We can only hope." If our experimental snails actually got infected, I figured on no particular basis, that it would take about a month for them to show infections by dissection. They would begin releasing cercariae even later than that. With that in mind I told Annie that she should get at least two more batches of snails going by the method we had used for the first batch. That would increase the odds on having some success infecting snails before the summer was over. She readily agreed and said she would arrange that. Before too long there were four aquaria in the lab with 10 supposedly experimentally infected snails in each.

About a week later the journal that published the wound-healing paper hit the stands, that is, the libraries. I called Provost Bigelow to tell him that had happened. He had already gotten a copy of the paper somewhere and commented on me having sliced myself up some as an experiment. He said, "I hope you don't use students that way." I assured him I have not and would not. The 250 reprints I had ordered and paid for came in shortly thereafter. The 250 reprints weren't enough. Almost immediately I got enough reprint request cards in the mail to use them up. I sent out 240 and kept 10 for my use. I quit sending out reprints, but it was a short article and people could easily xerox a copy in a library. There was much interest in it and that pleased me immensely.

Before too long I had gotten 15 letters and a couple of phone calls from medical outfits of various sorts requesting information on *Cercaria loossi*. Where could the host fan worm be collected? Where could parasite infected worms best be found? What is the best way to remove the worm from its tube, the parasite from the host? Could a visit be arranged with you to get some instruction? These were the types of questions asked. I quickly got the idea that I could spend the entire summer and more, just responding to, never mind satisfying all these requests. With my one man operation that would quickly become prohibitive on my time and I wanted to undertake other research projects, Annie's work being prime among them. What to do? I needed a plan.

There was no department structure on this campus. Faculty sort of worked through Dean Terkel's office. At least that's where everyone's mailbox was. So there was no biology department to help me out with secretarial work or any of these requests for help. I thought that Annie in particular, but also Timothy and Toby might be able to help. They had all been involved with the recent experiment and could help someone learn how to handle fan worms and the parasite. But, their time shouldn't be used up or uncompensated either. I would have to avoid getting myself or them over used, which could easily happen. More requests for instruction were coming in all the time. I would have to develop a hard-nosed policy wherein if someone wanted instruction on this parasite I could provide it, but it wouldn't be free. That someone would have to pay for an instructor's time. I also had to think about the possible decimation of the fan worm population on the pier pilings. The worm *Eupomatus dianthus* occurred in other places besides the pilings, mostly attached to the rocks of jetties and groins and in the subtidal zone. The worm occurred on the east coast from Cape Cod to Cape Hatteras. At other universities and colleges local marine invertebrate zoologists would be aware of this serpulid fan worm and if asked could lead someone to populations of it. But, if my instruction were needed for some reason there would have to be a cost. A policy such as this goes directly against my instincts. Assistance of this sort should be free for the asking, but it just couldn't be that way if I and my team were going to have time to pursue our own interests.

I contacted Provost Bigelow and told him of my developing problem. He might as well be aware of some of the problems that might arise from faculty engaging in research. He handled this in a very efficient manner. He first said that his secretary, Gail Pratt, would handle answering the letters asking for assistance. I would have to give her a basic form letter, with any needed changes for particular people, my signature would go on them, and she would see they were sent out. That would be a big load off. If anyone wanted to come for instruction, the University would charge $200 for one day's worth. Annie, Timothy, and Toby would be hired by the University for the summer and their job would be to instruct folks on how to handle the host worm and its parasite. There wouldn't be a lot of money, but at least they would be paid for their efforts. As for me, I wouldn't be paid extra. Mostly I would have to correspond with instruction seekers and organize their visit. That would be quite a bit, but it would be the price of momentary fame.

Beyond that piece of work done earlier, I did not get too much in the way of research done during that summer. Assembling my promotion dossier took a lot of what time I had. The biggest thing was getting my student evaluations organized. Summary tables of evaluations from each course taught in each year had to be assembled and the original evaluations had to be organized so they would be available to anyone who wanted to check them. Believe me that was very time consuming. I had done quite a bit of research, five published papers, the manuscript in review, and the experiment done early in this summer, but not too much that could be called service. I had been on a couple of committees and that was it. And of course, there was a self-evaluation to write. When I finished my dossier it was exactly 50 pages long. Whew!

Annie had good luck with her thesis research. She had tried to infect 40 oyster drills with *Parorchis avitus*. Of those 40, 25 (62.5%) had picked up infections and ultimately (before the summer was out) began emitting cercariae. That spoke well for her method of experimental infection. She had dissected a total of 150 drills after passing them as uninfected by failure to release cercariae and coming from the pier. In the end she found 2% of those to be infected. So, infected snails that had passed her screens might explain perhaps one or at most two of her 25 experimentally infected snails, but no more than that, certainly not all 25. In other words, in this summer she had successfully infected quite a number of oyster drills.

On top of that she had written, as I saw it, a top notch proposal. Her thesis was in very good shape, with which both she and I were very happy. She could hand her proposal to the other members of her committee when she got back to the main campus for fall courses. Both professors she asked, Drs. Lang and Berkowitz, had granted her request that they would become her committee members. This fall would be the beginning of her junior year and she already had her senior thesis pretty well in hand. When she came home next summer she could finish up any loose ends and write her thesis. It should be very good.

Another happening during the course of the summer was that a paper got accepted. It was the manuscript written by Annie, Timothy, and me on the different prevalences of *Parorchis avitus* in drill populations on pilings and the jetty and why they were different. Some small revisions were pending, but... wow! I was pleased to be able to tell Provost Bigelow about that. He seemed genuinely happy to hear it. I was even more pleased to be able to tell my coauthors. Annie spent three days about a foot off the floor. She was to put it mildly, absolutely ecstatic. Timothy wasn't far behind her, though a little more reserved. I had no reprint yet to include in my promotion dossier, but it was great to have one more accepted paper to cite and that with two undergraduate coauthors. I would have a total of six published papers. We did the revisions and quickly sent the paper back to the editor. It would be out sometime this coming spring.

I found time during the summer to take a preliminary cut at writing up the manuscript about cleaning up the methods in the host-switching paper. The question was about the need for blending the fan worm parasite fluid or the need for host worm fragments in the fluid as it affected the demise of mussel parasite infections. Neither blending the fluid, nor host worm fragments in the fluid are needed to kill off the mussel parasite. It was good that I started the writing during the summer when all three of my coauthors were around to review and make comments on the manuscript, but I got it nowhere near finished. I planned, though I didn't actually accomplish it, to get the final version together this fall semester. Anyway, in the process of all this, I did have occasion to tell my three prospective coauthors that they were to be included as actual authors. They were all elated when I told them. On the other hand, Annie, Timothy, and Toby were to be on the main campus this fall pursuing their biology degrees. Good grief! All my established help would be soon gone. Both guys were thinking about research, maybe a senior thesis, but they would be just sophomores in the fall and thought they would give it some time to see what developed before making up their minds.

There was another thing that accounted for much time during this summer. A total of 21 different outfits sent people to get lessons on the host fan worm and its unusual parasite. The University hauled in over $4000 from them. My three students did an admirable job. They all were able to give effective instruction on collecting and handling the host worm and its parasite. An experience was had by all of them and they made some actual money using what they know. I got used up some and didn't get any new research done. I spent time with all the people who came. A common observation was the smallness of my operation here, but all seemed happy with the information obtained. The fan worm population on the pilings and jetty got only minimally damaged from all this and I was glad for that. We would have to see what the information seekers did with their knowledge. That would take time. Not me, but maybe at least one of them will make a fortune on the wound healing capabilities of *Cercaria loossi*. Well, I foresaw all that when I decided to just write the note and publish it. I still liked that decision.

The University's Local Branch Gets Under Way Anew

My reputation had gone up some and I figured it was time to apply for a grant. The Provost had figured out a University plan on how to administer grant money. I thought it would be nice to have some money with which to operate, if I had any time to operate. The summer was about over. I was disappointed that I hadn't yet found time to finish writing up that experiment done with Annie, Timothy, and Toby at the start of the summer. I had to get on that. Maybe next summer wouldn't be so cluttered. If it weren't, I could spend my time more profitably investigating, thinking, and following my research instincts.

Chapter 11

TEACHING, RESEARCH PROPOSALS, AND A NEW ABODE OCCUPY MY TIME

The fall semester began. I was teaching Biology I and Invertebrate Zoology and both classes were chock full, 24 students each. Apparently word about my interest in research projects had gotten around. On the first day of class five different students in Biology I, three guys and two girls, came up and asked if there was a project they could be involved in. All five were taking both courses. I took note of their names, but had to tell them that at the moment I didn't have anything underway. Annie and Timothy were not around, but they all indicated knowledge of what they had done, get a paper published while an undergraduate, and that sounded astoundingly interesting to them. For now I suggested they just pay attention to the classes in front of them. Get that off to a good start. Maybe something would come up.

Actually my thoughts were on something new. The existence of a fairly large population of a snail, the periwinkle *Littorina littorea*, on pilings out near the end of my long pier was beginning to interest me. This is a snail population at the southern edge of the species' geographic distribution. It occurs in abundance in the north, for example on New England rocky shores. Based on a very small sample of eight snails, the population on the pier pilings appeared to be uninfected with trematodes. Is that actually correct? Are there other populations of *Littorina littorea* in this area? How many periwinkles are present on those pilings anyway? As with many marine organisms, periwinkles get distributed about the surface of the earth by larvae that drift in the plankton at the mercy of currents. Do waves of larvae regularly get delivered to the piling population, *i.e.*, are new juveniles regularly recruited from the plankton, or is it a population made up of older individuals that the plankton delivered long ago?

To answer any of these questions would require getting out there toward the end of the pier in my canoe, which had gotten somewhat battered with its extensive use transporting instruction seekers this summer. That would be dangerous duty and I wasn't sure I wanted to expose students to that. Anyway, this would be a good topic for some future research.

The idea of getting research funds did occupy me for a while. Provost Bigelow had set up a system to administer any funds that faculty obtained. The charge for overhead expenses to be paid to the University was a fairly standard 30%. Whatever total amount you might get in a grant, the University would take 30% of it. That would be figured in the grant's budget, *i.e.*, you would have to ask for that much more in the budget to cover overhead. What I mainly wanted was money for equipment (a good quality dissecting microscope with a camera was prime among my needs), student wages, possibly a new canoe, and supplies. Faculty here were on nine month contracts. Pay, however, was spread out evenly over 12 months. I could therefore put some of the budget toward paying me during the summer session. An added two ninths of my annual salary would be nice to obtain.

There was an outfit to which you could apply for a grant for the type of research that I did *i.e,* marine invertebrate zoology and ecology. Basically you had to write a research proposal and submit it for peer review and evaluation. Not the least problem was coming up with a budget and a time line for the research: how much would it cost and what did you expect to get done and by when? At the heart of any proposal, of course, is a research idea and that was my first challenge. Undoubtedly the most "erotic" thing I had done in the past was the topic of my wound-healing note. To develop that line of research further would certainly be interesting, but at the same time the sort of research needed would definitely be outside my resources and expertise. I didn't think that was a good avenue. The work that Annie was doing with the drill parasite was expandable, but that was her province. Don't touch, I thought.

My mind kept coming back to thinking about the periwinkle population on the pilings. With my resources the pier piling population was workable only in the nicest of weather. All by itself that population would make for a limited research proposal. However, along the open ocean coast and in estuaries near the ocean in the local area there were a number of stabilizing beach groins and inlet jetties. These structures were put in decades ago and they are a small scale likeness of the New England rocky shore. Just possibly the plankton had brought periwinkle larvae to one or more of those habitats. There might be populations of the periwinkle on those as well as on the pilings. I would have to do some searching. If there were populations of *Littorina littorea* in at least one of those rocky habitats, it would open up a comparative approach to studying the periwinkle in this area. I am using Annie's original idea relative to the oyster drill, but with a different snail. As third author on Annie's paper it was O.K. to use the idea. There is a good chance that periwinkles on the pier were less often parasitized than a population on a jetty or groin. Birds, the definitive hosts, would visit the pier less often resulting in fewer infected snails. Thanks again to Annie and Timothy. This snail has the additional, sort of sexy, problem of existing at the southern extremity of the species' spatial distribution. Did that situation have any effect on any parasites that might be found infecting the snail locally?

When I explored the jetties and groins, sure enough two other local populations of the periwinkle were found. Both were on open coast beach groins. These were essentially strings of large rocks extending out across the beach into the water. There is something called the along shore drift. In the local situation waves approach the beach predominantly from a southern angle and sand is moved slowly northward in a sort of saw tooth pattern. The purpose of groins and jetties is to hold beach sand in place, that is, keep it from moving north along the shore. Some periwinkle larvae had settled and taken up residence especially on the offshore pilings and others had colonized rocks in the local area. So the comparative approach had an opening.

Here in outline is what I decided to look into with respect to the three discovered local periwinkle populations. (1) What are the sizes of individuals in the three populations? This snail lives for 10-12 years (maybe longer) and reaches shell heights of around 30 mm (about 1.5 inches). If a population consisted only of snails near that maximum size, that would indicate that larvae were recruited to the population long ago (~10-12 years) and not since. The presence of smaller individuals in the population would indicate more recently recruited larvae. (2) What is the size of each population? Can more snails exist in one or the other of the two habitat types? This would be the most difficult to assess in the rocky habitats, lots of nooks and crannies and more surface area. (3) If any, what trematode species parasitize snails in each population? In more northern climes on the east coast of North America three trematode species have been identified in the periwinkle, two commonly observed and one observed only once. An assessment of parasitism would be most interesting in populations of this snail at the southernmost tip of its geographical range. Did any of the three parasites make it this far south and become established in local snail populations? The details of how I designed this project are as complicated as were the ones on the oyster drill population on the pilings done previously. I won't go into all those details here. The three areas of research indicated above give enough of an idea of what I had in mind.

I kept pecking away at the proposal all that semester. Aside from teaching and putting time into Sylvia's project and I did not get much else done. An item that was weighing on me was the manuscript on the experiment done at the beginning of last summer that needed to be finished. My coauthors deserved that writing. If the paper was to be published, it would be nice if it came out while they were still students. I guessed maybe that will have to be put off awhile.

I did manage to get the research proposal finished. It was more work than many of the papers I had written. The research proposal, per se, was kind of fun to do. The rest of it, budget, time line, etc., was a bigger drag than looking for a job. Now all that was needed was to send it in and wait to see if it got funded. The first part of that duo, the research proposal, got done near the end of the fall semester. For the second part, the work was supposed to start next summer. So I sent it in and would be hearing yeah or nay on funding during the spring semester.

The question of whether or not funding would be coming had to be put out of my mind for a time. Sylvia made some moves relative to getting faculty going on research. I tried to help her with all of it. She didn't much need it, but there I was. Her first item was the biggest: get local grants organized for which faculty could compete. My recent experience with grant writing made me useful in writing up her proposal to Provost Bigelow. What she wanted to do was have the University set aside a parcel of grant money for which faculty could compete. Her proposal held that $50,000 would be enough for the immediate future, five grants were to be awarded each year, and the most that anyone could request was $10,000. The Provost could think of it as an investment. If outside grants later materialized, the University could get their outlay back in the form of grant overhead. Besides, it would stimulate faculty research. If that activity got going, maybe the University could solicit contributions to keep the money replenished.

I accompanied Sylvia to the meeting with Provost Bigelow to pitch this and other proposals. It didn't require any curves or fast balls. He was remarkably receptive to the idea of an in-house research grant system. He said, "It will take a while to organize the money for the first year, but I don't see a problem with getting this up and running for next fall semester." To which I said, "We will need to appoint a committee of at least three to review proposals and make decisions about awarding grants. And, maybe we could set up a form for proposals." Of course, he immediately appointed me as chair of that committee.

The Provost would appoint two more. Well, that's what I get. Sylvia thought it was funny. A more minor thing that I proposed to my partner, which she liked, was that some effort should be expended to advertise the research accomplishments of faculty. There was a campus newspaper, *The Messenger*, and we could get the people in charge, students largely ran it, to include notifications of any research strides by faculty. The Provost was all for this idea. True to form, he suggested that some of my work might be first. He would take care of that. I pointed out that Sylvia's latest book had gone virtually unnoticed on this campus. I said that I had read her book through and it certainly should be placed first in *The Messenger*.

A third thing that Sylvia proposed was to change the promotion guidelines for this campus. The guidelines spoke almost not at all about the value of research activity and accomplishments in a potential promotion. She once again made it clear in that meeting that we didn't want to demand that research be a part of a faculty's promotion dossier, but we would be better off if it were recognized in the guidelines as a useful contribution. The Provost indicated that changing the promotion guidelines was in the province of the faculty senate. Now there was an organization that had, in my opinion, always been unwaveringly and uselessly in support of the administration. The Provost did say that he would talk to the Senate President and see if he could get something going in that vein. I thought to myself that doing something substantive would be a challenge to that venerable body. Sylvia had covered all the issues on her agenda and I had nothing further. The Provost called the meeting to an end and thanked us for our ideas. We said our goodbyes and left. We both thought the Provost had been helpful and reasonable.

Of course, the committee to which I had been appointed as chairman meant more time away from research projects. On the other hand, that in-house grant program could mean some operating money for my projects, particularly if the proposal just finished by me didn't get funded. Grant proposals are always risky business. Tales are commonplace of proposals that come back rated between good and excellent by reviewers, but still no money is awarded. If I had to try to get some in-house money for my research, it would certainly get crossed up with my chairmanship of the committee that sits in judgment on proposals. I would have to handle that somehow, but this potential problem was out in the future somewhere.

What I had decided to do with this winter session was finish that manuscript about a cleaner way to run my experiments on host-switching based on the fact that the fan worm parasite was cleanly emitted from the host worm via its genital ducts. The main points of that work were: (1) that mechanical blending of the fan worm parasite fluid was not necessary for the release of whatever chemical(s) resulted in the killing off of the mussel parasite in mussels, live parasite stages released them naturally; and (2) that fragments of the host worm in the cruder fan worm parasite fluid were not involved, which they might have been, in killing off the mussel parasite. My three coauthors were not around just now, but as first author and designer of the experiment I felt that I should take the initial crack at the writing. Anyway, on that manuscript was where most of this winter session was spent and it got written. It couldn't be submitted to a journal before my coauthors had a chance to review and approve it. I would mail copies of it to them.

The spring semester in 1979 had me scheduled to teach Biology II and the Introductory Human Physiology course. I did not like teaching the physiology course. Ecology and invertebrate zoology were more fun to teach. Dean Terkel knew that and I supposed she scheduled me that way as a little jab to make me pay for the recent success of Sylvia and myself at getting the ban on faculty research removed. There was no problem with that yet for Dean Terkel, but if faculty started doing research, it was considered a legitimate activity, and it contributed to promotion it would eventually become a diminution of her power on campus. There was one big benefit to this schedule. There was no laboratory associated with the physiology course and that meant much less time had to be devoted to the course. On the other hand, I hadn't taught the course for a few semesters and that meant lectures would require updating and therefore much time. Well, in academic politics such is the way Dean Terkel could wage a little war.

The other big deal for me during this spring semester was going up for promotion to Associate Professor. My promotion dossier had been finished and handed in at the appointed time during the fall semester. It was to be decided upon by the various committees during the spring semester. Fortunately, there was nothing further for me to do on this, my work was now done. From this stage the committees and committee members, mostly on the main campus, would bear the brunt of it. It was a bit of a test case; nobody other than Sylvia had previously gone up for promotion from this campus with research credentials acquired while on this campus. I suspected success would be mine. If so, it would mean a good raise in pay and that was certainly good.

Another pending issue was, within the next year there would be a need to move out of my current abode because the owner had retired and wanted to move in. I had really grown fond of living there and moving out would be a trial. It would be expensive over near the shore, but maybe a place could be found to buy. My savings now were about $20,000 and if promoted I would be able to arrange and support a mortgage. Talk about big deals! If it turned out that way, I would be in the position of owning some property. For a guy with my history and predilections that would be a momentous change indeed. Life was getting complicated.

The committee that Provost Bigelow had appointed me chairman of came into play during the spring semester. The Provost had lined up the $50,000, the administration of it, and two more committee members to read and sit in judgment on proposals. He would take the recommendations of the committee and make the final awards. Depending on the proposer's choice, awards would be started either in the next summer or next fall. A total of four proposals came in. The Provost appointed the Full Professor in Economics, John Landsby, to the committee, which was cleverly named the In-House Grant Committee. Landsby was a good man to have on the committee. He may be uninterested in doing research at the moment, preferring to concentrate on his artwork, but in the past he had a rich experience with academic research. The third person that Provost Bigelow had appointed was a female Assistant Professor who taught English named Alice Quigley. I was aware of her, but did not know her. We would have to see what she was able to contribute to the committee's work.

Of the four proposals that had been submitted one came from a biologist. Eric Mortimer, who after eight or nine years was still ranked as an Assistant Professor, had submitted a proposal to study a problem in genetics. Not yet having even read it, still I was pleased to see that contribution. An Economist had submitted another, the historian Sylvia Armbruster had contributed a third, and there was one from a person who taught Chemistry. There would be no University overhead charges on these grants. So a proposer would not have to figure that into the budget for his or her project. It would be tough making judgments on proposals outside of my area, but we did have a pretty good breadth on our committee. As there were four people who would do the judging, yours truly, John Landsby, Alice Quigley, and finally Provost Bigelow, the proposers were instructed to submit quadruplicate copies. I, as chair of the committee, took in the proposals and distributed the copies to the necessary people and arranged for the first meeting of the committee in three weeks.

With regard to the manuscript I had just written, copies were sent to my three co-authors who were on the main campus. With her usual efficiency, when Annie got her copy she responded quickly. Timothy and Toby were not far behind her. Both guys liked the manuscript and had virtually no comments. However, I noted that Timothy's letter was masterfully done with good English. Good for him. Annie made a couple of quite good corrections to it, but was basically very pleased with it. If I would attend to her few comments, questions, and suggestions she would not have to see it again. As far as she was concerned it could be submitted to the parasitology journal I had selected. There wasn't much to be done with the manuscript. It was in very good shape. After fixing a few things I got it together and submitted it to the chosen journal. It was a good piece of work. If the editors and reviewers thought the experiment worth doing, it would probably be accepted. It was a lonesome contribution, but at least that was one submitted manuscript for this year.

With regard to Annie's thesis proposal she had already given copies to Drs. Berkowitz and Lang. They had read it and given positive comments to her. This semester we had to arrange a committee meeting to officially judge her undergraduate thesis proposal. That would mean I had to make my first ever trip to the main campus. Well, it was about time. Besides, I really would like to meet Annie's two other committee members. I communicated to Annie that a Friday meeting would make it easiest for me to come up to main campus. Understanding that, she could arrange a date, time (late morning or afternoon), and room when and where we could all meet. And further, I was pleased that her thesis procedure was coming along so nicely. A trip there for her meeting would be a pleasure. Next summer before her senior year we should be able to get any experimental work for her thesis finished up. We could even get it mostly written. We would give it a good try. The University had quite a set of hoops to jump through to get an undergraduate thesis written, submitted, and defended. I had faith that Annie Hall could professionally handle all of that.

I of course had to stay on top of my two courses, but at the same time there was not much time left to review and judge those four faculty research proposals. A lot of time would have to go into that in the immediate future. Logically, I was most interested in what the biologist, Eric, was proposing, but though they were out of my area of expertise my full attention would have to be given to the other three proposals. Eric had a well-defined problem with fruit fly genetics. He had found an unused University room that he could set up to raise fruit flies and pursue an answer to his question. He had requested $10,000 because he needed quite a list of equipment to get his fruit fly operation going. He would be a very busy guy. The proposal was very well written and clear. I was the closest to the subject area and committee members would have to recognize what I thought about the validity of Eric's proposal. Unabashedly, after reading it my idea was to award him the money.

The proposal from Steve Wagner, who taught economics, was clear enough and seemed to me to make sense. He was requesting just under $7,000 to make his study. I was glad John Landsby would be there to help us make a judgment.

The proposal from Sylvia in history was pretty straight forward. She wanted to begin a fourth book about an aspect of the Revolutionary War. She needed about $6,000 to travel to libraries where the necessary references could be obtained. I would not qualify as the most unbiased judge, but saw no reason to not fund her project.

The faculty member in chemistry who had submitted a proposal, Benjamin Givens, was new on the faculty just this year. He wanted about $9,000 to study the dynamics of a particular chemical reaction under the influence of pH, temperature, and reactant concentration. I understood what he was proposing, but the proposal was unclearly written and he never made any attempt to explain why he wanted to know what he was proposing to find out. What would be the importance of learning what he wanted to learn? I had quite serious reservations about funding this proposal. When we had our meeting in a few days, we would see what the other committee members thought.

When the In-House Grant Committee got together for their first meeting I was pleased with the way it went. All three of us were well prepared to discuss each of the four proposals. As a biologist I started right in with Eric's offering. In effect I held that it was a well written proposal that asked a legitimate question about genetics. It was well laid out and, in my opinion, likely to be successful. Eric needed a lot of equipment and supplies to get started and the amount requested seemed logical and well justified. He should be awarded the grant. John Landsby agreed. He liked the way the proposal was written, understood pretty well what he was proposing, but was a little hazy on the significance of the question asked to the science of genetics. Alice Quigley too thought the proposal was well written. However, she confessed to not knowing enough about genetics to judge the question asked or its importance. She would go along with the recommendations of the other committee members. Alice was an attractive, pleasant and petite woman in her middle twenties. She had been on the faculty here for two years. After her short speech on Eric's proposal, I thought her to be reasonable and I found myself liking her. She was very well spoken and presented herself with precision. We took an official vote and all voted to recommend funding of Eric Mortimer's proposal.

Alice wanted to discuss the chemistry proposal of Benjamin Givens next. She did not feel competent to judge the problem addressed, but was appalled by the way it was written. I agreed with that last criticism and went on by stating that he did not address how chemistry would benefit by finding out what he was proposing to find out. John felt about the same way. He didn't get any help from the proposal's author in terms of the importance of the question being asked and the writing was not of the highest quality. When we took our vote we all thought that this proposal should not be funded.

The historical proposal of Sylvia Armbruster was then discussed. I informed the committee of my personal relationship with the author of this work and my judgment might be considered biased. On the other hand, I had read all of her three existing books and knew her to be a very capable scholar. If her proposed book turned out as good as the others, it would be a worthy contribution to the history of the Revolution. Then I asked for the thoughts of other committee members? John said that he had some knowledge of the historical issue that Sylvia wished to address in her new book. He could attest that it was a great idea for a book. It should be well received by other scholars of the Revolutionary War as well as by the more general public. The costs of the project are modest and well justified. Alice added that she too had some knowledge of the issue to be treated in the proposed book. It is a valid issue and is a great idea for a book. That she plans to involve students in her research for it is a definite added value. She had no problem recommending Sylvia's proposal for funding. So we all had about the same idea about Sylvia's proposal and thought it should be funded.

Steve Wagner's economics proposal was the last discussed. This little study had the purpose of looking for a resolution to the question as to why and how people make personal decisions with regard to their finances. John Landsby was the committee member best equipped to lead off the discussion. He said,

> I too, sort of as in the case with Blake Turner and Eric's proposal, am happy to see this proposal submitted. The people dealing with economics on this campus need to have a model for the discovery of new knowledge. This study may just serve that purpose. As you may know, in the past I have dealt successfully with that general question. That Steve has decided to pursue research along those lines undoubtedly stems from conversations with me. He has a new angle that is well defined and it is very likely that his proposed study will make a contribution to our understanding. Importantly, what he wants to accomplish with this study can probably be done with the money he has requested.

He finished by saying that it was a small study, but potentially a very important one. My comment was that the proposal made good sense to me. I liked the way it was written and relative to what he was proposing the budget makes good sense. Alice's comment was that she liked the question he was asking and thought it was an interesting approach to the problem at hand. The proposal was well written, comprehensive, and suggested an author who knew what he wanted to do and why. We all voted to recommend it be funded.

We had been meeting for about an hour and a half when I said,

> We should probably bring this get-together to a close. I propose that we meet one more time, say next week. In the meantime I will attempt to write up the sense of the committee with respect to these four proposals. My write up of that will be available to you before that meeting. Let's set that meeting up for the same day, place, and time next week. Does anyone have problems with that? No, then that's what we'll do. If anyone has changed their mind about any of these proposals, they can bring it up then. What we have to do is make the committee's recommendations available to Provost Bigelow. The final decisions will rest with him, although I expect that he will agree with our recommendations. Let's keep it a secret what went on in here today. Ideas and comments will not be attributed to individuals in my little report, just the way the total votes went and the general comments by the committee. We could have had to award as much as $40,000, but only awarded about $23,000. That means that there is already $27,000 of the $50,000 in next year's grant budget. Not bad. And importantly, this should stimulate more research on this campus. Thank you, I'll see you in a week.

That night I got my committee's-sense document written. My hope was there would not have to be too much change to it. Anyway, it was in the other committee member's mailboxes the next day. I called Provost Bigelow and told him that we had met and would probably have our recommendations to him next week after we meet again. Now, if nobody on the committee changed their mind in a major way, we could make a few changes to my document and be done with the In-House Grant Committee's duties until next year. I already knew John Landsby quite well, but it was good to have had a chance to meet Alice Quigley. She was pretty cool.

At the next meeting nobody had changed their positions on any of the proposals. There were a couple of suggested changes to my document covering the sense of the committee. I finalized the brief meeting by telling them that I would attach the document we just corrected to a letter from the committee to Provost Bigelow. We probably don't need to meet again. Before Provost Bigelow's letter is sent, I will get a copy to each of you. If there is something to change, we will handle it. Not hearing from anyone, let's say by Thursday, the letter will be sent. I said in closing, "I think this committee did a pretty good job. Thanks to you both for your contributions. And, now we are adjourned."

The members stayed around for a few minutes and then left. By Thursday there were no corrections to Bigelow's letter and it was sent. Let this be the end.

At about this time in the spring semester the paper by Annie, Timothy, and myself concerning the oyster drill came out. Its major claim was a connection between the frequency of visitation by definitive hosts (gulls and terns) and the prevalence of infection in the snail. It only took up four pages in the journal, but for me and especially my coauthors it was a big step forward. For me I could point to students as coauthors, which I thought was pretty cool. For the students they would get the interest of fellow students. They would realize that the authors had accomplished a new thing. As undergraduates they had done a piece of work and published something. They were down in the literature for posterity.

Soon the 250 ordered reprints came in. I sent 75 to Annie and 75 to Timothy. As the identified corresponding author, I kept 100 to honor reprint requests. It turned out that 87 requests came in so I ended up with 13 copies. For Annie's upcoming committee meeting it was good to have reprints to advertise her previous work with the oyster drill and its trematode parasite.

Another thing that happened about coeval with that paper's publication was that word came back concerning the research proposal I had written about the periwinkle. It was astounding to me, but it was funded in full! Clearly the funding agency felt that studying that snail at the known southernmost extreme of its distribution was well worth the money. My grant was for a total of $80,551. The main single expense was for a truly well-equipped dissecting microscope. I had selected one with a clever lighting system, very good powers of magnification, and a mounting system for a camera with a light meter. With all the equipment the damn thing cost nearly $30,000. I could also buy a separate camera with a variety of lenses ($500) for use in the field and lab. The University got some overhead ($24,165.30). Most of the rest of it went for student wages and lab and field supplies. I could afford to hire Annie and two other undergraduate students this summer and pay them reasonably well. It wouldn't be great pay, but as such things go, not bad. I didn't include any funds to pay me for my summer labors. Getting this thing going would be a lot of work and very challenging. Well, I did ask for it.

The first thing to think about was lining up student assistants. Those five students that had approached me early in the fall semester were all doing well in my courses, and would be quite well informed. Come summer they all would have Invertebrate Zoology and Biology I and II under their belts. I decided on three main ones and kept two in reserve. Sophie Timmins was a tall athletic sort of girl. She was a member of this branch's women's softball team. Alive with wit, her personality made her fun to be around. She had done A work in all three courses and was an excellent student. She would be an asset. If I was going to work around those far offshore pilings, I needed at least one fit and adventurous guy. Zachary Trumble in his conversations with me had mentioned a number of canoe adventures he had been on. He had pulled a B out of Biology I, was getting a B in Biology II and had gotten an A out of Invertebrate Zoology. He was smart enough, but sort inconstant as far as scholastic effort was concerned. Zachary was a bit of a gamble. Be that as it may, he was definitely worth taking a chance on. A third student I decided to ask was Tilly Strathman. She too was excellent, pulling an A in all three biology courses, but it turned out she had taken another summer job and was unavailable. When I asked Zachary and Sophie whether they would like to work with me this summer they both immediately said yes. Both had planned to take the summer off before going up to the main campus in the fall. The money wasn't all that great, but they were both pleased to be able to get involved in research and make a few dollars before going. As far as field work was concerned, I would not have to worry about either of them being a hopeless spasmodic in the field.

The other two students were not forgotten. Those two guys had several times expressed an interest in involvement in research. I told them I was very sorry, but my budget wouldn't allow me to offer them a job. I would try to work them in when I had something needing doing. Each was disappointed, but agreed to take part when extra help was needed. So I had a crew of three recruited to do research during the summer. Annie would of course work out and we would see how the others did.

When I told Provost Bigelow the news about the grant he was most pleased. The money the University would accrue as overhead would virtually cover the amount needed to refurbish the $50,000 needed for next year's In-House Grant budget. He said, when I talked to him, "I congratulate you on being able to get that grant. I am especially happy to hear that you plan to work with three students this summer. You never know what that might open up for them." Getting overhead funds into the coffers of this branch of the University was simply a great thing as far as the Provost was concerned. Such funds might cause a few administrative problems, but those were outweighed by the good they would do.

Another event coming up in this spring semester was Annie's advisory committee meeting for her proposal. The day for it, was about two thirds of the way through the semester. She had arranged the meeting on a Friday in the early afternoon. It was about a four hour ride up to the main campus. I figured I could drive up in the morning, go to the meeting, stay overnight on Friday night somewhere, and drive back the next day. Annie passed along to me a little knowledge of what she planned for the occasion. She wanted to have time to talk with me and there was a gathering of a few students and her committee members later in the day. She offered to let me stay at her place that night, but I asked her to reserve a room in a motel near campus. She was living a student's existence and there was no need of any extra expenses for her that my visit might incur.

It was good that I would have a chance to get acquainted with the other members of Annie's committee in a situation less formal than the official committee meeting. I welcomed a chance to talk with faculty from the main campus. I also was eager to see a little of Annie's environment on the main campus. Annie had sent me a final version of her proposal. I had read it again and noted that she mentioned only 10 of the snails she infected last summer. Further, she mentioned only some of the snails that she had checked for infection by release of cercariae, found them to be uninfected by that method, and later dissected to see if they carried "silent" infections. Mentioning only some of her results was a good move. There was no reason to put all possessed data in the proposal. The day for that meeting was approaching. I thought her proposal was just great. Now all that would be needed was to make the trip.

When that Thursday night arrived I went to sleep early. I got up, dressed in Levis, a shirt (no tie), and a sports coat. After a substantial breakfast, I began my drive by about 7:00 A.M. The way to the main campus was unknown to me. I looked at a map and chose what looked like the best route. The way was mostly rural and the long ride was enjoyable. At one point I ran into a large used book store and stopped in for a break. They had an amazing number of old Edgar Rice Burroughs novels, in which I had gotten interested of late. I spent some money on "Tarzan of the Apes" published in 1914. It cost me $90, but it was in good shape and a first edition of his first Tarzan book. It was a great find. I also picked up a few others of his novels, they too had dust covers, but were not first editions. All were published by Grosset & Dunlap or A. L. Burt at about that time and all these were $10 or under. It was unlikely that I would run into such a collection any time in the near future.

I got on my way again and about 11:30 -12:00 rolled into the town of the main campus. There was an hour before Annie's meeting and some time to get a sandwich. Just before 1:00 P.M. I had found the room in the Biology Department where the meeting was to be held. Annie was outside the door and happy to finally see me. She was concerned that I might not get there in time. But, to her relief there I was and I did not fail her. She characteristically wasn't nervous about defending her proposal. There were a few students there in attendance. Among them was Timothy. We greeted one another. He was mostly just quietly there, but it was good to see him again. On entering the room Annie introduced me to her two other committee members. Dr. Herman Berkowitz was her parasitology professor. He was a man in his late 50s or early 60s sporting a graying beard and quite distinguished looking. The meeting was due to start so we just shook hands by way of greeting. Dr. Jed Lang had taught her an ecology course. He was a younger man, probably in his late 30s. We too shook hands and started the meeting.

I introduced things by saying, "Annie Hall is pursuing an undergraduate thesis entitled "The Experimental Infection of the Gastropod *Urosalpinx cinerea* with the Trematode *Parorchis avitus*." I am her advisor, Dr. Blake Turner, from the branch campus of the University where she is doing her work on this project. Let's begin by letting Annie summarize what she proposes to do." Annie then talked for 20 minutes on her proposal. Her talk covered the overall distribution and habitat choices of the host snail, where the parasite had been seen, and finished up with the fact that no one had ever experimentally infected this host snail with this parasite. Simply put, that was in effect what she was proposing to do.

After her talk I said, "Now let's open this up to questions. When we are done with questions the audience and Annie will be excused and committee members, that is me, Dr. Berkowitz, and Dr. Lang will meet in this room to discuss our decision on this proposal. If it is passed, then Annie will be able to go on and finish her research and write her thesis. If not, she will have to go back to the drawing boards and fix the problems that have been brought up. We will let the general audience ask questions first, then Dr. Berkowitz will ask his questions, then Dr. Lang, and finally I will cover questions that have not been already answered. Let's begin."

A couple of what I took to be students raised a hand. I called on one of them. The young lady said, "I have not taken a course in invertebrate zoology, but I know pretty well what a snail is. The one you are working on I have heard you refer to as the oyster drill. Why is it called that?" Annie launched into a description of the drill's feeding habits and included the fact that she had been maintaining her drills on young oysters. She finished up with a good description of the rasping tongue-like structure (the radula) the drill possesses to drill through an oyster's shell.

Another student asked a question that betrayed his having taken invertebrate zoology at some point. He said, "I have read your recent paper on the prevalences of this trematode in two populations of oyster drills. How does this snail reproduce? Is there any chance that trematode-infected drills moved preferentially from the piling population to the jetty population? Could that explain the higher infection prevalence among drills found on the jetty?" Annie related that, from the egg case where larvae develop, embryos (veligers) are not released into the plankton. Rather, from the egg case juvenile snails just crawl away. Juveniles and adult snails have limited dispersal capability. They stay pretty close to wherever they are living. The jetty and the piling populations are separated by some three or four miles and lots of habitat unsuitable for drills. There is virtually no chance that a drill, uninfected or infected, could disperse that far. So, the answer to your question is no. We couldn't explain differences in parasite prevalence by movement of infected snails from one habitat to another. A third student asked, "What do we need to know about marine parasite life cycles for anyway?" Annie said in response, "Right now the study of marine parasitology is, compared to freshwater parasitology, an area of investigation that is pretty much in its infancy. Not that many people have been studying it. Almost anything we can learn is very valuable. The trematode infecting drills, *Parorchis avitus*, has been known to exist as a distinct species for about 40 years. There is a 1932 paper by Stunkard & Cable. They found it possible to feed common and roseate terns with encysted cercariae (metacercariae) of this parasite species and the birds became infected with adult worms, which they described. But, until now nobody has infected the first host oyster drill with miracidia from adult worms. That is the goal of my proposed research." There were a few other questions from the audience. About a half hour had been used up and for my money Annie had handled herself very well.

The next challenge was due to be Dr. Berkowitz, the parasitologist. He opened by asking, "To which Family of trematodes does *Parorchis avitus* belong?" Annie said, "It's an echinostome." Then he further asked, "And how might we characterize that family?" She said, "There are freshwater and marine forms and they all have a collar of spines around the mouth of the adult worm as do the cercariae and metacercariae." He then said, "You have used herring gull droppings as a source of miracidia to infect snails. Why?" Her response was, "Well, that is the known natural host of adult *Parorchis avitus*. Adult worms have been found by dissection of herring gulls taken from the field." His next question was about the common and roseate terns she had mentioned in a previous answer. Annie said, "They were host birds that were more easily obtained and handled in the laboratory than herring gulls. They could be infected in the laboratory, but are not (so far) known to carry natural infections in the field." He went on to ask about other echinostome trematode species known to infect herring gulls. She said, "Yes, there are other echinostomes known to infect herring gulls. In fact there is another species in the same genus as the drill parasite. That one is *Parorchis acanthus*." Dr. Berkowitz then asked, "How can you be sure you are trying to infect drills with *Parorchis avitus* when there is also this very similar species possibly infecting herring gulls?" Her response was, "*Parorchis avitus* is uniquely viviparous. That is, the adult worms have active, alive miracidia within them and those live miracidia appear in the bird's feces. This is not the case with *Parorchis acanthus*. For that species miracidia have to develop from eggs produced by adult worms that are released in the bird's feces. If you find active miracidia in fresh herring gull fecal material, they are the miracidia of *Parorchis avitus*. Besides, the few experimental infections I have accomplished with these miracidia have produced the rediae and cercariae of *Parorchis avitus* in those drills." Dr. Berkowitz then said, "Well, that finishes my questions for now and Dr. Lang can take over."

The ecologist, started out, "I picked up in the last exchange that only the herring gull is a known natural host for *Parorchis avitus*. However, in your published paper you counted both herring gulls and terns as they visited the sites of drill populations. Was that a mistake?" Annie responded, "Perhaps it was. But, terns can be experimentally infected with adults of *Parorchis avitus* and it seemed wise to include them in our counts. Even if you separate out visits by herring gulls and terns, the number of visits by herring gulls to the jetty drill population was much greater than to the piling population."

Dr. Lang then asked, "What proportion of herring gulls is infected with your trematode?" She said, "Of all the herring gull droppings I have collected, about 20-30% of them had active miracidia in them, suggesting about that proportion of birds carry infections." Thinking like an ecologist Dr. Lang then said, "Meaning, using data from your paper, that if 20-30% of gulls are infected, then that is sufficient to produce about 30% infection in the drill population on the jetty. What are some of the factors that might affect such a conclusion?" Annie answered as follows, "How can parasite prevalence be about the same in bird and snail hosts? Well, the snail lives for years and the infections with this parasite may persist. That may explain how parasite prevalence gets to be about equal in the snail and definitive host. Infections in the snail may accumulate over time. Anyway, that's a promising question. Further, I suppose season of the year might figure in. It could be that adult worms do not release miracidia into gull fecal material during the winter months. Even if they do, it may be that the miracidia cannot accomplish snail infection when the temperature is low." He then said, "Let's go with those. How would you go about testing either of those latter ideas?" Her response was, "To answer the first question, whether adult worms release active miracidia into bird feces at all times of the year, I suppose you would have to collect herring gull feces at all times of the year to see. The second question, whether miracidia can accomplish snail infection when temperatures are low, would require a lab experiment under cold conditions. With the techniques I have developed so far that would be a doable experiment." Dr. Lang then wanted to know if anything besides temperature was likely involved in winter transmission of the parasite to a snail. She said, "Yes, temperature would be the first thing to go after, but I think there might be other factors, for example the condition of a potential host snail. During winter snails bury in the sand and shut down. Their buried state may remove them from any active miracidia and moreover in its shut down state a snail may not be able to be infected. But I'm intrigued with your initial observation, Dr. Lang. How can the parasite prevalences in birds and snails be about equal considering the vagaries and chancy nature of miracidial transmission between them?" Dr. Lang nodded and gave up the floor to me.

I said, "You and two other undergraduates, one of whom, Timothy, is sitting in this room now, are authors on a manuscript that is currently in review. Could you please summarize for the present audience what that piece of work was about?" Annie said, "In a previous publication you documented that a trematode parasite of the fan worm, *Eupomatus dianthus*, sometimes switched- hosts and infected the blue mussel, *Mytilus edulis*. You were able to show that when a blended fluid containing host fan worm fragments and stages of the fan worm parasite, *Cercaria loossi*, was added to an infected mussel it would cause the demise of the trematode species infecting the mussel. This was held to be why the fan worm parasite was able to dominate another trematode infecting a mussel host. The questions we addressed in the manuscript you asked about were: was it necessary to homogenize the fan worm parasite and the fragments of host worm before the fluid would kill off the mussel parasite in a mussel and did the host worm fragments play any role? The answer to both questions was clearly no. Homogenization, or blending, of the fluid was not necessary and host worm fragments did not play any role." I responded, "Thank you, and that was a great little summary. I'll have to get you to write the next abstract that comes up. Now, tell me two things: (1) what question would you like to see answered about that specific system and (2) how would you extend the capabilities of the fan worm parasite to investigate the trematode that infects the oyster drill?"

She answered, "Well, with regard to the first query, a question that has arisen in my mind is whether before the fan worm parasite can infect a mussel, switch-hosts, is it required that the mussel already be infected with the mussel parasite?" I then asked, "And how, briefly, would you undertake answering that question?" She said, "Most first hosts for trematodes are gastropods, but the fan worm is a polychaete. I suppose you would have to come up with infective fan worm parasite miracidia. You could then see if they can infect mussels that are not already infected with the mussel parasite. Assuming you could do all that my question would be answered."

I said, "Fair enough, now what about the second question I asked." She hemmed and hawed a bit, but finally answered,

> In another paper you were able to show that quite outside the host-parasite relationship the homogenized fan worm parasite fluid had the ability to dramatically speed up the healing of human wounds. I suppose that a good question about the drill parasite is; can the fan worm parasite also kill off a *Parorchis avitus* infection in a drill? Before you ask, you could investigate that in much the same way you did it with mussel infections. It would be more difficult to do, but you would have to expose a drill infection, put some fan worm parasite fluid on the drill infection, and wait to see what happened. If the drill infection was killed off and the fan worm parasite became established in the drill, that would be another host-switch and that would be extremely interesting. It would suggest that the fan worm trematode might be involved in many host-switching events. But, pending actual data, that however is a speculation."

At that point I offered that this question and answer session had gone on long enough. It had been over an hour. "What I would like to do now is excuse everybody except us three committee members so we can talk over what has happened here." Everyone, including Annie, got up and filed out of the room.

When the last person was gone and the door was shut we committee members were sitting there looking at each other. I said, "Does anyone care to start?" Jed, Dr. Lang, spoke up, "I would like to begin by saying that Annie conducted herself very well here today. It's not as if I'm surprised, but she did. Let me also say that you Blake Turner have delivered to us a fine student from your far away campus and you are to be congratulated. She handled all the questions asked of her with poise and while demonstrating a thorough knowledge of her field. My graduate students should rise to such an occasion so well." Dr. Berkowitz, Herman, chimed in with something similar, "Jed, I am glad you felt as I did about Annie's academic acumen."

I then said, "I think she is a pretty wonderful student and person too. When she approached me about getting involved with research a couple of years ago little did I know how great she would be. She even recruited Timothy and got him interested in pursuing research. One or the other of you probably knows, Timothy Holt. Herman said, "Yes I do know him. He is taking my parasitology course now. He was asking the other day whether there was a research project he could help with. I have a project underway. He is a very good student and I believe I will use him." I said, "You won't be disappointed." Herman returned, "You know, I have only been vaguely aware of your branch campus for a number of years, but never have I taken special notice of any students from there until now. Jed indicated that he had another student in class last semester from that branch and his name is Toby Gillus. I said, "He's another good student, a coauthor on that manuscript in review I mentioned today." Herman went on, "I don't know how you got your research going under conditions at that branch. There has been almost no research out of that place and I guess that's why almost everybody on this campus has been ignoring that branch campus."

I said in answer, "Well maybe that is about to change. A history professor, Sylvia Armbruster, and I have been working on getting faculty interested in doing research. The new acting Provost is sympathetic with us. He has put together an In-house grant program to begin the process. We had four applications this spring. Further, I have been lucky enough to get some outside grant money. But now let's get back to Annie. I take it that we are in agreement that Annie passed her research proposal defense. If that is the case, let's sign the paper and let her know." Sort of in unison they agreed and we all signed.

We opened the door. Annie, Timothy, and some of her friends were waiting there. With a little hug I told Annie, "Congratulations we all were very happy with your defense of your proposal. You passed, and now all you have to do is finish the research and write your thesis." She was obviously very pleased, but still poised. She lightly said, "Oh, is that all?" Drs. Lang and Berkowitz said their goodbyes and told her they would see her later on at her gathering. I indicated that I would like to go and check into my motel and relax a while. It had already been a long day. I said goodbye to Timothy, who couldn't make Annie's party. He didn't say a lot, but I could tell that he had improved his English quite well. It was good to see him again and I complimented him on that accomplishment. I quickly left to get a little rest.

Annie's gathering was at her apartment. Her roommate was running it. After getting a small supper I managed to get there about 7:00 o'clock. I was somewhat refreshed after taking a little nap. Annie introduced me to her roommate. Her name was Nancy Burke, a history major who was also doing an undergraduate thesis. She was aware of Sylvia's work on the Revolutionary War. She was a pleasant girl and fun to talk to. We spent several minutes getting acquainted before she was drawn away with other hosting duties.

I got a chance to talk with Annie alone for about 20 minutes. I told her that she did a wonderful job with her proposal defense. I was impressed and proud with the way she handled all questions. We had previously talked over most of the subject matter of those questions, but she handled it all very well indeed. She said, "I felt good about my answers and was glad you had prepared me so well for today's challenge." I said, "I was just having fun doing my job with a quality student. In any case you deserve the credit for how you handled yourself today, not me. I couldn't be more rewarded." She asked a couple of questions about how we should busy ourselves during the upcoming summer. I told her that there wasn't much more, if any, research to be done. She had much more data in hand than she had to use in her proposal, certainly enough for an undergraduate thesis. The main thing to do was take the information she had and get her thesis written. That was the main job for the summer. I related that I had some grant money coming in and could hire her for the summer. She said, "That is really great! I need to earn some money this summer." I finished our conversation by saying that I would buy us breakfast before I went back tomorrow morning and we could talk more about this then.

Dr. Lang showed up and shortly thereafter Dr. Berkowitz. Jed said on arriving that he did not often come to such festivities as this, but he was impressed enough with Annie that he thought he would make an appearance at this one. He asked, "How did you ever get started in research with Annie? She would have been only a freshman at first. Here she is in her junior year and she comes off as incredibly accomplished. In her proposal defense today she did a really good job." I replied, "Well, it was certainly more her idea than mine at the start. She approached me. I had already started with oyster drill population ecology on the pilings of a long pier. I had run into trematode infections in fan worms and blue mussels by the time Annie came on the scene. I wanted to see what the state of their infection was during the winter months. So her first exposure to research was collecting specimens from a canoe in winter. She impressed me with how she handled that work." By this time Dr. Berkowitz silently joined our conversation and began to listen. "Anyway, that experience didn't turn her off. She became a very high quality assistant, capable of many things. That winter and the next summer I was very lucky to have her around. Not least, she got another student interested in research and he in turn yet another. We spoke of those two earlier today. Annie is an impressive girl." At this point Herman inserted, "I certainly agree with that. I am thrilled that she has taken an interest in parasites. She will likely become a very productive scientist. In fact, I would love to work with her and plan to try and convince her to apply here to graduate school. I would not like to see such a promising student go elsewhere." I responded, "I'm happy to see such things open up for her. She deserves it. Of course, the challenge at hand is to guide her through the writing of her thesis. First things first, and Annie will want to continue getting an A in all her courses." Herman added, "And let me say one more time that you Blake deserve accolades for getting her started and beautifully guiding her thus far. If she is any portent of what can come out of your campus, then we on this campus had better begin paying more attention." I simply said, "Thank you for that. We are trying hard to keep student involvement in research going on our campus." More time was spent in essentially idle conversation, but before long Drs. Lang and Berkowitz got drawn off into other conversations and shortly thereafter they both left the gathering.

After Jed and Herman left I was sort of on my own for the rest of the night. Annie did check on me a couple of times and I had another brief conversation with her roommate Nancy. I found myself longing that Sylvia could have been there. It seemed as though we never wanted for stuff to talk about. Sylvia and I had a date for dinner on Sunday night after I got back. I was eager to talk with her, but that would have to wait until then. In the meantime this was a gathering of university students. There was, of course, alcohol around and being consumed. There was some rowdiness afoot by this stage. I decided I should leave. I got hold of Annie and claimed I was tired. She was a little bit tipsy. I had never had occasion to see her in such a state, but she carried that off well too. Anyway, I confirmed our breakfast meeting. Annie did not have a car on campus and I told her I would pick her up at 9:00 A.M. and left. Some sleep would be a welcome respite after a very full day.

When I collected Annie the next day she had a little trouble getting going. In private she asked if her roommate could come along for breakfast. I said I would like that. We went to a restaurant that Nancy recommended. I was pretty hungry, but in their somewhat debilitated condition that was not so for them. I ate a full breakfast. They only got toast, coffee, and juice. I apologized to Nancy because Annie and I needed to talk business for a bit. She said, "That will be O.K. with me. Have at it. I'll be happy sitting here for a time just drinking my coffee."

I began by telling Annie that I, Dr. Berkowitz, and Dr. Lang were all very pleased with the way she comported herself during the defense of her proposal and that she was to be congratulated. She had done a nice job! She said, "Thank you for telling me that. I felt good about the way it went. Now, what do we need to think about for the coming summer?" Even with a touch of a hangover she cut right through to the meat of the issue. I said, "There are two things you have to do. I have a grant and can afford to pay you for your labors. You would be required to work about 20 hours per week. The other thing on the agenda is writing your thesis. I think you have enough data to make a quality argument for your case." Her immediate response was, "What if I want to do some new investigation?" I answered, "I would never forbid such an endeavor, but you will need to shut off such things somewhere and get the writing done. Your thesis should be pretty well written when you come back here to campus next fall. That will be a big job for you. A schedule will have to be set up: you write a section, I will read it, and we will go over it together. With about three months of this your thesis should be in good shape by fall." Her next question was, "What sort of investigation(s) are you planning?" I told her about the grant proposal I had written and gotten funded about periwinkles and their trematodes on the pier pilings and local jetties. I indicated in closing that you and Timothy get credit for the original approach you used on the oyster drill and its parasite.

I then said, "In a nutshell that covers what I needed to say to Annie this morning. Nancy, feel free to rejoin the conversation if you are so moved." She said, "I'm feeling better now." Our talk began to revolve around campus events. As I had intuited last night, Nancy was a very bright girl. She asked me about Sylvia Armbruster. She had read most of her latest book because her undergraduate thesis had to do with the American Revolution. I told her that I too had read that book. It was interesting to her that Sylvia operated from a branch of this University that was not known for original contributions to history. What was she like? How well did I know her? I said, "I know her pretty well. She is a hardworking, beautiful woman. The picture on her dust cover doesn't quite do her justice. We have been out together quite a number of times and we are cooperating on trying to encourage faculty research on our campus. I think highly of her."

At this point I allowed as how I had a long drive to get back home today and needed to get going. I paid the bill and took them back to their apartment. Annie thanked me for making the trip and ordered me to drive carefully on the way back. Nancy said that she was very pleased to get a chance to meet Annie's much vaunted advisor. I returned that I too was glad to meet Annie's roommate. They went in, probably to take naps. Having earlier checked out of my motel, I climbed in my pickup truck, filled my gas tank, and got directly on the road home. It was about 11:30 and quite a nice, crisp day.

The trip back was uneventful and took a little longer than four hours. I was pretty rested and my thoughts were mostly on satisfaction with Annie's progress, and my own. We had both done well in the last couple of days. I pulled into my abode on the coast at about 4:30. The first thing I did was call Sylvia. I wanted her to know I had gotten back safely, had missed her, and also about the conversation I had with Annie's roommate. She was glad I was back and said that she had also been thinking about me over the last couple of days. News of a history student that had read her recent book was welcomed. I allotted being tired from my trip and was looking forward to our dinner date tomorrow. We then signed off.

When the next night came I went to pick up Sylvia. She immediately started in gathering the details of what had happened in Annie's proposal defense and afterward. How did Annie do? What did Drs. Lang and Berkowitz think of her? Were there many students there? Did anybody take notice, besides Annie's roommate, of research activities on our campus? Over dinner I related the doings as completely as I could. Sylvia was very pleased, as I had been. It was particularly rewarding to her that people on the main campus had begun to notice the research accomplishments of faculty at this University branch. When I told her about the gathering at Annie's apartment and how I had ended up sorely missing her company. She said, "Well you've got it now. Suppose we finish eating and go back down to your place." A suggestion like that from Sylvia was not going to be missed out on by me. We finished and made the trip back in my pickup. We continued talking things over and she stayed the night. Her intellect would be enough, but her wonderful body added immeasurably to it. The form and feel of it has always intrigued and excited me. Sylvia is one voluptuous woman. After my trip I so wanted this commingling to happen and was happy that she had a similar idea.

I did not have any classes the next day, but Sylvia had to get back for a 9:00 o'clock class so we got up pretty early to head back to campus. A trip to her home allowed her to change clothes and freshen up. After that I drove her to where her class was. She was only two or three minutes late. In my office, some organizational things for tomorrow's classes were take care of and then I drove the half hour back home.

It was getting close to the end of the spring semester. In a matter of about a week I would be hearing whether I was to be promoted to Associate Professor. I certainly hope so. In any case, I needed to begin looking around for a new place to live. My landlord wanted to move into his beach cottage and I supposed that I had been renting long enough. So I put the rest of that day into looking for a potential abode. I found a couple of possibilities. One that I really liked was a smallish place nestled up right on the shore of a local estuary. There would be a danger of flooding when the tides rose abnormally high, but it was built for that. The living space was up on pilings and if flooding occurred, which would happen very rarely, no damage would be done if you moved any valuables up out of the way. I guessed my truck would be alright. The view out across the water was to my mind breathtaking and the idea of having my canoe right there on the water, just slide it in, was very appealing to me. I went to check on what the deal was at the realtor whose sign was next to the short driveway. I found it

Teaching, Research Proposals, and a New Abode Occupy My Time

would be expensive, but thought I could handle it if I got promoted. I told the realtor I was definitely interested. I had a promotion decision coming up this week and my decision depended on that. If the owners would accept $10,000 less than they were asking I would likely buy the place. Apparently the place had been for sale for quite some time. They might accept my reduced offer to be done with it. The realtor said she would ask the owners.

Before the week was out, word came down that promotion was mine. It would have been nice if tenure came with it, but even so the news was very good. Anyway, I was now Associate Professor Blake Turner. How about that! The Provost sent me a note of congratulations and Sylvia took pains to tell me how great my promotion was. Within a day I invited her on a trip down to the coast to take a look at the place I was planning, assuming all went well, to buy. On seeing it she really liked the setting. She predicted I would see a visitor often. Her, and I was attracted by that prospect. The promotion meant more money would be coming in and I called the realtor to see what the owners had said. They had said that they would do the deal for $5,000 less than the asking price. I thought about that for a minute and decided that, over the length of a mortgage, $5,000 wouldn't make much difference. I told the realtor that selling price was acceptable to me. She said she would draw up a contract and I could come in and sign it in a couple of days.

Visitopolis University had a deal whereby under their auspices a faculty member could arrange a mortgage. The University's involvement meant that the interest rate would be a little lower and the whole deal seemed pretty good. In fairly short order I had signed up for a 15 year mortgage. Over that short term monthly payments would be about twice what I had been paying in rent, but that could be dealt with. In a couple of weeks the ten mile move was executed between my former place and my new place. Buying a house was a major undertaking for me, but probably a wise one.

If the need arose that I had to leave this University, there might be some problem about paying off my mortgage. It didn't look like leaving would be a problem any time soon, but if that turned out to be the case, somehow I would handle it. For now, however, I had a great place to live. The front yard was protected from the estuary by a bulkhead. I loved having the water close to my doorstep and the look out over a picturesque view was inspiring to me. The estuary was about a mile wide with some tall treetops visible on the opposite shore. Starting this business of buying a house, taking on a mortgage, and moving in had only taken up about a month's time. The semester was just over. Annie was back and ready to start her important summer labors. I had a lot to get quickly organized for the coming summer.

Chapter 12

A LAST RESEARCH SUMMER AT VISITOPOLIS GETS UNDERWAY

All the people I planned to have work for me this summer, Zachary Trumble, Sophie Timmons, and of course Annie Hall, had to get started. That would take some doing because though Annie was tried and true neither of the other two had yet been involved in research. My grant would pay them all. Another major deal was my periwinkle research had to be put into action.

My first concern was to get Annie on her way. We met in the lab. My initial comment was, "The main thing I want you to do this summer is write your thesis. You already have more than enough data to build a perfectly good undergraduate thesis. Getting it produced will probably take you all summer so you better get started immediately. Do it your own way, but I suggest you begin with Materials and Methods. I will pay you for 20 hours per week and, if you do nothing but write, that will be fine with me. Of course, if help is needed in the lab or field with my research project I'll be happy to call on you, but you will be wise to stick to writing your thesis as much as possible. Let's set up a day next week when we can go over your first cut at Materials and Methods or whatever you attempt to do first." To which she responded, "I agree that Materials and Methods should come first and I will look forward to helping with your research project. It will be something I want to do and a good break from writing. Right now I will go home to get started on my thesis." She left and there ended our first meeting of the summer.

The first thing I wanted to do on my project was wait for a good day and get out to the outermost pilings to see exactly what I was going to have to deal with as far as that periwinkle population was concerned. I decided that the outer pier pilings would be potentially too risky for three people in a canoe on this first trip and I asked Sophie not to go. Two days hence a day came, but there was too much wind and I put it off until the next day. Zachary and I had got things ready for the first day and therefore were ready to go for the next. As it turned out I didn't need to, but on the first day I spent some time warning him about the tippy nature of the canoe in amongst those pilings. He responded by saying that he had read my paper about wound healing and was forewarned about what could happen. I commented that the water would be much deeper out at the end of pilings and it would be more difficult to recover from any mishap. We shall need to be very careful and watch out for ourselves. He agreed to take the best care he could.

On the next day the weather cooperated at least reasonably well. Zachary and I got down to the pier and launched the canoe. There was some wind, as is common out of the northwest, but not too bad. We used the protection of the pier to paddle out. Zachary was a proficient canoeist and I was happy to see that. When we got to the site we nosed in among the pilings. It was a little rough in there, but handle able. I wanted to examine at least the six pilings in one row in considerable detail. Out farther the pier expanded out in a T-shape so there were more pilings there, rows there consisted of about 30 pilings. We couldn't see them from where we were down on the water under the pier, but on the upper surface of the T part of the pier there were several nifty bollards to which ships could be moored. Cool! They are not all that common in my experience. Anyway, we made a count of all periwinkles we could see in the intertidal zone on the last row of six pilings before the pier got wider, measuring the shell height of the ones we could, and collecting ten of them to check for trematode parasites. We counted 63 periwinkles in that row on the six pilings. We could measure only 42 of them and all were quite large. In that row at least, there were no younger snails and this indicated no recent settlement of periwinkle larvae had occurred. The 10 collected snails were sequestered in a sealed plastic bag for transport back to the lab. After getting this done we ventured forth to check out other pilings.

At the offshore end of the pier there are 15 rows of pilings with 30 pilings per row. It formed a wide cap on the pier, which is simply referred to as the pier's T. That's because from above the pier looked like a giant T. Just shoreward of the T was the row of six pilings on which we had just counted periwinkles. I needed to know how far shoreward there was a similar population of periwinkles and what the situation was on the pilings of the pier's T. The periwinkle population remained substantial for 20 rows shoreward of that. Assuming (a big assumption) the counted row of six was representative of all pilings (an average of 10.5 periwinkles per pole), that would mean a total of 576

A Last Research Summer at Visitopolis Gets Underway 187

pilings and a population of 6,048 periwinkles on the pilings of the T and shoreward. If that estimate is anywhere close to accurate, it would mean that I have a considerably large total population with which to work at this site. On return to the lab we would see if any of the 10 collected snails had trematode parasites. While we were paddling back in Zachary, who had been pretty quiet, said, "It is pretty calm today, but I can see how it might get very risky around those pilings if there were more waves. It wouldn't take much at all to make what we did today undoable. But, I enjoyed the hell out of it." I then said, "Yeah it was fun, but let's guard ourselves and try hard to not get in trouble. I don't even want to think about getting dumped so far away from shore." We made it to shore, loaded the canoe and gear, and headed back to the lab. Sophie was going to meet us to help with the dissections.

We got back to the lab in the early afternoon. Sophie was there and Zachary spent time giving her a rundown of what we had done in the morning. He made quite a colorful tale of it. I told her that her main responsibility would be associated with jetty populations of periwinkles. In fact, tomorrow we would make our first exploration and I invited Zachary to come along too. He might as well get a look at the whole system. I explained to Sophie my calculation of what the periwinkle population might be on the outermost pilings and said, "We might have collected more than 10 periwinkles, but 10 are what we've got." I followed that with, "So let's see if any of these have parasites. It is unlikely we will find any because bird definitive hosts, which would be required, don't hang around those pilings much, but let's look." We commenced to put the ten snails under the hammer and then microscope for examination. My two assistants had done some of this sort of thing in their invertebrate zoology course so it wasn't entirely new to them. Not one of the ten snails was infected. I was pleased with their interest and the way they went about things.

The following day found us working at the first of two groins where there were periwinkle populations. This string of rocks will be referred to as jetty #1. We had also driven by the site of the other groin (jetty #2) just to show them where it was, but checking that jetty population was for another day. There is only so much time to work on one low tide. Sophie and Zachary would help each other out whenever needed, as would Annie, but these jetty populations of periwinkles would be Sophie's main venue for the summer. She certainly came across as eager to see where she would be helping with my project and was ready to go. I told the two of them that today would be a day of just looking this habitat over, much like what Zachary and I had done with our first visit to the pier. Today on jetty #1 I needed to see what sort of distribution periwinkles had on that particular intertidal jetty and get an idea of how many snails there were.

We also needed to assess what sizes of snails were there and collect a number of larger snails to check for parasites. The reason I wanted to collect larger snails was because they were older, had been around longer, and therefore had more time to take on trematode infections.

We arrived that day at jetty #1 when the tide was still going down and went to rocks on the jetty that were at or above the waterline as far out as we could go. The rocks making up this groin were about a cubic meter. Waves and currents would not move these rocks. They were of course festooned with algae and of irregular shape. When you looked closely down in between the jetty rocks, the environment in there had a character all its own. The confined air was still, laden with moisture, and the algae made for a sort of musty smell. It was just the kind of place where many types of invertebrates could predictively survive low tide. The algae growing attached everywhere made the rocks slippery. I had to caution my two compatriots to be very mindful of their footing when climbing about on them. Well, maybe I didn't need to harp on that, but I felt better having done so. My situation was still to be getting around without any trouble and they were both young and agile. We made it through our initial exploration without any missteps. That was fortunate. I didn't want me or either of my assistants injured.

We searched for periwinkles for about two and a half hours and our observations that day were kind of surprising to me. First, there were quite a few snails. We counted the snails on 10 larger rocks that were distributed pretty evenly along the length of the intertidal groin, trying to do a complete count of all snails present. We marked those 10 rocks with a magic marker we had with us so we could find them again and use them consistently. More visible and permanent marks could be put on later. There was an average of 35 periwinkles per rock. That is not many compared to other places where that snail occurs. In New England I could recall seeing periwinkles almost literally carpeting intertidal rocks. How much total surface area was available to these snails? Methods were needed for figuring the amount of surface area available on different sized rocks. That was a big problem. We would have to work on that.

Interestingly, there were a few smaller snails among the mostly larger ones observed. I couldn't be absolutely sure, but based on existing growth data they appeared to be something like two maybe three years old. That meant that within that time, at least within five years, these snails were larvae in the plankton and they had happened on this jetty and settled. It appeared so far that the pier piling population had not accrued any new members, but on jetty #1 the population had recently recruited smaller snails into it ranks. To get an idea of how the snails were distributed on the jetty, we made more cursory searches of various rocks from the beach out to where the water got too deep to go farther. Snails could be seen out beyond this.

There was an upper level on rocks above which snails were not found. The snails occurred downward from there all the way into the water to the bottom. Therefore periwinkles have a zone in which they live from that upper level of occurrence to somewhere down in the water. Intertidal ecologists refer to this phenomenon as zonation. We would have to account for that in our estimation of available surface area. Near the end of our field trip to jetty #1 I decided the population on the jetty could easily afford to lose 15 snails to check them for parasites. The unlucky chosen snails probably didn't appreciate being selected. We collected larger snails from here and there as we headed shoreward. Examining rocks farther out first when the tide is lowest would be a helpful idea. As the tide crept up nearer that upper level of periwinkle zonation we left and headed back to the lab. My new dissecting microscope should be in pretty soon. I eagerly awaited that, but in the meantime we would just have to muddle along as we had been.

Annie was there when we got back. She wanted to help with the dissections of a new snail species for her. Even if I wanted to, I don't believe I could have kept her away. As it was, I was happy to have her on the scene to serve as a creative model for Sophie and Zachary. They were both headed to the main campus in the fall and needed to know a little of what Annie was doing, what she was capable of, and what her situation was on the main campus. Besides, Annie was always an inspiring force to have around and on the job. We four got right into looking at snails. I held back and let Annie take the lead with the two students. Sophie and Zachary had already looked at pier periwinkles and knew basically what to do. Before long 10 of the 15 snails had been examined by them and by me, but no parasites were found. They all seemed very happy as they worked, jabbering away about this and that. When snail number 12 was measured and the shell cracked, lo and behold there was a trematode parasite infection. It was *Cryptocotyle lingua*.

Many species have been observed infecting the periwinkle *Littorina littorea*, but only two main trematodes use this snail as first host on the east coast of North America. This one in a periwinkle infects the snail's digestive gland and gonad. The parasite stages in the snail are rediae that produce cercariae. Second hosts are marine fish, in which the cercariae that are released from the snail embed as metacercariae. Definitive hosts are birds, gulls and terns that get infected when they eat fish infested with metacercariae. The last three collected snails were not infected with trematode larvae. Nevertheless, at least one parasite had made it to this southern extremity of the snail's distribution.

The miracidia that infected this particular snail probably came from an infected gull or tern that had spent time in more northern latitudes where it had eaten an infected 2nd host. Interesting! Would we find other species infecting the snail? Maybe the other often encountered species with sporocysts in the snail would be found, or maybe just more snails infected with *Cryptocotyle lingua*? Well, this is the stuff of science and why we will do what we will do. After we put the infected snail and its parasite in 70% alcohol for future reference, we decided to leave for the day. Sylvia had offered to cook me a dinner at my place so I had to get going. She did seem to like my new abode. On the morrow Annie needed to work on her thesis, but Sophie and Zachary and I would explore jetty #2 and the other population of periwinkles there. What would we find? What indeed?

I was glad I went home when I did. Sylvia, who took the key I offered her, was there. At my invitation she had apparently enjoyed most of a summer day right there, next to the water. She had gotten some tan. It looked invitingly good on her. I liked the idea of her feeling so comfortable in my new house. She is certainly a sought after guest. There was an open deck above the stilts on the water side of the place with an enchanting estuarine view. When I got there Sylvia was already getting set to cook some hamburgers on a grill out there. She had made some potato salad and fixed a green salad. It was a pleasant time getting that simple, excellent meal consumed.

We drank about a six pack worth of beers between the two of us. Eventually, she became sleepy and fell asleep on the couch in what I called the living room. Through a picture window it looked out over the estuary. She was sleeping very soundly and looked content, happy to be there. I threw a light cover over her to ward off any chill and went into my bed and went to sleep myself. The next thing my awareness settled on was Sylvia getting ready to leave the next morning. She had some writing to do back at her place and needed to get on with it. Only partly awake I muttered, "Thanks for that wonderful dinner and the great company" and off she went. From this place it was about a 25 minute drive to campus. She would be at work before too long. I crawled out of bed and availed myself gratefully of some of the coffee Sylvia had made. The low tide was just after noon at the jetty due for exploration today. I got some breakfast together and got ready to go and meet Zachary and Sophie.

During my early arrival at the site and under my gaze the water, with seeming purpose, ebbed down off the rocks. Tides are pretty damn cool. Jetty #2 was a little smaller than the one we had explored yesterday, but probably made at the same time from the same rock source. The individual rocks were essentially the same size. One of our soon to be completed tasks was to get a pretty good sketch of the chosen rocks in these jetties so we had a record of the nature of each and they could be found again and again for snail counts and sampling. But, not to be done on this day and about a half hour before low tide my team showed up. Having been through this yesterday, they knew what had to be done and over the next two hours or so we explored this jetty as we had the other. We counted and measured snails on 10 larger rocks distributed along the jetty's intertidal length. We marked these rocks so we could find them again. It came out that there were an average of 18 periwinkles per rock and they were all over 25 mm in shell height. It had been many years since larvae had been recruited from the plankton onto this jetty. Before we left, 15 snails were collected from various rocks to examine for parasites. In our conversations while exploring I mentioned that we needed to make a drawing of the rock situation on these jetties. Sophie responded that she might be able to do that. She had some artistic ability and would like to try. I pointed out that we had a camera on order. When it came in we could take photos from the jetties' sides on a low tide to help her out. If she were successful, then we would have a reasonable map of the snail habitats in which snails were counted and measured. We finished up in the field and went back to the lab to dissect snails. Annie came in shortly after we got there to join in and help. We found one of the 15 periwinkles from jetty #2 infected, again with *Cryptocotyle lingua*.

Well, that trematode is not very abundant, but that's twice we have seen it. Interesting, was it just due to an occasional infected bird that wandered down here from up north and led to occasional infected snails, or was the life cycle of the parasite being completed locally? The latter was possible because all of the hosts for the parasite, the snail, marine fish to serve as second hosts, and definitive hosts, gulls and terns, were present in the local area. If there were many infected periwinkles that would suggest local completion of the life cycle. We would try to see.

We took the next day off from fieldwork. I went up to campus and discovered that a big shipment of ordered equipment and supplies had come in, prime among which was my new dissecting microscope with a camera. There was also a field/lab camera that was meant to operate away from the microscope. The whole day and into the evening was spent getting that all up and working. The microscope was nicely equipped and gorgeous. Magnification went all the way to 60X, damn good for a dissecting microscope, and the lighting system was superb. The microscope camera was metered and arranged so it would mount directly on the microscope. That microscope and camera would really add to the equipment I had at hand. Grant money is nice!

Apparently Sophie couldn't wait to get the drawing of jetties underway. While I was fussing around with my new microscope in the lab she had made a trip down to the jetty we had been at just the day before. Late in the day I was in the lab dealing with the microscope camera and other equipment when she got back. She showed me the drawing she had already made of jetty #1. It was a creditable job, a little less detail than we would need, but very good. She possessed some real talent. The independent camera that arrived this morning was there and I had familiarized myself with it. I went over the camera's features and operation with her. Photos could be taken from about where she was standing when she had drawn to add the necessary detail to her drawing. Measurements of how tall and wide certain rocks were from that viewpoint would give us a good size scale for the jetty. Based on seeing what she had so far, it was predictable that she would come up with a very nice drawing of the snail habitat on which we could include the positions of the rocks we had chosen to count and measure periwinkles on. A representation of general snail distribution would thus also be gained. We could take more detailed photos of our selected rocks from various angles later. With my artistic talent, which is all but nonexistent, I could not have drawn even one rock successfully. So, how to go Sophie! You never know what wonders you might run into among the student ranks. A career path as a scientific illustrator would be open to her. There was a receding tide at jetty #1. She thought she could get there and take some photos. I gave her the camera, asked her to be careful of it, and she was gone. I finished ordering things in the lab in the next couple of hours and then I went home to eat, have a beer, and read a book. An adventure novel was yet waiting for me and it was that first edition of *Tarzan of the Apes*. That would be fun to get to.

The two days of weekend were about to arrive. There was no need to do any field work so Sophie and Zachary were not on call. They had worked well during the week. Annie called me at home late on Friday afternoon. She had a first draft of her Materials and Methods completed and wondered if we could meet to discuss it. Yes, we could definitely do that. Annie had not yet seen my new house and I couldn't think of a more pleasant place to work. Would she like to come down tomorrow? We could have our discussion then. I told her that if she couldn't find me when she reached the neighborhood she could give me a call for directions in. At about 9:00 A.M. the following day she knocked on my door. Of course, she was there and already knew of that infected snail we had found on jetty #2. She said right away, "Finding that second *Cryptocotyle lingua* infected periwinkle was interesting and spectacular." She commented further, "That may mean the parasite is completing its life cycle in the local environs." As usual Annie was having suspicions similar to mine. She had her first draft with her. It was 20 pages typed double spaced. I needed time to read it. I suggested she go out to the water's edge and kill some time while I did that. She could even put the canoe in the water and go for a paddle if she wished. It was a pretty day, the water calm, and she thought that was a sterling idea. Last summer she was a competent canoeist so I told her where there was a paddle and a life preserver. I would help her with the launch if she wished. She didn't need my help. She expertly launched the canoe and paddled away. While I was reading and making notes I watched from my deck as she traveled nearly out of sight. She couldn't have done that when I first knew her.

In an hour and 15 minutes I finished going through what she had written. By that time Annie was about half of the way back. I went in and made a pot of coffee. By the time it was finished Annie had gotten the canoe back on land and it was on its stand.

She was ready to begin talking about what she had written. First she gleefully related, "It was simply marvelous out there. I really enjoyed that. This sure is a great place." I offered her a cup of coffee. Accepting the offer she set about doctoring it as she wanted. We were ready to begin. I opened by saying, "You really have done a competent job on this. I can understand the somewhat heavy detail on this your first draft, which we can talk about in a minute. I just want to say that your whole thesis might be as much as maybe 100 pages and no more. I think you can tell the story in that amount of space and you don't need to overwork a reader with more than that." Her reply was, "That's good to know. I was wondering where to set the level of detail and length." I then gave her a specific. "For example, much of the information about when and where you collected herring gull feces to try to obtain live miracidia and how much time elapsed until you actually exposed supposedly uninfected oyster drills to them could be put in a table. That would save you maybe two or three pages." I added that in the same vein much of the data on the conditions under which the snails were maintained to wait and see if they had become infected could go more appropriately in another table. "Right there the Materials and Methods would be perhaps five pages shorter and still contain the needed information." She said, "That is a good approach and I will do that. It seemed as if all the text involved was unfortunate. Thank you for that." I then went over some nit picking things I had noted that needed correcting.

When I finished making my comments it had become early afternoon. It had been a time since I had eaten and Annie had done a lot of exercise. I asked if she would like a sandwich or something. She responded, "I sure would. I am pretty hungry." Nothing fancy, but I put together a couple of PB and J and we ate. We talked for a while after that, but she soon decided that she should go. She wanted to work on her thesis. I imagined she was tired. So off she went. I gathered that she was happy with her canoe excursion and with our session afterward.

Sylvia was coming down on Sunday to spend the day and I was looking forward to that. The rest of that afternoon involved a trip to the grocery store and more time with *Tarzan of the Apes*. I crashed early. On Sunday I got up at 7:00 A.M. and on the quiet day went for a canoe tour of the Bay. I came back and fixed an elaborate breakfast and by shortly after 10:00 Sylvia arrived. It was a sunny day and the rays she had previously caught made her mysteriously attractive. By now her tan was getting darker. I know, I always attribute good looks to her, but she was quite something. She had a meeting early the next morning and went home that night. As was my want I treated her finely and we had a first rank day. We both were pleased with it.

I went into the lab on a cloudy and windy Monday morning. Both Zachary and Sophie were already in there. They wanted to know what was on tap for this week. First I gave them a lesson on dealing with the new dissecting scope. Then I related that if the wind let up Zachary and I had to collect more snails from the pier. Sophie had taken the film on which she had photos of the two jetties to a 24-hour film developing place. The pictures should be in today so she could make use of them to increase the detail of her drawings and indicate the height of the rocks we had chosen to count periwinkles on. Next day Sophie could continue getting her artwork together. Low tides were very early and were predicted to get very low. If the weather cleared, Zachary and I could run our canoe trip.

It was a little blustery the next day. The low tide at the pier was about 7:30 A.M. and we had to get on the job early to get out to pier's end and do our work. The wind was mostly out of the west and northwest. While paddling out we were happy to be on the east side of the pier and enjoyed having its protection. I was glad that Zachary knew his way around a canoe. I had plans to find, identify, and mark 15 random pilings on which to count and measure all periwinkles. The 15 pilings had been chosen with the aid of a random numbers table. There was just no way to get that done. The waves were too frequent and energetic. The pitching, yawing, and rolling the canoe was doing would have scraped too many snails and other life off the pilings we were trying to assess. We would have to come up with a calmer day to get that job done. On the protected side of the pier we found we could approach pilings and collect some snails. Off four different pilings we collected 30 periwinkles. We put them in a sealed plastic bag in a satchel tied to the canoe. Individual pilings could be identified by noting the row number and the piling number in that row. I recorded which pilings they came from. Rather than writing things down, which involves keeping a pencil and paper handy under sometimes adverse conditions, I had adopted using a microcassette recorder. It was much easier to keep notes with that little bit of technology. The major danger in keeping notes that way was that the recorder might be dropped in the water. Were that to happen it was certain curtains for the recorder, but if it could be retrieved the tape would usually survive and could be played back on another tape recorder. Keeping the recorder in a plastic bag to protect from a dunking was sometimes a pain, but it was overall a good system.

After we had put our snail catch away a larger than usual wave crested through the pilings and upset the canoe. It was an unfortunate conspiracy of events. A canoe is pretty stable if you keep your weight centered in it. When the wave came through I was reaching out for a rare organism on a piling at that location, a sea star. I never got to identify it for sure. It got sacrificed with some other stuff into the deep as we went over in about 15 feet of water. It was only June and the water was still pretty cool and uncomfortable. Of course, there was no harm to the sea star, but we were put to considerable trouble as a consequence of the spill. The canoe was still afloat, but filled to the gunnels with water. Fortunately we were both unhurt. No pilings came into play to cut up either of us. But, we still had a big problem on our hands. We had to somehow get the water out of the canoe and get it floating on the surface of the water again. Doing that in deep water is a challenge. We swam the swamped canoe in close to some nearby pilings and I steadied myself and it against them. There was a two by four crosspiece between a pair of pilings there. You had to kick and reach up more than an arm's length above the water to get hold of it, but it was nailed in place, sturdy, and not covered with grasp foiling mussels and barnacles. It was a major aid in solving our problem that day.

We had a bucket onboard. It had drifted a distance away after the dump. I kept my hold on the canoe while Zachary expertly swam to retrieve the bucket. I secured the stuff in the canoe that had not disappeared into the water. The snails and the recorder in their sealed bags were O.K. I used the bow line to fasten the canoe to a piling and swam a little way after the retrievable paddles. They were with the life preservers floating nearby that had gotten loose from the canoe.

When Zachary got back to me he was in good humor. He came up with a string of wisecracks about our predicament. Most of them had to do with my having caused the canoe to be upset. I couldn't argue. We both thought the jokes we traded were amusing under the circumstances. They lightened up the situation considerably. The thought came to me that I could be damn glad it wasn't winter time. Were it that time of year this would all have been very deadly serious instead of just a little uncomfortable. Anyway, Zachary got busy bailing out the canoe with the bucket. It was a difficult job what with not being able to touch bottom. He got about half the water out of the canoe and at that time we switched positions. He steadied the canoe and I took to bailing. When I finished our next problem was to get back aboard. By using that crosspiece I pulled myself up to it and with Zachary steadying the craft I managed to get seated in it without upsetting it again. Then using the crosspiece in the same way he too neatly got in while I steadied the canoe. We still had some water sloshing around in the bottom, but we were afloat, underway, had our snails, and could get back to shore. We were in the water for something like an hour and a half getting all this done, but nobody was hurt and paddling in we both thought this little adventure was mostly just humorous. After this episode I felt that I knew Zachary much better. He was steady under fire. Good.

We loaded the canoe and other gear on my truck and in our separate vehicles made the drive back to the lab. Annie and Sophie were both there. Sophie had worked some on her drawing of jetty #1 and it looked very good. In my mind's eye I could see it in a future publication. I complimented her and thanked her for an excellent job. She had put the whole length of the jetty on paper and no single photograph could encompass that. There was no reason not to, but Zachary was eager to tell of our morning trip. At the telling Annie remarked that she could remember a similar circumstance. She added, "But, I'm glad it wasn't in such deep water. That would have made things much, much more difficult." Smiling Zachary said, "It was a bit of trouble, but we got through it O.K." Never one to be afraid to bring a moment down I said, "We have 30 periwinkles to examine and we better get at it. We will have quite a good sample of snails from those pier pilings after this: there were eight that I examined early last summer, 10 more from the last time we were out there this summer, and now these 30." I told Annie that I had seen a few oyster drills out there on those distant pilings this morning, but not nearly as many as on pilings in closer to shore. I wondered why there were not so many out there. What explains that? For that matter, what explains why there are more periwinkles on the distant pilings compared to nearer shore?

I basically let the three students examine the snails. They were well experienced and Annie above all would pick up on any trematodes to be observed. They came up with a little system and went through the snails pretty quickly. They all looked at all snails after removal from their shells, as briefly did I, and no trematodes were found. So far all together that was 48 piling periwinkles that were all uninfected. I mentioned to Annie that I was unable to explain that except by noting that, as she, Timothy, and I had found for the oyster

A Last Research Summer at Visitopolis Gets Underway

drill, the bird definitive hosts of the parasite just don't spend much time around those pilings. I did not see any at all around there this morning. I said, "Periwinkles can't become infected if there is no source of *Cryptocotyle lingua* miracidia. It may be that the point of our previous paper applies to more than one snail and one trematode. It may also be that miracidia are available there, but for some reason they can't often get to snails."

I asked Sophie to go and fish my mail out of my mailbox for me. Upon her return I glanced through the mail and immediately noted a letter there from the journal I had submitted the manuscript to by Turner, Hall, Holt, and Gillus. With heart in mouth I opened it. I was relieved to read that the manuscript had been accepted, and with no revisions! I immediately passed the news on to Annie. She was simply thrilled. That made two publications as an undergraduate for her. I thought she might enjoy passing the news on to Timothy and Toby and I asked if she would do that. They had both found research jobs on the main campus and were spending the summer there. She said, "I would be more than happy to do that. And, Timothy will be especially happy to learn of the apparently parallel situation between the trematode in the oyster drill and the one in the periwinkle. Let me go now and see if I can get hold of one or the other of our coauthors." She disappeared to do that.

Sophie and Zachary were deep in thought. I don't think that publishing something as an undergraduate had ever seriously entered their thoughts. Well, it had now and so they said. Based on something that had been said this morning Sophie had an idea about which she wanted to talk with Zachary. They too disappeared. We needed to go back to jetty #1 day after next. But, until then they were both free. As for me, I went to a phone and called Sylvia to tell her the good news. She liked to hear of student successes and as expected was happy to hear this news. She was busy writing and we didn't talk long. I called Provost Bigelow to spread the word. He was in his office and was glad to hear of the three students listed as authors. I gave him their names. I also took the opportunity to tell him that the three students I had hired this summer, Annie among them, were productively working. Here it was only the middle of June and we were making progress. I left out the watery mishap Zachary and I had today. He not knowing was best.

Chapter 13

AN UNDERGRADUATE INVESTIGATION TAKES PRECEDENCE

I thought I was done with this, but all of a sudden two letters came in asking about the fan worm parasite. They came from two medical people that wanted some instruction on collecting and dealing with that trematode. They both intended to investigate its wound healing properties. I wrote back and told them that the University had a policy wherein there was a charge of $200 per day for my time explaining things about this parasite. If that was no problem for them, then we could make an arrangement when they could come. I would be happy to accommodate. In fact, I wasn't looking forward to taking time away from this summer's project, but I would do what was required for both groups.

When I next saw Sophie and Zachary (the next day) they had spent a lot of time talking. They had a question to answer and thought they knew how to answer it. The question was: why are oyster drills so much more common on inshore pilings than on offshore pilings? I thought that was a good question, one that had occupied a little of my time as well. In the broadest sense it had to do with a basic query that ecology tries to explain: what controls the distribution and abundance of organisms? Their plan was to release somehow marked oyster drills around the base of pilings from which all drills had been removed to see if they repopulated those pilings. It was an experimental approach to answering part of their question. I thought it would be relatively easy to do such an experiment in shallower water, but to answer the whole question it would be necessary to also perform the experiment in deeper water out near the end of the pier. When I mentioned this to them they were puzzled about how to run the experiment far from shore. I offered that there are two possible reasons why oyster drills are markedly less abundant on those offshore pilings. First, the snail may be less abundant on the bottom out there, and second they may not be able to unerringly climb a piling to the height necessary to get into the intertidal zone on pilings in deep water. Maybe they are there, but lower down. They had more to think about. I liked the question and the basic approach and I told them so. The topic of Annie's thesis was the oyster drill and they might profit by talking to her. I did not offer anything else. I would wait to see what they came up with. It was left there for now, but I predicted a return to it in the near future.

One thing they got right onto trying to do was developing a method of marking oyster drills. They made a trip down to the pier and collected 20 drills. They tried to glue bits of paper on the shell of five of them. The paper didn't last more than a couple of days in the water of an aquarium. I suggested that they try a spot of red nail polish on shells. It might as well go on what would be sort of like the snail's "back," the part routinely kept away from whatever the snail was sitting on. They found that if they buffed the shell with sandpaper before putting the nail polish on, the mark stayed on the shell for at least days on end. Before long they had a reliable method of marking live oyster drills. Now they could run a field experiment.

We were due to go back to jetty #1. When we were last there we counted periwinkles on 10 of the larger rocks. We needed to count and measure snails on those same rocks again. Maybe they were not the very same snails in the second count, but at least we would know whether the number of periwinkles on rocks stayed pretty much the same. On jetty #1 we successfully found the 10 rocks on which we had previously counted and measured snails and this time marked the rocks more visibly and permanently. As an estimate of the amount of surface area available to snails we considered how many faces of a rock would be habitat for snails, which would generally be four or five. (That depended on whether or not the top surface of the rock was higher than the upper level above which snails cease to occur.) Measurements of the dimensions of each face would allow us to calculate a surface area for that face. This was of course only a crude estimate, as rock faces were not perfect rectangles and not perfectly flat, but at least the faces of larger rocks would add up to more surface area and smaller ones to less. It was a rough, but reasonable estimate. It took a long time to take rock measurements and count and measure snails on 10 rocks. That was all we were able to get done before the tide came back in, but it was a good day's work. On the next day we would have to do essentially the same thing at jetty #2. With that in mind we didn't collect any snails for parasite examination on this visit.

Next day, after we had done the 10 rocks at jetty #2, Zachary and Sophie wanted to talk more about their proposed experiment. For starters they first wanted to do the experiment in shallower water on more inshore pilings. Their plan was to: (1) denude the six pilings in a row completely of oyster drills, releasing them off pilings onto the bottom; (2) release 100 red marked drills on the bottom between pilings three and four (collected from other pilings); and (3) over the next few days observe how many drills (marked and unmarked) came back onto the drill denuded pilings. I thought about this for a minute and then commented, "This seems like a good plan. You are wise to start out with the shallower water experiment first. You should be able to spot red marked drills (as well as other drills) on your denuded pilings and I predict you two will have some success. The deeper water experiment will present big problems, however. But, let's not worry about that too much yet." They had most of their marked snails assembled with only 10 to go. Annie had helped with marking and was going to help them with the experiment, which was scheduled for Friday, Saturday, and Sunday in the coming weekend. They couldn't have better help than Annie. Me, I would stay in touch to help if needed, but I planned to stay away and let them run the experiment.

Sophie took a minute to show me the finished drawing of jetty #1. She had done as fine a job as on jetty #2. I thanked her for putting in extensive effort on these drawings. They will be of great aid when it comes to publishing something on this project. I salted them away for that purpose and suggested that if she could come up with a scaled down drawing of the four or five faces of a rock on graph paper, we could come up with a better estimate of the total surface area on the faces by simply scaling up the smaller drawing to the actual dimension of the rock. For starters let's begin with one of our 10 rocks on jetty #1. It still wouldn't be a perfect estimate, but it would be much better. All 20 rocks would be a major effort, but the doing of one would give us an idea of how difficult this would be to do and how good the estimate was. She seemed intrigued with the idea and said she would try it out at the next opportunity.

I didn't schedule any field trips for the rest of that week. Sophie, Zachary, and Annie could use the time to set up and run their drill experiment. Tides were predicted to be extra low this weekend. Now if only the weather would cooperate. Rain would make the work less pleasant and the wind might blow in from the ocean, which would keep the water in the estuary and make for a higher low water. Or, the tides might just not go as low as the astronomical prediction, which would make searching for marked snails on pilings very much more difficult. This will be a first experience in trying to run an actual experiment in the field for all three of them. The scientific structure of what they were going to do was as follows: (1) the basic observation was that there are clearly more drills on pilings moderately closer to shore where the water is shallower and fewer on pilings far from shore where the water is much deeper; (2) the hypothesis to explain this observation was that in shallower water drills could more easily climb up into the intertidal zone because that zone it is nearer to the sand at the base of pilings, but in deeper water they would have to climb much farther (up to about 12 feet) to get up into the intertidal zone on a piling; and (3) the manipulation to see if this made sense was to, in shallow and deep water, clear all drills off a row of six pilings and place 100 marked oyster drills at the base of the central pilings in that row and observe if and how fast marked (and unmarked) drills repopulated the pilings. If the hypothesis was true, drills in shallow water would repopulate pilings fairly quickly, but in deep water it would take longer.

Running the deep water experiment among the outer pilings will be much more difficult. Out there, depending on tide, the water can be 15-20 feet deep. In deeper water, are there drills on pilings below the intertidal zone? Is it a matter of drills not being able to climb on a piling all the way up to the intertidal zone without getting dislodged, or are there just fewer drills in the sediment around piling bases out there? Are both factors involved? These are just some of the questions that will require some difficult-to-obtain data to address. Given those data maybe then we will have a good explanation for why there are more drills in the intertidal zone on landward pilings. Field experiments, even relatively simple ones, can be troublesome to run, but running them is valuable practice for an inspired student. If my students can get their experiment to run and produce a result, I too will be inspired. They decidedly deserve the right to try.

On Friday there was a good low tide. The three of them got out there and examined very carefully the six pilings in the chosen row. It was June and the number of drills on them was substantial. They did keep track of how many there were on each piling, but on all six they were able to find and remove 211 oyster drills. To avoid inflating the population of drills on the bottom around that row, those drills were taken shoreward 15 rows of pilings and released. Once they had done that they placed their 100 marked drills on the bottom in the middle of the experimental row between pilings #3 and #4. All this about used up the time of low tide.

They went back for low tide the next day (Saturday) to see what happened. At that time they examined the pilings again. They found a total of 42 drills on the six pilings that were cleaned of drills yesterday, 19 marked (mostly on pilings #3 and #4) and 23 unmarked. So the pilings were repopulated with oyster drills in the intertidal zone in fairly short order, about 24 hours. They checked again on the Sunday afternoon tide and were able to find a total of 38 marked and 42 unmarked snails in the intertidal zone of one piling or another. More had come in. Drills found their way back into the intertidal zone of pilings pretty rapidly. So, as far as the shallow water site goes, the stated hypothesis was supported by the results of the experiment.

I kept out of their way all weekend and let them run the experiment. I was in the lab on Monday morning when they all trickled in. They excitedly told me about the results they had gotten. I congratulated them on successfully running the experiment. Annie was thinking a bit ahead of Sophie and Zachary. She already knew how important it was to somehow run the experiment in the deeper water among offshore pilings. Until that was done, nothing had been shown yet except that drills from the bottom could quickly repopulate the intertidal zone of shallower water pilings. The demonstration of it was nice, but we sort of already knew that. A comparison experiment was needed if anything was to be explained about why drills were less abundant in the intertidal zone of offshore pilings. As soon as she said something to that effect Zachary began to ponder seriously how they might run such an experiment out at the end of the pier. He of the three, after all, had the most experience with being out there. Sophie was thinking too. She said, "In the pilings we worked with when the tide was low, there were drills on pilings below the water line in the subtidal zone. Are there drills in the subtidal zone on offshore pilings and if so, how many?" At this point I said, "I have been thinking about this and that's one thing that we have to somehow assess on those outer pilings. And, if I might now interject, how many oyster drills are available in the sediments around the bases of those offshore pilings? I guess we will need a similar estimate for the pilings closer to shore as well. It might be that there are very few drills out that far and that is why there are fewer drills up in the intertidal zone there."

Zachary then said, "Dr. Turner and I have spent some time in the water out there and I think I can use a face mask and flippers to examine pilings for drills below the intertidal zone all the way to the bottom. That would be difficult, but possible. I confess that I am at a loss as to measuring how many drills are in the sediments around the base of those pilings." I responded, "In my original paper on the oyster drill population on those pilings I sampled them in shallower water during winter using a modified clam rake. I've still got that rake, but it won't work in deeper water. We ought to use the same method to sample the bottom in the nearer shore and offshore parts of the pier.

I said to the group, "There is a bottom grab I saw somewhere around here. It was probably purchased by some former faculty member for some purpose or another. We could dig that out and use it to assess the oyster drill population in the sediments. That should work." A bottom grab is a fairly hefty piece of equipment that is lowered to the bottom in the open state on a line, the mechanism of the grab is then triggered by sending a weight down the line, the grab then closes on a sample of sediment, and the sample can be brought to the surface. If operated properly, it grabs a known volume of sediment from a known surface area. I thought I had seen the bottom grab in a certain storeroom. Annie knew where that was and went to look. She shortly came back struggling to haul the approximately 30 lb. grab, its line, and its messenger weight. Zachary jumped to help her into the lab with it all. We put it on a bench, put some oil on its hinges, and got it working. It hadn't been used in some time. Anyway, before long all four of us had its workings figured out. We had to now get back to doing the work of studying the periwinkle. However, it had been a productive morning. Details of procedure would follow, but we had a basic plan for what had to be done.

What Zachary and I had to do was get out to the outer pilings again. When I proposed this trip to him Sophie was in the room and immediately said that she would like to go as well. She did need to get acquainted with the system out there. When I asked if she could swim the answer was a definite yes. So I said, "You are welcome to come, but be warned. We will, as always, try to pick a day with good conditions, but there are always apt to be unstable conditions out there and you might get wet." Sophie responded that she thought she could handle that and we then started to plan just exactly what we were going to do on this trip. We needed to see if the number and size of periwinkles on those 15 random pilings I had selected for the last trip out there could be determined. We couldn't do that last time out. We would need some way to mark the piling rows in which those pilings were located. We could then count our way to the desired piling in the piling row. A mark from a can of spray paint placed well above the water should work to mark the rows. Counting and measuring periwinkles would require minimal wave conditions, but it was essential to get that done. We also needed to collect 30 more periwinkles from various other outer pilings (not among the chosen random pilings) to examine them for parasites. A third thing we needed to accomplish was a count of oyster drills, intertidal and subtidal, on a row of six pilings. The last row of six pilings before the pier got wider seemed like a good bet. Zachary would need to spend some time in the water with mask and flippers to see how difficult it was going to be to search the subtidal extent of those pilings for drills (and periwinkles). I closed by saying, "If we can get that done, it will have been a great day. It is supposed to be a beautiful day tomorrow and the low tide is in the later afternoon. Let's see if we can do it then." They agreed to that and left for the day. I went to buy a can of spray paint and then went home.

An Undergraduate Investigation Takes Precedence

When the next afternoon came along I met Zachary and Sophie at the pier. It was an ideal day, almost no wind, sunny and warm. We got the canoe in the water and loaded with the necessary equipment. Sophie had not done any canoeing. I told her it was most stable if she kept her weight centered in it. She had command of the middle of the canoe with me in the stern and Zachary in the bow. The paddle out to the end of the pier was very pleasant in the calm water. I was thankful for the tranquil day. We found on the east side of the pier's T the desired rows of pilings and marked them with painted numbers. We had gotten out there ahead of low tide and Zachary could briefly stand in the canoe to get the marks up high enough on the poles. With all the rows marked we went to the outermost row and counted our way in to piling 12, the first of the 15 pilings on which periwinkles had to be counted. The tide was still ebbing and just above low water. We counted and measured all the periwinkles, as best we could without dislodging them, in the intertidal zone on that piling. It took some time to progressively find and go through the other 14 pilings. As we went we took 30 large periwinkles from other pilings to be examined for parasites. There were between 15 and 35 and a mean (average) of 21.3 periwinkles per pole in the intertidal zone on the 15 random pilings.

Of note is the fact that we found and measured a few small snails that represented larvae that had settled out of the plankton and onto pilings early this year or last. As before, if there are 576 pilings with an average of 21.3 periwinkles per pole, that suggests a total population of 12,268. That's a higher population than we thought we had on our first trip out here (~6,000), but in the same ballpark and probably more accurate. This higher estimate is based on a larger sample of pilings (15 random versus six in a row).

We had one more official thing to do: we needed to count the oyster drills in the intertidal zone on that first row of six pilings just shoreward of the pier's T. Zachary wanted to get in the water with mask and flippers to see if he could find any drills in the subtidal zones of those pilings. We went to where that handy crosspiece was and he used that to lift himself out of the canoe. In the process Sophie scraped her arm a little on some barnacles on a piling. It wasn't a bad scrape. I sort of humorously noted that I knew of a parasite fluid that would heal that scrape up in a hurry. She nodded understandingly, but said that probably wasn't necessary. Meanwhile Zachary swam over to the row of six pilings we wanted to make our count of drills on and we followed in the canoe. Sophie and I endeavored to count drills in the intertidal zone on those poles while he attempted to do the same by swimming down into the 12 or so feet of subtidal water on the same pilings. He wore gloves to protect him from anything sharp on the pilings. We could locate only a total of two drills in the intertidal zone on those six pilings. Down in the water Zachary did not have any luck looking for oyster drills. He saw none on the pilings, but said that visibility was pretty good. He would have seen them if they were there. On the other hand he could see periwinkles well down the poles.

So, periwinkles are quite abundant out there on the numerous pier pilings in the intertidal and subtidal zones. The few smaller periwinkles in the population on those poles indicated that planktonic larvae had been recruited recently from the plankton. It is important to know that, as on one of the jetties, the piling population there too has recruited new members recently.

On the other hand, unlike on more inshore pilings, oyster drills are not very abundant on those offshore pilings. In fact they are outright scarce in the intertidal and subtidal. We saw a few up in the intertidal zone, but none were seen on the poles in the subtidal. Neither adults nor larvae of oyster drills swim and they must crawl vertically on those poles through the subtidal zone to get up into the intertidal zone where there are potential prey organisms for them, e.g., a few oysters and blue mussels. Not that many pass through the subtidal and probably that is why no drills were observed down deeper on the poles. The distribution and abundance of oyster drills on the pilings of that pier mean that my students are asking a valid question: why are drills distributed the way they are on that pier with many on inshore pilings and many fewer on offshore pilings? Good for them. They need to use the bottom grab we resurrected to sample the sediments for drills. The experiment with marked drills also needed to be run at the offshore site. There was yet a lot to be done, but we did pretty damn well today because the Sophie and Zachary team worked out very well. Sophie operated with care. Even if the waves were worse she would have been O.K. Zachary's ability to go under water to examine those six pilings was really quite striking. It involved going down about 12 feet and he was remarkably adept at it. I suppose I could have done it, but was glad I didn't need to.

My assistants had keys to the lab. They were instructed to take our 30 periwinkles back and leave them in a bucket with a little sea water until tomorrow. At that time we would have to abuse their shells and use a microscope to examine for parasites. I went home and took my canoe off the truck. I hosed it off and cleaned up the paddles, life jackets, and such. Sylvia was there when I got back, had been most of the day. Working out there on the deck on her portable typewriter, her tan was becoming very sharp indeed. I wanted very much to tell her what we had discovered today. She listened with interest and carefully, and had some news about her current writing project, which was coming along nicely. We spent an interesting evening together.

On the following day we both went to campus fairly early. In the lab all three of them, Annie, Sophie, and Zachary, were already there. Annie handed me her Results section, which I said I would read as quickly as possible. Sophie's arm looked O.K. Annie had suggested to them that they might as well get started on the periwinkles. They had done 10 of them and had found none of them infected. Shell heights had been measured with vernier calipers and recorded. All 10 of the dissected snails were laid out in dishes of sea water for me to make my own judgments. I agreed they were all uninfected. These three were getting damned good. I told Annie that if she didn't think snails were infected that was good enough for me, but if any of them showed up infected I wanted to see that. I went to my mailbox and office to work on a few things while they completed doing the dissections. There were return letters from the two groups that wanted instruction on the fan worm trematode. They included proposed dates for their visits. I used the phone to get hold of the people and said that we could make one of those times work.

I started reading Annie's Results section, but it wasn't long before they came in to tell me that none of the 30 periwinkles were infected. So, as of now, that is 78 pier periwinkles that were uninfected, but two out of 30 (6-7%) from the jetties were infected. It looked like those two jetties could afford more periwinkles for dissection. We shall have to take advantage of that. A better estimate for parasitism among jetty snails was needed.

They all found seats in my office when I proposed that we spend some time thinking a little more about oyster drills on the pier and what was yet to be done. I started, "As you all well know, there are two main things to be done: run the marked snail experiment near the outer end of the pier, and assess the abundance of drills on or in the sand around inshore and offshore pilings. The bottom grab sampler grabs a surface area of sand half a meter on a side. It digs in for 13 cm, but we don't care whether the drills come from down deeper in the sand or near the surface. So let's do our figuring on the basis of area sampled rather than volume sampled. Let's consider the shallower site first. I deem that six grabs on either side (offshore and inshore) of the experimental row of pilings should give us a pretty good estimate of drill abundance in the sand around those pilings. Samples would be taken midway between the experimental row and the next rows to the inshore and offshore sides. We could use the poles in our row as a guide for where to take samples. That's 0.25 m^2 per grab times 12 grabs, or a total of 3 m^2 of sand sampled. At least in the shallow water that should be manageable. What do you think?" Zachary spoke up and said, "That grab is no lightweight to handle. Even at the shallow site, I suggest we bring the canoe along to give us something to work off." Sophie said, "That's a good idea." I added that in the shallower water people could help out with canoe stabilization from alongside. I then said, "At the deeper site we are dealing with at least 12 feet of water and all grab work there will obviously have to be done from the canoe. Getting that heavy grab over the side and down and up will require some canoe balancing, not to mention calm weather. I think Zachary and I could do that without mishap.

After counting the drills we obtain at a site we could replace them on the bottom, thus not disturbing things any more than we have to." Annie said, "If we think about sampling the inshore site first, we could get busy finding drills to mark as we did before." I said to that, "At the deeper site we probably should release more marked snails, say 200. Because we have already done the experiment at the inner site, we could mark any snails we get from the sand at that site for release at the offshore site. If we need more, we could take drills from nearby inshore pilings for release at the offshore site (which we might even mark differently). Then we could do the experiment around the offshore row of pilings that Zachary was just swimming around on our trip yesterday." We agreed to attempt taking bottom samples from the inshore site on the next early morning low tide. We had to wait a few days for that to come around so I suggested that we make another trip to jetties #1 and #2 to collect 30 periwinkles each, from rocks other than we are going to count and measure snails on. They will be dissected to examine for parasites. Maybe we could hit the tides at both sites tomorrow on the late afternoon tide. I told Annie I would read her Results section today and we could talk about it tomorrow morning if she could make it down to my place. She said she would be happy to do that and would be there at 9:00 A.M. And so we left it for that day.

For some reason I was very tired, getting to be an old man I guess. Anyway, I headed home and stopped at a local restaurant to get supper. When I finished that I went home to read Annie's production. It was almost 40 pages because she had included a rewritten Materials and Methods section as well as Results. I made some coffee and started in. She had improved her methods section and it now read very well. Results were pretty good, but there were some problems. I made a few notes and then crashed. I was not aware of anything until next morning. I had just barely gotten out of bed and made some coffee when 9:00 o'clock rolled around and there was Annie. I invited her in, gave her some coffee, and told her that tired as I was I had managed to read her work last night. I said, "Your rewrite of the section we last talked about looks very good and we can leave that alone today. The Results section has a few problems, which we need to cover this morning. But, let's drink this coffee first. Then we'll get started."

She was getting admirably good at the written word. The problems I saw had to do with tabular and graphic presentation of data and with some statistical oversights or unawareness in her analysis. In some of her graphs, for example in showing conditions in her infection cultures (water temperature and salinity) over time, there is a useable trick with which she had apparently not yet learned. Instead of two graphs, say one for temperature and one for salinity, at left and right on a single graph you can put two vertical axes and use the horizontal axis for a third variable, say time. That way you could plot temperature and salinity versus time on one graph instead of two. Use two curves on the same graph plotted with different symbols and/or line styles. There were several cases where this might profitably have been employed. Also, in graphs and tables there were problems with titling them. A table or graph along with its title should be able to be interpreted, read and understood, without reference to any other text. It is tricky business writing such titles. I gave her some examples of how to do it so she could make corrections.

The other errors I saw had to do with statistical practices and presenting statistical analyses. In her work she had tried to infect the oyster drills on several occasions over time. She wanted to make the point that it didn't matter when she exposed snails to miracidia; the success rate of infection was statistically always the same. That doesn't mean the infection rate was always exactly the same. Rates were quite similar, but she wanted to back up statistically that they in fact were essentially the same. That's always a good idea.

She had made four attempts to infect drills with mira0cidia gotten from gull feces. The number of snails that were infected and the number not infected for each attempt were set up in a four row (the times) by two column (became infected or not) table. She used something called a chi-square contingency test that could be used to see if any of the tabled values, in the infected and not infected columns, were statistically different from the others. If they are not, then infection success was always the same. I won't describe the test here, but it is a test that would work for this job. Her mistake was that she did the test based on percent of snails infected and percent not infected, a statistical no no. Suppose at one of her four times she attempted to infect 20 snails and eight became infected and 12 did not. In the test she should have done the calculations on the raw number infected (8) and the raw number not infected (12), rather than percent of each (40 and 60%). Annie had not had a statistics course yet and I have seen this error from people who should know better. Anyway, this and some other errors needed to be corrected. I finished by saying that despite the pointed out errors her results were quite clearly presented. She was to be congratulated. By this time it was approaching noon. My hungry self, invited her to lunch (peanut butter sandwiches again).

We ate our sandwiches and drank some milk. In our conversation she said that she felt she had done a pretty good job of writing, but she definitely needed advice about such things as I brought up. I accepted her thanks and told her with a grin that it was good that she recognized me for doing a good job. For such a student as her it was nothing but a pleasure.

Later this afternoon I was to meet Zachary and Sophie at jetty #1. I told Annie that if she wanted to come along she could hang around here, maybe take a canoe ride, until then. Otherwise maybe we could see her in the lab tomorrow to help dissecting our 60 snails, say at 9:00 A.M. She thought she would go back home and fix some of the things in her Results section while it was still fresh in her mind what had to be done, but she would come into the lab to help with dissections. After that in very short order she was gone. I killed about two hours and then left to get to the jetty.

This time it was Sophie and Zachary that were there early and watching the tide recede off jetty #1. The two were getting along famously. We just needed 30 large periwinkles from that jetty and there was no reason to waste time. The tide was a little more than half way down. We all waded in, climbed about on the rocks, and came up with our periwinkles from various places along the jetty, avoiding rocks we planned to do repeated periwinkle censuses on. In fairly short order we could get on to jetty #2. We drove over there and with the lower tide by this time we easily collected another 30 periwinkles. Again I instructed them to put these snails in the lab in two separate and marked buckets with a little seawater for overnight. Annie will be in about 9:00 to help with dissections. I was curious to see how many snails in this larger sample were infected.

Next morning all three of them were there at the appointed hour. By now they were a pretty well-oiled machine and got started processing snails right away. They knew what to do and I just stayed out of their way as much as I could. Annie in particular was sure to pick out any infected snails. To measure, dissect, and keep the data straight from a single uninfected snail requires maybe 10 or 15 minutes. Infected snails take longer. It was about four hours before they finished dissecting snails. The results were that two snails from jetty #1 were infected with *Cryptocotyle lingua* (6.7% of 30 snails) and one from jetty #2 (3.3%) with the same species. So, the prevalence of this parasite in this larger snail sample is not much different from what it was in the previous 15 snails examined from each jetty. Prevalence of the parasite was low, but it seemed to me that local infections arose because the life cycle was being completed locally. The other possibility, which did not seem to be the case, was that local infections were based on an occasional infected gull or tern wandering down here from somewhere up north. Of course, both things could be happening.

I didn't have anything planned for myself on the day before we could continue work on pier oyster drills. A call to Annie fixed that. The pier low tide that would allow us to continue with the drill investigation was coming up early tomorrow and I wanted to make sure the team was ready to go. Annie said she would contact Zachary and Sophie to remind them that this was coming up. I said, "The low tide is just after dawn tomorrow and I will meet you all at the pier then. Almost regardless of the weather we ought to at least be able to get drill samples from the sand at the site closer to shore. It will be good practice working with the bottom grab. With that little piece of introductory business out of the way Annie told me that she had reworked her Results section. It was a key part of her thesis and she would like to get my idea of its state. Could she come down to the coast today to discuss it? I said, "Sure, give me time to read it first and we'll go from there." She would be at my place about noon and would bring lunch for both of us. I guessed she didn't want peanut butter sandwiches again. Well, O.K., that's fine with me.

True to her promise, Annie rolled in around 12:00. She brought some tuna fish sandwiches and french fries she had gotten somewhere. I had some iced tea and provided that as a drink. We rapidly finished with the food and very soon I was reading the new version of her Results. It was a fine day and Annie went out on the deck while I did that. When I had finished reading I was happy to tell her that her graphs and titles were much better. With the exception of a couple of minor changes that I would suggest they were now pretty fine. She had fixed the statistical errors and as far as I could tell the Results section was in pretty good shape. She could leave it for now and go on. I suggested that she tackle the Introduction next. In that she would have to set up the question being asked, give any previous work on the general topic (a literature review), and indicate the benefit of seeking the answer to the question. The Materials and Methods told how she answered the question and the Results presented the results she got. After the Introduction she could start on the Discussion, always the hardest to write. My comment was, "Well, there isn't much to talk about today. I congratulate you on a nice Results section. It's a big step forward. You will come back to it and it will change, but for now you can leave it." Annie said, "I felt quite good about it the second time through. After your comments it all fell together quite comfortably."

We were done for the day. I invited her to hang around here if she wanted, maybe take a canoe ride or just sit in the sun. Her decision was to head back home to begin work on her Introduction. She had told Sophie and Zachary that she wouldn't be down here to work with them next morning. The three of us could handle sampling at that inshore site without her. If she came we would be one too many, and she wanted to work on her thesis. If later in the day they brought back oyster drills to mark for that offshore experiment, she would be around to help with that. Before long she got in her car and left.

With that early low tide tomorrow I thought I had better load the canoe on the truck tonight. The students were going to bring the bottom grab, buckets, plastic bags, and field camera from the lab. The near shore experiment now done we could mark all the snails we grabbed up from sediments. However, we might need more from pilings away from the experimental row. Collecting our marked snails mostly from inshore pilings seemed like a good idea. They would have a history of having climbed pilings. We needed 200 marked drills for the offshore site plus a few more snails for contingencies. After marking them we could get tooled up to run the offshore experiment. Zachary and I could go out there the day before the experiment started to take the 12 grabs to see how many drills were available in the sediments. However many were grabbed up at the offshore site would be returned to the bottom by dropping them overboard so they could potentially help repopulate the pilings.

Next day I rose early while it was still dark and left for the pier and the inshore sampling. The first light of dawn came into being about 5:15. It was a quiet day, no wind. The stars, twinkling in the dawn sky, forecasted that it was going to be sunny. About 5:30 Sophie and Zachary pulled in. We got the canoe unloaded, down to the water's edge, and the gear loaded into it. On the falling tide we could simply walk the canoe out to the near shore site. When we got there is was about 6:30, right at the time of low tide. Zachary would have to do most of the bull work with the bottom grab. It is good to have young and strong men around. I suggested he get into our craft and work the grab from there. It would give him a chance to see the problems of that work. He might learn something for when we were out in deeper water. He worked sitting facing the middle of the canoe on the bow seat. Sophie and I steadied the canoe from along its sides. We started on the offshore side of piling one in our row. We two charged with steadying the canoe made it a point to not walk where a sample was to be taken and did our steadying of the canoe from near the stern. The water was only about one foot deep. The grab settled to the bottom and was triggered. It grabbed its sand and Zachary lifted it back on board. We needed some sort of board to put across the canoe's gunnels to empty the grab's contents on, but we hadn't thought of that beforehand and the sample had to go on the canoe's bottom. There were six drills in that sample. Sophie gathered them up and put them in a plastic bag marked #1 offshore-side. We cleaned as much sand

An Undergraduate Investigation Takes Precedence 213

as possible out of the canoe and moved in to the offshore side of piling #2. After rinsing it off the cocked grab was lowered into that position and triggered again. This sample had four drills in it. Basically we worked our way progressively through the 12 samples in this way. Samples produced 6, 4, 10, 4, 3, and 7 drills on the offshore side of our experimental row and 2, 13, 5, 4, 6, and 4 drills on the inshore side. That comes to 68 drills in the total 3 m^2 of sand sampled, an average of 5.7 drills per 0.25 m^2 sample. These snails were left in their bags for return to the lab for marking. We needed another 135 or so drills for marking so we set about collecting those from nearby pilings. They went into a separate bag. The tide had been rising for a while and today's job was done. We walked the canoe back to shore, unloaded it and brought samples and gear to my truck. After hauling the canoe back to the truck it was loaded on. It was now about 10:30 and we needed to go back to the lab. In our two vehicles off we went.

When we got back the main job was to take care of the oyster drills we had collected. I called Annie to tell her of the data we had gotten, 68 drills in 3 m^2 of sand and 200+ drills to mark. The number of snails from the bottom was more than she expected. She wanted to talk to Sophie or Zachary. Apparently the message was that she would be in there early tomorrow to mark snails. I suggested to Zachary that we two could go to the pier tomorrow morning and sample the offshore site with the bottom grab to see how many drills were present out there. There was supposed to be very little wind, especially at that early time of day. He immediately said that a board across the gunnels to empty the grab onto when it was pulled up would make things much easier and he had a piece of wood at home that could be made to work for that purpose. He needed to get some measurements off the canoe and would get sample bags ready to go and the board fixed up. We would meet at the pier just after dawn. That should give us time to get out to the site by low water. In the morning Sophie could meet with Annie in the lab and busy their selves marking drills. Drills from the sand would be marked with a white dot of nail polish and drills from the pilings with a red dot. We might as well see if drills from the sand or from pilings were more likely to climb. Plans made, Zachary went home to work on his board and the sample bags. I called it quits for the day.

I got in touch with Sylvia. She was in her office. We went out to lunch. That was a good place for two faculty members, "out to lunch." She had something she was busy doing and needed to get back. We just ate some food and then she went back to work. Sylvia was appropriately interested in what we had found this morning. She wished us luck, which we might need, getting those samples in deep water tomorrow.

As it was just getting light out I met Zachary at the pier. We got the canoe and gear down to the water's edge. The board he had come up with was a nice piece of work. It was a 3/4 inch thick plank, a little more than two feet wide and a little longer than the canoe was wide. On the underside on both ends he attached pieces of wood to come up against the inside of the gunnels and keep the board from slipping off the canoe. Along the board's crossways edges that went between the gunnels, he had screwed on lengths of one by three inch wood that formed boundaries at those edges. They stuck up two inches above the upper board surface and kept stuff from falling off into the canoe. It was a convenient bench to work on. You could pull up a sample, unload it on the board, pick out the snails, and then wash the sand over the side to get ready for the next sample. I complimented him on the board and told him that it should be a great help.

We got all our stuff onboard and made the trip out to the site. The very light wind was a blessing. In this deep water we didn't need to worry about trampling on future sampling sites. Care had to be taken to avoid damaging the assemblage of life on the pilings with the canoe. We got into position for the first sample. Zachary got turned around on the front seat so we were facing each other. Using the board as a bench he cocked the grab and lowered it over the side. When he would have to lean out one way, I would lean out the other. With practice we eventually got pretty good at successfully balancing the canoe so it did not roll over and put us into the water. The wind remained minimal. Were there more wind we would have had a very difficult (maybe impossible) time getting these samples. Down went the grab and settled on the bottom about 12 feet below. He sent the messenger weight down the line to trigger the grab. It tripped, grabbed its sand, and Zachary hauled it back up. There was lots of balancing then. With effort he got the grab with its captured sand onboard and dumped the sample on the board. We looked through the sand, but found no drills in this sample. After washing off the board we were ready to move on to the next sample site.

We sequentially proceeded on through the other 11 samples. Several times we damn near got tumbled into the water when our balancing act wasn't up to par. But fortunately that never happened. It would have been a real pain getting things back in order if it had. Even if tied to the canoe and not lost, that heavy bottom grab would have been challenging to get back aboard from the water. Oyster drills found in the 12 samples were: 0, 1, 0, 2, 0, and 0 on the offshore side of our experimental row and 1, 1, 0, 0, 2, and 0 on the inshore side. That comes to 7 drills in 3 m^2 of sand (versus 68 at the inshore site), or an average of 0.6 drills per 0.25 m^2 of sand. Obviously, there were many fewer drills on the bottom out here. The few drills on/in the bottom at the offshore site must be a large part of the explanation for why there were fewer drills seen in the intertidal zone on pilings out there. Why didn't snails make it that far out? Could it be that out here they couldn't climb very high on pilings without getting knocked off and they need to do that for some reason? Maybe they needed to get up to the intertidal zone to get at prey species of some type. It may not be worth it to live where that prey is so far off the bottom. Well anyway, we had accomplished our task for the day. It was a couple of hours of hard work, done mostly by Zachary. I said, "If the weather allows and the girls have finished marking snails, we could come out here tomorrow morning and begin running the marked snail experiment out here." Zachary responded, "I'm for that and we will definitely need light wind conditions like today and a sun in the east would aid in finding and counting subtidal drills on our row of six pilings." We decided to head in as the tide had come up quite a bit by now. Paddling in was a pleasant trip and we pretty quickly got the canoe and other stuff loaded on the truck. In our separate vehicles we drove back.

On arriving there we found the girls hard at work marking snails. They had a sort of assembly line going. The 200 snails had to be gotten out of their aquaria to dry off. Once sort of dry each snail had to be buffed with sandpaper to further dry and make a clean spot on which to put the mark. Next was the nail polish mark, white for snails from the sand, red for snails from the pilings. After the mark was on, it had to air dry for at least an hour, maybe two. Then a snail could go back into its aquarium until time for deployment in the field. The marks of all 68 of the drills from the sand were already sitting out drying. They had 30 of the snails from pilings in the process of being marked at the time.

We took a moment and told them what this morning's samples had revealed. In 3 m^2 of sand there were just seven snails. They do exist out there, but in much smaller numbers. Sophie said, "Well, that will be a major piece of information in answering our question." I said, "Yes, and what this marked snail experiment will show is whether oyster drills in short order can even climb up all the way into the intertidal zone. Obviously a few make it, but how long does it take to accomplish the feat. Maybe we will get an answer. Zachary and I have decided that, weather permitting, we should try to start the experiment tomorrow morning. That means we will have to get these snails all marked today." The three of them got right into it and before the afternoon was out they finished all 200 snails and 10 more. I told them I would hang around for at least an hour to let them air dry before putting the last of them in the aquarium. Zachary and I could run the experiment by ourselves, but there is room for one more if somebody else wants to come. Annie wanted to work on her thesis and Sophie had another commitment so just the two of us were going to be it. I told Zachary he would have to pick up the marked snails and meet me at the pier about an hour after sunrise. We would go out and examine the six pilings for drills below the low tide line and then release the marked snails between pilings three and four of our experimental row. Over the next few days as the weather cooperated we would have to get out there to see if there were any climbers among our marked snails. In fact there were very few high on the poles out there and we would be interested in unmarked snails as well. Annie chimed in, "If there's not much wind, I'll go with you the day after tomorrow. That much agreed on, they left me alone in the lab. It was intriguing being in there alone. I hadn't recently had that experience.

My partner and I met at the pier at the appointed time. Wind was very light and the sun was low in the eastern sky. We loaded the marked snails, Zachary's mask and flippers, and paddled out to the site of the experiment before the time of low tide. He used that handy nearby crosspiece to hoist himself out of the canoe and into the water. I paddled over to our experimental row of pilings and he swam. It had entered my mind to get a mask and flippers to aid Zachary in the subtidal searches, but decided it was better to have one of us in the canoe in case something untoward happened, maybe a shark, an injury of some sort, or some other eventuality. Zachary had some experience doing this before. He hadn't found any drills on the pilings that time. The way he did it on this day was as follows. When he came to a piling he slowly made two trips down about 12 feet to the bottom, one for each hemisphere of the pole. He kept his face mask close to the pilings so he would see any drills. The sun slanting in from low in the east aided in visibility. It usually took four or five gulps of air per dive and two dives. Upon completing his examination of the first piling he came to the surface and told me he had seen one drill on the piling down there and lots of periwinkles. He moved on to the second piling in the row and did the same thing. No drills were seen on that one. On the third piling, there were no drills. On the fourth, there was one. On pilings five and six, no drills were observed. I counted a total of one drill up in the intertidal zone in our row. At this point Zachary announced that he had only one more dive to the bottom in him. He was getting exhausted, but volunteered to take the 210 marked drills down and place them on the bottom between pilings three and four. That way they would not be scattered by drifting down though all that water. That was a good plan if he was up for it. I passed the snails over to him contained in a plastic bag and he delivered them to the bottom. All together that was a lot of swimming and diving and Zachary is to be commended for being able to accomplish the feat. Outstanding! Even he did not know he was so valuable. He was pretty worn out, but we made our way back to the crosspiece and he helped himself back into the canoe with that. He had been in the water for about an hour and a half and said then he was glad to be out. The gloves he wore had protected his hands working his way down the pilings and the hand ware made the job less traumatic than it might have been. Nevertheless, he was pleased to be out of the water and back in the canoe.

There was nothing else to do at the experimental site on this day so we made our way back in. We loaded things up. I told him that if we can do it I expect to come out here tomorrow with Annie. He well deserved a day off. Following that short conversation he drove back to campus and then probably home to take a nap. I went home to relax the rest of the day.

I called Annie to tell her if tomorrow morning is anything like this morning we ought to be able to visit the site of the ongoing drill experiment. I said, "Zachary did real yeoman service this morning. He deserves a lot of praise for all the swimming and free diving he did. It took a lot of effort. About now he is probably sleeping." Conditions were very good for this part of our work on this problem. His examination of the six pilings revealed only two subtidal oyster drills, one on piling #1, and one on #4. I counted only one up in the intertidal. Also, he delivered the 210 marked snails to the bottom and placed them on the sand between pilings three and four. So we did get the experiment going. I finished by saying, "Could you call Sophie and tell her what happened and could you and I meet at the pier tomorrow at 9:30?" She said, "Yes." That was all and we hung up. I made some lunch and spent the rest of the day reading, a good part of it out on the deck. My own tan was getting pretty bronze now.

When Annie and I went out to the experimental site next day, there was considerable wind out of the northwest. The water was choppy and a bit of a challenge, but we didn't need to do much besides look around for marked snails that had climbed up to the intertidal zone on those pilings. We both thought that we should try to go out and look. We bounced around a bit, but didn't see any marked snails in the intertidal zone of our experimental piling row. Annie unabashedly enjoyed dealing with the wave action. Having been out there the last two days, I was a less thrilled with it. If oyster drills were going to get that high on the pilings at all, they apparently had not done it yet. That's not really a surprise given the small number of snails at any level on those pilings. But, as of yesterday there were 210 oyster drills in place between the center poles in the row. That represents a comparatively very dense drill presence. If drills can climb to the intertidal zone on pilings, they should do it there. It was a useful observation to have made that the snails apparently couldn't reach the intertidal zone in some 24 hours. It would also be useful for Zachary to go back down there and see how high they had gotten. We paddled our way back to shore and put the canoe on the truck. Given the way things were going, it will be necessary to check the site again in two or three days. Maybe Sophie would like to make the trip. Annie left to go work on her Introduction some more. I had some scientific articles from the library to read and I went home to do that.

From home I called Zachary. I wanted to tell him that we looked, but didn't find any marked drills up high on the pilings today, either with red or white marks. I guessed it was too soon. Also, in the next few days we had to do another count and measurement of periwinkle snails on the pilings and on the two jetties. There will be afternoon low tides for the next few days and we might use them to make more periwinkle observations. On our next trip to a jetty Sophie should try out making a detailed sketch of the faces of one of our rocks to improve our assessment of available surface area. We could help her make the necessary measurements. Zachary could do a jetty trip three days hence as he had to do something with his family for the next two days. I agreed to that schedule. So the plan was for on a later day tide three days from now. We then terminated our brief conversation. I next put a call into Sophie. She had to be informed of our plans for the next few days. I was able to get in touch with her and told her the experimental news and that Zachary was tied up for the next couple of days, but we thought we might make a trip to one of the jetties the day after that. It will be in the afternoon. That was O.K. with her. I said a couple of words about making a detailed sketch of one of the rocks and then we hung up. I settled down to do some reading.

So here it was just approaching July. Things were going pretty well, but as things turned out this was to be my last productive summer of research at Visitopolis University. Annie's thesis was coming along nicely and she was doing enough field and laboratory work to keep the summer interesting for her. In addition I had two other students who were working out very well. They were dedicated workers on the periwinkle project and to boot they had asked a workable question about the ecology of the oyster drill. The experiment to answer that question was well under way and it looked like there would be an answer. Possibly a publication would come out of that work. Maybe I should just give whatever aid I can and let the students write it up and have the publication. For my periwinkle work a lot of information was coming to light. It is difficult at this stage to see what all will come out of it, but I think that work too will result in at least one publication. With the sum of all our activities, that is, me, Annie, Timothy, Toby, Zachary, and Sophie, we are contributing a bit to mankind's knowledge. As I have said many times now, in addition to disseminating knowledge, that is what a university is all about. So this summer and others thus far are an unqualified success.

Chapter 14

BOEUF BOURGUIGNONNE AND A CONFESSION

Here it was at the beginning of July in 1979 and I had a couple of days with no research activities. I called Sylvia to see if she could go out to dinner with me tonight. She said, "I have something to talk with you about. If you have some empty time, I think I would rather come down to your place and cook you a dinner, unless you are set on going out." I came back, "No, I'm not set on that. If you can swing it tomorrow, let's do it then." She said, "Yes, I can do that and don't worry about getting any groceries. I have something in mind and will handle that." Her expected arrival time was early afternoon tomorrow. I closed our conversation by saying, "Sylvia you are definitely a classy woman and I'm looking forward to it." Then I went on home. It was about dusk when I got there and with the sun in the process of disappearing across my estuary there was a superb sunset. I enjoyed it for a while then watched some TV. A western novel by Owen Wister occupied a little of my time and then I went off to sleep.

In the morning I arose about 6:30. After eating some breakfast I put the canoe in the water. I thought I would go for a ride. It was cloudy with a steady wind out of the northwest and I had to labor pretty hard to get away from my place and out into the estuary. I put a five gallon jug of water up in the canoe's bow. The bow rides high out of the water when you alone in a canoe and sitting on the stern seat. The weight of that water-filled jug kept the bow down and helped keep it from being pushed to the left by the wind as I paddled out. It was easier to stay on the course I had decided upon. The conditions were exhilarating. The waves were not that big or dangerous, but they did keep you busy. You didn't want to allow them to hit the canoe too much from the side. Moving against the wind and waves you had to keep the canoe properly angled into the waves or else it might be rolled, upset and swamped, which would have meant a long swim to shore. Spray came over the bow, but this little trip was my election and its challenges were welcome.

In roughly an hour I made it over to the other side of the estuary, about a mile distant. There was some protection from the wind there. I was a bit worn out and paddled around near that shore for a while. Then I headed back across the bay. With the wind almost directly on my back going that way, it only took some 20 minutes to be back at my shore. By the time the opposite shore was mine, the wind had pushed me to the south of my house and I had to fight my way north to regain my target destination. That was a fun ride. I got the five gallon jug emptied out and took the canoe out of the water at about 10:30. It sat there on shore high and dry as though nothing had happened. As for me, I recognized this had been a sterling time. My house up there on its stilts received me nicely. The clouds were starting to break and from my deck and in the new sunshine the bay was dancing about with sparkles. I made some coffee, poured it, and took my refreshment out on the deck to just look and take it all in. I was happy to be there.

At 12:30 Sylvia arrived with a couple of paper bags full of groceries. I kissed her hello and said, "My goodness what might you have planned?" Her reply was, "It's a surprise and it will take two or three hours to prepare it." My rejoinder was, "Well, if that's to be dinner, then maybe you need something for lunch. I have some bread and some tuna fish." Sylvia's reply was, "No, I've got that covered too. Just leave me alone for a few minutes." I went into another room and very quickly she invited me back into the kitchen. She had some homemade turkey sandwiches and other things, including warm purchased french fries, iced tea, and a simple salad, all put out on the table. Everything was delicious and after my exercise this morning certainly was welcome.

She cleaned things up and organized the other stuff she had brought. Then she said, "Let's go out on the deck for a while. It didn't look too good this morning, but it has become a wonderful day." She probably wanted to work on her tan some more, which was a great idea as far as I was concerned. I went on out and she changed into her bathing suit and, looking very fine, she followed.

Sylvia had some news. The simpler thing was that she had taken up with a student who had proposed to pursue research toward doing an undergraduate thesis. Sylvia was genuinely thrilled by this and thanked me for indirectly inciting this student to try this. Apparently this girl knew Annie and what she was doing. The plan was to investigate a local occurrence of about a hundred years ago that was noteworthy and of historical importance. I said, "If this student is any good, I think you will be amazed at how she will progress once you open up her intellect by searching for the answer to a real question. Congratulations! That is a wonderful thing to do for both of you. Do I know her?" She said, "Her name is Agnes Moore and I believe she was in a non-major's biology course you taught. She is indeed very good. I've had her in two courses and she expresses herself in writing very well. I have high hopes for the way this will turn out." I said, "Yes, I remember her now. Agnes handled my course nicely. As I recall, she got an A."

She went on, "For another thing, I got word just the other day from Provost Bigelow that my in-house grant has been funded. That money will come in very handy." I responded, "Another congratulations to you. I haven't been following the status of that lately. I'll have to see who else got funded." Sylvia said, "I can tell you. It was me, Steve Wagner, and Eric Mortimer." I replied, "Having sat in on judging those proposals, I'm glad it came out that way. For Biology I am very happy that Eric got his money."

The other news was not so simple. Provost Bigelow had offered her a job. He had said that he was very impressed with her initiative and the way she had handled invigorating research on this campus. He wanted her to become something to be called the Dean of Research on this campus. I thought immediately when she said this that it sounded like she was being kicked upstairs. But, it wasn't that bad. It would mean a substantial raise in pay for her and an operating budget. She would still have to teach two courses per year. And, she would have to oversee and facilitate all faculty and student research done on this campus. I said with a smile, "Sylvia, I guess that would mean a new boss for me." She smiled becomingly in return and said, "I'm not sure I'm going to take the job. It would make things quite different, but it has possibilities. What do you think?"

I silently thought for a while and then expressed this to Sylvia,

> Well, it would make you an administrator, but if we take Provost Bigelow as an example that need not necessarily be bad. In fact it might be good. If you decide to do it, I can't think of anyone who would do a better job in such a role. In that capacity you stand to raise the respect that faculty have for administrators. But, I do worry about how much you will be separated from your teaching and research. You need to remain open to new ideas. That you will be teaching two courses a year ameliorates that worry a bit and I suspect that you will maintain your interest in scholarly activity. Teaching and research seem to be part and parcel of being you. It would be a shame to see those strong interests of yours disappear, which for many administrators they do. At least you must maintain your

connection with students. They keep you alive. The University would suffer great loss if you were to allow that connection to lapse. On the other hand, your existence would be less structured. You wouldn't have to teach so many courses, which would free up time for other endeavors. Not only that, but the administrative job you would take on is a noble one and one you have been expressly working toward for about a year and before that. You could do even more fostering of research by faculty and students with a quite powerful position such as Dean of Research. On balance, it will mean big changes, but I come down in favor of you taking the position. Getting swept away into the wasteland of administration is a danger. If you don't let that happen, this is a position where you can really put forward what we have been promoting for the past year. The pay Provost Bigelow has offered, roughly a 50% increase over your current salary, suggests that he is dead serious about this offered position. He wants something from it and you.

After sitting there in the sun and patiently waiting for me to finish, Sylvia responded with a question, "Do you really think the Provost is that serious about this position?" I said, "Yes I do. He would not come up with a pay scale like that for you if he didn't want you to move research ahead on this campus." She replied, "The money is very attractive, but I wouldn't want to become Dean of Research unless I thought he really wanted me to do something." My response was, "Well, he hasn't led us astray so far. And, he has wisely picked up on you as the person for the job. The $50,000 dollars he arranged for the In-House Grant program certainly suggests he's serious about the future implementation of research on this campus." She said finally, "The Provost wants an answer by the end of this week and right now I'm thinking about accepting the position. I'll have to make a final decision soon. I thank you for your thoughts on the matter. I especially liked the bit about the need to maintain my connection with students. I will have to make a plea to him for it to be understood that I need to do that. They do keep you alive. All too often administrators become insulated from students and I'm thinking of making that a condition of accepting the job." At this point she shut off this topic. We had been out on the deck for nearly two hours and she had gotten enough sun for the day. Anyway, she had to go into the kitchen to prepare that surprise dinner and got up to do that. What was it to be?

I left her alone to do her thing and busied myself down in the yard turning the canoe over and stowing the paddle, jug, and life vest. While I was puttering around something that had been bothering me for a time came into my mind. I had been debating with myself the necessity and advisability of telling Sylvia

Boeuf Bourguignonne and a Confession

about my involvement with former Provost Flannery's death. Except for that I had always been honest with her. I felt bad about keeping this a secret from her. It had been more than a year since it happened and I had not been drawn into it in any way. To my knowledge it was not being further investigated. It didn't look like I would in any way be involved. Apparently his death had been chalked up as an accident by all concerned. My reservation was: should I even bring her into it? Especially because of the job in the administration it looked like she was going to take on, was that fair to her? Should this information clutter up her world? This was a debate with myself I could not settle in the abstract. I would have to make a decision at the moment when it felt appropriate to bring the subject up.

When I went back into the house Sylvia was being very busy in the kitchen. I couldn't tell what she was preparing, but there was some kind of cooking meat involved and the place smelled better than it ever had. She didn't want me nosing around where she was working so I went into the office I had set up and busied myself with the novel I was reading. Something like an hour later she called me to the kitchen table, the only one in the house. "Dinner is now served," she announced. The table was nicely set. There were four pots. Through the glass covers on three I could make out a vegetable (fresh string beans), some mashed potatoes, and what looked like a soup. The main entree was hidden from me by a metal cover. We had some delicious vegetable soup. When the cover came off the main dish I didn't recognize it. Such is the state of my culinary expertise. She rescued me by saying, "It's Boeuf Bourguignonne." In the pot the beef and other things were festooned over with mushroom caps, small onions, and parsley. When I tried some I could taste olive oil, garlic, and cognac plus there were a variety of spices on my palate. It was superb tasting. The beef must have been a very expensive cut because a fork was all that was needed and it almost literally melted in your mouth. After consuming goodly quantities of everything, I said, "Now that was an experience! I have heard of Boeuf Bourguignonne, but never had it available to me. Really excellent and my stomach thanks you profusely." She said, "I haven't put that together in a long time. It takes quite a while and I have not had an occasion where it seemed worthwhile. I'm really glad you liked it." I answered, "I sure did, in spades." We poured some of the cognac and had an after dinner drink and talked a bit. She explained some of the steps that went into making that dish. There were lots of them and my appreciation for all the trouble she went to went up. After the cognac had been consumed, against her wishes I helped her get things cleaned up and put away. When it was all done I said, "Thank you Sylvia, I don't know where we could possibly have gotten such a marvelous dinner out."

It was warm out and there was a breeze that kept mosquitoes from being an issue. We lit a couple of hurricane oil lamps and sat down out on the deck. It was very pleasant out there as we drank some coffee. After we got done commenting on the spectacular evening there was a lull in the conversation and thoughts about telling Sylvia of the former Provost came flooding back into my head. There wasn't anyone anywhere nearby and no danger of somebody else hearing. If I was going to do it, this was the opportune moment. I thought to myself, should I? Honesty is the best policy and it seemed to override any other considerations. Additionally, it would be a load off my mind so I decided to go ahead. I began,

> There was a time, even though the way you thought you handled it was not very good, when you felt it necessary to tell me of your tense experience with Provost Flannery in his office. And, I'm so glad you did. It prepared me for what might happen to me in a similar meeting with him and it allowed me to maintain something of an upper hand. But I have told you all that before. There is more to tell and I believe I should tell you. I hope it is not a burden to you. It has bothered me that I couldn't tell you of this before and I want to be right in doing so now. I do it for the sake of our personal relationship, which I value very much. In a nut shell, I was with the Provost at the time he died. I did not do him any harm. He brought that on himself. After it was over I gambled that no one knew I was there and I decided to just leave.

At this point Sylvia interjected, "Damn! What happened?" I returned, "I don't know if you were ever at his house." She said, "No." And, I continued,

> He personally called me up in my office and invited me out to his house the next night. He said he had hopes we could have a discussion and maybe come to an agreement about our differences. You had just left to go to that historical meeting that spring and you weren't here to discuss this strange invitation, which I certainly would have done if were you here. You being gone changed the whole situation. At his house there's a deck something like this one. It's situated over a driveway at the rear of the house. We were standing out there on that deck talking with drinks in hand. While I was there I had two beers. He was drinking some pretty stiff bourbons. Our talk went well enough at first. He ventured an offer. I would be allowed to publish one paper a year. To explain why that might not do, I told him about the wound healing paper being reviewed and the notoriety it might bring if published. I also told him about my two student assistants

and our submitted manuscript and the general enhanced interests of students in research activities. I think he perceived all that as a threat to his idea of how this place should be run because the whole character of the evening was different when I finished. He became noticeably unfriendly and challenging to everything I said.

Unwisely I pushed it. I asked him why he didn't want faculty doing research on this campus. I didn't bring up the story you passed on to me about his unsuccessfully trying to publish a book on his dissertation, but I did press my inquiry by asking why he had never published anything. Finally, I accused him of abandoning his academic discipline and training leading him to not want any faculty under him to be involved with research. He didn't answer, but I must have struck a nerve, too much truth I fancy. His demeanor told me he was really pissed off. I was standing with my back to the deck's railing and the next thing I knew he was coming at me with a martial arts punch of some kind. You may recall that he had a black belt in taekwondo. I saw it coming and luckily managed to sidestep it. His forward momentum took him right over the railing. Down he went about 15 feet onto the driveway's pavement. A look down showed him quietly lying there next to my pickup. I gathered myself and went down there to check on him. He was dead. It looked like he had broken his neck in the fall. Very upset, I left him there as he had fallen to go back inside and call the police. I started to call, but then had reservations. What was I going to tell them? Why was I there? What were we talking about? He had threatened my job and eventually the questioning would lead to a motive for pushing him off the porch. I thought about that for a short time and decided it would be best to just leave and hope that nobody else even knew I was there. My fingerprints are not on record anywhere, but I spent some time cleaning up wherever I might have left them. I got in my truck and left with him lying there in the driveway. That was the last I ever saw of the place.

Sylvia said, "My goodness! I don't think in your place I would have had the nerve to leave, but it seems to have worked out O.K." I came back, "Yes, that was a tough call to make." Her reply was, "I just need a moment to think about what this all means." After a little while she said, "This all seems to have worked out for the best and I certainly won't say anything to anyone, but how did you feel about all this?" I responded, "Well, not good, but I had to play it out. Once I started it what else could I do? For a time I worried rather a lot about the police showing up to question me, but that never happened. It has been more than a year and I guess it's all settled now. I sure hope so."

Then Sylvia said,

Well, it is too bad you (and he) had to go through that, but it certainly opened up possibilities for this campus. Bigelow is definitely a better Provost than Flannery ever was. His backing of our faculty research agenda has been a boon. It will mean a lot to this campus. The job offer I am presently considering would never have come to be had he not taken over the role of Provost. The other big benefit is that you are not going to be terminated, which is most likely what would have happened had Flannery continued. It will be nice to have you around at least for a while. It seems that it all resulted in things looking up for me and I am thankful for that. As of this moment I have decided to accept the position of Dean of Research. I plan to use it to try to make something out of this branch campus of Visitopolis University. Wish me luck.

I replied, "I think you will be an unqualified success and I thank you for taking the opportunity. It will do great service to this University."

We let it drop about there. Sylvia was filled with thought the rest of the night. She did take time out to exclaim twice, "I know I have said this before, but I can't believe you decided to just leave." She didn't have to be on campus until late tomorrow morning. Eventually what I had told her quieted down in her and we lay down together. We pleasantly stayed there until morning. After some breakfast she bundled up her stuff to go back to her office on campus. I thanked her again for the wonderful dinner. She thanked me for a very interesting evening. She said, "I am so pleased you told me what happened. I wouldn't like something like that to be hidden from me." After that she left and that was it. Evermore, we spoke not at all about Jacob Flannery events. That business was not necessary to cover again. I was relieved to have told her. I did hate to have that dishonesty resident between us.

Chapter 15

SNAILS, FAN WORMS, AND A HINT OF TANGLED WIRE TO COME

Back to research - I was thinking about getting back out to look over those pilings for drills, but after Sylvia left I chose to ready for the next day's jetty trip. I thought we would tackle jetty #1 first. At this point we had our 10 rocks picked out and counted and measured all periwinkles one time. How dynamic are the periwinkle populations on those jetty rocks and pier pilings? We needed to do that again to see if the numbers of periwinkles on rocks stayed pretty constant or what. If the population on a rock had the same sizes of snails in the same proportions as the first time, it would suggest that probably the same snails were present on the rock on both occasions. If, on the other hand, the proportions of size classes changed from one time to the next, that would suggest that the population of snails on that rock had been invaded by new members or that members of the old population had left. Numbers and measurements of snails, collected in so called size-frequency distributions, would give us a clue to the stability of populations on groin rocks and pier pilings.

Suppose that from one time to the next on a rock the proportion of 20 mm snails went up dramatically. That would suggest an invasion of 20 mm snails on that rock. By comparing the size-frequency distributions (graphs) through time we could determine whether the population on a rock stayed stable or not. When we finished gathering data for this run through we would have two graphs to compare for 20 jetty rocks and 15 randomly chosen pier pilings. I didn't guess that periwinkle populations on pilings would change all that much. After all, snails can't swim from pole to pole. To change pilings an intertidal snail would have a long trip down one piling and then up another. Populations on jetty rocks had more chance to change because the rocks are closer. The first job was to get the data for jetty #1 and make the graphs. Zachary and Sophie could make those graphs. What I needed to do was make a model graph to show them how to do that. I spent the rest of the day hunkered over my desk at home making up model graphs for them to use.

When the next day came, I met up with Sophie and Zachary at jetty #1 on the afternoon tide. It was a little blustery, but O.K. for working on the jetty. We had two things to do. The faces of one of our rocks had to be sketched and measured in some detail so Sophie could attempt to draw it to scale and then we could figure out its surface area for periwinkles more accurately. We chose a rock and the three of us set about getting the best measurements of each of its faces habitable by periwinkles. As a start they would allow Sophie to make pretty accurate sketches of that rock. Having done that, we started counting and measuring the periwinkles on our 10 rocks. We just barely finished before the tide rose and routed us out of there. It was too late to do much else today. If the weather was good tomorrow, little wind, we could try and make a pier trip in the afternoon. We could count and measure the intertidal periwinkles on our 15 random pilings. Not only that, but we could look around for any marked oyster drills that had made it up into the intertidal zone. Tomorrow it will be five days since the marked snails were placed out there at the bases of pilings three and four in our experimental row, maybe enough time for a drill to climb up into the intertidal zone. Possibly Zachary could get in the water and see if any marked snails were down lower on the pilings. If the weather wasn't suitable for pier work, we could go and work jetty #2. With that decided the two of them headed for home. I went home to load up the canoe in case the weather was good tomorrow afternoon. Also there was a lot of data on the three tape recorders that we had recorded the counts and measurements of periwinkles on the 10 rocks today. After putting the canoe on the truck I got busy getting the data off the tapes and onto paper. It was late night before that was done.

The next afternoon it looked like we might be able to make our trip out to the end of the pier. There was some wind, but we erroneously thought we could handle it. We paddled out and started in on the chosen 15 random pilings. Maybe that was too many and it should be cut down to 10. Anyway, we labored to do 15 pilings today. Sophie was in the middle of the canoe and Zachary in the bow. As we bounced around in the wave action they endeavored to get counts and good measurements on the intertidal periwinkles on pilings. They relayed the data to me and I entered it into the recorder. We got all 15 pilings done and managed to not scape off any snails or other life on the pilings. Bravo I thought as I put the recorder away. I didn't think we were going to get all those data today. Off pilings, other than the random 15, we also collected 30 large periwinkles to examine for parasites. They too went in a bag and were put away.

That piece of work done we then hurried in to that last row of six pilings while we could still see any oyster drills up in the intertidal zone. The sun was streaming in from high on the west side of the pier. That made visibility in there pretty good. Zachary used that handy crosspiece to get out of the canoe and into the water with his flippers and mask on. He started to swim over to where he could go down and check on the snails he had placed five days ago. I paddled over and Sophie and I looked around that row for marked oyster drills up high on the pilings. The wind seemed to be more fiercely blowing in from the west now. We managed to look over the nearest pilings just offshore of our row. No drills were visible. We got turned around and made a pass by the pilings of our row. No drills were up in the intertidal zone there either. About this time Zachary had dived down to observe as best he could what the situation was down deep on the pilings. Sophie and I were now making a pass along the inshore side of our row checking the pilings in our row and the one just shoreward of it. Zachary surfaced and told us that he had seen one red marked drill about a foot up on piling #3. He couldn't see any other drills anywhere including where he had placed the 210 marked drills 5 days ago. I quipped, "I'll take it. It's nice to have seen at least one of our marks."

Sophie and I proceeded through to the west side of the pier and were in the process of turning around to get back to the east side. That's when it happened. A larger than usual wave hit the canoe sideways at an inopportune moment. In a flash the canoe rolled and into the water both of us went.

The wind and fairly steady waves pushed us and the swamped canoe up against the pilings. Sophie bobbed up and I told her to get to the side of the canoe that was away from the pilings. That would give her and me some protection from the cutting barnacles and mussels attached to the pilings. I wasn't hurt and she didn't think she was. She maybe had a premonition of things to come and wisely already had a life jacket on. Not so wise, I did not. I grabbed a life vest from the overturned canoe and slipped into it. I also corralled the paddles and two buckets that were drifting away partly sunk. Zachary was there by then helping to gather things and wanting to know if all was O.K. I said, "As far as we know, yes. What we better do is push this swamped, but still afloat canoe over to where that crosspiece is and get it bailed out. Maybe then we can get back to shore." "That's a good enough plan," was Zachary's response.

It was late afternoon and we had at least three hours of light left. First we rolled the canoe over so it was at least right side up. It didn't move through the water easily, but the three of us guided the canoe through the width of the pier back to the east side. Waves and wind were less over here. We got to the crosspiece and I steadied the canoe there while they worked with the buckets I had retrieved to bail it out. Between the three of us in about 45 minutes we had most of the water out of the canoe and it was partly afloat. I hauled myself up on the crosspiece and got seated in it and worked to bail out more water. Zachary also pulled himself up on the crosspiece and got back in. Sophie didn't think she could manage that maneuver. So Zachary said wryly, "Well, I guess we'll have to leave you out here because we've got to get back to shore." I commented, "Yes, of course, we'll have to do that. I don't see any other solution." She saw that we were just having fun and came back, "You guys don't want that on your conscience. I will haunt you until your dying day. Now, you wise guys help me over the side." I used the crosspiece to steady the canoe with one hand and helped her in over the side with the other. We almost entirely finished bailing out the canoe, checked around for any more of our gear we might retrieve, and then started paddling back in.

I was slightly concerned about Sophie and this little adventure. I didn't know how she would take it, but her high spirits on the way back in indicated there was no reason for concern. When we slid into shore I said, "Boy, I don't want to have that happen in winter, but today I think we did pretty well." They both voiced agreement. We had not lost any data. The recorder and data tape were safe in their bag, as were the 30 bagged periwinkles and further we had seen one of the marked drills. The canoe and gear was loaded when I said, "Let's not go out in the field tomorrow. We deserve a light duty day. I'll see you in the lab at 10:00. How's that?" They both thought that was great and left for home.

I drove back to my place and unloaded the canoe and gear. The snails would be fine in their bag with some seawater until tomorrow. A phone call to Sylvia with a report of the day's activities was much appreciated by her. I wanted to get the data off that tape. Some water had leaked into the bag and the recorder was history, but the tape played O.K. in another recorder and I got the data onto paper. I would want it tomorrow. After some food a welcomed hard crash came on. Nothing more was known of that night.

The next morning I gathered up my periwinkles and the data that I had transcribed from the tapes and headed up to campus. When I hit the lab Annie, Sophie, and Zachary were already in there. As I came in I interrupted the animated telling of yesterday's events by Sophie. She stopped, but I asked her to please go on. There are all kinds of research experiences and those who experience them do love to tell the story. With humor Sophie was telling of the time when we threatened to leave her behind in the water out there. She allotted she couldn't have pulled herself up high enough on that crosspiece to get herself

Snails, Fan Worms, and a Hint of Tangled Wire to Come

into the canoe so she was happy to have some assistance getting over the side. Her enthusiastic rendition without any rancor made me think that she was grateful to have had the whole experience.

Annie was paying close attention. I'm sure she recognized that same thing easily could have happened to us when we were out there the day after the deep water drill experiment was started. At the moment Zachary was just standing there taking all this in. Anyway, this research experience forever bonded the three of us.

I said, "Well, I hate to break this up, but we have some business to attend to. For one thing we have 30 snails to dissect. For another Sophie and Zachary have some graphing to do. For yet another item we need to get Sophie started on the detailed drawing of that rock we took data on the other day. First let's do the dissections." The three of them fell back into their routine and in about two hours had all 30 snails examined. As I had come to expect of pier periwinkles, they were all uninfected. Keeping track of parasite prevalence on the pier pilings, we now had 100 periwinkles that were dissected and found to be uninfected.

I said to Annie, "Thanks for helping with those snails. Unless you want to you don't need to hang around for the graphing we are going to do now." She returned, "I'll stick around and listen for a while." Further, she handed me a copy of her Introduction. I said to her, "I'll get to it later today and we could have a talk about it tomorrow if you want." She said, "I would like that."

Then I hauled out the data I had transcribed and the graph models and started in,

> Based on the data we collected on size and frequency of periwinkles from the pier and from each of 20 rocks on the two jetties we can make what are called size-frequency graphs. They should be made this way. We can put snails into size classes. Because we measured with a simple ruler and not calipers, the measurements were not more precise than the nearest mm. Let's put snails into 3mm size classes. That will be classes of 1-3 mm, 4-6 mm, 7-9 mm, 10-12 mm, 13-15 mm, 16-18 mm, and so on up to about 30 mm. You probably know this, but to figure the proportion of snails in any one of these size classes you take the number of snails in that class on the rock or piling and divide it by the total snails measured in all size classes on that rock or piling. We counted more snails than we were able to measure. For these purposes consider only the measured snails. Here are copies of a size-frequency graph to use as a model of what I want. Let's use the pier as an example. Right now we have data, snail measurements and counts, to make size-frequency plots for 15 randomly selected pilings

at two times. The outer pier is Zachary's province. Here is the data we gathered yesterday. Data from the first time out at the pier will have to be transcribed from the tape before it can be plotted. We can see on the model graph the proportions of snails in the various size classes are plotted on the vertical axis and the different size classes are plottled on the horizontal axis. Zachary, initially you will want to make a couple of plots for one of the pilings. Then let me see those plots. We will make any necessary corrections before you go on to do the other 14. Here is the graph paper to use. Sophie, you will have the 20 rocks on two jetties to deal with. Here's a data sheet from jetty #1 the day before yesterday. The first day's data will have to be transcribed before plotting. Initially, as with Zachary, choose one of the rocks and make up the two graphs for the two days, then show them to me, and we'll make any needed corrections. I want to be sure all plots we make are in the same format. We will start a notebook (and keep a copy) and keep it up to date with data sheets and size-frequency plots. We can thumb through the plots looking for changes. When you show me your sample graphs we'll discuss what they might mean. If you have any questions about making these graphs, ask them now.

Zachary said, "Where can I find that first day's data for my piling?" I answered, "I have the first day's piling data right here, as well as the first day's data on the jetty rocks. Of course, we only have one day's data for one of the jetties at present. Sophie will have to work with a rock on jetty # 1 for her two graphs. You will both have to get the first day's data off the tape. Here's a data sheet indicating how I went about transcribing other data. Here are two recorders that you may take with you. I'll be in here tomorrow morning. In addition to talking with Annie I will be able to look at your graphs." Sophie indicated that she would like to go and work on her graphs and not mess around with doing that detailed sketch of the rock just now. That was alright with me. Before she left and true to form Annie expressed appreciation for my explanation of how to do a size-frequency graph. She was not the type to brown me up and I was glad she liked it.

At my office desk I gave Sylvia a call and talked to her for a time. That was enlivening as usual. Then I went home to read Annie's Introduction. It was 15 pages long and was quite well done. She laid out the question asked, why it was important, and cited the necessary literature as a literature review. I had only a few comments. She was getting better at this business. I thought I had done a pretty good day's work and relaxed the rest of the evening.

My arrival at the lab was at 9:00 A.M. No students were there then, but it wasn't long before Annie came in. I said to her, "We don't have much to talk about today. Your Introduction was good. Except for a few grammatical alterations I would not change anything." She intoned that she felt good about the way it came out and liked it herself. I then went over my few comments. About this time Zachary wandered in. I suggested he have a seat because Annie and I were going to be done here shortly. I opined to Annie that she probably had her biggest challenge upcoming, writing the Discussion. Just to tell her again, I went through what that section is supposed to do. The data you obtained are presented without comment in the Results. In the Discussion you get to say what you think your data mean and how they relate to other work on the specific and general topic. I expect that the Discussion section will be some 30 pages in length and you can build off of what you put in your Introduction. I wished her luck. She stayed to listen about what Zachary had done with his graphs.

Zachary hauled out his pencil and paper graphs and at about that time Sophie came in. I suggested she get hers out too. They had the idea. Their graphs were well constructed and I was glad for that. I admonished them that these graphs might sit in a file folder for years on end. It had better be clear exactly what they are when pulled out again. I corrected a couple of things about labeling axes and went through what they had to do to title them. Zachary had made size-frequency plots of periwinkles found on a certain piling on the two dates. The plots were pretty similar. There was no indication that the proportion of any size class of snails had changed appreciably from one date to the next and the total number of snails counted remained about the same. I offered to Zachary that on both dates probably the same snail population was measured.

Sophie's graphs told a different story. She had made plots for one rock on jetty #1 on two dates. Proportions in certain size classes were pretty variable from one date to the other. It could be seen that there were three size classes of periwinkles that changed proportion pretty dramatically from one date to the next. They were size classes 10-12, 16-18, and 25-27 mm. The first and last classes just listed had increased in proportion while the middle one had decreased. It seemed that 10-12 and 25-27 mm snails had increased in the intertidal zone on this rock between the dates, moved in from other rocks or came up from the subtidal zone, and 16-18 mm snails had decreased. The number of measured and unmeasured snails counted on that rock on the two dates was quite different. I observed out loud that to change pilings from the intertidal zone of one to the intertidal zone of another a snail would have to make quite a lengthy trip. To change rocks, or move from the subtidal, on a jetty was comparatively much easier. It appeared from the data that periwinkles moved from rock to rock, or zone to zone, on a jetty much more often than from pole to pole on the pier. That was interesting and accorded well with the two situations. These were still the days, at least in my world, when computers were not everywhere. It would be a lot of work, but we needed to make plots for the other 14 pilings and for the other 19 rocks, homework for Zachary and Sophie. We would see whether piling periwinkle populations were routinely so constant and rock periwinkle populations were routinely so changeable. Also, influxes of very small snails would indicate recruitment of periwinkle juveniles from the plankton. There stood to be much revealed in this way about the ecology of periwinkles at the southern end of their geographical distribution.

All three of them were impressed with what they had been a part of when I finished with that little exposition. There was much chattering. They were all amazed that life for a snail on a rock versus on a piling could be so different. Both Sophie and Zachary were eager to plot more graphs, which was very heartening to me. Annie was just happy to have listened and been in on it. It was now well past lunch and I, and they, wanted to eat. I thought we had done enough today. If we allowed this day and another to go by, there would be an early morning low tide at jetty #2. I proposed that we go and take advantage of that to get data for a second date from that jetty. Sophie and Zachary agreed to do that. They left to attend to their hunger needs and I hoped to build more graphs. Annie stayed around and told me she had really learned something from my treatment of those two sets of plots. She observed that you could learn a lot about the ecology of a beast by paying attention to size (age) classes, a lot indeed. I said, "And, we only barely looked at what can be found out today. Some statistical analysis would yield much more." With that she left to go get some lunch and start thinking about her Discussion.

I spent the next day with Sylvia. She was happy to come down to my place, get my supposedly scintillating company, and some more sun. The day was beautiful. Sylvia had never done any canoeing. I took her out for a fairly lengthy ride. Sitting up there in the bow she got her paddling down pretty well. When we got back to shore and took the canoe out of the water she said, "That was very cool. I can see why you like canoeing so much." Up on the deck over a couple of beers she was most interested in what had transpired with my students over the last few days. Her own student, Agnes, the one that wanted to do a senior thesis, had started her investigation into that local historical event and was making good progress. Sylvia was having daily interactions with her student, sort of similar to what had been happening with my students. She said it was an invigorating experience and she was really glad she took that student on. She could see that student's intellect waking up. Sylvia had told Provost Bigelow that she would accept the position of Dean of Research if, and only if, it was recognized in writing that she would put considerable effort into maintaining her dealings and contacts with students. The Provost was all for that and thought it would be a critical part of her job. He happily put that in her contract.

That job would officially begin with the start of the fall semester. It would be a big change for her. She would be teaching one course in a semester rather than the two, sometimes three, that she normally taught. Her power on campus would be increased. I wondered how Dean Terkel felt about that. I had not dealt with her much lately, but I thought I knew. There were nearly two months to go before she would take on the duties of her new position. She seemed excited about the coming possibilities. Coming soon she would have to be away for a while. She had plans to put some of her grant money to use. A library some distance away had to be visited to obtain some reference material that only it had. It would be necessary to fly there and back. Viewing these references at this library was a major rigmarole. She would have to sit in a reference room under lock and key to use copied documents. The originals were too valuable to be copied over and over again or handled much. That would stand to damage them. So she had to sit and use copied documents, even those with gloves on, to find out what she wanted to know. It was quite a procedure. Sylvia would be away for two weeks. This was coming up soon and as usual I would miss her, but I had enough to do in my future to keep me busy.

For one thing, the first outfit this summer that wanted to know about the wound healing parasite (*Cercaria loossi*) and its polychaete host (*Eupomatus dianthus*) was sending a team of two people to come and learn. That will probably use up most of two days. It will be happening this coming week. On top of that I wanted to keep the periwinkle project on track. The summer was going fast and there were many things I needed to get done before it was gone.

Anyway, Sylvia and I enjoyed the rest of the day. She left for campus early in the morning because before dawn I had to get up to meet Sophie and Zachary at jetty #2 just after dawn. We needed another periwinkle data set, more graphs. We got to the site and started in. My "guys" knew what they had to do. We all started counting and measuring periwinkles on one or another of our chosen rocks. The trip went well. My practiced team and I got our work done in about two hours, including the collection of 30 large periwinkles to check for parasites. We hadn't collected any snails from jetty #1 last time out and I thought if we got moving we might be able to do that today. So we got in our vehicles and motored over there. The tide was rising, but we didn't have much trouble getting our snails. We packaged up and headed back for the lab.

I called Annie and told her we had 60 periwinkles from the two jetties to check for parasites. She indicated that she needed a break from working on her

Discussion and was glad there were some snails to dissect. She would be right in. Pending her arrival I got Sophie going on that detailed treatment of the rock on jetty #1. This rock was roughly a rectangular cube. There were only four faces to consider because the upper surface was above periwinkle zonation, but the back face that was up against the groin was only partly exposed to snails. I said to the two of them, "Let's take these faces one at a time. What we need to do is make the best scaled-down drawing we can of these four faces on a piece of graph paper." We commenced with one of the rock's faces. That face was wider at its base, less wide half way up, and it became wider again up toward the top. We had measurements of many subtle width changes on this rock. Before long Sophie had quite an accurate drawing of that face on graph paper. Zachary got busy counting the little squares on the paper that were included in the drawing of that rock face. Knowing what the scale of the drawing was we could extrapolate to a good estimate of the actual surface area of that rock face. When we finished all four faces we could add them up to get a quite good estimate of the total surface area on that rock available to periwinkles. Sophie was already working on a second face of that rock. She was kind of into it.

At this time Annie came in. She was intrigued by the way we were estimating surface area on that rock. It was about lunch time and Zachary went out to get some take out for all but Annie. She had eaten before coming in and began dissecting snails right away. After lunch I let the three of them use their system to process those snails. They finished in about three hours. In all they found four infections, two on each jetty, and all infections were by *Cryptocotyle lingua*. That was turning out to be pretty predictable. Some 6% of snails were infected on both jetties and, at least so far, always with that one parasite species. My two graph artists had done three more plots each. Zachary had done three more pilings for the two dates. The story for all three was the same as it was for the first piling, no change. Sophie had done three more rocks on jetty #1. One of them showed no change, the proportions of size classes were about the same on both dates. The other two rocks were similar to the first rock she did. Some size classes showed a pretty clear increase in proportion of snails making them up while others showed a decrease. That indicated that on the jetties, periwinkles moved around from rock to rock pretty commonly. I thanked them both for their good efforts. For the rest of this week there wouldn't be any field work to do, but they should continue making these graphs for the remaining 11 pilings and 16 rocks. It is tough duty, but we need to get all these graphs copied and into notebooks.

Now let's finish with the surface area of that rock. Among the four of us we finished up the other three faces and calculated the total surface area available to periwinkles. It came out to 6.4 m² for about 150 periwinkles. Something you might do is, make measurements on other rocks so similar detailed drawings can be made. From the other day you know what to do so you won't need my guidance.

Figuring the available surface area on pilings is much easier. This is essentially the surface area of a cylinder (not including the two ends, that's = $2\pi rh$) with a radius (r) of 0.15 m and the intertidal zone on a piling is an average of 1.1 m tall (h), which comes to 1.04 m². So let's consider there to be 1.04 m² available on a piling in the intertidal zone for an average of about 21.3 periwinkles per piling. That will give us a pretty good estimate of the number of periwinkles in that amount of space on a piling.

Tomorrow Sylvia was going to leave and the first of my information seekers were coming in. I suppose I could have gotten Annie to instruct them, but I figured I would give them my undivided attention. They arrived late in the day. I met them and showed them where their accommodations were. One was a medical doctor, the other an assistant of some sort, and they were from a university medical school. Dr. Bruce Gallagher was about 30 years old. He said to just call him Bruce and was very interested in the potential for good that my discovery might do. He wanted some firsthand experience in dealing with the parasite and didn't want to delegate that to an underling. His assistant, Steve Forbes, struck me at first as a guy who was just along for the ride. They had a car and there was a restaurant and bar right near to their motel. So they would be O.K. tonight and tomorrow morning. They would be on their own tonight. At a propitious moment I told them what was going to happen. I said, "Tomorrow morning there is a low tide and we can go out and collect some worms. We will go to the pier where I did my work. I will meet you down by the coast at a place that is easy to find and we will go to the pier together. Our meeting place is about a half hour drive from here. I will have a canoe with me and we will use that to go out and collect some worms. After that we will come back up to campus to do some lab work." They seemed like nice guys and were agreeable to that plan. I left them there saying I would see them in the morning.

I met them in the morning at the appointed time and place and led them over to the pier. Neither one had any experience with a canoe, but we got it off the truck and down in the water. We paddled out a way with Bruce in the bow working a paddle and Steve in the middle. I offered,

> Here are the calcareous worm tubes in those skirts around the pilings you can see there. You can also often find *Eupomatus dianthus* living attached to rocks, for example on an inlet jetty. The parasite in these

polychaetes is more common farther out on the pier. Not much is known about the parasite's life cycle, but the definitive host, the source of worm infections, is undoubtedly a marine fish. Out there, where the fish hosts are resident most of the time is where a worm is most likely to get infected. We can stay in pretty close to shore where it is safer and about 30% of worms are infected. I've had quite a few misadventures with the canoe getting upside down out farther. The water is pretty quiet today so let's go over there and get a sample of worms. I might add here that you can see many blue mussels on pilings above where the skirts of worm tubes are. Blue mussels are host to another trematode, the one that is killed off by the fan worm parasite when a fan worm parasite also infects that mussel.

We went over to a piling and chipped off a piece of fan worm tubes. We then visited a couple of more pilings and got other fan worms. I said, "we'll take these back to the lab. Are there any questions I can answer while we are here?" Steve wanted to know where the host fan worm was found geographically. I told him that the worm occurred from Cape Cod to Cape Hatteras. Bruce wanted to know more about the relationship between the fan worm trematode and the mussel trematode. I related that I had found about 4% of mussels on this pier infected with the fan worm trematode, never a fan worm infected by the mussel parasite. Further, I had demonstrated that if the fan worm parasite infected a mussel that already harbored a mussel parasite, the mussel parasite was killed off. What is the relationship between the fan worm parasite's ability to kill off mussel parasites and the ability to heal human wounds, asked Bruce? I answered, I did not know, but thought there must be some connection. There were no more questions we so headed back to shore. We loaded up the canoe and headed for the lab.

In the lab we immediately separated some worm tubes and took to making holes in them and pushing worms backwards out of their tubes. We got a number of worms out, I showed them the orange strips along the belly, and told them that's where the parasite infection is. There were sporocysts and cercariae of the fan worm parasite in those strips. In my first efforts I very carefully cut the strips out, but I found that parasite stages exited through the worm's genital ducts when the worm was placed naked in seawater and the released, intact parasite stages had the same negative effect on the mussel parasite. Bruce wanted to know whether the intact parasite stages would also heal wounds. I said, "Well, they do kill off the mussel parasite. I expect they would also heal wounds, but I haven't tested that and don't really know. What I did was cut those strips out and blend them up in seawater. That fluid worked very well as a wound healer."

We had been working on worms for about three hours and it was getting late in the afternoon. We were about to quit. Bruce said, "I am particularly fascinated with the wound healing properties of this parasite. Could we blend up some of those parasite stages. I'd like to take some of the blend back with me. We have a number of patients in our hospital that have recalcitrant wounds that won't heal. I want to try some of that parasite fluid if patients are willing." I responded, "Sure we could do that. If you can help some of those people, I would be very pleased." I blended up some fan worm parasite fluid and Bruce carried a bottle of it away with him. They thanked me for all my help and my day's efforts and then left to go back to their motel. They were heading back tomorrow morning. I told Bruce that he had best keep that fluid somehow refrigerated. And so my first visitors were done. Maybe some good will come of it. We would see. They seemed like useful guys. The next pair of instruction seekers would be in next week.

That night I called Annie to see how she was doing with her Discussion. It was still in the works. She had about 10 pages written with about twice that to go. It was giving her a time getting everything in there. Discussions don't just roll off your pen, so to speak. That section is always the most demanding part of a manuscript to write. I could sympathize with her predicament. But, her thesis was well under way and it looked like she would accomplish it this summer. I let her bitch about her writing challenges for a while and then we signed off. I was sure she was up to any difficulties she ran into.

I didn't want to bother Sophie and Zachary too much just now. They needed time to get their graphing done. But, tomorrow it would be 13 days since marked snails were put out to the distant pilings and six days since we had last been out there. If those marked drills were ever going to rise to the height of the intertidal zone, it would be about now. We needed to get out there in the next couple of days. So I called Zachary. He was in good spirits. He and Sophie had done some more plotting. They had even gone and measured three more of the rocks on jetty #1 for detailed drawings. They were steady workers. Through Zachary I thanked them both for doing that. I mentioned that we needed to visit the pilings to look for marked drills. He said he was getting cramped up with all this paper work and would appreciate a trip out to the pilings. I suggested we go tomorrow if the weather permitted. He said that would be fine. The low tide would be in the middle of the day and we made plans to meet at the pier. I made an encouraging subsequent phone call to Sophie to thank her personally for her good work. I told her that we were planning a trip out to the pilings to look for marked drills tomorrow. She did not need to come along unless she wanted to.

She declined, preferring instead to work on making her graphs. And, so we left it.

Zachary and I made the trip to the outer pier pilings. The weather conditions were very cooperative for the occasion. We didn't have much to do except look for drills. There was not much likelihood that many marked oyster drill would have made it up into the piling intertidal zone, but it was important to make the observation. By now the snails had just shy of two weeks to make the trip. When we got out there we looked pretty thoroughly at our row of pilings and at the three rows landward of that. In the offshore direction we looked at the inner six pilings of the next three wider rows of the pier's T. In the intertidal zones of all 42 of those pilings there were a total of two marked oyster drills, one red and one white, to be observed. They were right on pilings #3 and #4 of the row where they were released. On those 42 pilings there were also two other unmarked drills to be seen. So as expected there were few drills, marked or unmarked, on those pilings and the marked ones were right on the pilings near where released and it took them almost two weeks to climb up the poles. The fact that they were in the intertidal zone on those poles suggests that the abnormally high abundance of drills (210 of them placed there) at the bases of those poles at one time increased the likelihood of them getting that high up. Zachary would have gone in the water, but even if a few marked snails were observed on pilings there would be no real gain for the effort. We already knew the basic story and we decided to leave. On the way back in we stopped at that inner row where we had released marked drills. This was day 25 since they were released there. We counted 15 marked drills on that row in the intertidal zone, only four less than on the day after release. Apparently, at that site drills readily get up into the intertidal zone on those pilings and basically stay there. I suppose the unanswered question is: why don't more drills get farther offshore in the sediments around the bases of those pilings? For some reason few occur out there. What's the barrier?

Anyway, we were done for the day and we packed up and left. Only two marked drills had managed to climb up into the intertidal zone on those distant pilings and after all this time there were almost the same number of drills in the intertidal zone on the inner piling row as right after they were released. Data from this day pretty well tells the whole story about drills and pilings. I called Annie and Sophie to fill them in on the drill lore we had found today.

With respect to the periwinkle project the main thing to be done was give Sophie and Zachary time to finished making their graphs. The ones they had were beautifully done, but we needed to get them all made so they could be put in that notebook. Sophie had those detailed drawings of the jetty rocks to finish as well. I would have to ask Zachary to help her out with those. During the first two days of next week my second pair of information seekers would be coming in and I contacted my two helpers and told them they would have those two days to work on the graphs. On the following day I wanted to see the notebook up to date. They both thought they could manage that.

Late in the day the medical doctor arrived to learn about *Eupomatus dianthus* and its parasite *Cercaria loossi*. She was a woman named Dr. Agnes Wilson. The helper she had with her was Candy Porter. I met them on campus and took them to their motel and pointed out a restaurant where they might get dinner. Dr. Wilson talked a mile a minute. She had lots of questions and I had to curb some of them. I claimed that it would be easier to explain most of this tomorrow when we went out to collect some worms. The tide would be in the afternoon and we would be going to the pier where I worked. We would probably be into the evening getting our work done. It would be their choice whether they used the motel for another night or drove back home after we were done. I lived down on the coast and if they would make the half hour drive down, I would meet them there. I was moved to get clear of the pointless and incessant questioning. After making sure they had everything they needed, I said I had to go. It was a thankful guy that got out of there.

When we met at the agreed upon place the next day the questioning began again. She was determined to get her money's worth out of this visit. I would do what I could. We went to the pier and the three of us took the canoe and gear down to the water. Of the two, only Candy had done any canoeing. She climbed in the front seat with a paddle and we pushed off. The tide was low enough to expose the fan worm skirts and except for the constant questions it was a quiet day. At one point I caught a look from Candy making note of her boss' constant jabber. I launched into essentially the same spiel given my two previous visitors. We went to pilings out a little farther than I had gone with visitors last week. It would be good to get more likely infected worms. As we approached some worms in a skirt I cautioned Candy that we did not want to allow the canoe to scrape off any of the organisms attached to the pilings. She did well at avoiding doing that. After collecting some worms Candy was interested in collecting a few mussels. Apparently she had read my host-switching paper and she wanted to see if we could find a mussel parasite infection when we got back to the lab. I thought that might be interesting and agreed to do that. We collected a few mussels and then headed for shore. After loading the canoe and gear on my truck we headed back to the lab. Candy rode with me. She didn't say much, but made a brief comment on the constant talk of her boss, "She seems to be unable to keep quiet, but behind all that Dr. Wilson is a very caring person. She has always treated me with respect and well," she said. I took in her statement and believed it.

When we got back in the vicinity of the lab it was about 6:00 PM. My two compatriots and I needed to get something to eat. We got some takeout food to bring back to the lab. That over with we began to look for some infected worms. I showed them how to push worms out of their tubes. We happened on some infected individuals immediately. I showed them the two longitudinal strips along the bellies of infected worms and described the way parasite stages (cercariae and sporocysts) get emitted from the host worm via the host's genital ducts. From three worms I excised the parasite strips to show them how that was done. Dr. Wilson requested that I blend up some of the parasite stages so she could take some of the fluid back with her. She had a patient that had given her permission and she wanted to see if it would heal her wound. After mixing up the fluid I made it a point to recommend that it be kept refrigerated. Whether that was actually necessary was not known, but that had been my practice. With the jar of *Cercaria loossi* blend in hand Candy was interested in looking at some of the mussels. The time had marched ahead to 9:30 PM. We found a mussel infected *Protoeces maculatus*. That was what Candy wanted. She wanted to see the effect of putting some of the *Cercaria loossi* fluid on the mussel parasite. I warned them that it would take a couple of hours for any effect to be seen.

Both were game to try so I removed one of the mussel's shells to expose the infection and treated it with some of the fluid. While we were waiting for some effect on the mussel infection Dr. Wilson began with some questions again. That led me to produce a reprint of the last paper on the cleaner way to get parasite stages out of a worm, which answered most of her questions. It wasn't too long before the mussel infection began to show signs of being killed off. By midnight it was apparent that the mussel parasite was in real trouble. They were both mightily impressed. It was time to call it a night. We cleaned things up and were out of there by about 12:30. I said goodbye to them in their motel parking lot. Candy thanked me for sticking with it through the demise of the mussel parasite. She really wanted to see that. Dr. Wilson was thankful for the day. She was able to learn a great deal. Their home base was about 150 miles away and they would be heading back tomorrow morning. I lied a little to Agnes and told them I enjoyed their visit. With that I left them and my second visitors were finished.

Last summer I had spent a little time with each set of visitors, but I did not fully realize the total time they took up. All visitors were reported to have gotten what they wanted from their visit. Annie, Timothy, and Toby had borne the brunt of that. Sure, they got paid, but not much and I owed them more appreciation than just that. At the next opportunity I would have to express that.

It was now the first part of August and I received a surprising and inconvenient request from Provost Bigelow. He asked me to come to his office and there dumped this on me. It seemed that the President of the Faculty Senate, Dr. William Foster, one of the Sociology faculty, wanted to resign his position. Because I had recently been promoted and done some research as well, Provost Bigelow thought I would be a good candidate to fill that role. Talk about things to soak up my time! After he asked, I immediately said, "You have been such a great help with the faculty research agenda of Sylvia Armbruster and myself. With your help, finding the money to start the In-House Grant Program is certainly not least in this regard, we have gotten some faculty renewing their interest in research. It's may be only a beginning, but I have confidence that it will take off and make our service to this community stronger and stronger, especially with Sylvia as Dean of Research." He said thanks to that. Then I said, "I am honored by your belief in me and for that reason alone don't want to refuse your suggestion out of hand. I must say, however, that I do not wish to spend my time in pursuing and serving in such a political role."

Not one to be easily dissuaded the Provost came back, "Faculty have to take on these responsibilities. Many don't want to, but they must. You are now one of very few faculty on this campus with an advanced academic rank and you have achieved that through excellent teaching and the amazing research you have done. This puts you in the position of a leader whether you like it or not. In my view you are just the person for the job." My response was, "As I said, because I respect the moves you have made in your current position I won't flat out refuse you, but there is little enough time to carry out research as it is. This will only clutter up my time with activities in which I am not interested." The Provost returned, "I can't and won't force you to run for this office, but I see in you qualities that would be useful to the whole faculty and to me in that position. As a consequence I really wish you would accept this responsibility and run. Filling that position would be one of the best things you could do for this University branch." I asked who would be running against me and he told me it would be the French teacher on campus, Dr. John Ferguson. I thought to myself, "Well at least there would be an opponent." If the Provost felt so strongly that I should do this, then against my instincts, and maybe it was a mistake, I would put myself on the ballot. So ultimately I agreed to do it.

When I left the Provost's office I wasn't happy. My fervent hope was that less than a majority would vote for me. That would be the desired outcome. Just late yesterday Sylvia had gotten back from her trip. I tried to find her in her soon to be old office. She wasn't there so I called her at her place. She was tired from her trip, but I talked her into going out for some lunch. I wanted to talk over the thing I had gotten myself into this morning. I picked her up and we headed for a local restaurant. It was rejuvenating to see her again. I asked her how her trip had gone. She said that it was a lot of hard work, but she had picked up a lot of information that would be of superb use in writing her new book. I commented, "That sounds like an unqualified success and I am happy it all worked for you." Then I told her that I was not happy about it, but the Provost had just asked me to run for faculty senate president and I reluctantly agreed to do it. She thought that me as the senate president was probably a good idea and said, "In my soon to be assumed position as Dean of Research I can see real benefit to having a senate leader with an attitude sympathetic to mine." I retorted, "That may be the case, but research time is short enough now and I worry that the available time will be utterly dried up." Her comeback was to the effect that if I were elected, there would be a demand upon my time, but maybe it is time to redirect a parcel of my effort to another possibly more pervasive line of action than my own research. "You have already done quite a bit. Perhaps you could put some time into developing the research activities of other faculty. Promoting that on this campus would be a meaningful service." I wasn't pleased with her view of what I should do with my future. To my mind the main role of a university faculty member is to teach and discover new knowledge. Besides, those are the things I liked to do and what I am pretty good at. I expressed those feelings to her without getting too strident. She did not agree with my feelings on the matter, but she tacitly accepted what I said. The Dean of Research let it lie there and we went on to other things in our conversation. As I was afraid would happen, she was reasonably enough already taking on some administrator qualities. Well, I suppose some of that is unavoidable.

Chapter 16

THE END OF MY FINAL SUMMER AT VISITOPOLIS ARRIVES

It was into August. My three students would be leaving soon to take up main campus life and I would soon be involved with teaching Biology I and the Invertebrate Zoology course. If I got elected, I didn't know exactly how much time would be taken up, but it would be a problem finding time to keep up my research. For Sophie and Zachary I had at least two things that had to be completed. Before the month was out we had to do one more episode of taking periwinkle data from the pier and the two jetties and they needed to finish their graphing of results. Annie had her Discussion to finish.

Another thing that probably should be done was to find out how the abundance of oyster drills in the sediments changed as you went offshore along the pier. The inner row of pilings at which drill samples had been taken was at piling row 55. The water was only about a foot deep at low tide and we found an average of 5.7 drills/0.25 m^2 of sand around those pilings. Around piling row 107 (the offshore site) the water was about 12 feet deep at low tide and there was only an average of 0.6 drills/0.25 m^2 in those sediments. How did drill abundance change as you went offshore? Did it just gradually decline or was there a critical depth beyond which the number of drills fell off rapidly? This would be important to know for any publication coming from this work. It would be a lot of work, but if we kept track of water depth, perhaps we could sample drills with our grab between pilings three and four from row 55 to row 107 in about every tenth row. I would have to propose that next time I saw the team. Next day I was supposed to meet with them all in the lab.

When we got together I was very pleased with what they all had been doing. Annie had finished a first draft of her Discussion. It was almost 40 pages long.

She handed it to me and I told her to give me a couple of days to read it and we would talk about it. Sophie and Zachary had finished their graphing jobs. He had the results from the 15 random pilings all done for the two times periwinkles were counted and measured out on the pier. The message still seemed to be that proportions of periwinkles in various size classes on pilings did not change much. Those data could go into the notebook. Sophie had finished with data from all 20 rocks from jetties #1 and #2 for the two times data had been taken. It seemed that periwinkles did move around quite a bit on jetty rocks. There were lots of examples where proportions of size classes had markedly changed. Another thing she had done was finish the detailed drawings of the faces on all 20 rocks. Zachary had helped her complete the measuring of rocks. How to go Sophie and Zachary! That meant that we could estimate pretty accurately the total surface area that could harbor periwinkles on each rock. We could likely finish those estimates up today. I said to them all, "You students have performed very well this summer and I thank you for your efforts. It has been a pleasure working with you all." I then told them what I had planned for the rest of the summer. Sophie and Zachary had to complete one more round of periwinkle data collection and the new graphs would have to be added to the collection. It was important that Annie finish writing her thesis. The other thing I mentioned was finding out how the abundance of drills in the sediments changed as you moved offshore and the water got deeper. That would represent a lot of canoe and grab work. We also should count drills up in the intertidal zone as we went offshore. Our answer to why drills were less abundant in the intertidal zone on offshore pilings was getting to be pretty complete. Knowledge of how drill abundance changed with distance offshore would enhance our answer. All three of them were avid to see what those data would show. They were eager to see them collected.

    I suggested that we could get busy today counting up the surface area on the remaining rocks based on Sophie's drawings. It would be a bit of work, but it needed to be done and this was as good a day as any to do it. We each took the drawings of the faces of one of the rocks and commenced to figure the surface area habitable by periwinkles. We worked for about three hours and had the job finished. Now the number of snails on rocks could be related to surface area available to them. I then said there were a series of early morning low tides coming up in a few days. The first useable one would be three days hence. If that works for Sophie and Zachary, we could, depending on weather, try to do the pier periwinkles. Failing that we could do one of the jetties. They said they would be ready to do one or the other at that time. In the next couple of days Annie's Discussion had to be read. I told her I would be finished with it by tomorrow. If she wanted to come down to my place about 3:00 PM we could discuss it then. Annie said she would be available to do that. At that time we all left. I immediately went home to read.

Before getting to my task, which I was looking forward to, I called Sylvia. I told her about the happenings of the day and how happy I was with the performance of my students. She said that her student Agnes had found some interesting material and her work too was also coming along fine. Sylvia was quite well known on the main campus. They had arranged for two other faculty from the main campus history department to sit on Agnes' thesis committee and when she went up there this fall she would already have that settled. I thought that was better than good. Eventually we would likely have at least two students from this campus with a senior thesis. Sylvia talked some about taking on her new position as Dean of Research. She maintained all her composure, but I detected that she was somewhat perplexed, anxious about the prospect. I said, "Maybe you should be a little nervous about that. It will be a huge responsibility, not just maintaining what we have accomplished so far, but coming up with new directions for promoting research." I offered a few comforting words, "You are the best person I can imagine for this job. You have been and are engaged in your own research and have produced a number of scholarly contributions. No one else around here is better qualified to take on the position of being the first Dean of Research. I am so happy with the Provost's choice of you to play that role." She said in return, "One thing I plan to do is encourage faculty to take on students wanting to accomplish a senior thesis. And, the only other person that the Provost might have chosen is you." To which I said, "Maybe so, but I wouldn't want the job and in any case I expect you will be much better at it than I would be. I have great faith in you Sylvia." We talked for a while more and then I indicated that I had to get Annie's 40 pages of Discussion read before 3:00 PM tomorrow. I hoped I had been a source of some comfort to Sylvia. Probably not, but we both took the cue to say goodbye for now.

Then I began reading. It took me about three hours. I liked the way she had set it up. She first took on the question of whether she had tried to infect snails with miracidia belonging to *Parorchis avitus*. I was already convinced she had, but it was an important point to make. She then went on into the issue of whether the snails she tried to infect were initially uninfected. In the first place she used snails from the pier where few were infected. Annie had further tested drills for infection by looking to see whether they released cercariae. She subsequently dissected the tested, but unused, snails to see how often snails tested as uninfected, but bore an infection nevertheless. Very few tested and supposedly uninfected snails turned out to be infected. Of 150 snails that had passed the cercarial release test as uninfected and were later dissected to see if they were in reality infected, only three (2%) were infected. Among the 40 snails she tried to experimentally infect, 25 (62.5%) had infections when they were examined later that summer. Some 2% of these 40 snails (about 1 of them) that she attempted to experimentally infect might have sneaked through with an infection that it came into lab with. You certainly couldn't explain more than one, maybe two, of her 25 laboratory infected snails as being already infected when they came into her procedure initially. Annie's next point in the Discussion was that the cercariae and rediae in her experimentally infected snails fit the published descriptions of *Parorchis avitus* cercariae and rediae.

Having treated those potentially contentious issues, she went on to discuss her main results. There were no reports in the literature of anyone attempting to experimentally infect *Urosalpinx cinerea* with *Parorchis avitus*. She had produced 25 infections in the lab. By any standard that was a nice accomplishment. She finished up by taking a look at avenues for future research on this system. My only criticism was that this section went on too long. There was no doubt that more research could be done and her suggestions were good. However, using 10 pages doing this is a bit much. She should make an effort to shorten that section by at least five pages. There were a few grammatical things to fix, but other than that shortening I had no substantive changes to promote for Annie's Discussion. She had done a quite professional job with it, which pleased me no end.

When Annie rolled in at 3:00 the next afternoon I told her right away that she had done a very professional job on her Discussion. I then made my case about shortening that last section. The session did not last long. I had an accomplished student on my hands. The only real job that was left was to construct her bibliography, a tedious undertaking that didn't take much inventiveness, just pointed care. She had expertly handled all the referencing. I said, "Here it is only early August and your thesis is in pretty good shape. I like it. I suppose you will be walking through fire to get it into the official format for the University, but you have come a long way." Annie returned, "I suspect you are right about the complications of the University thesis requirements on format. I guess I shall have to hire an experienced typist to type it, but I am very pleased to have gotten it to this point. Above all it is critically important to me that you like it." I answered, "I surely do and I expect that you will have great success defending it once you get it in final form."

I then told her that in the next few days there would be 90 periwinkles to dissect and we also should take more grab samples of sand to assess the pattern according to which drills become less abundant as you go offshore along the pier. If we get that piece of information, we should have a pretty good story to tell about the why of oyster drill distribution. After writing the paper we could submit it for presentation at a scientific meeting and you could present it. Zachary or Sophie might not be quite ready to do this, but you certainly are and it would be good experience. Doing that was a way off, but Annie thought we would have a good explanation of what makes for fewer drills on the offshore pilings. Presenting a paper was a promising idea. After that exchange she needed to go and work on shortening that section of her Discussion and constructing her bibliography. So we respectfully parted company.

The next day I met with Sophie and Zachary. I laid out the need to take one more periwinkle data set from the pier and from the two beach groins. They were well experienced at this and if the weather cooperated there should be no problem getting that done. I also told them that to complete the drill experiment we should take a series of grab samples along the pier to see if there was a pattern according to which the drill population declined between inshore and offshore sites. A paper could then be written to tell the story. I thought that probably Zachary and I would mainly have to do that sampling, but this underestimated Sophie. She spoke up and offered that she could probably paddle the canoe while Zachary took samples. I responded that what I thought they should do is take a sample between pilings three and four in every tenth row. It would be a lot of work and you would have to pick a very nice day to do it, but if you two think you can handle it I will let you try. Sophie was an able girl and likely up to that job and I had faith in Zachary's ability to correct any happenstance that might occur. Sampling drills wasn't the most pressing thing and for the time being and it was left that way. There was a morning low tide on the morrow that would be appropriate for doing the pier periwinkle sampling and I thought we should attempt to do that. If the weather wasn't suitable, we could sample one of the beach groins. They quickly agreed to that plan and left.

As it turned out the next day was very quiet, almost no wind. We took the canoe out to outer pilings. Sophie and Zachary were in good form and we worked our way through the 15 random pilings, counting and measuring periwinkles. On three pilings we observed there was an influx of newly settled snails. That would show up as a population change on those pilings. We also collected another 30 large snails to look for parasite infections. The day and the whole expedition went smoothly. Zachary could now come up with 15 more graphs, probably mostly uneventful except for the new juveniles, of any changes in the periwinkle populations on those poles. When they got together with Annie and dissected those snails none of them were infected. So, the summer's periwinkle sampling on the outer reaches of that pier was now done.

Sophie and Zachary wanted to take a crack at sampling sedimentary oyster drills in the very near time frame. In fact, the next day seemed appropriate to them. I thought that, if they wanted to try, it would be O.K. with me. In the afternoon we went back to the lab and put our plans together for doing that. Among other things we loaded the gunnel to gunnel plank and bottom grab into the truck. I would stay out of taking the samples and the two of them would pick up my truck and canoe in the morning. Plans and gear arranged we left it at that for the day.

The following day was weather-suitable and they collected my two modes of transportation at about 8:00 A.M. I wished them good fortune with this endeavor. They quickly disappeared. I had some library materials to read and happily busied myself with that and some coffee out on my deck. Maybe I've told you, I liked it out there.

Before noon they came back and they had good success. They had to sample between pilings three and four in rows 45 (water depth 10 inches), 55 (1 ft.), 65 (1.9 ft.), 75(3.5 ft.), 85 (7 ft.), 95 (12 ft.), and 105 (13 ft.). They were able to get all seven 0.25 m^2 samples with the grab. The drills they counted at each location were (row/count): 45/8, 55/6, 65/7, 75/1, 85/0, 95/0, and 105/1. Drills were pretty abundant at the first three rows sampled and fell off pretty clearly and dramatically from row 75 on out. For some reason not many drills occurred where the tidal depth at around low tide was 3.5 ft. or more. The reason for this would be interesting to know, but it is nevertheless important to know where there is a break to much reduced drill abundance in the sediments. From row 45 on out drill abundance does not simply and gradually decline with greater depth. It falls off sharply at a certain point.

I said to Zachary and Sophie,

> That makes for a reasonably complete story about why drills are less abundant in the intertidal zone of offshore pilings. I think this is a publishable piece of work, but I don't believe I will be an author on any paper that comes from it. It was an idea of you two initially and Annie was a big help in getting it done. I do recommend that you make extensive use of Annie in accomplishing the writing of the manuscript. Having been involved in authoring two previous papers and now her thesis, she has become quite expert at writing scientific papers. In terms of order of authorship I don't care how you settle that. Get together and negotiate. I think it is appropriate that you three-author this manuscript. I will, of course, help you out as much as I can, but I will not be an author. You students should take that on.

Both students seemed quite taken aback by what I said. As was their way they asked to be excused for a minute to discuss things. They went out on the deck and I could see them conversing. On their return Sophie did the talking. She indicated that they were both excited about the prospect of writing a manuscript and attempting to get it published. The idea of publishing a scientific paper while a student in college really appealed to them, but they thought that I would be in on writing it. They were flattered that I thought they could manage without me being involved. But, never having done anything like that both were sort of intimidated by the prospect in front of them. They didn't think they could do it well. I made the following point, "What you need to do is make a deal with Annie. She was in on the project and deserves to be in on this aspect of it. Moreover, she has demonstrated the ability to contribute greatly to the writing of a scientific paper and would be a valuable colleague for you. You two may have not experienced producing a publishable manuscript, but I have faith that you guys will do a fine job."

Zachary piped in and made a statement, "You have guided us successfully through three courses and have made us more than mere assistants in the research work this summer. I am grateful as I know both of us are. If you think the manuscript would be well served in student hands, then I think it should be done that way." Sophie said, "Well said Zachary and me too. And thanks from me too." I closed with, "Many thanks to you both as well. The oyster drill project this summer was your original idea. It's right this way and based on the way Annie is I think I know what arrangement you three will come up with, but that is up to you. All of you will be on the main campus this fall and that will facilitate working on the manuscript. As always, I will help as much as I can." We left the prospective paper there for now. I suggested that we should figure to work one of the jetties, say #1, on tomorrow morning's low water. They agreed to do that. With their help I unloaded the canoe and gear and shortly they left to go back to campus to put the grab and plank back in storage. They had many plans afoot to be discussed.

That very afternoon Sophie, Zachary, and Annie had a meeting of the minds. The two I had spoken with this morning passed along to Annie what I had said. As later related to me, they came up with an agreement that, knowing Annie pretty well, was essentially what I had expected. Basically, Sophie would be the first author, Zachary the second, and Annie the third. This was largely at Annie's behest. She felt that with her knowledge of the oyster drill and experience with writing she could make a significant contribution to the paper, but the original idea was Sophie's and she and Zachary had done most of the work. Based on a later conservation with her, Annie was happy as the third author. That was where she felt she belonged.

The next morning we met at jetty #1. We found our rocks and started counting and measuring the periwinkles on each. We behaved like a competent team and in about 2.5 hours we had the job done. We collected another 30 larger snails, all 25 mm or over, to examine for parasites. That afternoon they were dissected with Annie's help and three of them were infected, again with *Cryptocotyle lingua*. After completing that we agreed to take on jetty #2 tomorrow morning. Annie wanted to come along and aid in the counting and measuring periwinkles. She had not done that before and wanted the experience. We were happy to have the extra help. The four of us worked over jetty #2 the next day. It went quicker with the extra worker. We collected 30 snails to examine for parasites and did the dissections that afternoon. Two had *Cryptocotyle lingua* infections. Prevalence of that parasite in jetty snails was amazingly constant, always about two or three out of 30 snails.

So, this summer's field work for my team and I was completed. It was about two weeks into August now. What Sophie and Zachary had yet to do was make their graphs up, 20 for Sophie and 15 for Zachary. Once they were added the notebook this summer's work would be completed. Of course, they also had to get ready to go to the main campus. They would both be sophomores. Annie had finished her bibliography and showed it to me. It was nicely done. She had her thesis in very good shape and could go back to the main campus for her senior year with it basically written. There would of course be official formatting to do, but I had faith that she would make it pass muster. I hoped they would find time to also work on the drill manuscript.

As for me, in my last two weeks of the summer I had to make my final decision about declaring myself a candidate to become president of the faculty senate. I know, I know, I had agreed to do it, but I still had not convinced myself that it was a good idea. That election would be held midway in the fall semester. Talk about a useless encroachment on my time! To do my kind of research you need to be in good measure flexible and free. You must be able to accommodate the timing of tides and the vagaries of weather. Time that had to be invested in teaching courses was problem enough, but having your time cluttered up with a myriad of senate duties would make research a virtual impossibility. I did not want this to be how my time was used, but felt I was somewhat obliged to Provost Bigelow. One more attempt to talk him out of that endeavor seemed worthwhile. So I made an appointment with him to do that. Right now the Provost was away at a meeting and I had to wait a week before I could see him. His secretary, still Gail Pratt, was on the job and set me up with an appointment for the Tuesday after he got back. My meeting was essentially a week before fall classes would begin.

Chapter 17

THE WIRE STRANGLES ME: GOODBYE TO VISITOPOLIS

Early in that two-week time frame Annie and I had a meeting. She wanted to talk about the manuscript Sophie, Zachary, and she were going to write and about her thesis in the upcoming year at the University. I told her I was pleased with the arrangement she had made with her two coauthors. Their agreement was pretty much what I expected and seemed appropriate. She asked me for my assessment of what should be covered in the manuscript. I thought a minute and said,

> Well, let's see. We are looking to explain why there are fewer drills in the intertidal zone on offshore pilings. Just to list the main things out without too much detail: (1) where the water is shallower drills can repopulate the intertidal zone of drill-denuded pilings very quickly; (2) there are very few drills in the offshore sediments compared to inshore sediments; and (3) even when numerous drills are placed at the base of offshore pilings, very few manage to climb up the ~10 - 12 ft. into the intertidal zone of those pilings. So the explanation seems to have two factors: first there are very few drills around the bases of offshore pilings (it's an open and important question exactly why that is); and second, even if drills were more numerous in the sediments out there they mostly wouldn't be able to climb on pilings all the way up into the intertidal zone. They either have no impetus to climb or fail in the attempt.

Annie asked, "Would you agree that the whole thing should be cast in terms of explaining one aspect of the abundance and distribution of *Urosalpinx cinerea?*" I answered, "Yes, as you already know, explaining the distribution and abundance of organisms is one of the main purposes of the study of ecology." She then said, "Well, that lays out the basics of the manuscript. We plan to start the writing before we go up to main campus. In keeping with your usual advice, we'll start with the Materials and Methods."

With regard to her thesis she only wanted reassurance that I thought it was now in good shape. I said, "Yes, it is. It will undoubtedly change some as you put the finishing touches on it, but you can be proud of what you have done as it stands now." Her next moves were to check on formatting instructions, do a final arrangement, and engage a typist to do the final copy. After our brief meeting she left almost immediately to go and arrange a session with Sophie and Zachary. Before she left she mentioned that she was scheduled to take a statistics course this fall. That was a good move. It would make her even more dangerous.

I had to put most of that week into getting some lectures organized and ordering laboratory supplies for Introductory Biology I and Invertebrate Zoology that I was teaching this fall. The week went quickly. At the end of it I had things pretty well ready to go. A dinner date with Sylvia was coming up on Saturday night. For the past couple of weeks I hadn't seen much of her. She was about to embark on her new job and I presumed she had been devoting herself to that. When she got her first swollen paycheck this fall I would have to get her to take me out to dinner. Anyway, she came down on Saturday to spend some time in the sun. Before going out to eat we spent two or three hours out on my deck. She was looking marvelous! That striking symmetry of hers together with a tan was something to behold. It was a pleasure to have her in my world.

On the deck we talked some about the Dean of Research position and what it would mean for her. She had thought through some of the things she was going to do in her first year. I was happy to hear the list and it sounded good. For one thing she planned to broaden the In-House-Grant Program. As an advertisement for the program, she had made good use of her particular grant this summer. She wanted to increase the potential number of $10,000 grants awarded to seven or eight. That would increase the interest in research and the number of faculty and students involved. I liked that idea, but wished to not be running the committee that had to judge proposals for much longer. A new batch of proposals was due in the spring semester. I could most likely expect to chalk that wish up as a disappointment. Another thing Sylvia wanted to encourage was students pursuing undergraduate theses. Annie was set to be the first from this campus to accomplish that. She was very happy with the progress of her own student, Agnes Moore, and found that a most satisfying and rewarding thing to do. Agnes was thoroughly into it too and liking what she is going after. Provost Bigelow had assigned her a discretionary budget of $50,000 to support her initiatives as Dean of Research. Some of that was to be used to fund faculty and students deciding to take on senior thesis projects. No doubt this would stimulate research on this campus. A third thing Sylvia had in mind was the better integration of our campus with the main campus. Basically she wanted to somehow foster relationships among faculty on the two campuses. If faculty from our campus were involved in prospective senior theses, such relationships would need to be developed because of the necessity of getting committees together to sit in judgement on those theses. Of course, faculty interactions between campuses cannot be forced, but the plan was to encourage them whenever they could be fostered.

    I thought the three areas she had focused in on were very promising in terms of a research leader on this campus. I told her out loud that was my thought. Then I mentioned my upcoming appointment with the Provost and my reason for it. It was in essence to get him to remove his request that I run for president of the faculty senate. Sylvia did not hold my wanting to avoid that in any higher esteem than the first time I expressed it to her. Well, we could disagree, but nevertheless I still thought it was a good reason, absolutely fundamental to what I wanted to do as a faculty member.

    My tanned beauty and I eventually made it out to eat. Work matters were forgotten and we had a quality time at a very good restaurant. The food was good, but not as good as that Boeuf Bourguignonne Sylvia had put together for us. That occasion and the food was a fond memory for me. Another such memory was to come. We went back to my place afterwards and had a couple of drinks. She announced that tomorrow morning she would love to take a short canoe ride. With a twinkle in her eye she allotted that with that in mind she would like to stay over. Well, all I could say was, "That sounds better than O.K. with me. The canoe ride sounds good too." We indulged our senses and shortly thereafter we got to sleep. At 7:00 A.M. I arose and put together some juice, bacon, eggs, potatoes, toast, and coffee for us. It was a beautiful, quiet Sunday morning as we ate. Early in the next hour saw us off in the canoe. We both took a paddle and went completely around my private estuary. No adventures, it was just an exceedingly peaceful, scenic, and nice trip. We returned and took the craft out of the water and put the gear away. Sylvia had some work she wanted to get done and, after saying how much she enjoyed the afternoon, the dinner, last night, and the canoe ride, she left to go home. It was a beautiful two days with her.

Later that Sunday morning Sophie called. Her message was that she, Zachary, and Annie had written a draft of Materials and Methods and would very much like to have me read it and discuss it with them tomorrow. I said I could do that. I asked how long it was and could you get it to me tomorrow morning? It was 16 pages and she could even bring it down to me today. I thought that would be best. I expected to be home all day. She said she would be by sometime this afternoon. At about 2:45 she appeared. I took the manuscript section and told her that I would get it read and would meet them in the lab tomorrow at about 9:00 A.M. She left and I settled down to read around a bottle of beer out on my deck. What would I do without this place?

I could see Annie's hand in the organization. The grab itself was well described, as were the methods of taking drill samples from the sediment with it. They had also well covered the marking of drills and their deployment. The method of counting and taking snails off the inshore pilings, leaving them denuded of drills, was neatly handled. The scarcity of drills on offshore pilings made the denuding unnecessary out there, but there was a nice treatment of the method of observing for drills below the water on those poles. Zachary's hand could be seen there. As far as it went, this was pretty damn good for a quickly written section. What was missing was a section dealing with methods associated with statistical analysis of data. They would need a statistical reference book and probably some time to learn some statistics.

Let me briefly set out the data to be statistically analyzed in a couple of informal tables.

In Table A are presented the numbers of *Urosalpinx cinerea* found in the 12 sediment samples taken on either side (landward and seaward) of the inshore and offshore experimental rows of pilings used in the drill investigation. Table B shows the number of drills in the seven bottom samples taken at 10 piling row intervals between the inshore and offshore experimental rows. The depth to the bottom (during low tide) at the time of sampling is indicated for each of the seven samples. The patterns noted just below are pretty clear from merely looking at the data, but using a statistical test (something called the t-test) to compare some of the mean (average) values in the tables above would help. Some "official" statistical points about these data follow. In Table A drills in the sediments at the nearer shore site were significantly more abundant (inshore mean of 5.67 versus the offshore mean of 0.58 drills/0.25 m^2). Also, especially at the inshore site, but also at the offshore site, drills exhibited a patchy distribution, i.e., some of the samples had a quite a few drills, others had fewer or zero. In Table B if we divide the seven samples into two groups, the first three samples and the last four, and compare the mean number of drills in the two groups an interesting result emerges. Samples at rows 45, 55, and 65 had a mean of 7 drills/0.25 m² whereas the mean number of drills in the other four samples, more offshore, the mean number of drills was significantly lower at 0.6/0.25m². There was a significant reduction in the number of drills in the sediments where the depth at low tide was 3.5 ft. or more. That was a break point beyond which drills became less abundant. This agrees with a result noted above for Table A: there were more frequent drills in sediments around the inshore site.

Table A. Numbers of *Urosalpinx cinerea* (oyster drills) in 12 sediment parcels (0.25 m² each) at two sites, inshore and offshore, along a pier

	Number of Drills	
Parcel #	Inshore	Offshore
1	2	1
2	13	1
3	5	0
4	4	0
5	6	2
6	4	0
7	6	0
8	4	1
9	10	0
10	4	2
11	3	0
12	7	0
Total	68	7
Mean #/0.25m²	5.67	0.58

Table B. Total number of oyster drills in a parcel (0.25 m²) of sand with increasing piling row number and depth as you go offshore along a pier

Row #	Depth (ft.)	#Drills/0.25 m²
45	0.8	8
55	1.0	6
65	1.9	7
75	3.5	1
85	7.0	0
95	12.0	0
105	13.0	1

When I met with them I would have to explain the workings of a t-test. That is not too complicated and shouldn't be much of a problem. In the time we would have, I can be thankful that more involved statistics were not necessary. Anyway, Annie had obviously had a major hand in writing that draft. Absent her input it would not have come out nearly so well, but the three of them had produced a fine product. I felt good about sending them off to the main campus for further collaboration. They should do nicely with the rest of the manuscript.

At 9:00 A.M. the next day I met with the three authors of the drill manuscript. After compliments on what they had done so far, I then launched into my coverage of the need for and the workings of the t-test. That took about 45 minutes. Following that it was time for goodbyes. They only had a little time left to pack up and get ready to go to main campus. To Annie I said, "It has been a good summer, you were a great help and we got done what we needed to do. Your thesis is in great shape and you should not have a problem getting it finished this coming year. I of course expect to be on hand when your defense rolls around." She indicated that she too felt good about the way the summer had gone. Her farewell words were brief. She had much to do and then left to do it. Sophie and Zachary had to go as well, but stayed around for a few moments. Sophie said that, "No one had previously had so much faith in me and trusted me to do so many things. You gave me quite an experience this summer. I really appreciated your attitude and help. Thank you." Zachary then added, "I too would like to thank you for allowing me to be more than just a dishwasher. That is what I thought I would be doing most of the time, but it was so much more. I have gotten a sense of what fieldwork is all about and I think you have shown me what I want to do with myself in the future. As it is I am really looking forward to going up to campus and taking courses. That's something I never thought I would say." I then said, "You both have been great students and more than just helpers. It has been an unqualified pleasure working with you. I wish you luck with your approaching main campus adventure and so long for now." They left and there I was all alone in my lab once again.

The meeting with Provost Bigelow was the very next morning. There were no preparations needed for that, but I was a little anxious about it. Before leaving for the day I wanted to check my mailbox. My mail was most interesting. Aside from a good bit of junk there was a letter from one of the people, a Dr. Amos Ferguson, who had come to campus to learn about the fan worm and its parasite. That was right after the self-inflicted wound paper had come out. He dealt with Timothy, who had apparently done a fine job as guide when he visited. The good doctor had been able to locate a local population nearer the university hospital where he worked. He gave me the name of a marine invertebrate zoologist that was on hand at that university to help him with that. I recognized the name. The assistant he had brought with him for the instruction had taken on learning how to collect worms, find infected worms, and make up a parasite fluid. Ferguson had a medical paper coming out relating the effects of that parasite fluid on skin infections of a number of his patients. He had seven patients and, even though infections in the seven were caused by four different bacteria, on all of them the fluid had been a resounding success. Within a day or two the infections cleared up. All of the infections had been resistant to the antibiotics they had been using and Dr. Ferguson viewed this as an unmitigated success. He was going to continue studying the fluid further. That was just the kind of test I was not equipped to do and I was thrilled by his results. Maybe this lucky discovery will actually help some people, in fact it already had. I wrote a letter back right away. I told Dr. Ferguson I was very pleased with his results and thanked him for letting me know what happened. I was glad that my little discovery had been able to help some people. His visit here had been in summer 1977 and that was before acceptance of the paper by me, Annie, Timothy, and Toby about the cleaner way to obtain the fan worm parasite fluid for testing on infected mussels. He couldn't have seen it. So I enclosed a typescript copy and sent the letter off that day.

When the next morning came I went to keep my appointment with Provost Bigelow. I was in for a shock! Our meeting started out innocently enough. Before long however things went unexpectedly very bad. The Provost was lining things up for the coming fall semester and did not want any of his plans upset. After some beginning amenities I began explaining what I was thinking about offering myself as a candidate for the senate presidency. I said, "I know I have agreed to do it, but want to tell you again that this is something I really don't want to do. I have always taught what was asked of me without argument or grousing. It has been difficult scheduling my research around my teaching. Especially this fall I will need to use my time to focus on completing the research associated with my grant. The time devoted to the election and if elected time taken up doing the job will not be compatible with that. More generally, feeling the way I do about it will likely lead to me doing a poor job." The Provost responded, "These are the kinds of things that faculty must be willing to accept doing." I answered, "Yes, you have made that point before, but you seem to want research on this campus to increase. You must realize the great amount of time a successful investigation takes." His response to that was surprising,

> I understand that you are not thrilled with the prospect of leading the faculty senate, but I have made a judgement that your value to this campus resides not in doing further research. You have done enough of that for what I envision. It's time to cash in on what you have accomplished. Your better role will be to lead others into the research arena. Your example will serve to show what can be done. A promising place for commencing on that role is the presidency of the faculty senate. If you bring yourself around to it, you have great potential in such a position. Your drive to develop research on this campus coupled with your leadership potential could have a major influence on the development of this campus. I have developed a very strong feeling about this.

I said, "I realize that you have a position of leadership on this campus, but think it presumptuous of you to make such a decision about what I will do. Getting research under way on this campus is a goal of mine, but just promoting research by others is not what I want to do. I want to do it myself."

At that the Provost discharged his big gun. He said,

> Considering your expressed attitude and feelings concerning your taking on the role of President of the Faculty Senate, I have something to say to you. I've wondered if I'd ever have to use this, but I think this the time. I know something about you that may cajole you into accepting my design for your future role. Two springs ago, just before his death, Provost Flannery told me of his invitation to you to meet at his house. He said that short of not renewing your contract, he wanted to see if he could resolve some issues about the research you had been doing. That was on the Friday afternoon before his body was found on Saturday. I don't in fact know if that meeting ever took place, but that was his plan and I assume it did. That would mean you were one of the last people to see him alive. At the time I thought hard about what I should do. Should I tell the police or not, about that proposed meeting? At that time, I decided not. I thought that this branch of the University would be able to get over the event of the Provost's death more easily, if there were no additional questions or intrigue surrounding his death. Your role in that death, if any, was and is unknown to me, but from what I knew of you then I didn't think you were causally involved. I just salted my knowledge away, maybe to use later, maybe not. This is the time when I have decided to use it to try and influence you to see your future role the way I do.

Needless to say, at this point he certainly had my attention. It was unlike anything I expected from Provost Bigelow. He had always been most helpful and straightforward. But, here he was proposing to blackmail me into signing onto his plans for me. I was not amenable to the attempt. Revealing of the information he had to the police would certainly be a problem for me, but it would also be a problem for him. Were he to do that now, why did he wait so long to tell them? Could it be that he had something to do with Flannery's death? He had in fact gained a lot as a result of his death. Those and other questions would likely arise. In stunned quietness I thought about all this for a minute. My silent conclusion was that come what may I simply would not stand for it. I had just recently signed another annual contract so at least for another year I could not easily be fired. If the son-of-a-bitch was going to get what he wanted by blackmailing me, I would ultimately have to gamble on him not actually giving any information to police. And, I would have to get the hell out of here. If he did decide to reveal his information, then I would have to take the consequences and somehow deal with that. Except for pissing him off, I didn't do anything that night to cause Flannery's death. He did that himself. With the Provost's tactic the present situation was utterly untenable and, as much trouble as it would be, I had to make arrangements to leave.

What could I say to him, in his office, right at this moment? I had already let him know what I thought of his plan for me. It was a transgression. Should I admit that I had met with Flannery at his house that Friday, or should I deny everything? Counting Sylvia, only two people know I had been there that night or there was a plan to be. Things were bad enough now and, if the Provost chose to tell the police what he knew, I did not want to create an extensive lie to further complicate matters. So I said, "Yes, I did meet with him on that Friday. If you tell the police about this, I will tell them in detail what happened, but failing that I will keep my own counsel about what that was. I will only say to you that I did not cause Provost Flannery's death." To this Provost Bigelow said, "I reiterate that from what I have gotten to know about you that does not seem a likely possibility to me, but I can't claim to know." I returned, "Well, I am at least glad that you feel that way." The Provost went on to say again that he felt strongly about my value to the campus in being a purveyor of the ideals of research. I responded, "Maybe you see something in me that I do not. There may be something of which I am unaware, but I do know that what you would have me do I don't wish to do. Teaching and research is what I want to spend my time on."

The Provost then said, "Of course I am very much interested to know what you know of Provost Flannery's death. But, if you choose to not tell me more than that you did meet with him, I suppose we will have to leave the rest within your knowledge." I responded, "Yes, that is my choice." My thought at the time was that I had made a good decision to leave it at that. Anyway, I gave him no further information about what I was going to do. The salient features of my future plans were that I would not be running for senate president and would be looking for another job. However, I said nothing and that plan was left hidden. Our meeting ended there. I walked away upset with what had transpired and with a personal commitment to follow up on my unvoiced plan. Even if no job turned up, I would have to leave. There would be no staying here with a threat of blackmail always in the background. I could not have the Provost thinking that such a ploy would work.

My first move was to have a talk with Sylvia. She needed to be warned about Provost Bigelow's threat to blackmail me with an eye to getting me to behave in the way he wanted. If she was going to work directly under his control, she should be aware that he was capable of such a nefarious tactic. Also, we had been good friends and lovers for quite a while now and the necessity of my plan to look for another job and leave should be made known to her.

Associated with her coming duties as Dean of Research, she was moving into her new office. A secretary had been hired to filter calls, but Sylvia also had a direct line to her desk. I called her on the direct line. She answered and I told her that my meeting with Bigelow had just taken place and I needed to talk with her. She needed to take lunch and said we could do it then. We agreed to meet at the restaurant. I hadn't seen her for a few days and when the time came she was her usual pleasant, inspiring self. I repeat myself about this, but so she always affected me. We got seated in a booth with no neighbors and talked quietly. I began,

> As you know Provost Bigelow wants me to run for senate president. He has the idea that I would be more use to this campus if I were to promote research by others, rather than continue to do it myself. For me to take on that role he did something mystifying and unexpected. Apparently, on the Friday before his death, Provost Flannery told Bigelow he was going to meet with me that night at his house to try and iron out our differences. To 'cajole' (Bigelow's choice of words, not mine) me into taking on the role he had in mind for me he threatened that, were I not to agree, he would give that information to police. In effect he proposed to blackmail me. In our meeting I went so far as to admit that I had in fact met with Flannery, but awarded him none of the other information I gave you when we talked about my meeting with him that night.

I explained why I had admitted that much. Sylvia interjected, "I am astounded that the Provost would take to blackmail to get you to assume that role, really astounded." By way of agreement with her, I expressed my own surprise, "Based on his previous behavior, it was unlike anything I expected from him. Maybe powerful administrators just can't help themselves." Next I went into what I felt I had to do about the situation. That would be of special importance to her because it would put our relationship in jeopardy. I said, "He is not aware of my plans, but there is no way I can continue to work here with his blackmail threat hanging over my head. I just signed a contract for the next year, but I will have to see if I can find another position as a faculty member somewhere else." Sylvia had a question: "But what if he goes to the police and tells them what he knows?" My comeback was, "I have thought about that. I would certainly have a big problem if he did, but concluded that if I weren't around here to threaten, he would not take that action. There would be nothing to gain for him, except possibly making life miserable for me. Besides a lot of time has gone by and he would have to explain why he waited so long to inform them, which would raise a number of questions he would prefer not to have to answer." Sylvia thought that was true.

Sylvia then said,

> As I said, Bigelow resorting to blackmail really surprises me. It is about the last thing I would have expected. On top of that I don't see what he expects to gain from such a threat. I mean you might have the potential to do a lot of good in the path he would have you follow. In fact I sympathize with his desires along those lines to some extent. But the tactic is reprehensible and betrays a serious misunderstanding of how to deal with you in particular and faculty in general. It's as if he had no experience with you at all. Not only that, but he under values your contribution to this campus if you were to do nothing else than continue along your present course. You are at least a high quality faculty member and he shouldn't want to lose you. Bigelow should have known that the effect of his tactic would be to drive you away. Aside from our personal relationship, in my new job I mourn your loss to this campus. There will be less to work with around here and I am sorry for that. My job will be more difficult.
>
> As to our relationship, I understand why you will have to leave. It won't happen for a while yet, but envisioning a future around here without you makes me sad. You have made things adventuresome and fun. I hope I won't be too lonely and we can maintain our connection to each other, even if it must be at a distance. I have developed a dependency on you.

I responded, "I feel the same way about you. You are a special woman and of the greatest importance to me. I do have to leave, but moving away from you will be the most difficult aspect of that. If I have any power over it, we will keep on with our connection. My love for you will not disappear." I had never said anything about love to anyone before. To her it was a real emotion and I felt good about it. To that she said, "I have never been comfortable with that word, have never used it, and don't really know what it means. I'm a little surprised to hear you use it." I added, "Well, it wasn't an accident and I meant it. The word is equally mysterious to me and I've never used the word before either, but I am at a loss for another word to use." "We feel similarly about each other and that's enough. It makes me very happy," was her response. That was good enough for me too. We finished eating, paid the bill, and left. Both of us had things we needed to get done this afternoon.

I needed to get started looking for a job. At the time I was aware of two main publications that listed advertisements by colleges and universities looking for new faculty to hire. One was the weekly journal *Science*, to which I had a subscription, and the other was *The Chronicle of Higher Education*, which was available in the library. A trip to the library and a perusal of the last few months of the *Chronicle* produced five possibilities. I made xerox copies. I had months of back issues of *Science* in my possession. Looking in those gave six additional current possibilities. All were adds for faculty related to invertebrate zoology and ecology, which were not too numerous. My next endeavor, which I did that day, was to write a basic letter of application for these positions. Every application requires different components and emphasis. My basic application would be adapted to suit the requirements of each prospective employer. Of the 11 applications I had to assemble some were more likely to be successful than others, but none of them were ultimately all that likely. One was for a smallish (~3,000 students) place called Haven University on the east coast about 200 miles south of my current location. They wanted somebody to handle invertebrate zoology and ecology classes and to pursue research having to do with those areas. Haven University did offer a master's degree in biology, but most highly prized undergraduate research. From a distance it is hard to tell, but I had great hopes for that one. I hoped it would come through. Anyway, I wrote my basic letter with that university in mind.

It was coming into the academic year of 1979-80. An academic year, such as this one, would encompass the fall semester of 1979, the winter session of 1980, and the spring semester and summer of 1980. I had been at Visitopolis University since fall 1973 and my seventh academic year was about to begin. Given the circumstances my plan was it would be my last year here. What wonders might my adaptable application letter contain? Basically it had to summarize what had been accomplished and under what conditions during that time. It was decided to come up with a summary, a *curriculum vitae* (CV), which would contain all the vitals of my accomplishments. A copy of this CV would go with all applications. This would allow me to make the application letters shorter and deal with my fit to whatever the receiver of the application seemed to want. Different things could be emphasized to make the letter suitable for various applications.

A listing of my degrees obtained (which would include Bachelors, Masters, and Ph.D.), where and when awarded and papers published would certainly be included in my CV. In the summer of 1975 and in the fall of that year two papers based on my Ph.D. dissertation were published. The paper on my initial Visitopolis research, the drill work done in 1974, wasn't published until the fall of 1977. In spring 1978 the host-switching paper (the fan worm parasite could also infect the blue mussel) was published and in summer 1978 the note on the human healing properties of the fan worm parasite was published. The paper by Hall, Holt, and Turner (Annie, Timothy, and me) on the comparison of infection prevalence in pier and jetty populations of the oyster drill saw print in spring 1979. My current last paper, the one on the cleaner way to produce and make use of the fan worm parasite fluid to kill off mussel infections, was accepted this past summer (1979), but it was not yet out in print. Of course, author, year, title, journal name, volume, and page information would be given for each published paper, but I won't take up space with that here. Anyway, I had managed seven publications in my six years at Visitopolis University. Considering the conditions set up by administrators during most of that time, the list is not shabby.

My history at this institution might be variably emphasized in some application letters. Let's briefly review some of that. At my first faculty meeting in 1973 there was some flap about a faculty member (Sylvia) desirous of getting some support for research. In that meeting I learned that faculty research activities were frowned upon by administrators. No one had said anything about this during my job interview. I was flabbergasted by this attitude on the part of leaders of a university! I decided right away that despite the dictates of the administration I would quietly find a research project and pursue it. There was no apparent problem from the two papers published from my dissertation. Those were O.K. because the work was done elsewhere. With the first publication based on work done here I began to accrue problems. My local research at Visitopolis began when the drill work on the pier pilings was done, between March and November in 1974. In summer 1976 I began working with parasites and discovered that the fan worm parasite could switch hosts into the blue mussel. In the summer of 1977 I found that the fan worm parasite kills off the mussel parasite. In fall 1977 I discovered that the fan worm parasite had wound healing properties. At that time the paper on my first local research was published and problems with administrators began. Naturally, the episode with Provost Flannery would be left out, but I would indicate my role in getting the faculty vote to change the research policy of administrators as well as a part of my interaction with the new Provost.

In my CV I would also, of course, make note of my $80,500 research grant. My one official claim to service performed was my chairmanship of the In-House-Grant committee. I also wanted to cover the students I had worked with, their accomplishments in research, and little of their subsequent history. I guessed all that, depending on what had to be related, would make for letters about two or three pages in length. Some striving to keep them interesting enough for a reader to get through with ease would be wise.

I was working in my office at school. A look up told me that 6:30 PM had arrived. I had made considerable progress this afternoon, but was now tired and not thinking straight. That being the situation a bit of cleverness won out. There was no point in trying to officially write my first letter. That would best wait until tomorrow. So I left and stopped for a single beer and a sandwich at a bar a mile or so from my house and then went home and crashed.

The next morning I was up by about 5:00 A.M. I had slept well, but could not wait to get at those letters. Notes had been jotted down about what was to be included and my typewriter was waiting. My want was to write the Haven University letter first because that was the job I thought I most desired. But, there were 11 to write and I thought maybe it would be wise to wait until I had a little experience with formulating these letters before writing that one. My decision was to make Haven University number five. Over coffee, my best cookery item, I tackled my first letter. All there was to go on in this case was the ad in *Science*. That was enough. My letter, pointing to the fit between me and the advertised job, came out pretty well. At least I was happy with it. There was much still to get together for these applications and I set my first letter aside for a while. The second letter required about the same content as the first. It was approaching noon and time for a late breakfast. I was ready for it.

It was a useful break to eat something. Fortunately, there was no need for me to go to campus on this day, but I was teaching Biology I and Invertebrate Zoology this fall and classes were starting next week. Things were pretty well in hand for lectures and labs of both courses, but I would have to rethink my way through the lectures and laboratories again. This day, however, was devoted to writing more letters. I managed to get six thought out and on paper, a good day's work.

Another thing, it was necessary to decide who would be asked for letters of recommendation. My choices were Dr. Veblen Postelwaite (my Ph.D. advisor) and Dr. Stephen Victor (my friend and an ecology professor at my Ph.D. institution) and Dr. Dustin Filbert from where I got my master's degree. I would have to write letters to all three requesting that they write letters to the places where I was applying. It was a lot to ask of them, 11 letters. Well, they all had secretarial help and I would be properly solicitous. Solicitousness would have wait until tomorrow when I got back at work on all this. I would dearly like to finish this application process before classes begin next week.

A big necessity was coming up. A couple of students had to be hired to help with at least two, possibly more, sets of periwinkle samples on the outer pier pilings and the two beach groins. Trips to the outer pilings would have to be outlawed when it turned colder. I did not want to take a chance on getting me or a student dumped into in cold water out there. Selecting students would be a problem! All my experienced students, most recently Annie, Zachary, and Sophie, were gone up to the main campus. I wished them all a successful year there, but their absence presented me with a problem. Useful students would have to be found that had no course work yet and were untried and unknown to me. We would have to wait and see what turned up on the first day of classes.

The very next day I completed the other five letters of application as well as the three request letters for recommendations. It was kind of fun writing to my former professors. My three choices for letters of recommendation had all, in the deep dark past, agreed to write letters for me. It had been a while since I needed one, but I was confident that their willingness would be unchanged. Along with the names and addresses of the 11 people to whom they needed to write, I would enclose a copy of my CV. My referees needed to be abreast with my current activities.

Some of the secretaries around campus were beginning to work with computers and the word processor programs they ran. By today's standards they were pretty primitive, but they made it possible to produce finished letters quickly. On a typewriter it would have taken me at least two days (probably more) of tedious typing to produce the finished three referee and 11 application letters. One of those secretaries, her name was Shirley, said she would be happy to help me out with her word processor. She claimed it would be good practice for her. I can't thank her enough for that. Because of her typing skills it only took her part of a morning to get the letters, names and addresses, and CV into computerized form and the necessary copies printed out. I thank you, Shirley. It was great! I was amazed. At about this time there were desktop computers becoming available. I would have to get one and learn how to use it. Indeed I would.

So, all my letters were finished and ready to go. No contact with my chosen referees had been made for quite a while. I decided it would be good to give my referees calls to let them know what I was doing and talk with them a bit. They would not need to know explicitly why I felt the need to leave, only that I was looking for a position where my talents and desires would be better appreciated. That afternoon the calls were made. It had been a while and it was good to have made contact with these three. They all said they would get their letter written and copies sent off as quickly as possible. That little bit of conferencing finished I could and did send out the 11 applications right away. There was no denying that my main hope was for the Haven University job. That would keep me reasonably close to Sylvia. None of this was within my power and I would just have to see how all this turned out. The matter of applying for jobs being done for a time, the rest of the week went into preparing to begin teaching. My first day of classes would be next Tuesday.

During the weekend I spent a classy day with Sylvia. She was about to officially begin her duties as Dean of Research and needed that day to relax a bit. I did my level best for her. She wanted to talk at length about her upcoming position and wanted to know the state of my application process. To her appropriate exclamation, I told her how much work that was. She was particularly interested in Shirley's use of a word processor and printer to hasten the job. She too thought she would have to look into getting a desktop computer. We both thought that the use of them would become a very common thing. Sylvia and I ate dinner out on my deck and she stayed the night with me. We both needed that. In the morning we had some breakfast and then she left to go home. She had many preparatory things to do.

In my first classes I was amazed at the number of students wanting to get involved in research. Apparently word had gotten around about what Annie, Timothy, Toby, Sophie, and Zachary had been doing. No fewer than 10 approached me to express their interest in trying their hand at research. At various times all were told that I needed to get help from two students this fall, but at the moment it wasn't clear how to do that. Of course, I knew absolutely nothing about any of them. Perhaps a show of a little aggressiveness would reveal the best of them. I would wait a bit to see which of them would pursue their application. It didn't take long. A couple of them actively campaigned for the job, a girl named Alexis Higgins and a guy named Paul Ambrose. Somehow the others were less impressive. Alexis was a fit looking girl, well spoken, and who sported an infectious smile. She claimed that she knew Annie and really wanted to do what she had done. It was very inspiring to her. Paul was well above average height. He had been a basketball star in high school. He came up and said that he was very interested in participating in research because he thought that was what he would like to do in the future. Well, they were both pigs in pokes, but I decided to take these two on. Maybe they would work out. Well, I hoped so.

I needed to get to know them a little bit. An appointment was made with them to come in and listen to a brief characterization of the periwinkle project that would be paying them. At the appointed time they both appeared and sat to listen. I gave them a rundown of the three sites and what had happened at each. Sophie's drawings and photographs were a big help in doing this. With regard to the pier I made the point that we could only work that site when the water was calm and warm. Paul said he could swim, Alexis on the other hand said she could a little bit, but not very well. I made a mental note that she at least would have to wear a life vest any time she was in the canoe. Neither of them said much about what was in front of them. What could they say? It was all utterly new to them. Both listened with attention and seemed to understand pretty well. We made an arrangement to go to one of the jetties on Friday of this week. We had to get going before the water turned cold. It was September and we could figure to work through October and maybe part of November on the jetties. The pier's available time would be shorter. My plan was to get data at least two more times at each site.

They both came down in Paul's car on that Friday. About two hours before low tide I met my two aspiring researchers at an agreed upon place and led them over to jetty #2. The smaller of the jetties seemed appropriate for their first day. A little time was devoted to telling Alexis and Paul how slippery these rocks could be. So they should move with care. I introduced them to *Littorina littorea*, the most abundant snail species on the jetty. Two very shoreward rocks were chosen and I showed them how the snails on a rock could be counted and measured without dislodging them. If a snail could not be measured without taking a chance of dislodging it, it was better to leave it alone and just count the little bugger. After that demonstration I turned them loose to get some experience with this procedure. Each of them worked on an unmarked rock we had not been counting and measuring snails on. Observations of how they proceeded revealed that both were being careful and thorough. Work went slowly at first. Before too long, however, they both finished counting and measuring periwinkles on the rock they had been assigned. It looked as if both of them would work out O.K. The tide was about used up at this point. We could take a run at getting official data when we came back. They were both ready to do that on Saturday or Sunday and we decided that the next day would be best. Thirty large (older) periwinkles were collected to examine for parasites. They went into a bucket and were due to be examined on our return to campus, which came up next.

In the laboratory I gave them a lesson on measuring and dissecting snails. The use of calipers to measure shell height was brand new to both of them, not to mention the use of a hammer to crack snail shells. Alexis didn't like doing that. I can't blame her for that. It wasn't my favorite thing either. She and Paul hung in there while I, for the most part, went through the 30 snails. Three of them were parasitized; again it was with *Cryptocotyle lingua*. We spent a good deal of time going through the life cycle of this parasite and I showed them the rediae and cercariae. They also learned the features and use of the microscopes. It would take them some time to get comfortable doing all the things they had done today, but it seemed like a good start.

I was pleased with the way both of them had acted during our field and laboratory experience. It seemed they would work out alright. They had come across as genuinely interested. Paul was a mentally agile and capable guy. He asked some good questions and did things carefully and well. Alexi's' infectious smile alone made her pleasant to be around. She too was at least very bright and seemed to learn quickly and remember things. I had lucked out. It was late in the afternoon and we decided to quit for the day. We separated after agreeing on a time to meet at jetty #2 on the next day.

At the appointed time on Saturday I met them at the aforementioned jetty. I said, "To get actual data today, I don't care how slowly we have to go. It's always best to move through data collection as slowly as you need to and get good, accurate numbers. The practice rock on which they had measured and counted periwinkles yesterday was not among the 10 that needed to be done at this site." Paul and Alexis were given tape recorders and taken to one of the 10 marked rocks and requested to start counting and measuring. I hung around them for a while to make sure they were doing things correctly and then went on to work on a third rock. That rock was finished and I was on to a fourth rock while they were appropriately plodding through their rocks. The tide did not go all that low on this day and we were only able to get to a seventh rock before low tide was over, but we had seven out of ten rocks now completed. On Monday we could go on to a little of the graphing that would ultimately be required. A time was found that did not conflict with either of their class schedules and we agreed to meet then in the lab to do that. They left to go home and I went home to take a canoe ride. It was a beautiful day and my little canoe trip was again nothing short of spectacular.

When that was over I called the Dean of Research at home to see how her first week on the job had gone. She said it was kind of underwhelming. On the other hand, the course she was teaching was quite inspiring. It was a sort of upper level history course on this campus. It began well and there were three students that approached her to ask about the possibility of pursuing an undergraduate thesis. All of these were aware of what Agnes Moore was doing and thought that was pretty cool. Students do communicate with each other and they are willing to take on challenges. Sylvia found that to be very encouraging. It made things look good for her plan to promote such theses on this campus. She would attempt to get something going with these three students. I told her about the students that had approached me about doing research and my good experience so far with Alexis and Paul. She thought that was a very excellent start. She wasn't in any particular hurry for me to get off the phone and went on to comment that the fact that I had gotten 11 job applications sent off was a definite step in the right direction for me. With sincerity she wished me luck in that endeavor. I would need it. Eventually Sylvia closed up our conversation with a great idea. We had not seen each other all this week and she wondered if she could come down tomorrow. She hadn't spent much time in the sun over the last couple of weeks and wanted to spend some time on my deck to spruce up her tan. I said, "That's definitely worth sprucing up and any reason you want to come down is more than O.K. with me. Please do." She would be here about 10 A.M.

I was up at 7 A.M. Over coffee I spent some time finalizing the lecture topics for the coming week. Laboratory exercises for the two courses I was teaching this fall would also begin and I had to think those through as well. After I spent about three hours on these matters, at 10:30 Sylvia rolled in. She was still thinking about senior theses and had come up with potential projects that her three new students might undertake. She described them to me. I told her that if Agnes' project and three others as well got going that would be a major commitment on her time and effort, but it would be worthwhile and time well spent. Setting a personal example for other faculty would be a good way to proceed in promoting undergraduate theses on this campus. After this brief exchange she wanted to get out in the sun, which was gleaming brightly. Sylvia went into a back room, my bedroom, to change into her delightfully brief two-piece swimsuit and with something to read went out to get some sun and decorate my deck. It seemed like a good time to leave her alone for a while. Except for bringing her a cup of coffee, I did that.

After about two hours she signaled that she would like to get some lunch. I volunteered to make a trip to the sub shop. That took around 45 minutes and then we ate our submarines in the glorious sunshine on my deck. She was ready to talk some more and we pleasantly whiled away most of the rest of the afternoon out there. Sylvia had to be on campus for an early meeting the next day and had to return home this night. When the sun had lost most of its tanning power we adjourned to the inside to enjoy one another for a time. By about 7:30 or 8:00 P.M. she had saddled up and was gone. Tomorrow was not a class day for me. I fixed myself a meal, hot dogs and beans, and ate. There was not much left in me and I did little else but sleep that night.

The next morning I traveled to campus early. My two students were coming in at 10:00 o'clock. I had to show them how to make size-frequency graphs using two of the seven rocks we had completed on jetty #2. I gathered up the notebook of data and graphs on that jetty that Sophie had generated this summer. The new data was all on audiotape and the first job was to get the data onto paper. What we needed was a total count of all periwinkles on a rock and the sizes of all those that could be measured. Sizes of snails would obviously be used to build the size-frequency graph. Once data were on paper the data tape could be erased and eventually reused. These guys would not know what they were doing or why. As long as they followed instructions carefully the data and the graphic representation of it could be made part of the notebook.

They came into the room adjacent to the lab. Alexis was her usual smiling, cheerful self. Paul for some reason came off as particularly serious. We had about two hours before they both had a class to attend. I showed them an example of what Sophie's transcribed data looked like and gave them each a rock to do. Listening to what they had entered on the audiotape would train them in how to do that in more orderly fashion in the field. Getting data off a tape took them both about 45 minutes. At the end of that time there were two jetty rocks worth of data on paper. The next thing was to build a graph (a histogram or bar graph) of size-frequency. This involved the setting up of 3 mm size categories (e.g., one would be 4.5-6.4, another would 6.5-8.4 mm). Size classes would go on the horizontal axis of the graph. They would then have to figure the percentage of snails falling within each of the size class, which would be represented by the height of a bar on the vertical axis of the graph. By the time they had to go to class each of them had a start. They could finish their graphs on their own time. For now I told them just to copy the axis titles and graph title that Sophie had correctly done. All they had to do was change the date and place (rock #) to reflect their particular data. They could learn the intricacies of title construction later. Two students filled with thoughts went off to class. It had been a good session. They were both taking both my courses and we will see how their graphs came out in labs this week or soon thereafter.

I went to check my mail. It was too soon to expect any response from any job applications, but there was a surprising letter from Dr. Agnes Phillips, the talkative visitor that came this summer with an assistant named Candy. They took some parasite fluid from the fan worm parasite back with them and tried it out on a patient with a troublesome infection. Based on the account of my experiences with that fluid, I presume they had permission and felt safe in doing so. The infection had been resistant to a variety of treatments for quite a while. The letter said that the parasite fluid worked marvelously. In about two days the infection cleared. She also thanked me profusely for taking the time to show her all that I did. Apparently Candy had a new job. She was in charge of collecting parasitized worms and making more fluid. Candy loved it. Dr. Phillips was thrilled with the success of the *Cercaria loossi* fluid so far and expected to continue on with the work. I was very happy reading this letter. That makes two people that had independently cured infections with "my" fluid. I sat down and wrote an answering letter. I said (a small lie) that it had been my pleasure to give what instruction I could and I mentioned the work that Dr. Amos Ferguson was doing. I said that he was having some great success healing up infections as well and that he had a paper in press that would be out before too long. She would be interested to know that. The letter was put together with a typescript copy of the paper about the cleaner way to make the parasite fluid and I committed them to the mail.

The week of classes went very well. I enjoyed them all. The weekend was coming on and I made arrangements with my two helpers to go and get data from the other three rocks on jetty #2. We did that on Saturday. Suffice it to say that my helpers performed nicely. We had the equipment on hand and they had the know how to do the job. Neither of them had brought graphs in for me to look at during the week, but they both had them on Saturday. Before going out to count and measure periwinkles I had a chance to look them over. With only a few minor corrections their graphing had come out fine. We thought we could do jetty #1 on the next day and we did that. Thirty more snails were collected from jetty #1 to be stored and dissected sometime next week. The next major challenge was to do a trip to the outer pier pilings. There were low tides early in a day next weekend when that could be done. I gave Alexis the option to not go out with us, but she would have none of that. She wanted to go. I figured she would be safe enough if she wore a life vest. Being able to swim well, Paul would probably be O.K. even without one, but I wouldn't allow that. I would have to see him in action out there at least once before I would even think about giving him that liberty. He claimed to have done a little canoeing. I sure hoped the weather would be favorable and we would not get dumped.

During the next week we found occasions when those snails could be dissected. It was their second time through this procedure and they were more help than the first time. We found four snails infected with *Cryptocotyle lingua* on jetty #1. With the three on jetty #2 that was a pretty good round of data taking with respect to parasites. To boot we had all 20 rocks done and with their recently gained expertise they could get busy with the graphing. With the approaching weekend we got ready to make our pier run. I spent probably too much time admonishing them about the dangers of working out there, but they needed to be forewarned.

When Saturday morning came to be the tide was at 7:00 A.M. and we met at the pier an hour before that. The canoe was taken off the truck and it and all the necessary equipment was gotten down to the water. They put on life jackets. With me in the stern, Paul in the bow, and Alexis in the middle we began the paddle out to the end of the pier. Going slowly, it took us about 20-25 minutes to get there. Alexis was upbeat about what we were undertaking. Maybe that was to hide what she was really feeling. Whatever the case, she showed a sense of adventure, which was applaud able considering where she was going and not knowing how to swim very well. Fortunately there was almost no wind. I didn't know how many pilings we could get examined, but we would do what we could. Out of a tippy canoe counting and measuring snails is tricky business. My two novice helpers took some time getting onto the task, but they did quite well. We managed to get quality data from five of the 15 pilings. Then the tide rose and made work impossible. We collected 30 large snails and at that time I said, "That is pretty good for today. Let's quit now and get back to shore while we are still dry." They both agreed with that sentiment and off we went. Back on shore with the canoe loaded and tied down and with the other equipment taken care of, they both said they would come back tomorrow and see how many more pilings we could examine. I said, "You have been very good help this morning. Good going." Alexis' rejoinder was, "I didn't know how I was going to make my way out there, but it was kind of fun and I'll be glad to come back tomorrow." So, thus far anyway, the pier was a success.

The weather cooperated fine the next day. We met at the pier and made the trip out. My now practiced team was able to take data from the other 10 pilings. After getting back to shore and loading the canoe and other gear on my truck I said, "I am very pleased with what we have accomplished so far. When we dissect the 30 periwinkles we collected yesterday we will have one of the sets of data I need for this fall. We will have to work on those dissections this week.

You two have been a great help." They seemed happy as they left to go back up the road. I had to go get the canoe and other gear cleaned up and put away. The next morning I would meet my assistants in the lab and begin dissecting those snails.

When I hit the lab the next morning it was still too soon to expect any responses from the places to which I had applied, but low and behold there was a letter in my mailbox from a west coast university in the state of Washington. I eagerly opened it up. I was not letting myself expect too much, but apparently my application materials had found a home: they were impressed with my work with undergraduates and wanted to interview me. They gave me a couple of times when they could do that. If I would tell them when I would like to come, they would pay my way out there and back and put me up for the three days the interview would take. It was a short letter, but very friendly. I was amazed because I had not even expected to hear from them at all except maybe an acknowledgment that my materials had been received, but certainly not with an interview offer. This was super encouraging. At least one university was intrigued with my application. The interview was to be over a Wednesday, Thursday, and Friday. In a reply letter I chose a time four weeks from today. It would be a deal getting there and back. I had never been an airline passenger or that far from home before. It was unbelievable to me that they were willing to pay for the extensive travel involved. They must be pretty serious about wanting to interview me. It would be necessary to learn as much as I could about this university before I went. I was aware of it, but that was about all.

Some research in the library informed me that my interview would be at a medium sized university with about 10,000 students. There was a biology department serving about 700 undergraduate students. In addition they offered Masters and Ph.D. degrees. One of the strengths of the department was its marine science offering. It was quite well known for that and I had heard of that university for that reason. A diagram in their catalog showed a quite large campus. In photographs, it all looked attractive and there was also a nifty marine laboratory pictured. Basically, what they were looking for was someone to do research and teach in the area of invertebrate zoology. Well, I could do that.

I immediately put a call into Sylvia to tell her the news. She was in her office. Her reaction was, "Boy, that was quick and congratulations." She knew that an offered interview meant there was a reasonably good chance of actually getting the job. "If this comes through I will be unhappy to see you move so far away, but I am still glad for you." I responded, "Well, as you know getting another job is something I have to do. Moving that far away from you would be tough on me too. But, let's not get all excited now. Let's see what happens."

She was busy doing something and we left our conversation there and I went to meet my students in the lab. We had to get started dissecting those pier snails.

On getting there I did tell them that I had been invited for a job interview at a west coast university. It seemed useful to educate them a little bit about what is involved in looking for a job in academia. I, of course, did not tell them why I felt I needed another job. I said, "If it comes to pass that I should be offered the job and take it, that won't happen until at least next year." We did not talk about my interview long. They had no way to know how momentous a deal it was and we quickly got started dissecting snails. They both had a class coming up in two hours. Before they had to go we managed to dissect 10 of the 30 snails. They were pier snails and none of them were infected. We would get back to those dissections after their classes were over.

Unlike my interview at Visitopolis University some years ago these guys expected me to give a seminar. In the next four weeks I would have to put one together. Given the purpose of the seminar, seeking a job, I decided to touch on all of my bits of work rather than focusing in on just a part of it. That would include Annie's thesis work and the periwinkle project now proceeding. It would be a big job getting the slides made and the talk organized. I'd better start right away and make sure it is all well done.

When Alexis and Paul were done for the day with classes we got back together and finished dissecting those snails. That was 30 more from the pier that were uninfected. That was getting to be predictable and probably explainable. It had been a big day for me learning of my upcoming interview and I was pretty well exhausted at the end of it. Since I had classes tomorrow I thought I'd better get some sleep and home I went. On the way my thoughts went to Provost Bigelow. I wasn't going to tell him about my interview, but he was likely to find out somehow. How would he take the news and what might he do? It sure would complicate matters if he decided to go to the police with what he knew about my meeting with the former Provost the night before his body was found. Well, that was not anything I could control. I could only hope that he would not make the decision to do that right at the moment, not ever in fact. Sleep was a little fitful, but pretty sound.

I got up early and went over my lecture notes. There was no time yesterday and I was too tired last night. Before you give a lecture it's always good to think through what you mean to do. My 9 A.M. class went very well. After that I began outlining my talk. There was only about an hour before my next class. That's not much time to work, but I felt a need to get started on the talk. I wanted it to last about 50 minutes. Most of what I had to cover had been the subject of published papers. Skimming over that would be legitimate. I did want to spend extra time covering the discovery of the wound healing properties of the fan worm parasite, Annie's work on the drill parasite, and the current project on the periwinkle. That would be a lot to get through in an unrushed manner in the allotted time.

After my second class I went back to work on my talk. The outline was finished before the afternoon was out. Now all I had to do was put content in. Remember I thought, "Tell them what you are going to tell them, tell them, and then tell them what you told them." If I brought that off well, it would be an engaging talk. If only that were to be the way it came out, if only I would have to make it so. A few things had to be put in order for the Introductory Biology lab tomorrow afternoon. After taking care of those I took myself home. Following some supper a little time was spent thinking through my introduction for the lab tomorrow. Then I took up with a novel.

The next morning on campus brought another big surprise. My mailbox had a letter in it from the biology department at Haven University. In addition there were letters from two other places to which I had applied. As that was the job I thought I most wanted, the letter from Haven was eagerly opened first with great interest and some trepidation. That university was on the East coast in another state. It was only about 200 miles away from here and would keep Sylvia relatively close by, an important consideration for me. Amazingly, the letter offered me an interview for the advertised job! That was astounding, two interviews in about as many days! Their missive was informative. It took up nearly a whole page, unusual for such a letter. Apparently they were most impressed with the way I had been able to develop a research program even though this campus of Visitopolis University did not encourage faculty to do that. I was pleased they recognized that circumstance. The professor, who wrote the letter, one Greg Mortinson, seemed quite informed about this Visitopolis campus. That name seemed to ring a bell with me, but I didn't know him as a marine biologist. Where had I run across it? It would come back to me. They too requested a seminar and offered three times, two days each, when it was possible for me to come for a talk with them. One of them was three weeks after my other interview out west and I figured I would choose that time.

I would have to cancel that Wednesday and Thursday of classes. That would not be too bad, even with the other interview that also involved the same week days, because I had not cancelled any classes since I had come here. My letter, which was written and mailed that morning, told them that I was very pleased by the opportunity to come for an interview and gave them my choice of a time. I would drive down arriving the night before the interview days. The other two much less exciting letters in the mail were simply acknowledgments of receipt of my application materials. I filed them away.

I gave Sylvia a quick call to let her know about the second interview and when that was going to be. When I met my Introductory Biology lab that afternoon I informed students of my need to be away on two of the upcoming lectures and laboratory sessions this semester. I could shorten up the lecture material and adjust for those, but there was no one who could or would take over and run those labs for me. I could not afford and didn't want to cancel two labs out of the 12 that semester. We would have to make up at least one of them. What I decided to do was put off the lab practical exam for one week at the end of the semester and run one of the labs in the freed up week. That way, students would not miss both scheduled laboratory exercises. The students were not happy about the extra week's activity at the end of the semester, but that was the best I could do. Similar accommodations would have to be made in Invertebrate Zoology lectures and labs when I met those students the next day. I hated short changing students on course time, but there are occasions when you have to do these things.

Following the laboratory that afternoon I went back to into the attached room that is my lab and started gathering materials to make slides for my talk. Most of the needed graphs and tables were already in journals, but a lot of things not in that state had to be gathered. I grabbed my good quality camera and began taking photographs. I did not have a camera holding copy stand, which would have made the slides better, but once I rigged up sufficient lighting the camera took good close up views of what I had to photograph. Of course, I already had pictures taken through the dissecting microscope of parasite larvae. There were also photos of the periwinkle study sites. If the newer slides came out well (which ultimately they did), they would be good enough for the purpose. Especially for unpublished work an audience will tolerate less than absolutely pristine visual aids. Before about 11:00 PM, I had taken some 30 photographs that could be made into slides. The two lectures and a lab tomorrow begged me to go home and get some rest. The film was dropped off at a 24-hour film development place that had a night box (no longer necessary in this digital age) on the way home. The upcoming day would be demanding.

Over the next weekend, having picked up my slides, I stuck to business and organized my talk. Many hours of practice remained, but except for those it was pretty much done. Over the next week there were classes, labs to run, and I made two runs through my talk. The seminar I was going to give seemed like it was going to be good and I had it within the 50 minutes. That was important, as above all you don't want to stress an audience with an overlong talk.

The weekend after that, saw Alexis, Paul, and I at one of the groins getting another set of periwinkle data. We could figure to work in at least one more trip to the other groin. I was worried, however, that with the weather turning chilly another trip to the pier pilings might get away from us. I surely did not want to take a chance on getting me and my two assistants dumped into even moderately cold water. We might have to be in the drink for a long time.

Also on that weekend I managed to go see a movie with Sylvia. That woman is a light that illuminates my being whenever my eyes come to rest on her. It was a western, which did not make Sylvia happy, but it was pretty good and better than she expected. We both enjoyed the show. I was ever thankful that she had become part of my life.

I remember being exceedingly busy in the time between then and when it was time to go out for my first interview. A number of other acknowledgments concerning application materials received came in, but no more invitations to interview. It's probably a good thing because I had enough to do what with talk practices, lectures, labs, tests, and field trips to the jetties and the pier. We did manage to make one more pier trip. The pier was a little risky, but things went O.K. We would try to visit the jetties again, but even now I had enough data to draw some conclusions about the periwinkle populations on the jetties and the pier.

The week of my trip arrived. Early on that Wednesday I went to a nearby airport and began my trip to the state of Washington. There were two intermediate stops, one in Baltimore and one in Chicago. In both places the bustling airports were an experience for me, but I got through and my plane landed in Washington in the very late afternoon. A faculty member named June Allison met me at the gate. She welcomed me and related that she had a driver who would see that I got to my hotel accommodations and she back to campus. She had a printed schedule of events for this evening and the next two days. My seminar would not be until Friday. All day tomorrow and in the morning on Friday I was scheduled to meet with other faculty and administrators, sometimes over food, sometimes in their offices. The previous person with whom I met would deliver me to the next.

I asked and found that June was a vertebrate physiologist. She was talkative and very helpful. I found her to be engaging and attractive. My inquiry into what her area of research was produced a good and effective rundown of her research. It had to do with vertebrate endocrine systems, the study of hormones. I asked her a couple of questions to delve a bit further into her research. She seemed to take those questions as a compliment and answered them well and completely. We met up with the driver and proceeded to my hotel. I checked in. June left saying that someone else would come by in about two hours to take me to a gathering at a faculty member's house where I would meet several other faculty members. That sounded very interesting, but I was happy to have a couple of hours to rest after my long trip. There would be food available at the upcoming festivity. So far this place had things well organized.

Because they ultimately did not offer me this faculty position I shall not go into much detail about this interview. I spent much worthy time talking to faculty, several of whom I had previously known of as marine invertebrate zoologists. I learned a great deal and that alone made the whole trip worthwhile. One, a parasitologist, had some penetrating questions about the host-switching by the fan worm parasite, *Cercaria loossi*, I had been studying. He had read my papers and curriculum vitae thoroughly and he was himself in favor of offering me the job, but regardless of how all that turned out Aaron Lydecker wanted to stay in touch. In the next two days I had usually 15 minute meetings with a variety of deans, faculty, and other administrators. It wasn't long before they blended into sameness in my mind. My talk on Friday afternoon seemed to go very well. There were a number of interesting questions and my audience was in general very interactive. I was very pleased. My plane back was to be early the next day and that night I had mostly to myself. Two faculty members had dinner with me at a local restaurant. After that I collapsed in my hotel room. The next day, Saturday, my trip went off without a hitch. I made it back to my truck parked at the airport and was home late that night.

Even though it was late on arrival home I called Sylvia to say I was back and tell her a little of what had happened. Of course, at the time I didn't know whether they would offer me the job, but I said, "That was a good experience. They had things well organized and I believe my talk went very well." She said she was very happy it had turned out that way. Tomorrow she wanted to come down to see me. Then she threw in as a sort of aside that the Provost had indicated to her an awareness that I had gone for that interview. I said, "That's most interesting." We let our conversation stop there and said so long. Her last statement generated a wondering of what the Provost might do, if anything. At the moment I was very tired, but I would be glad to see Sylvia tomorrow. The wondering did not last long. Very soon I was asleep.

At about 10 A.M. Sylvia showed up at my door. It was a pretty day, about 75°. We had not seen one another for about a week now and were both were relieved to do so now. I made some coffee and the deck outside hosted us for a couple of hours. We talked over how the interview had gone in detail. Sylvia was intensely interested in it all. I asked her what the circumstances were when the Provost had mentioned knowledge that I had gone for an interview. She said it was a private conversation and did not go beyond that. He did not indicate how he felt about it just that he knew. I said, "Well, that's of interest to me. He probably won't, but if he decides to open up to the police, I should know soon. I do have to see him in the near future because I have to tell him that I have decided not to run for senate president. I guess that will bring this to a head." Sylvia answered, "I suspect so. If he's going to talk to police, it would likely be now because should you come up with another job he will lose all power over you. I truly hope he never passes along any information." I responded, "I can certainly agree with that." After that our attention turned to more personal activities. I certainly enjoyed the hell out of them, very fulfilling. Sylvia wanted to get some writing done tomorrow and needed to get back home tonight. We whiled away the rest of the day and about dusk she left. With a kiss she was gone. It had been a well spent day. That night I felt rejuvenated. Sylvia is always a good experience.

  I did not have any classes that Monday, but I did have a meeting with Paul and Alexis. I wanted to see them and follow their progress on graphing. They had both nicely finished with their responsibilities. Their graphs went into the notebook and I was very pleased with what they had accomplished. I thanked and congratulated them. I allotted that perhaps the water was getting too chilly to warrant going out to get more pier data, but we should do at least one more set of jetty data. I said, "In three weeks I have an interview at Haven University. Maybe we could do one of those jetties this next weekend?" They didn't see why not and we agreed to try and do that. At this point Alexis interjected that she had heard good things about Haven University and had applied there, but didn't get in. Knowing Alexis, I found that surprising and a little puzzling. We ended our meeting at this point.

  Immediately afterward, I got a call from the Provosts secretary. Provost Bigelow would like to see me today. Would I be available this afternoon at 2:00? "Yes," was my answer. I thought to myself that was even quicker than expected. What did that portend?

  I made my way over to Provost Bigelow's office at the appointed hour. Why he wanted to see me was unknown to me. It doesn't require too much imagination to see how much damage to my situation he could cause if he planned to go to the police with his information, as limited as it was. I could foretell a load of legal problems. While I was waiting for a few minutes I comforted myself by recalling the problems he would have waiting this long to come forward with his piece of intelligence. It had been some two years. If he did that, how would the police react? They surely would at least ask me what happened in our meeting. What would I say? After all, there is no statute of limitations for murder. If they suspected me of that crime, no doubt I would have to engage a lawyer. That was an ugly thought. If my meeting with Flannery became known to police, I decided I would not lie to them. That would only complicate matters. They would get only the truth. I might have some legal trouble over not having said anything about what happened at the time, a very big offense, but not as serious as murder.

My head was full of such thoughts when the Provost asked me to come in. His first words were, "I understand that you are looking for another job. I can't say I'm very pleased with that. As you know I have plans for you on this campus." I added, "Yes, and further I have come to the decision that I will not run for the presidency of the faculty senate, regardless of how this job search turns out. I plan to finish out my contract here. After the spring semester I will be gone." His rejoinder was, "Well, I thank you for being that definite about things. I now know what I have to plan for. I have suggested to you that I might go to the police with the information that you were supposed to have had a meeting with Provost Flannery at his house the night before his body was discovered. In view of my continuing belief that you did not do anything to cause the former Provost's death and because of your definiteness today about what you will do, I now decide that there would be no gain for anyone in telling the police anything." I replied, "For obvious reasons I am relieved that is your final decision. And, I suspect that we don't have much else to talk about. So I will now take my leave." He then said, "Yes, I guess that's about it." I walked out and closed the door quietly behind me. My goodbye to Gail Pratt in the outer office was sincere. I left considerably relieved. I could only hope that he would not revisit that decision.

On a stop by Sylvia's office I went in to see her for a few minutes to tell her the news. After giving a rundown of what had just occurred I said, "Needless to say that takes a load off my mind." Her response was, "Well, if we can trust him to stick by what he said, then yes indeed that is a load off my mind too." She had a meeting with a student and I wanted to go get a talk practice in. You have to keep on top of a talk. We parted quickly.

There were two weekends between now and my Haven interview. It had been about a month since our last visit to the jetties and I really did want to get another visit in before the interview. Between getting to the jetties, reading up on Haven, lectures, labs, and talk practice it would be a busy two and a half weeks. I was getting my hopes up for that job and wanted to be as ready as possible for that interview. In a contact with them they were informed that I would be driving down on that Wednesday and would arrive in late afternoon. At that time my first move would be to find the office of Dr. Greg Mortinson, the faculty member with whom I had been corresponding. Where that name had crossed my path in the past had come back to me. He was the biology faculty member that had quit just before I was hired by Visitopolis University. I had replaced him here and it was now obvious why he was so well informed about this place. To say the least, talking with him was high on my list.

I started in on the time between now and that trip. A recently acquired projector made a practice talk at home possible that afternoon. Not only that, but tomorrow's lectures were organized before the night was out. The next morning saw me eat breakfast out. My 9:00 o'clock lecture was given. The zoology lecture was just after that and both seemed to go well. Anyway, they felt good to me. A little later I met Sylvia for lunch. She was her usual sparkling, composed self. Her new job was going pretty well. She had come up with another student, besides Agnes, who seriously wanted to do an undergraduate thesis in history. Two others that started on that pursuit had backed out. Her greatest sense of accomplishment came from another faculty member. It was Dr. Alice Quigley from English. She had a promising student who wanted to do a thesis. I was happy to see that activity getting underway. Students need challenges. The rest of the afternoon was spent getting lab materials ready for this week. Later on at home the talk was practiced again. My plan was to give that talk once every day. I didn't want any flubs when it was given for real. And, so I occupied my time for about two weeks. When the next weekend arrived we managed to get but one jetty done. The weekend after that got rained out so the other jetty would have to wait a bit. Before I knew it the week of my interview was here. I taught my classes on Tuesday and on Wednesday I drove the 200 miles south to Haven University.

The drive down was mostly rural and quite pleasant. I drove into the town of Haven at about 3:30. I found the biology building, Wolff Hall, and went up to the third floor where Greg Mortinson's office was located. He was present and after I introduced myself he said, "Welcome to Haven University. I am very pleased to meet up with you. As you may realize I was employed for a while at Visitopolis University." After some niceties he got right to a meaty point, "I don't know how much you know about my time there." I said, "Not much, but a little." He went on; "Well you may be aware that I had a major problem with Provost Flannery. I understand that he died about two years ago under somewhat mysterious circumstances." I answered, "Yes that is so." It was going to be left right there by me, but Greg continued, "When I was there I wanted to get some research going. As I was being hired they said nothing about research." I said, "Yes, that was my experience too." He went on, "A Dean Terkel told me that faculty here do not do research." I interjected, "Yes, she's still there and even now would still like to tell people that, but things have changed now." He proceeded, "Well, that struck me as a ridiculous way for a university to act and I pressed the issue. Eventually Provost Flannery got involved. We had a meeting where he threatened my job over my wish to do some research. It was in his office and I actually thought he was going to attack me. He had expertise in martial arts you know. Anyway, I took the hint and found another job. I worked at that job for two years and then came here." Then I said, "I am aware of his martial arts expertise and had a similar meeting. Had he not died I doubt that I would still be there as a faculty member. A man by the name of Joseph Bigelow is now the Provost of that University branch." He said, "Maybe I should, but I don't remember him. Anyway it's time to get on out of here. I'll take you to your hotel and let you get checked in. You can rest for a while then later tonight there will be a faculty gathering where I can introduce you to everyone." I said, "Sounds good to me." Greg's rendition of his interaction with Provost Flannery was of great interest to me. Now that's four instances of that tactic being used!

On the way to the hotel Greg told me, as he had in his letter, that he and other people here were impressed with my being able to get research under way, conditions at that campus of Visitopolis University being what they were. He said, "I spoke about what the situation was like there and several people said that was hard to believe and wondered how you could overcome it." I answered, "At first it was a matter of finding a research topic and then keeping quiet about what I was doing. The new Provost thinks it is good for the campus and is outwardly supportive of faculty research. We even have an in-house grant program for faculty and my friend Dr. Sylvia Armbruster, an Associate Professor of History, is now the Dean of Research on our campus. Things are much better now." At the hotel I checked in and Greg said he would be back in about an hour and a half and we would go to the faculty gathering. A chance to rest a little was most welcome.

At the gathering 10 faculty members showed up. I met two physiologists, an embryologist, two molecular biologists, two anatomists, a microbiologist, a parasitologist, and Greg was an ecologist. There were three women and seven men. One of the women, a June Lockhart, was the parasitologist. She immediately pulled me aside, told me what she did, and asked me a number of questions about my research. In particular she wanted to know more about the fan worm parasite and its wound healing ability. I sorted out what I was going to cover in my talk and said, "I don't want to repeat what's in my talk, but let's see if I can answer your other questions. First, the southern limit of *Eupomatus dianthus* is Cape Hatteras and being a bit south of there that polychaete probably doesn't occur here." She asked, "Where could I find it?" I said, "Well, you would have to find a structure that provides hard substratum, a pier or possibly a jetty, north of the Cape. If you want to work with that species, I would guess the closer to this campus the better." She said, "Yes, I can think of a couple of situations just north of the Cape that might work." I added, "Since the definitive host of the parasite is undoubtedly a marine fish, the farther out from shore along whatever structure you find you can collect fan worms and the more infected worms you will find. At least on my pier that is what I have found. That goes for mussels carrying their parasite as well."

June had apparently gotten what she wanted and released me to talk with other people. For me, I made the rounds pretty completely. I learned much and provided a lot of information. It was an interesting time. About 10:00 PM the party broke up. Greg took me back to my hotel. He had a printed schedule of what I had in front of me tomorrow. It was to be a meet-the- administrator day. I slept well that night.

After breakfast I was delivered to my first meeting. That administrator was not too interesting, but we went through the motions. In the course of the day I met with two administrators that were of special interest to me, the President of Haven University, Dr. Gregory Howell, and the guy who was Dean of the College of Arts & Science. It was only 15 or 20 minutes with each, but I came to understand better what Haven University was looking for in their new biology professor. They both had pretty much the same story told with different emphases. Above all they were desirous of developing their undergraduate students. The main way the university meant to accomplish this was by involving students in the discovery of new knowledge, a tactic with which I could heartily agree. The President said that he was most impressed with the fact that I had persisted with research and involved students in my program even though there was a sort of ban on doing that on my campus. I thought, how about that! Here was one high-level administrator from a neighboring university that knew about the Visitopolis situation. He said, "In short, it is why we offered you this interview." Although I had included it in my application materials, I took the opportunity to explain again about Annie Hall's undergraduate thesis progress and how well she was doing. He seemed pleased with my description. I asked, "Do you have an undergraduate thesis program at this university?" He said, "Yes, indeed we do and we put quite a bit of emphasis on it. We do offer Masters Degrees, but it is the undergraduate students that we are most interested in. In the past an undergraduate thesis has produced many fine and successful students in their future endeavors." Our time was up, but that was the clearest depiction of this university I got all day and from right on top.

At the very end of this Thursday I got a chance to meet and talk with about 15 biology students. Not too often do undergraduates get to be an official part of an interview process. They must have been primed because they were most inquisitive about the students with whom I had worked. Most somehow knew about Annie, but they asked about the others as well. Where were they in their college careers? Had they been able to go on with research? How were they doing now? I explained to them that a student doesn't normally spend more than one or two years on my campus. They have to get up to the main campus to continue with course work for their major. So I often lose contact with them. They get on to other things, but several of them have gotten involved with other research projects. I mentioned Timothy, Zachary, and Toby as examples. I further told them of the three students that were currently working on an oyster drill manuscript, for which I predicted good things. This meeting only lasted about an hour, but I must admit that I was quite taken with the students around this place. Many of the ones I talked with were pursuing an undergraduate thesis. They were one and all a good experience.

The Friday of this interview was another very full day. In the morning I met individually with five biology faculty members. I had met them all and they all wanted to talk further with me, beyond our gathering two nights ago. I spent about half an hour each with Greg, June, the microbiologist, an anatomist, and the endocrinologist. All were inquisitive and gave me lots of insight into the nature of Haven University. I was very pleased.

In the afternoon I had to give my talk at 3:00. They gave me an hour to get ready to do that. I did not need it. My talk was well practiced. When the time came it went off very well, about as good as I wanted. I enjoyed telling of the discovery of the wound healing properties of *Cercaria loossi*, but the greatest audience interest was in the part of my talk dealing with Annie's accomplishments. How many undergraduate theses had been done on our campus? They seemed impressed when I told them none, hers was the first. There was a noticeable stir in my audience when I mentioned that there were more now in progress in various disciplines. Afterward, there was an hour long chance for students and faculty to discuss things and ask questions.

Greg, June, and two other faculty took me out to dinner. There were more questions, more discussion, and good food. I found it all thoroughly enjoyable. I felt that I had gotten a complete impression of the university from this interview and I liked this place a lot. If only I had adequately reciprocated. When dinner was over everybody said their goodbyes. Greg took me back to my hotel and said in closing that they would make their decision about to whom the job would be offered in the next three to four weeks. They now had two interviews completed and the third would be next week. I said, "Thanks for a wonderful interview process. I learned a great deal and I hope that I too have been forthcoming. I freely admit that I have gotten worn out over the last three days and look forward to getting some sleep." His rejoinder was, "I'll just bet that is the case. Let's get you right to it. Perhaps I will see you again." With that and my so longs he left. I thankfully went to my room to collapse.

The next morning, Saturday, I got up fairly early, checked out, and began my drive back. It was a beautiful day and I felt good about the interview. We would see. Except for stopping at a book store to look around, my trip was uneventful. I found and purchased a wonderful set of first edition Seaton's *Lives of Game Animals*. The four volume boxed set was expensive ($450), but in very good shape. There is a lot of great artwork in those volumes, which impressed me. I guess I bought them because I was feeling so good. I wrote out my check, took the books, and left. Most used book sellers will accept personal checks without question. It took me about four and a half hours to get back on that Saturday. As usual my first move was to call Sylvia to tell her I was back and what a great interview it was. She said, "I'm so glad it went well. I would love to hear more about it, but right now I'm working on something and want to stick with it. How about I come down tomorrow? We can talk more then." I replied, "What with this interview coming up, it has been almost a week since I have seen you. By all means come down tomorrow." She then said, "I'll get there by about 11:00. Bye for now." I understood that she was immersed in some project and simply said goodbye. Sylvia should work as she saw fit. I ate some supper, thought through the events of the last three days, and then gladly went to bed.

When morning came I ate a good breakfast and took a relaxing canoe ride that lasted about two hours. By 10:00 I had that finished. It was a good thing. The early morning had been bright and sunny, but now it was clouding up and looked like rain was in the offing. At about 11:00, as Sylvia arrived, it got cool and the rain started coming down. There would be no lolly gagging about on the deck today. That did not slow us up in getting back together. I started in,

> I think I told you that the person I had been corresponding with at Haven University, Greg Mortinson, was a faculty member here and I took over his position after he quit. Maybe you remember him. He told me an interesting story about his quitting. Apparently he and Provost Flannery had one of those meetings in his office to dissuade him from doing any research, about which we both know firsthand. Anyway, Greg immediately saw the writing on the wall and looked for another job. He ultimately wound up at Haven University and has kept some track of what has been

going on here. I guess he told many people there what our situation was. Most notably when I talked to President Gregory Howell of Haven he seemed well aware of what our circumstance was here. He and a number of other people I talked to were impressed by the fact that I had been able to start doing research, involve students, and accomplish some things nevertheless. They looked very favorably on what I had done with Annie and took note of the fact that three more students (two of them yours) on this campus in different disciplines were taking on the challenge of doing an undergraduate thesis. I extolled your involvement as the new Dean of Research in getting things to that state. They make a pretty big deal at Haven out of having students take on undergraduate theses. Of course I don't know if the job will be mine. They have another interview to go, next week, and will let me know in three or four weeks. In any case, I was certainly well impressed with Haven University and would very much like to work there.

Sylvia responded, "I do remember Greg and find his continued interest in this place rather surprising. The fact that they push undergraduates to take on a thesis makes the place sound very attractive." I said, "Yes, that is a main tactic of theirs in developing high quality students and from the students I talked with it appears to be a success." Sylvia came back surprisingly, "You make the place sound very inviting. Maybe I could come up with a job there?" In response I said, "Now don't steal my thunder. Let's see if I can land one first. Then she intimated something I had not yet suspected. She said, "Well, I don't like the way Provost Bigelow behaved that is leading you to be driven out of here. Who knows when he will turn on me? I have to at least be thinking about changing jobs." I finished the train of thought with, "Well, if they like me, which remains to be seen, there is no reason they wouldn't like you too. You are certainly as accomplished as I am, even more." As was her way she figured the point was made and went on to other things. She told me a little of their projects and how the three students working on a thesis were doing. They were all making good progress and I was enthused by that. Also, she related how her job was going. As far as I was concerned, mostly due to my own busyness, I had heard too little about that of late. Provost Bigelow had left her pretty much to her own volition. Not being called on for much, she was quite happy with the way things had been going. The increase in the In-House grant money was due to kick in soon. That meant more work for me when it did. Well, I could think of worse ways to satisfy my service obligations, but who knows maybe Provost Bigelow will decide that someone else should take that up. With regard to promoting undergraduate theses she repeated herself, unusual for her, and said she was very happy and pleased with the way that was going. A number of faculty had expressed interest in that possibility and she was very encouraged by that. At that point I said, "Maybe more students from here will avail themselves of that opportunity. It will do much good for them and this campus." She returned, "If only it would go that way. You and Annie can be proud of starting that."

I took an opportunity to show her my new book acquisition. She was appreciative of Seaton's fine artwork. Then she deviated, changed topics and wandered off into what a crappy day it was outside. There was a new restaurant in the neighborhood and we decided to go and try it out for lunch. That was a rewarding decision. Later that afternoon she needed to get back home. She was busy writing something and wanted to get back to it. We spent a few minutes making out and then off she went. I was sorry to see her go so quickly, but did have some lectures to prepare for the coming week.

When I went to campus the next day I had a meeting with Alexis and Paul. Alexis asked whether my interview had gone well. I said I thought so, but you never know how these things will turn out. It was well into fall now and pier trips were out of bounds, but since I was done with interviews we could figure on getting some jetty data collection in on the next weekend. They both could do that. Beyond that, there's nothing much to cover. I was paying them for 20 hours per week, but did not want to interrupt their studies too much. Having the upcoming week for them would be productive enough. A trip to my mailbox produced a couple of more acknowledgments of receipts of application materials, but no new interviews were offered. This being a sunny, bright day I motored home to read some in my new set of *Lives of Game Animals*. I put in a couple of hours on the deck doing that. Those books are so cool. It was an informative pleasant experience. I looked ahead to reading more, most interesting.

There was not much new and different about the next month or so. It was mostly teaching, research, and angst worrying about whether a job would come through. Paul, Alexis, and I did manage to get data from the jetty we had not been able work before the Haven interview. The pier was out for them. I might have taken myself out there, but it did not seem wise to expose especially Alexis to the chance of getting dumped in quite cold water for an extended period of time. We would have to be satisfied with as much pier data as we had already gotten. It seemed unlikely, but if the opportunity presented itself maybe we could get one more set of pier data before I left in the coming year.

One thing that did happen was that the university in Washington, where I had that other interview, sent me a letter turning me down for that job. Well, I couldn't complain. It was a good interview and I learned a lot from that experience. There was no word from Haven University yet, but the absence of that other possibility put more pressure on whether the Haven job would materialize. At the moment I had no other prospects if the Haven job failed. At the time, I thought maybe I could land a job pumping gas somewhere, maybe.

After about four and a half weeks a letter from Haven showed up in my mailbox. With some fear I hastily opened it. Son-of-a-bitch, they offered me the job!! The letter was signed by Gregory Howell, President of Haven University. It was quite brief and said they in the University were impressed by the way I handled students. The relief I felt can't be overstated. Not only was it a job, but a job as a tenured Associate Professor. It would begin next fall at about a 20% increase over my current pay, a good recommendation for believing they were happy with their choice. That same day my letter of acceptance was composed and put in the mail. I also called Greg and told him my letter was on the way and I was very pleased with Haven University during my interview and looked forward to working there.

Of course, having gotten that done my next thought was to see Sylvia and tell her the news. I made a try at her office. She was there. I walked in, closed the door, and with a smile seeping out I dropped my happy news on her. She walked over and planted a kiss, one that I wouldn't be able to soon forget. I said, "Maybe I should look for another job if that's the kind of reward at stake. Well, maybe not. Such luck would not be mine on two occasions." Sylvia said, "The kiss is always yours, but I am very pleased that you will not have to move all that far away. I was afraid you might get that job way out on the west coast." I said, "No, a little while back I got a missive turning me down. As it turned out, I'm glad they didn't want me because I really like Haven University. They put much more emphasis on undergraduate education." She returned, "I can understand your feeling that way." We agreed on a dinner date to celebrate the very big deal of me getting a new job and after another inappropriate kiss in her office we parted.

I had at least one more thing to immediately do and that was to tell Provost Bigelow the news. Here it was well into the fall semester and there would have to be someone hired to teach my courses next fall. That would take some time. Maybe Bigelow knew already. He had ways of being informed. Anyway, I would get some satisfaction out of telling him. It would be strong notice of his failed tactic. I had no desire to piss him off, well maybe I did. In any case he should be informed. I called his office to make an appointment. Gail Pratt said he had an open time tomorrow at 9:00 A.M. I said I could make that. When the time arrived at 9:05 I walked into his office and gave him the news. Bigelow said, "I am not pleased by that, but am glad to know about it in a timely fashion."

He didn't seem upset, only surprised. I said, "I'm glad for Haven's acceptance and to have it all over with." It seemed like a good time to end our little session. The message had been delivered. I was still exercised about his attempted blackmail and all I stood to do with further engagement was to anger him somehow. So I did a sort of lame goodbye and went out of his office. That little meeting was my last personal engagement, except a couple of times by phone, with Joseph Bigelow. He never stirred things up with police. For the trouble it would have caused him, not to mention me, and with Blake Turner being elsewhere employed I guess he decided in the end it just wasn't worth the trouble.

An announcement of my coming departure was made in my next classes. Of course, students were not told any of my motives, just the fact that next year in the fall I would be at Haven University. After the Introductory Biology class Alexis came up and congratulated me. When she was applying there she was certainly impressed with Haven. Another student came up and said that he was going to transfer to Haven next fall. His name was Henry Fortis and he had been doing very well in the course. He said that he wanted to get involved with my research project at the beginning of the semester, but did not do enough to make that happen. That was why he was transferring to Haven. There were more opportunities at Haven for undergraduates to do research. To that I said, "Well, it will take me some time to find a project and get things organized, but please do keep me in mind." Henry closed up with, "I will do that and good luck."

A few days after this a letter arrived from a Dr. Regis Philbin. He had been one of the first people to come summer before last to get some instruction on how to find and deal with the fan worm (and its parasite *Cercaria loossi*). I remembered him, but only met with him for a short time. Annie had been his instructor and had apparently done a wonderful job. He was very complimentary to her in his letter. His purpose in writing was to tell me that he had collaborated with a biochemist named Paul Berg. They had done some work with the parasite, and they had a paper coming out in the spring. A typescript was enclosed with the letter. It wasn't overlong and I had it read in short order. In brief they had isolated a compound, a metabolite, from the parasite. It is a small protein. There is a way, because of its amino acid sequence, to change it and render it inactive. When that metabolite is left active the wound healing properties of a parasite fluid are evident. When inactivated the wound healing properties disappear. Wild!! We not only know that the parasite has wound healing abilities. We now have a very strong notion of why. It's partly or wholly brought about by that small protein metabolite. They are currently working to find out whether that metabolite works alone to heal wounds or in conjunction with other chemicals.

To determine this it will be necessary to get a purified extract of the metabolite and see if it works all by itself or requires that other chemical(s) be present. A question came to my mind. Let's assume for the moment that this protein is related to the ability of *Cercariae loossi* to kill off the mussel parasite when it co-occurs with it in a mussel. Now, is this protein produced by the parasite as an evolved adaptation to remove the mussel parasite *Protoeces maculatus*? Or, is the metabolite an adaptation of the fan worm parasite for some other use and its negative effect on the mussel parasite on co-occurrence is accidental? After thinking about these questions the hypothesis I came up with was that it was probably accidental. The fan worm parasite and the mussel parasite do not infect the same mussel very often. The idea that one parasite species could evolve an adaptation to deal with another parasite species when the two seldom co-infect the same mussel doesn't seem likely. But, maybe the two parasite species encounter one another in mussels more often than I think they do. Only further work on what possible function this small protein may have in the fan worm parasite's metabolism will answer this. But, at least we now know where to look, which we didn't before.

So at this point I knew of two medical people that had cured infections with the fluid from *Cercaria loossi* plus another medical person, working with a biochemist, who had isolated the causative compound from the parasite. I might not make any money from having made this discovery, but it was a nice finding. It sure is wending its way out there in the annals of science, but the way I look at things that's enough for me.

I wrote back to Regis Philbin and told him I was excited about what he and his collaborator had found. It was something I could not do myself and I'm glad someone else did, a nice piece of work. I will be sure to tell Annie Hall about this. She will be most intrigued. I added that Annie is currently in her senior year at Visitopolis University and about to defend her undergraduate thesis. I didn't imagine that Dr. Philbin would be too interested in my question about the adaptive role of that protein molecule, but I also spent a few sentences on that question in my letter. My suspicion was that we were on our way to someone making some real money out of this. If that purified protein works on its own, then we might be on the verge of having something of a wonder drug, something marketable.

Having done that letter I thought it would be good to also write to Annie. She should be told about the success she had with Regis Philbin and about his further work. I got the letter off. When she wrote back she was very pleased and thoroughly interested in that big step forward. She wrote, "That will open up a lot of possibilities." Indeed it will. Enclosed with her return letter was a manuscript by Sophie Timmons, Zachary Trumble, and Annie Hall. They had a Materials & Methods section before they left this fall. This contained also the Introduction and Results sections. Annie said that they had a three-hour meeting every week to accomplish the writing. They wanted me to read it and make comments before they tried to write the Discussion. As it stood it was 30 pages long. That was probably overlong. Undoubtedly shortening would be necessary. I sat down and did my reading and made a few comments in the margins. They could have written it more efficiently, fewer words, but all in all it was pretty good. I was very surprised that they handled the statistics as well as they did. I supposed that Annie's statistics course had an effect there. I made some suggestions on where and how they might shorten it, but it told the story pretty well. I made a copy of the manuscript with my notes on it and quickly put the original back in the mail to Annie. They had done a quality job with this manuscript and I told them so. I've always felt that it's important to let students know of my complementary opinions, as well as the other kind when they have earned them.

A lot of changes were suddenly in front of me. One got handled very quickly and I didn't have to do it. By means of the phone Provost Bigelow communicated to me that because I was leaving next spring he would designate somebody else to run the committee to make judgements on the next proposals for In-House-Grants this spring. I had a premonition that it would be the Economist John Landsby, but did not comment. My canoe was getting old and had seen a lot of use. It was too large to haul south and I decided that when I left I would donate it to the University. It was more of a convenience for me and not so much a big gift. Anyway, I took the opportunity and told the Provost that the canoe would be left and he accepted. Maybe someone would get some use out of it.

The big thing was that I would have to put my house on the market and see if I could sell it. I contacted the real estate agent through whom I had bought the place and told them to list it. I would miss that wonderful domicile in the extreme, especially the deck and the view of "my estuary" from there, but so it goes. Almost immediately a potential buyer got in touch with the listing real estate agent and made an offer. The buyers must have really wanted the place. They sweetened the pot by offering $5000 more than I paid for it. That was welcome and acceptable to me. If they would take it as it is now, furniture and all, and wait until next June to take possession, that would be what I wanted. The buyer found the deal acceptable and the agreement was made. The real estate company made 10% on the deal. I was happy to have the deal done and so was the realtor. So on June first I would be out. The mortgage would be paid off. The bank and the University would be happy with that and I would be gone. I was thrilled with the way that all worked out and come June first I would be among the absent, on my way down to Haven University. It was fortunate to have all that settled so quickly.

Well, all the drama went out of my existence throughout the remainder of the fall semester in 1979 and the spring semester of 1980. In terms of accomplishments my time at Visitopolis University was pretty good. The former negative attitude of the administration about research didn't help. However, I was pleased with the courses I had taught, the research I had been able to do, and the students with whom I had worked. The last group mentioned does not only include students with whom I had been involved in research. There were many students in various classes that had found their footing in academic pursuits. Many students learned how to think and learn more. A lot of them went on to finish their majors on the main campus or at other colleges. There is an old idea that success has many fathers. I can't claim to be the only reason for those student successes, but I had a hand in it and that is most satisfying.

Most of my remaining time at Visitopolis was winter or early spring. My decision was that no further data would be taken on the periwinkle project. In the fall semester Alexis, Paul, and I did do a final jetty measurement, but that was it. My two helpers remained on the payroll to the end of that semester. Both were very appreciative of what they had been able to do and what they learned. Both ended up with A grades for Introductory Biology I and Invertebrate Zoology. Next semester they would be students in Introductory Biology II. Come next year both of them were to be on the main campus seeking a biology degree. One could predict a good outcome for their future.

I basically had a summer and fall of periwinkle data and I thought that would be enough to write a substantive manuscript about my findings so far. It was necessary to stop collecting data at this point, although I would have preferred to get another summer's worth of data. A compare and contrast of jetty and pier periwinkle populations at the southern extremity of the species' geographical distribution seemed called for. It was my hope that the agency that had funded the project would also think it was worth it. The periwinkle does not occur as far south as where I was about to take up existence next year and I would have to let that species go as far as research goes. But, there are lots of species and lots of parasites everywhere. Something would turn up. My last months at Visitopolis were devoted to teaching and writing my periwinkle manuscript. Since I was leaving, the administration did not come up with anything extra in the realm of service for me to do and it was basically a relaxing time. Oh yes, in the spring Annie's thesis defense would be coming up. For her and for me I really wanted that to be a success. Knowing Annie, I had little doubt that it would be.

During the break between fall and spring semesters I made a trip down to Haven University. It was necessary to look into a place to begin living in June. Haven was an inland town, but close to the coast. From the campus it was only about 15 miles to the Atlantic Ocean. I wanted to see if maybe there was a house to buy or a place to rent near the water. That really mattered to me in terms of proximity to a future research site. The residence that had been just sold was right on the water and I was longing for a similar place. It wasn't as though the sale price was entirely mine. Most of what I would take in had to pay off the mortgage, but there was some equity in the house and at Haven University I would, by university standards, have a quite good salary coming in. I could buy if I found an attractive deal. If not, I could as well rent for a while. As I was looking Sylvia was most in my mind. My expectation was that we would trade visits and I wanted a reasonable place for her to come to. After contacting some real estate agents and generally looking around I found some available places that looked good. There was nothing directly on the water that was affordable to buy. Even if I could afford something I was not particularly interested in a place right on the ocean. Perhaps in error, I kept looking for a place similar to my current house, on an estuary. Such a spot would be a little more protected and when I got my new canoe it would be a better place for that activity than the open ocean. Wave action there would be too rough much of the time for comfortable canoeing.

It got to be toward late afternoon when I eventually found a suitable place that was rentable. It was not a place with an estuary lapping at a bulkhead in the front yard. The water was across the street in a somewhat protected bay off the open coast. Access to the shore was part of the deal for the place. The house itself was a bit fancier than my existing house. It did not afford a view of the water to match what I had gotten used to, but still the place seemed to fill the bill pretty well. It was a handsome place, a single story on three foot stilts. The stilts would be useful protection if the tide came up, which according to the real estate agent it only very rarely did. I hoped I could believe him. It was about six months before I would need the place, but I signed a year's lease beginning in five months and put down two months of deposit. The deal was reasonable and I could live there for a year while I looked for a place to buy. I thought to myself, thinking that way my circumstances must have improved substantially, certainly since graduate school. No way could I have even thought about such a place back then.

Before this trip was made I had contacted Greg Mortinson and told him I would be in town. He invited me to dinner at his house. He wanted me to meet his wife and two sons. So, when finished with my real estate deal I found a motel, checked in, and then went over to his place. He greeted me at the door. Greg came off as genuinely happy to see me. I had no reason to doubt he actually felt that way. An offered beer opened the way into our conversation. There hadn't been much chance during my interview for me to find out what he was doing in the way of research. So I asked him. He was a terrestrial ecologist. The project he was working on was a study of praying mantises. The questions were: what happens when you exclude praying mantises from a habitat where they normally occur? How are the relative abundances of other species in the habitat (e.g., mantis prey, and other predators, such as spiders) affected? Once you remove mantises, which are removed manually, they can be kept out of a chosen area with something called tangle foot, a wide strip of material with adhesive on it. Then, you measure the abundances of other species in areas where mantids have not been excluded and compare with abundances of those species in areas where mantids have been excluded. I found it informative that the tangle foot apparatus could hold mantises out of an area. Most cool!

The recent developments of my periwinkle project did not need to enter our conversation because that project had been covered in my recent interview talk here. However, I did arouse a lot of Greg's interest with a brief discussion of the things other people had been doing with the wound healing properties of *Cercaria loossi* from the fan worm. The work of Regis Philbin and his coauthor Paul Berg brought forth quite a discussion of what that all meant. He could see that would put us on the cusp of a marketable product. I said, "Yes, but I doubt that I will get any of the proceeds. I just put the discovery out there. People could do with it as they chose." To which he said, "That's too bad. What on earth made you do it that way?" I returned, "Well, at the time I would have needed medical collaborators who were not available to me and moreover I was keeping my research activities as quiet as I could, which seemed wise at the time. So I just made the decision and now I get to take the outcome."

Greg jumped to another topic, one that he obviously wanted to get to. He said, "I am going to take a chance on you and tell you something rather personal that has been bothering me. During your interview for some reason I came to have a lot of trust in you, maybe because of our similar histories. Anyway, since my wife and kids are out I will do it now. It's about how it was that Provost Flannery died. I read a newspaper report, but maybe you can fill me in some more." As much as I did not want to talk about it, I felt that he deserved some sort of answer so I lied by omission. I said, "You probably got this from the newspaper report, but he pretty obviously fell off his porch and broke his neck." I further said, "The police don't know how that happened." I went on to say that his body was found the next day by his housekeeper, but then stopped. Greg then said rather hesitantly, "My dealings with the man were unexpected, unnerving, and violent. The event I wanted to talk about here took place in the early 1970s just after I was hired at Visitopolis. We were in his office and as I already told you he had just strongly laid down his law that I was not to involve myself with research on this campus. I mistakenly got pretty strident. I told him just as strongly that was a very un-university attitude to take and no way was I going to give up pursuing research. He got very angry and took on a pointedly fearsome look. He came around his desk and to my utter surprise he hit me in the chest with some kind of karate punch." I interjected, "I had a similar interaction with him in his office, but it did not extend to actual violence." He went on, "The punch took my breath away for a few moments. As you can see I'm not a very big or imposing guy. I was frankly unnerved and just wanted to get out of there. He threatened me with more violence if I told anyone about this. At that I left. Afterwards, I was ashamed of myself and never did tell anyone. I got another job and left as soon after that as I could." I told him that I knew of one other who had a similar experience and that apparently when challenged he ruled repeatedly by intimidation. I said, "But I never heard tell of him actually hitting anyone." Greg said one more thing, "I've never felt very proud of the way I handled that situation, but maybe Flannery should be thanked. I ended up here and this is a great place to do research and teach." I said, "I wouldn't worry about how you handled it. Flannery could be a frightful guy. At the time and under the circumstances you did the only thing you could, especially to take the opportunity to get out of his office." At this point his wife and kids pulled into his driveway. The topic was dropped and I was grateful for that.

His wife, Angela, came in with their two boys. I was informed that Jimmy and Ted were six and seven years old. My experience with kids of that age was pretty minimal, but they seemed to be pretty well behaved. Angela was not a pretty woman. However, personality wise she was a bit of dynamite, funny and sharp of wit. She directed the kids out to play and quickly made me feel at home. Dinner would be put together in fairly short order. She invited us into the kitchen and while preparing the food entertained at least me with tales of her day of activities and what she thought of the doings in the department of biology. It wasn't that big a campus and I gathered that she was interested and involved with much of what went on. She worked part-time as a secretary in another department. My learning curve trended sharply upward about this place just by listening to Angela. The dinner assembled, we all gathered round the table. It was delicious and due to her good humor a wonderful time was had. Everybody there seemed jovial and content. The kids were eventually put to bed and I stayed there until almost 10:00 that night. After thanks and goodbyes I left to go to my motel.

My plan for the next day, a Sunday, was to spend some time looking around at a variety of coastal habitats, salt marshes, beaches, sandflats, inlets. In the time I had I could not look too far into these, but I could at least familiarize myself with what was available. It would be my first chance to consider possible avenues for research and before going home I was eager to do it. A different set of marine invertebrates existed south of Cape Hatteras, but not entirely different from what I knew and had been working with for years. They would nevertheless take some getting used to. There were no sites similar to the army pier I had been working with, but I did find an interesting inlet stabilized with jetties. It was in an estuary, but very near the open ocean. On looking in amongst the rocks lo and behold there were periwinkles existing there! There were not many, but a few. I had no idea they had made it this far south, nor apparently did anybody else. I was even surprised when previously I found them some 200 miles north above the Cape. They were all large and I took three back to my truck with a little water. There had been some herring gulls around that inlet, a definitive host for *Cryptocotyle lingua*, and I would check them for parasites when I got back to my microscope. I can't say there was much else of interest that day, but I found that pretty exciting. Tomorrow I would dissect those snails. (None were parasitized.)

On my return home Sylvia got a phone call. I wanted to tell her I was back, some of the trip's occurrences, a little about the house I had rented, and about my unexpected find of periwinkles down there. She listened politely to all of this, but was most interested in hearing about Greg Mortinson's interaction with Flannery in his office. That was not long before the time when she had her situation with him. I said, "I sure am glad he didn't take it to the level of striking you. It was bad enough as it was." "Amen to that," she said. I then noted, "And that makes at least three people to whom Flannery has done something similar. I wonder how many more there are." At this point I told her that, "I'll make it a point to see you tomorrow morning. She stated that, "I expect to be in my office all morning." I said, "That's good to know and I'll see you then." We hung up. Her reactions to bits of intelligence always interested me.

The spring semester began and was underway. In terms of events at Visitopolis there is not much further to tell. It was a quiet time devoted mostly to teaching. One event was quite notable. It was the occurrence of Annie Hall's thesis defense. About midway through the semester Annie scheduled the time for it. She sent me a copy of the final version. It ended up 105 pages long. I had about two weeks to read it between when I got it and the time of her defense. Not surprisingly, after that reading Blake Turner found it to be a masterful job. The story had not changed, but she had paid attention to detail in a polished way. There was almost nothing negative to say about the writing and it would be a challenge to come up with some meaningful, worthy, and interesting questions for her defense. After all we had been over it all before. I would leave the stock and trade questions for somebody else, like where would you take it from here, and try to hit on more interesting fare.

For one thing, I decided to challenge her on what could be a weak point in her study. That was the fact that she had depended upon finding live, active miracidia in gull feces to be sure that she had *Parorchis avitus* with which to try infecting oyster drills (*Urosalpinx cinerea*) in the laboratory. The question was: how dependable was that as a criterion? I could guess what she would say (the miracidia matched those of *Parorchis avitus* and the rediae and cercariae that developed from these miracidia matched those of that parasite), but it is a fair question and I thought I would see how she would handle it. For one more thing: how old must an oyster drill be before it can be infected with *Parorchis avitus*? Not a lot was known about the age of oyster drills at various sizes or how long they live. Again, I could guess what she would say, in the field the smallest drill that was infected with this trematode was 12 mm in shell height and that must be at least two years old, the smallest one that she was able to infect in the lab was 16 mm, this all suggests that a drill must be 2-3 years old to be infected, that is, the snail must have attained sexual maturity. That would be about the best she could do with what was known. A final thing: can you put together what you learned last summer about the distribution of oyster drills on the army pier pilings and what you know about the infection prevalence in oyster drills on that pier? There are a number of ways she might answer, but key among them all would be to note from the paper that she and Timothy wrote that fewer drills are infected on the pier because gulls spend less time around those pilings than for example around a jetty. In short, because the drill parasite uses gulls as definitive host, the parasite is not adapted to transmit to drills existing on pilings. There are lots of drills on pilings closer to shore, very few out away from shore. Why that is, what about drills causes it? That's an unanswered question. Those three questions would be fair and would challenge her a bit. I figured I would be well prepared when the time came.

When the time did come for Annie's defense, on that Friday morning I drove up to the main campus. I left myself a little extra time so I could stop on the way for a while in that used book store where I had purchased my copy of *Tarzan of the Apes*. Maybe they would have something else to feed my interest. They did. I purchased two other first editions. These were also published by A. C. McClurg. One was *Tarzan and the Jewels of Opar* (1918) and the other was *Thuvia Maid of Mars* (1920). Both still had their dust covers with some great art work on them and were in beautiful shape. They were $21.50 each. I felt lucky to find them.

When I got to the main campus I checked into the same motel I had used previously. I found Annie about an hour before the defense was to begin. Not having seen her since last summer, the degree to which she had matured really struck me. Her experiences during the year (writing her thesis, that manuscript with Sophie and Zachary, and whatever else) had made a real difference. For the occasion she was nicely dressed and brimming with confidence. I told her that she came off as a professional young woman. The news that she had been recently been accepted with support to pursue a Ph.D. in a high quality graduate school with a strong program in parasitology was especially good news. I wrote her a letter of recommendation, but I was unaware that she had been recently accepted. That she was going to leave Visitopolis surprised me a little, but she should definitely go to the best possible graduate school. Nancy Burke, still her roommate, joined us. She was looking good and had just defended her own thesis two days ago. It wasn't long before Drs. Jed Lang and Herman Berkowitz showed up. It was good to see them both again. Jed asked me how things were going at my home campus. I told them whereupon about my new job. Both said something to the effect that this university should and would be sorry to see me go. They said you sent us a number of good students. They even listed them: Timothy, Toby, Sophie, Zachary, and of course Annie. That they had all these students in mind to list was meaningful and a reward for me.

The defense started. The room was packed with students and several faculty members. It was a local event. Since almost no one there would know me I gave a short introduction of myself. I introduced Annie and her talk. She spent about 25 minutes going through it. Then I opened the questioning by asking for any question from the general audience. Following that the members of Annie's committee came next. Not surprisingly she answered all questions fully and with style and aplomb. Total time for it all was one hour and 10 minutes. Everybody but her committee was dismissed and we spent some time talking over how Annie had done. We all readily signed off on her having passed her defense (with flying colors) and emerged to tell her so with congratulations. So, there was the first completed undergraduate thesis stemming from the branch campus of Visitopolis University. How to go, Annie!

After a while she introduced me to a fellow biology major by the name of James Blake. I gathered quickly that the introduction was special to her. She and James were an item. I had never known Annie to take a special interest in a particular member of the opposite sex. She was often too busy. It may well be that I just wasn't paying attention. She said that James too had been accepted as a Ph.D. student at the same graduate school as she had been. Then her big news, after graduation, next summer, they were planning to get married. I was, to say the least, astonished. Well, such things do happen. I somewhat hid the degree of my surprise and offered my congratulations. They seemed to complement each other. I learned that he also was interested in parasitology and was working in Herman Berkowitz's lab. That was where they had met. I had to admire his taste in women. Right then and there it was not possible to make much of a judgement on him, but I liked James. He was well spoken and engaging. My prediction was that they would do well as a team. I was happy for her. As is always the case, in all likelihood she knew exactly what she was doing.

Each in their own way both Jed and Herman came up to me and indicated that they had enjoyed serving on Annie's committee. It was the easiest committee job they had ever done. Herman thought the quality of her undergraduate work was at least at the master's thesis level. It was too bad she had not done the work for that degree. Annie mentioned to me that Dr. Berkowitz had suggested she skip the master's degree and go straight for the Ph.D. She could certainly handle that. Jed commented that he had heard nothing but good things about Haven University. He said that they are well known for the quality of their undergraduate students and you should be very happy there. I said, "During my interview I was very favorably impressed and I certainly hope it will turn out that way. I am looking forward to getting started there. To my surprise when I was down to Haven I even found a small population of the snail, *Littorina littorea*. As you know I have been working on that species and it's not supposed to occur that far south." Annie, in on this conversation chimed in, "Is the population big enough to study, is it recruiting new members from the plankton, or is it the product of just a few larvae that happened to drift down there and settle?" I answered, "Those are unanswerable questions. It will take some investigation to find out. I shall have to look around some more. The mere three I examined were not parasitized." She came back, "Well, it's pretty wild that you found any periwinkles at all that far south. That would be worth a short note anyway." I returned, "Yes, it would at that." It had been a while since the occasion had presented itself and I had almost forgotten how much fun Annie could be discussing such things. I thanked her for her thoughts. Her roommate Nancy, who was listening, said, "If you guys are going to get into all that stuff,

I'll be going. There is a party later on and I've got to see to that." And abruptly off she went. Then, at my expense I invited Annie, James, Jed, and Herman out to dinner. I was hungry and it would give me a chance to deal a little more with James. It was a well spent $120 or so.

We finished dinner and went to Annie's party at the apartment she and Nancy rented. Herman and Jed only stayed for a little while and then left. When I left later, James was still there. My motel room was eagerly sought by that time and I went there. On Saturday morning prior to my leaving, Annie, Nancy, and I once again went out to breakfast. Nancy told me a little about the thesis she had just defended. Annie and I had no more thesis business to discuss. That was over. I congratulated her on the thesis, her defense, and not least on her coming wedding. I told her James seemed like a great guy and I wished them well. She said, "We will have the wedding near my home. Please come. We'd love to have you there." To that I said, "Well, I'll be gone by then. I have to give my place up at the beginning of June, but I want to come. Let me see what I can do." Then, Annie produced a finished manuscript entitled "The distribution and abundance of oyster drills (*Urosalpinx cinerea*) on a quarter mile long pier." I said, "I shall read it with great interest." After breakfast I dropped them off at their apartment, said goodbye, and started back. It took about four pleasant hours to get home.

The first thing I did on my arrival back, as had gotten to be my way, was find Sylvia. It was very good news to her that the first senior thesis to come out of this campus went off marvelously. Annie defended her work nicely in front of a packed room. Then I dropped the news about Annie's wedding plans. I said, "That surprised me more than a little. His name is James Blake and both have been accepted to take on a Ph.D. program in parasitology at the same prestigious graduate school. Good for them!" Sylvia returned, "That is really good to hear. It sounds as if things are nicely underway for the two of them." She was interested in what I could explain to her about Nancy's thesis. She liked that her own work had been referenced several times in the thesis. Being pretty tired, I needed some sleep. We made a dinner date for the next night and home I went.

On arising the next day, having finished with events associated with Annie's thesis, my thoughts were mounted on what was going to happen to me next. There was just about a month and a half left before I would have to be out of my house and moving on down to Haven University. I was still positive about that move and looking forward to the job I would be taking up. My time at Visitopolis had been no picnic. It was from fall 1973 through spring 1980, seven academic years. There were some very unfortunate events, the business with Provost Flannery prime among them and Provost Bigelow's attempted blackmail. But there were some very good occurrences too, Sylvia especially, discoveries made, papers published, students worked with, and courses taught. Lots of good things, but I found myself worried about moving away from Sylvia. I would miss her terribly.

In a category by itself, a special remembrance was what had transpired in research with some very capable students. Except for Alexis and Paul they were all away and into other things by now. Undoubtedly the one that had so far gone the furthest into biology was Annie. The others were at an earlier stage, but whatever they may or may not ultimately do with biology that subject had become a major piece of their lives. By exercising their intellect on biological matters they have become more adult, more honest, better thinkers, and better people. Time spent with them was very rewarding. Such did my thoughts run for a while on that Sunday morning.

Later this day Sylvia and I had a dinner date and my thoughts ran back to her. We started an infant relationship within months of my arrival here. As it developed we never leaned on each other that much, but nevertheless we kept abreast of each other's activities, interests, and issues. From my end I can think of nothing that I wouldn't talk over with her. I think she felt the same way, although unlike me she seemed to have fewer pressing issues all the time.

Neither of us put much emphasis on our man-woman relationship. That was, of course, very enjoyable, but we were both pretty serious about our academic lives. We both had committed our lives to academics during graduate school and each of us always left abundant room for the other to pay attention to aspects of that, particularly research and writing. It was no accident that we worked together over promoting research on this campus. So we each had other things to do besides nurturing our love, or whatever it was, for each other.

But now, here it was some seven years after we had first met and I was about to take up existence away from her. It would be stupid of me to think I could not lose her. She was, to say the least an attractive woman, but that wasn't what endeared her most to me. Her honesty, good humor, caring, and straight forwardness contributed much more to that. She could definitely be lost to me if left alone too long. Some guy or other would eventually take up with her. A grievous loss like that I didn't want to experience. To have such a valuable person who had shared so much with me slip away by accident would be devastating. I had never thought about getting married. I once did use the word love with her. She immediately said she was uncomfortable with that word, didn't know what it meant, and had never used the word herself. At the time I couldn't define it either, but if I loved anybody it was certainly her. Saying it to her was easy and honest. I was now in my later thirties. So was she. Could I marry anyone? Could she? What did she think? Later on today, somehow I had better talk this over with her.

It was a cool, but a nice sunny day outside. In the afternoon I took a canoe ride. That always calmed me down and thinking along such lines made me need it.

Sylvia showed up at my place in the late afternoon. We planned to go to a local restaurant. She looked even more alluring than usual. Maybe she somehow knew what I had on my mind this day and put in some extra effort on her looks. Well whatever, but on this day she looked especially tantalizing to me. So there would be no backing out later on pretty quickly I told her that I had something to talk about with her, maybe over dinner. There was some cognac around the house and I offered her some. We consumed the bit of libation pleasantly. She didn't press me about what I had in mind to talk about. In her way, I supposed she thought I would get to it eventually. As for me I was perhaps being more introspective than usual, trying to formulate just what I was going to say to her. Having avoided the topic assiduously all these years, it wasn't easy to bring up. Anyway, we made it to the restaurant and were seated before seven o'clock.

We had another drink and ordered. Then she came right out with the question: "What did you want to talk about?" By then my opening was already in mind. I said, "We have known each other for about seven years now and have developed what can only be described as a beautiful relationship. But now, in a month and a half or so, I will find it necessary to move away from you. As it is now we see each other quite often and it is easy to maintain contact when we don't. That will soon come to an end and that is what concerns me." She interjected, "But, you will only be a couple of hundred miles south of here and we can still say hello and visit one another." I responded, "I intend to do that and it will work fine for a while, but in the longer haul I'm afraid we will drift apart." I paused, now where do I go? Not clear about what I meant to say next, I pressed on anyway. "I broached the topic of my love for you once before. You said you weren't comfortable with that term and had never used it. I respected that and never brought it up again, but now I feel it should be. It's the way I feel about you. The word love captures it like no other." She responded, "It's not that I don't love you. It's just that word. It's used too much and too loosely. As I said at that time, I feel similarly about you." I returned, "Well, that's good enough. We can leave the issue there, but what are we going to do to prevent drifting apart?" She came back, "I've been thinking about this too. The idea of you down there and taking up with some sweet young thing is perplexing to me too." Then she surprised me. "Ever since you came up with that job, described Haven University to me, and told me of your experiences there I have been thinking what a nice place to work it would be. My own job here is sort of O.K., but already I've been thinking I would like to get away from administration and more directly back into teaching and writing. If a job were to open up down at Haven University in history, perhaps I could apply for it." I said, "I don't know what might come up in the History Department at Haven, but I would be all for that. It sounds like the best of all worlds."

I was glad she had been thinking of me and possibly moving herself, but there was still that other issue that had been occupying my mind of late. I still needed to bring that up somehow. Dinner arrived and I got a reprieve for a while. There was a lot of silence as we ate. I guess we were both otherwise occupied, lost in our own thoughts. We ordered some coffee and after it arrived I finally got to it. I said, "Tonight we have expressed how we feel about each other. So we can leave that aside for a moment. I know you have some reservations about it, but I have been thinking about it lately. What I need to know are your current thoughts about marriage."

She came back, "Well, what have you been thinking?" In answer I returned, "Well, here we are both in our upper thirties and our time together is about to be seriously discombobulated. I've never talked about this with anyone, but I have come to the conclusion that being married to you is what I want. But, that can't be the whole story. I need to know what you think about marriage. Let me put it right out there just so there will be no mistake: Will you marry me?" My god, now there I've said it. I could see that took her by surprise too. She was actually taken back a bit.

After a few moments she regained herself and said, "Feeling about that the way I do, I thought nobody would ever ask me that. You have been a constant item in my life for the past seven years. I haven't had sex with anybody else in that time, haven't had any desire to. Considering how we have gotten along all these years, I believe you have done the same." I returned, "Yes, it has been exactly the same." She went on, "I do have a problem with marriage. People should commit to one another of their own volitions and for their own sake. Their relationship should not depend on the state of matrimony to maintain it. All too often it seems people stay together because they are married and for no other reason. I think we have a relationship that could survive marriage and not depend on it. After all, we have already lasted seven years." I responded, "That matches pretty well my own concerns about marriage. It is why I have never been led to ask anybody before. But you are different. I can't imagine getting along without you in my life. So will you?" Her response will live in my heart forever, "Yes, I will, but only because we don't need it and it won't get in the way of our relationship."

She went further, "Getting us both employed at the same institution will take some doing. We shall probably have to wait on marriage. But that won't matter. Nothing is going to separate us. I won't let it happen." There were many plans to be made, but we just settled for an after dinner cordial by way of celebration. After that we got the check, paid the bill, and left. We went back to my place and indulged one another's needs. It all went perfectly. Considering what had just transpired, that was only appropriate.

The next morning Sylvia had a meeting and got up early to get back for it. She gave me a long, thoughtful kiss and zoomed away. I was left with my own thoughts about what had passed last night. Maybe the way it turned out was a little further than I had initially planned to go. I had not intended to actually ask her to marry me in so many words, but it was good to have done it. On this, the morning after, I was pleased with her answer and damn happy about it.

What was in front of me in the next weeks was finishing the teaching of my courses and then getting moved down to Haven University. As far as the courses were concerned I had done both of them several times and they should not be a problem. They weren't. I would just have to be sure to keep the quality up. Once I started paying rent in May, my new place would be available for my use. Perhaps Sylvia could put together a weekend when we could make a trip down there and she could help me start to move in. I wanted her to have a look at the place and hoped she liked it. We settled on a middle weekend in May for the trip. We would leave on Friday and return on Monday. The place down at Haven was furnished and I was going to leave my place with the furnishings. There would not be too much stuff to move.

I had collected quite a few books since the last time I moved very far and I decided to move them on my first trip down. They would amount to a pretty full pickup truck and it would be good to get them moved first. There was enough empty shelving in my new place to hold them. I liked having my books around me and it was appropriate that they be moved in right away. Soon I would have to get some boxes somewhere and pack the books up for transport. As far as the laboratory equipment at school was concerned the only things I expected to move was my files, my field camera, and my only slightly used dissecting microscope with its camera. The microscope and cameras would be needed almost immediately. At least so I hoped. I had bought these with money from my grant. They were a major expense and not easily replaced and I thought I would just take them with me. Probably no one would question that. There was no need to move the remaining lab stuff. There was quite a bit of it, e.g., glassware, aquaria, but it could all be left at Visitopolis and replaced as needed down at Haven University. So on this Monday I made a trip to a local liquor store that I sometimes frequented and got a batch of cardboard boxes to use for books. Then it was time to prepare this coming week's lectures. Also, in a week and a half both courses had a test coming and they had to be made up. It was into the night before I finished my labors.

The semester proceeded along. All my responsibilities were admirably satisfied. Almost before I knew it the weekend of our planned trip south to Haven was on us. That Friday we left in the morning with a truck load of books plus the dissecting scope and cameras from the lab. It very fortunately wasn't raining, which was important for my books. The ride down was a pleasant time. Sylvia and I got a chance to mull over and discuss a lot of things, something we had not had a chance to do since our dinner date that Sunday night. Neither of us had experienced any second thoughts about what we had said. One question was paramount: What were we going to do about us after I moved? Her willingness to try and get a job down at Haven University was very helpful because I just could not stay at Visitopolis, but who knew when or if a position in history might become available. I had little doubt that Haven would find her accomplished self a desirable candidate. However, getting a situation lined up where we were both employed at the same university was an involved process. We thought we should hold off getting officially hitched until we had a better idea of the possibilities. Sometimes taking on a married couple as faculty members is a stumbling block for a university and we didn't want to impede anything because we were married. If she got a job there, a very big if, then we could get married. After all, faculty members do sometimes get wed and what could they do about it then. While our personal plan was on hold we would be relegated to talking on the phone and putting in quite a bit of time on inter-campus travel.

At my rented cottage we pulled in and unloaded the truck, moving the books, dissecting microscope, cameras, and our small amount of baggage inside. Sylvia liked my new place O.K., but said it wasn't as cool as my present domicile. I didn't think so either. This place was across the street, a Seahorse Lane, rather than right on the water and she would miss that elevated deck. She was glad I did not buy the place and it was only temporary. It could be predicted what sort of a place we could be expected to buy around here if our loosely constructed plans came to fruition.

On our arrival at my new place, we spent some time re-shelving my books. That made the place homey enough. I had not contacted anyone from Haven University about my plans to be here this weekend. The plan was to simply spend three nights and four days with my special woman. Essentially that's the way it went. There was one neighbor in residence a couple of houses down from us, but most houses were still empty this time of year. We found an inexpensive restaurant for our sustenance needs. Several meals were consumed there and on Saturday night we got a pizza and brought it back to 27 Sea Horse Lane for supper. I took the time to take Sylvia over to campus to show her around as much as I could. It was a much prettier place than our campus at Visitopolis and Sylvia thought it was an attractive, friendly environment. A couple of times I went across the street and took a swim. The water was still pretty cold and Sylvia didn't want any part of that, but after I got used to it the bracing water was tolerable. Lengthy swims were not in the offing. And so the weekend went. We packed and locked up the place on Monday morning. We had a pleasant trip back.

We got back in the early afternoon. Sylvia had some work to do and we parted company. The semester was almost over and after two weeks my house would have to be vacated and I would have to be moved. That there was much to do settled into my consciousness. For one thing I would be grading final exams to nearly the bitter end. The students deserved my best efforts. Alexis and Paul came into mind. They would not get the benefit of my continued presence at Visitopolis, as had happened with several other students. To help them out, in class I privately offered to write them each a letter of recommendation that they could use for any required purpose. They both were going to earn grades of A in my courses and had done a great job as research assistants. I was very pleased with both of them. Maybe the letters would help them out in some way in the future.

Other student research business included finishing reading the drill manuscript of Timmons, Trumble, and Hall. I had already read most of it, but the Discussion was new and I was eager to see how they did on that. On reading it, they had done an excellent job. I could see Annie's excellent hand in the whole thing. Sophie and Zachary were fortunate to have such a competent third coauthor. The final manuscript was a shortened 22 pages long. Its purpose was to explain how and why drills were distributed along the pier pilings as they were and as far as data in hand allowed the manuscript did that. They had chosen to send it to a popular, well respected journal. It was a nice piece of work by undergraduate students. I predicted to myself, and to them, that it would see publication. I was proud of them all. The proper writing of it must have required abundant attention to detail, negotiation, and ability to stick to the job at hand. All three would be better biologists for having done it. I made some minor corrections and notes on the manuscript and sent it back to Sophie giving them my congratulations. Not being involved as an author was a good decision. However, I did make it glowingly into their acknowledgments.

CONCLUSION

Before I knew it the two weeks had gone by. On the first of June I had cleared out of my house and I was on my way south. It was sad to say goodbye to that place. Sylvia took me out to dinner the night before. We sadly parted and said our goodbyes that night. I expected to be in my new place for at least a year. Annie had contacted me and informed me her wedding was planned for July 15. I wrote back that I was planning to make it to that occasion. Sylvia would put me up and as June went along I was looking forward to especially that more and more. Missing her was part of my daily existence.

But then, during that summer there was a lot to keep me busy. The biology department at Haven had decided that in the fall I would be teaching one course to allow me to get used to the place and find my way around. The course would be their introductory biology. I was glad that was their choice as I could easily handle that. The University also made $10,000 available to set up my lab. I was assigned an office and a connected and spacious lab. Such facilities, treatment, and funds were formerly unheard of by me. Haven University officially paid for work during the school year, but spread out the payments over the whole year. What that meant was that pay checks would start coming to me in June and the increase in pay would be immediately obvious to me. I opened a checking account at a local bank. My University checks would be automatically deposited. That was a new convenience.

In terms of research, aside from putting some time into setting up my lab, I used some time over this summer to look into how widespread *Littorina littorea* was in this region here below Cape Hatteras. The population I had found was unique and quite small. In all the places I searched, only one more very tiny population of periwinkles was found. The larvae must not often get this far south. Maybe a wider search would reveal more, but it did not look like a large scale research project on that species would be possible around here. Annie was right, only a small note extending the distribution of this snail southward a bit seemed called for. In any case there were lots of other species. My interest was grabbed almost immediately by the mud snail, *Ilyanassa obsoleta*. It was quite frequent in salt marshes, on mud flats, and on sandy intertidal flats in this area. That species occurred in abundance on the sandflat next to my pier north of here. It has been well studied by others with regard to its trematode parasites. I spent some time familiarizing myself with the trematode parasites that infected that snail species locally. There were populations of the snail in which trematodes were of very common occurrence. Maybe something could be done with that. Anyway, a number of possibilities presented themselves that students and yours truly might study. Here I was, underway at Haven University!

Naturally, there were administrators there, a faculty senate, and the usual academic politics. But, the place has an abiding understanding of what a university should be and why it exists. Haven does offer a few graduate degrees, but the emphasis of the place is on undergraduate education. Students are put first and to facilitate that it is understood that faculty, nearly all with a Ph.D., must be encouraged to follow their long inculcated predilections. From that will flow the best service to students. They, the students, can get involved in the search for new knowledge, gain faculty as mentors, and among other things take on and write undergraduate theses. The support and encouragement of students in these things makes them better, more accomplished people. That operating principle of Haven University is, and was on my first day there, something I could buy into.

When the time came for Annie's wedding I made the trip north to attend. The necessary confession is that while happy for Annie, I was most interested in seeing Sylvia again. We had talked on the phone, but it had been nearly a month and a half since I had seen her and I really wanted to get back together with her. Annie would naturally be interested in other things. Considering our plans, Sylvia was no longer concerned with me staying at her place. Given her position in the University we had been circumspect about using her abode before this, but she decided not to worry about that anymore. I was in agreement. We had after all already been an "item" for some time. If anyone had a problem with it they would just have to get used to us staying together. I doubted that anyone cared.

Not surprisingly, the first thing I did after arriving was to go and seek out Sylvia. It was late Friday afternoon, a Saturday wedding, and she was at home in her apartment. I walked in and she lived up to my, by that time, fevered expectations. She wasn't doing anything out of the ordinary, just being her.

Could I ask for more? We kissed a memorable kiss and simply took up where we left off a month and a half ago. She seemed a little more than just happy to see me. The news at the top of her list was that she had come across an advertisement put out by Haven University asking for applications to fill a position in the history department. It was for any rank, Assistant, Associate, or Full Professor, and preferably specializing in some aspect of American history. The advertisement had just recently come out and I was totally unaware of it. They were hoping to get the position filled by the spring semester of 1981. If she could get that position, for us it would work out exceedingly well. Sylvia said she already had an application in the works. I loved the way that woman could get things rolling. My previous and groundless suspicion was that she might come to her senses and decide marrying me was not a good idea. I did not worry a lot about much, but about that I could not help myself. The fact that she obviously had no second thoughts about marrying me bolstered my happiness about her news. A further statement by her, "Maybe tomorrow would not be the only wedding in my near future," gave me pleasure to hear.

There was some sort of dinner this night to which the wedding party had been invited and we had to get ready to go to that. I had a coat and even a tie in the truck. Before too long we were on the way. The dinner went pleasantly. In all my time at Visitopolis I had never had an opportunity to talk with Annie's Dad. On this night he made it a point to corner me. Just within the past few days she had made it clear to him that she would not have had any of the success that had been hers without my influence. By his lights that success had been substantial. She had found her future niche and interest. She was smart enough, but when she started college he doubted she ever would finish. But here she is going on to graduate school and with support funding to do so. He said, "I could not be happier." I returned, "I have worked with a number of students. Thus far Annie has been undoubtedly the best. I'm lucky to have had her as a student and colleague." He smiled, said so long, and went on to deal with other guests. I was grateful for what he had said. It made this dinner worthwhile. About 9:30 PM Sylvia collected me and said it was time to go. Once again, I agreed with her. We went back to her place and spent some very pleasant time. I can, I suppose, only speak for myself, but after a month and a half, I needed that desperately. Clearly, Sylvia was in agreement. I sure liked having her agree with me this time.

The next day at 11:00 A.M. we attended the wedding. In my time I had been to only one other wedding so I don't know how they are supposed to go off. Everything certainly seemed in order. After they had been married Annie came up to me. She said, "I suspect we won't be seeing each other for a spell and I want to try and express to you what you have meant to me." I said before she could get further, "Hold on there, whatever I have meant to you, you have meant to me, so there's no need for this." She returned, "Well, O.K., but this girl was able to find herself and feels she owes you a lot for making that possible. I guess I'll just leave it at that. We have always understood one another pretty well, so thank you." I answered, "Yes, you have meant a lot to me too." About that time James came up and suggested they had to go pretty soon and she had better finish with her goodbyes. So off she went to take care of that duty. When they drove away to start their honeymoon their car had been festooned in the traditional way. Streamers and tin cans followed them down the road. Annie waved to me as she left.

Of course that would not be my last dealing with Annie Hall. Because she had published under it she kept using her maiden name. We kept in touch by mutual agreement. Ultimately, after the drill paper by Sophie, Zachary, and Annie got accepted and published, Annie had three papers published as an undergraduate. To go into graduate school with those under your belt was the best of credentials. She went ahead and completed her Ph.D., and so did James. They eventually made a husband and wife team of researchers and two children were theirs. Over the years they have produced a steady stream of papers, some of them authored by the two of them, some by one or the other. Eventually they both worked for the same university and have become quite a phenomenon in the field of parasitology. I would have predicted it, but I am very proud of what Annie has been able to accomplish.

The other students I worked with at Visitopolis also went on to accomplish some things. Timothy Holt, who was second author on the paper by Annie, him, and me about why fewer drills on the pier were infected, did not become a biologist. Timothy was also was an author with me on another paper, along with Annie and Toby Gillus, on the cleaner way to extract *Cercaria loossi* stages from fan worms without contaminating the extraction with bits of host worm. Rather, after graduation he got a job with a fairly prestigious magazine and became one of their staff writers. As a result of numerous articles he has become quite famous. I would like to think that making some correction to his bad English when he was a freshman got him off on the right track. Toby Gillus got into pursuing biology. I have lost track of him, but last I knew he was in graduate school in a Ph.D. program. Good for him. Ultimately, both Sophie Timmons and Zachary Trumble became involved with biology. They of course, with Annie as third author, wrote and published the paper on the distribution of oyster drills on the pier. Sophie became a biological illustrator. I saw her once recently and she really enjoys her work. Zachary eventually followed my lead, becoming a field invertebrate zoologist. He said that was what he wanted to do and went ahead and did it. Zachary has a job teaching biology in a college and has had good success pursuing research in field biology and publishing. I am proud to have him in my footsteps. The last two students with whom I had worked at Visitopolis were both biology majors. Alexis Higgins and Paul Ambrose, I am afraid I have lost track. The very last I knew, years ago, they were on campus pursuing their degrees. Considering that, while Flannery was the Provost, our school expressly did not want students to be involved in research, this is all pretty encouraging.

As I write these final words I have been at Haven University for many years. I am a gray old codger now and retirement is just around the corner. My health is still pretty good. In my years here I have of course handled many students. Some did research with me. Three master's degrees and eighteen undergraduate theses have been completed under my direction. That makes me very proud. One of my first students was Henry Fortis. You may recall he was going to transfer from Visitopolis to Haven in the fall of my first year here. He has become a quality invertebrate biologist successful in research and was a pleasure to deal with. That's not to mention the myriad of students that I had in class, but with whom I did not pursue research. They were interested in subjects other than biology, or else other areas of biology. What effect I had on them is largely unknown to me. That is the way it often goes when teaching is so much of what you do.

As it turned out most of my own research and student thesis work was performed on the mud snail, *Ilyanassa obsoleta* and its several species of trematode parasites. As a research topic that snail and its trematode parasites have been a wonderful thing to study. I noted the vast populations of that snail on sand and mud flats when I first got here to Haven and it has proven to be a well-spring of topics for study. My students and I have produced many published papers dealing with these research problems, some of them containing quite influential discoveries.

It is now some 30 years since I published that note about the wound healing properties of the fan worm parasite *Cercaria loossi*. I never made any money off that discovery, but other workers have isolated, following the work of Regis Philbin and Paul Berg, the causative compound. It has since been made synthetically and is quite routinely used to treat infections. When other authors write about some aspect of dealing with that compound and what it can do, they routinely cite my note. I am appreciative of that and it was all I wanted. My life has been pretty comfortable and rewarding. All in all it was one long success.

The things I have done have been beneficial and a good way to spend my time. Nobody's perfect, but I feel pretty good about it all.

Sylvia has been and continues to be a true partner in all things. She did obtain an appointment as tenured Associate Professor of History at Haven University. She has been with me all these years at Haven. We were married during my second year here. I may have had my problems with the academic back street for a time, but I have been incredibly lucky having her as a compatriot. Sylvia has had continued academic successes. One of her favorite and proudest moments was getting her student, Agnes Moore, done with her undergraduate thesis before she left Visitopolis. Dr. Moore is now teaching history at a small college. Annie and Agnes started a small trend some 25 years ago. A number of undergraduate theses have been completed since the two of them did it at our former branch campus of Visitopolis University. Sylvia has kept track of such activities at Visitopolis and has continued to pursue that endeavor while being here at Haven. So far, 16 students have completed undergraduate theses under her direction. That makes Sylvia most proud. Not only that, but at our old Visitopolis branch campus there are quite a few faculty that have engaged in research in the years since then. Apparently her one and a half years as Dean of Research had its effect. Certainly not least, in her time here at Haven, Sylvia has published three more books that were well received. Royalty checks show up in the mail every now and then to bolster our combined income. Looking back on it I am thrilled that Haven University has worked out so well for both of us.

Sylvia if I have had a good life, it's largely because of her. The fact that we are married we mostly leave in the unsaid background, but our connectedness has not waned. We both enjoy our jobs here and administrators seem very pleased with what each of us does. She has emphasized teaching and, even though she has had the option, has not gone back into an administrative position. We are both Full Professors now and like me she has put on years and is nearing retirement. For my money she is still as beautiful as ever. Sure, if somebody younger were to look at her they maybe would not see it, but they would be wrong. Her face and body still have that wonderful symmetry to them. Of course, our sexual proclivities of younger days have largely waned with the years. Nevertheless, we still love being together and she has been and is the author of some wonderful cherished memories. I remain ever thankful for her.

ABOUT THE AUTHOR

Lawrence A. Curtis, PhD
Email: lcurtis@udel.edu.

I was born in Hartford, Connecticut in 1942. In 1960-61 I attended Post Junior College of Commerce in Waterbury, CT – no degree. My Bachelor of Arts Degree in Biology was obtained a Nasson College in Maine in 1965 – that college since closed. A Master's Degree in Zoology was obtained from University of New Hampshire in 1967. My PhD Degree was gotten from the University of Delaware in 1973.

Exclusive of abstracts, I have published 32 papers, many with student coauthors, and a book. The book is A True Tale of Science and Discovery. 2010, Nova Science Publishers, Inc., New York.

In my active years as a professor I was a member of: American Association for the Advancement of Science; American Society of Parasitologists; Ecological Society of America; and Society of Comparative and Integrative Biology.

I believe in the liberal arts idea. I hold to the ideal that the function of a university is to promote the discovery, dissemination and wise use of knowledge. Over the years, I have devoted myself to this general notion. Experiencing new phenomena, ideas, and conceptual relationships for the first time is to me a source of joy, as is communicating them to others. I see research and teaching as interdependent endeavors, not decoupled and opposing activities, as they are so often portrayed. My goal is to improve my own depth of knowledge of biological science. Thereby, I hope to make significant contributions to the perspective and knowledge of other students of biology.